"An exciting, [...] [...]epherd has injected the same humor into this book as he did in the rest of the series . . . I really love these books and *Undaunted* is a great addition to the series." —*Fresh Fiction*

Praise for
Kris Longknife
INTREPID

"[Kris Longknife] will remind readers of David Weber's Honor Harrington with her strength and intelligence. Mike Shepherd provides an exciting military science fiction thriller." —*Genre Go Round Reviews*

"A good read for fans of the series and of military science fiction." —*Romantic Times*

Praise for
Kris Longknife
AUDACIOUS

" 'I'm a woman of very few words, but lots of action.' So said Mae West, but it might just as well have been Lieutenant Kris Longknife, princess of the one hundred worlds of Wardhaven. Kris can kick, shoot, and punch her way out of any dangerous situation, and she can do it while wearing stilettos and a tight cocktail dress. She's all business, with a Hells Angel handshake and a 'get out of my face' attitude. But her hair always looks good. *Audacious* maintains a crisp pace and lively banter . . . Kris Longknife is funny and she entertains us." —*Sci Fi Weekly*

continued . . .

Kris Longknife
REDOUBTABLE

Mike Shepherd

ACE BOOKS, NEW YORK

THE BERKLEY PUBLISHING GROUP
Published by the Penguin Group
Penguin Group (USA) Inc.
375 Hudson Street, New York, New York 10014, USA
Penguin Group (Canada), 90 Eglinton Avenue East, Suite 700, Toronto, Ontario M4P 2Y3, Canada
(a division of Pearson Penguin Canada Inc.)
Penguin Books Ltd., 80 Strand, London WC2R 0RL, England
Penguin Group Ireland, 25 St. Stephen's Green, Dublin 2, Ireland (a division of Penguin Books Ltd.)
Penguin Group (Australia), 250 Camberwell Road, Camberwell, Victoria 3124, Australia
(a division of Pearson Australia Group Pty. Ltd.)
Penguin Books India Pvt. Ltd., 11 Community Centre, Panchsheel Park, New Delhi—110 017, India
Penguin Group (NZ), 67 Apollo Drive, Rosedale, North Shore 0632, New Zealand
(a division of Pearson New Zealand Ltd.)
Penguin Books (South Africa) (Pty.) Ltd., 24 Sturdee Avenue, Rosebank, Johannesburg 2196,
South Africa

Penguin Books Ltd., Registered Offices: 80 Strand, London WC2R 0RL, England

This is a work of fiction. Names, characters, places, and incidents either are the product of the author's imagination or are used fictitiously, and any resemblance to actual persons, living or dead, business establishments, events, or locales is entirely coincidental. The publisher does not have any control over and does not assume any responsibility for author or third-party websites or their content.

KRIS LONGKNIFE: REDOUBTABLE

An Ace Book / published by arrangement with the author

PRINTING HISTORY
Ace mass-market edition / November 2010

Copyright © 2010 by Mike Moscoe.
Cover art by Scott Grimando.
Interior text design by Kristin del Rosario.

ISBN: 978-0-441-01956-4

ACE
Ace Books are published by The Berkley Publishing Group,
a division of Penguin Group (USA) Inc.,
375 Hudson Street, New York, New York 10014.
ACE and the "A" design are trademarks of Penguin Group (USA) Inc.

PRINTED IN THE UNITED STATES OF AMERICA

10   9   8   7   6   5   4   3   2   1

Lieutenant Commander Kris Longknife paused just outside the bridge hatch. She steadied herself, one hand on the bulkhead, the other heavy on her cane, waiting for the wave of dizziness to pass. The docs said these episodes should be getting fewer and fewer.

So far, the docs were bloody optimists.

Kris measured her breathing and fixed her eye on a hatch farther down the passageway of the Wardhaven Scout Ship *Wasp*, and thought, TIME, NELLY?

YOU'RE STILL TWENTY-ONE MINUTES EARLY TO RELIEVE THE WATCH, KRIS. ARE YOU ALL RIGHT?

I'M FINE, Kris lied to her personal computer, acquired at a cost greater than several ships of the *Wasp*'s value.

YOUR BLOOD PRESSURE, PULSE, AND RESPIRATION DON'T LOOK FINE, Nelly pointed out.

AND TO THINK, THIS TIME THE BOMB WASN'T EVEN AIMED AT ME, Kris thought.

IT WAS, Nelly countered. IT WAS JUST THAT THEY WERE AFTER THE GUY WITH YOU FIRST, AND YOU SECOND.

ENOUGH OF THIS, Kris thought, let go of the bulkhead, steadied herself without the help of the cane . . . without *much* help from the cane . . . and marched onto the bridge of the *Wasp*.

A glance showed her that tonight's watch was double the norm for a scout ship . . . and huge for the merchant ship *Mary Ellen Carter* that the *Wasp* claimed to be.

Sulwan Kann, the *Wasp*'s navigator, was Officer of the

Deck. In her usual cutoffs and tank top, she, like most of the *Wasp*'s original contract crew, refused to let the added Marines and sailors now aboard make her drop her easygoing ways. Kris got a two-finger waggle toward Sulwan's brow for a salute. Kris returned a regal nod . . . as befitting the princess she was.

Still, the relief process went straight Navy. "I stand ready to relieve you," Kris said. "What is the *Wasp*'s condition?"

"Situation normal, decelerating at .85 gees toward Kaskatos."

"And the unknown?"

"The bogey is steady on her course. She will make orbit around Kaskatos at the same time and in the same space we do. What a coincidence." The OOD and ship's navigator tapped her command board, and the forward screen showed the star system, then zoomed in to show the two ships, the *Wasp* approaching Kaskatos from the system's Jump Point Alpha, the unknown from the nearest gas giant.

"It could be just a local entrepreneur, harvesting reaction mass to sell to any ship that comes by," Kris said.

"That would explain why it's aiming to make orbit right at our elbow," Sulwan said, raising an eyebrow.

Kris shrugged; out here beyond the Rim of human space, the logical answer rarely was the right one.

"And if that ship is just a nice, hardworking merchant, why isn't he on the horn, hawking his wares?" Sulwan added.

That was a definite strike against the business hypothesis. "It's not like he's got to worry about us buying from anyone else," Kris said. Kaskatos *was* also silent as a tomb.

Sulwan snorted. "They promote you, Princess, and suddenly you go all soft on us? I thought you Longknifes were supposed to get more bloodthirsty as you went up the promotion ladder."

Kris laughed. "I'm kind of enjoying nobody trying to kill me."

"Then how come you got us out here fishing for pirates," Chief Beni snapped from where he sat at Sensors. His uniform actually looked good on him. He'd lost weight and was wearing fresh khakis every day. Having an actual leading chief aboard the *Wasp* was definitely crimping his style. But even that couldn't change his perpetual devotion to avoiding harm's way.

"Cause those are our orders," Kris said. "Signed by King Ray himself."

"Couldn't you have told your grandpapa you preferred a nice quiet corner of the universe?" the chief asked.

"You've been with her longer than I have, Chief," Sulwan said. "It seems her granddad wants her far away from him first, last, and foremost . . . and usually in hot water up to her pretty ears." The navigator sank into deep thought for a moment, her finger tapping pursed lips. "Or is it she wants far away from him?"

"The feelings are mutual," Kris grumbled. "Now, if I relieve you, will you show me some respect?"

"Never, but I would like to be relieved."

"Have there been any communications in the last four hours from either the unknown or Kaskatos?"

"Not a peep," Sulwan reported. "Per captain's orders, we hailed both of them every hour on the hour. Not even a nasty word in reply."

"Any signs of life, Chief?" Kris asked.

"Kaskatos shows power lines in use. It has thermal plumes around cities and large structures, just like you'd expect. There is some but not a lot of activity on the roads and rivers. There are people there. They just ain't talking to us or to each other."

Kris would have cursed the inventor of the fiber-optic cable if she knew his or her name. Many start-up colonies were skipping radio and jumping direct to cable. That left little radio communications to eavesdrop on. That people were willing to put cable on their basic survival list said something about conditions out here beyond the Rim of human space.

Or what had been the Rim of human space.

Kris almost laughed out loud at the stale joke. The Society of Humanity had broken up for many reasons. Still, at the top of most lists was the difference between the staid . . . some might say decadent older planets, Earth and the like . . . and

the more vibrant . . . some might say malcontents . . . out on
the Rim. Earth said we'd found enough planets; colonies were
a drain on money better spent closer to home. The younger
worlds saw new colonies as places to make fortunes and get
elbow room. The politicians haggled for years, couldn't solve
the problem, and finally settled on splitting the sheets.

Six hundred planets went different ways . . . without a shot
fired. Thanks be to any god involved . . . and a little bit of mutiny by one Ensign Kris Longknife.

But when Kris took the *Wasp* out to find and map vacant
planets in unexplored space, she got a big surprise. The Sooners. These folks hadn't waited for any politician's permission
but struck out on their own. They picked up family, bag and
baggage, and headed out to wherever they found a good place
to "set" a while.

Just human nature doing what comes naturally. Simple
solution . . . or so it seemed.

Unfortunately, the same human nature that cuts the Gor-
dian knot also cuts throats. Where farmers and small business
went, lawless people like pirates and slavers weren't far behind. Those who go beyond the reach of law better either be
a law unto themselves or prepared to fight for what they hold
dear. If they didn't or couldn't, there was usually someone
only too ready to show them the error of their ways.

That was where Kris and the *Wasp* and the two hundred
Marines aboard her came in. And why she was covered with
shipping containers and squawking the false transponder of
the good ship *Mary Ellen Carter*, a week out from Brighton.

At exactly midnight, ship time, Kris announced "I relieve
you," and Sulwan replied, "I stand relieved," and the formal
transfer of godlike power took place. The *Wasp* was Kris's
to command through the quiet hours from midnight to 0400.

At least the *Wasp* was hers to command unless the one true
god of the *Wasp* showed up. Captain Drago was lord of all he
surveyed on the *Wasp*. Of that there could be no question.

He had the signed contract to prove it.

Exactly how the *Wasp* went from Kris's bought-and-paid-
for ship to a sovereign scout ship in the Wardhaven Navy

was something Kris could track. How it happened that the crew continued to be private contractors paid out of black funds by Wardhaven's Intelligence Chief was a bit harder to follow.

Probably, Kris's great-grandfather, King Raymond I to most, had his little pinky finger somewhere in the mix.

So, Lieutenant Commander Kris Longknife commanded Patrol Squadron 10 and its half dozen corvettes. She could order Jack Campbell of the *Dauntless* and Phil Taussig of the *Hornet* to convoy duty, escorting honest merchant ships around the routes between the Sooner planets. She tasked the *Fearless* and the *Intrepid* to faking it as independent—and stupid—solo merchants like the *Wasp*, hunting for unregistered start-up planets like Kaskatos.

Still, aboard the *Wasp* herself, Kris was only a watch stander.

Or maybe the problem was that she was *still* a watch stander.

Like so much of Kris's life as a Navy officer and a princess, there was no precedent. She could worry about it, do it, or not do it.

For the moment, Kris stood her watch.

"Chief, aren't you due for relief?"

"I asked to put in my eight during the quiet of the night."

"And the chief of the boat just let you do that?" If Kris knew anything of the *Wasp*'s new command master chief, Chief Beni was telling a boldface lie.

"He did, now that you mention it, have a problem with the idea. At first," the chief admitted with a cough.

"At first," Kris said.

"Then I explained to him that the unknown ought to be getting in range for us to find out some interesting things during your watch, and he decided to let me do things my way."

Chief Beni had been following Kris around the hooligan Navy long enough to pick up some bad habits along with a now-disappearing beer gut.

Command Master Chief L. J. Mong had spent a day aboard the *Wasp* before taking Kris and Captain Drago aside.

"This is an interesting setup you have here. Civilian scientists, Marines, contractors, and some newly arrived sailors. I understand I am chief of the boat. I think many people assume that extends only to the uniform sailors on the *Wasp*."

Neither Kris nor Captain Drago had affirmed or denied that observation.

The chief of the boat's grin grew tight as the silence stretched. "My grandfather told me that a wise man, given a rock, may use water to form it to his will . . . or a diamond drill. I have both in my footlocker, sir."

Captain Drago had studied the short, thin whip of a man for a moment longer. "I will enjoy watching a true artist."

And they had broken for supper. Kris and Drago to the officers' mess, L. J. to dinner with Gunnery Sergeant Brown.

SHALL I SEND A NANO TO RECORD THEIR CONVERSATION? Nelly had asked on the direct link into Kris's skull. Nelly, Kris's pet computer, was worth more than all the ships in Patrol Squadron 10, and smarter than all the computers aboard them, with the exception of the eight personal computers she called her kids. More often than not, Nelly was well ahead of Kris.

After a moment's pause, Kris had shaken her head. No, NELLY, LET'S PASS ON THAT. I'M LOOKING FORWARD TO THOSE TWO SURPRISING ME.

NORMALLY, YOU DON'T LIKE SURPRISES, KRIS.

Nelly's recent spate of surprises had caused some hard words and harder feelings between user and computer. Kris recognized where Nelly was coming from and chose her words carefully.

NELLY, AT OFFICER CANDIDATE SCHOOL, I FIRST HEARD THAT MASTER CHIEFS AND GUNNY SERGEANTS ARE THE PEOPLE WHO REALLY RUN THE NAVY AND THE CORPS. I DIDN'T UNDERSTAND WHAT THEY MEANT AT OCS. I'VE COME TO UNDERSTAND IT BETTER NOW. I SUSPECT, IF WE LET THOSE TWO OLD GOATS HAVE THEIR HEAD, THEY WILL SHOW US EXACTLY WHY THE NAVY NEEDS MASTER CHIEFS TO RUN IT.

IF HE IS HALF AS GOOD AS GUNNY SERGEANT BROWN, HE IS VERY MUCH WORTH STUDYING, Nelly agreed.

For the moment, on the *Wasp*'s bridge, Kris had other things to study. And, to be honest, she was glad to have her electronic expert sharing the watch with her.

"Can you tell me anything more about our unknown, Chief?" Kris said, coming to study his board over his shoulder.

"It's a system runabout, Commander. Its power source looks like a GE matter/antimatter annihilation reactor. Power plant is an Evinrude Z-20 or a good rip-off. A bit small for the job, but we are way out back."

"Anything waving at you 'Hi, I'm a bad guy'?"

"Nothing so easy," the chief answered. "Unless . . ." he added slowly, tapping his board and frowning at it. "I'm starting to maybe see something strange with the balloot."

"What kind of strange?" Kris said, holding tight to the blend of excitement at his words and frustration at their slowness.

"Balloots come in lots of different brands and sizes. We've got one loaded forward on the *Wasp* in case that crazy captain of yours decides he wants to go cloud dancing with this merchant ship. By the way, Princess, skimming gas giants for reaction mass is not recommended for ships loaded with containers and glued together with string and chewing gum like the *Wasp* is just now. You need a ship small, and tightly wound."

"Chief, I need an answer to the question you raised about that balloot."

"I know, I know, but I just thought you ought to know that the *Wasp* is rigged to do a gas-giant dive, but it's not really meant to. Us having a nice quiet midwatch, I figured now would be a good time to mention it."

"It's mentioned! Now what's strange about that balloot?"

"It's veined, I think."

"Veined?"

"Yeah, it's got these lines running across it. I noticed them about an hour ago. They're getting more and more pronounced."

Kris stared at the visual image of the unidentified craft. Basically, it was a big bag with the bare hint of the runabout's tail end sticking out from behind it. "I don't see anything?"

The chief tapped his board. The image grew to take in the entire forward screen. Kris still didn't see anything.

"I said it's just a hint of something running up and down and across the balloot. They come and go."

"Nelly, can you make anything out?" Kris asked.

"If you go to infrared," Kris's computer suggested, and the screen changed colors as the examination slipped from the visual spectrum to heat, "you can just make out lines running across the balloot that don't have quite the same temperature as the fabric behind them. They are slightly colder than the balloot and the reaction mass in it."

"I was about to show her that," the chief said.

"I know you were," Kris said. The chief and Nelly were both experts in sensors. And often in competition.

Sometimes that was good.

Sometimes.

"There's also a hint of the lines on radar," the chief added. "When you combine the hints on visual . . ."

"And infrared . . ." Nelly cut in.

"And radar," the chief finished, hands flying over his board, "you get the same set of lines, and they come through better."

Now the balloot was clearly crisscrossed.

"Are they reinforcements to the fabric?" Kris asked.

"None of the balloots from any company in human space have them," Nelly said.

"On a close pass to a gas giant, anything like that would disrupt the flow of plasma. They'd burn off. Might even burn up the balloot," the chief added.

"So they were put on after the pass. Why?"

"Commander, your guess is as good as mine," the chief admitted. Nelly seconded the human opinion with her silence.

Which left Kris staring at one lonely bit of information, which, balanced against the huge silence from all other sources, did not make her happy.

At the end of her four-hour watch, Kris knew nothing more than she had when she started. As Princess Kris Longknife, commander of Patrol Squadron 10, that really bothered her.

However, as Officer of the Deck, a quiet watch was a good

watch. As Kris was relieved at 0400, she tried to congratulate herself on having successfully stood a watch without starting a war or even firing a single shot.

It was getting to be a very pleasant habit.

2

Kris was in the wardroom later that morning at 0730. She spotted Penny, her intel lieutenant, at an empty table and joined her.

"How was your watch?" Penny asked.

"Uneventful," Kris said.

"Unusual," Penny answered.

"I'm trying to turn over a new leaf. No one tries to kill me. I try to kill no one. Did you have a chance to look at those news accounts I sent you yesterday?"

Penny gave Kris a wary eye. "Who is this Winston Spencer and why is he sending you news feed?"

"He's written some good stories from the Navy perspective. Digs deep, so he usually gets more about us right than he gets wrong. You remember that news dump my brother, Honovi, gave us last time we were at Wardhaven that pretty much showed me that being out here on the Rim left me totally in the dark about what was happening back home? I'd prefer not to give my brother that kind of a club to beat me with. So I asked Spencer to send me stuff he found interesting. Admiral Santiago recommended him."

Penny continued to eye Kris, as if weighing the words . . . and not finding enough truth in them. She had a lot of experience in the last three years listening to Kris tell the truth, or a small part of the truth, or a whole lot of bunk with a little bit of truth added in for spice.

Today, she made a face. "I guess I'll have to settle for that until you let me in on the whole story."

"What's the matter? Doesn't it at least sound plausible?"

"Oh, it sounds plausible. It might even be right. I just have this strange itch between my shoulder blades. Maybe my bra's too tight. Then again, I'm working for a Longknife. It could mean blood and gore. I'll just have to wait and see."

Since treason wasn't the kind of thing you discussed over breakfast in the wardroom of a commissioned warship, Kris changed the topic. "Have you found out anything about Kaskatos?"

"Not. A. Thing. I sent out requests for any data to both Greenfeld and Wardhaven sources. I actually got a couple of answers from Greenfeld planets nearby. All were negative. No responses at all from our own nearest planets. It's clear that the official databases are null. What I wonder about is if a bit of informal snooping around would be just as fruitless?"

"Are you suggesting we need to build up our own contacts on the ground around here?"

"It would be nice to have some Baker Street Irregulars to snoop around corners for what the officials don't know," Penny said. "You do know who the Baker Street Irregulars are?"

"I read the required classics in school," Kris admitted.

"My dad introduced me to Sherlock Holmes when I was just starting to read. I loved them."

Kris changed the topic. "You got replies from Greenfeld officials?"

"Yes. They know we're out here, and, at least to the extent that they are answering my search requests, they are cooperating."

"I wonder how long before a couple of Greenfeld cruisers come looking for us?"

"Depends on whether any can be spared from using their sailors to patrol the streets of this planet or that one," Captain Jack Montoya of the Wardhaven Royal Marines said as he slid into the chair next to Kris. He arranged his breakfast plate, attacked his eggs and bacon, and waited for Kris to comment.

"So far, we've had this space to ourselves," Kris said.

"Not even so much as a warning to get out of their neck of the woods?" Jack asked.

Penny shook her head. "Not a peep. All the other ships of PatRon 10 have the same report. An occasional merchant ship, usually glad to see us out here, but no sightings of the Greenfeld fleet. Not so much as a tug."

Jack shook his head. "If this were my stomping grounds, I'd be out here marking my territory with something. Things must be really bad inside the fraternal order of Peterwald good buddies to have the whole fleet tied up."

"I think the Navy is the only power that the Peterwalds trust to enforce their sway over their planets," Kris said. "Henry Peterwald got really lucky when he sent his daughter out to the fleet for an education."

That Kris had provided a bit of that education the rest of the table was kind enough not to comment upon.

"Penny, are you getting anything more specific from inside the Greenfeld Empire? We all know it's a mess, but . . ." Kris trailed off. She knew so little that she didn't even know how to talk about how little she knew.

"Sorry, Your Highness, but this little minion is deep down a dungeon's coal bin surrounded by black cats at midnight. Newspapers never have been all that trustworthy in Peterwald territory, and what with no one sure who's going to come out on top, you can't blame the media for not really wanting to stick their fingers into the ongoing catfights. Maybe Abby knows something from her informal sources?"

Abby, Kris's maid, settled at Kris's other elbow, her twelve-year-old niece right next to her. Abby really *was* a maid. Very highly trained and all. The problem was that she wasn't *just* a maid.

On Earth, where Abby had started maiding, personal help was expected to do other things . . . like shoot back when their Ladies got shot at. Abby got quite good at that. She also found out from others of the help that she could make extra money selling information to the gossip media. Abby got very good at that, too.

Working for Kris Longknife gave Abby plenty of chances to excel at all of her many skills.

Usually.

"Why do I hear you people taking my name in vain?" Abby said. She normally got up on the wrong side of the bed, and today looked to be no exception.

Kris repeated the question. Abby was shaking her head before Kris finished.

"No way, nohow am I wasting my hard-earned money on the rumors coming out of the Greenfeld Alliance. Best intel the info marketeers have even they admit is C-4. Secondhand idle rumors picked up by shady characters with only a passing acquaintance with the truth and that have dogs of their own in the fight. Princess, if you want me to waste your money on that untreated sewage, I'll do it, but you'd be better served spending it on some trashy suspense novel."

Colonel Cortez took this moment to join the breakfast club. He surveyed the growing silence with raised eyebrow. "My, aren't we quiet today."

"Not much going on," Penny said.

"Good. Would now be a good time for me to put in again for a transfer out of the princess's merry band of optimists to someplace safe and sane . . . like a Royal prison?"

Kris shook her head as she stood up. "Okay, boys and girls. Just because we've run into so many dead ends that it's starting to look like a holiday, doesn't mean that it is. Keep your eyes peeled. Our vacation will be over when you least expect it."

3

Kris's vacation ended abruptly next morning.

She had paused outside the bridge coaming to let a tiny bit of nausea pass. This spell was the shortest she remembered, and in a moment she expected to march across the bridge to her station, swinging her cane with a jaunty air.

All she needed was a few seconds' rest.

The speaker on the bridge crackled to life. "Freighter *Mary Ellen Carter*, vent your reactor to space and prepare to be boarded. Do this our way, and no one gets hurt. If you don't, we'll kill you all."

Captain Drago's response was not at all appropriate for pirate ears . . . or princess's either. The captain vented a long string of four-letter words ending in "Where is that bloody Princess Longknife when I need her?"

"Here," Kris announced, as she entered the bridge, cane and legs moving with purpose, aiming for her battle station at Weapons with all speed and only a touch of light-headedness she tried to ignore.

The petty officer second class at Kris's station kept the targeting crosshairs on the now self-proclaimed pirate ketch . . . and her finger well away from the firing button.

That was Kris's business.

"Do something about that," Captain Drago said, waving a hand at the forward screen that the pirate now filled. "And don't let them make a mess on my ship."

"Will do, Skipper," Kris told the contract ship captain, slipping into the seat just vacated by the petty officer. Kris had gotten just enough of a glance at the pirate to answer the question she'd had about the ropes and cordage crisscrossing the balloot.

At the moment, three or four dozen space-suited cutthroats used the ropes as handholds, tie-downs, or wraparounds for their legs. The space suits had been painted up with frightening sights. Tiger mouths roared, skulls gaped, and heads dripped blood and gore from their cut throats.

Kris knew this was deadly serious, but she had a barely controlled urge to offer the pirates candy and tell them their Halloween costumes were worth all the work they'd put into them.

She shook off that whimsy as she surveyed the rifles, pistols, machetes, and poles with gleaming hooks at the end of them that the freebooters were waving with bloody intent.

This was no time for a joke.

I COULD HAVE TOLD YOU THAT, Nelly put in.

NOT NOW, NELLY. "Chief, talk to me about those boarders."

From his station at Sensors, Chief Beni shook his head. "Their suits are not armored. Hardly any two of them are the same, except for a couple of dozen emergency suits. You know, the kind you find under your seat on a civilian shuttle. No telling how old they are. The paint jobs look nasty, but if you ask me, I think most of the paint's there to patch up the holes."

"But if they get aboard my ship . . ." the captain began.

"They won't," Kris cut him off. "Captain Montoya, are you watching all this?"

"From the drop bay, Commander. I've got four of my best sharpshooters in each of the four LACs. We'll be ready to launch as soon as the sailors get the canopies off them."

The LACs weren't going planetside this trip; the canopies would only block the aim of the Marines. And keep the pirates from seeing just how much of the wrong stuff they'd bit into.

"I've also got Marines in armored space suits at every entry hatch on the *Wasp* ready to either defend or step outside and sweep up our overly optimistic revenue collectors."

"At the moment, they aren't using the scam that they're

government officials," Kris said, though they could quickly fall back on it the instant Kris and Jack's Marines blew their pirate business to shreds. What Kris would do if their leader started waving the credentials of a customs officer or drug-enforcement-inspection warrant was something she'd think about when it happened.

"Jack, let me know when you're ready to launch," Kris said.

"*Mary Ellen Carter*, you are not venting your reactor," the pirate pointed out. "That's not smart."

"LACs away on my mark," Jack announced. "LAC-1 . . . mark. LAC-2 . . . mark. LAC-3 . . . mark. LAC-4 . . . mark. All LACs away."

"Running won't do you no good. The planet below is our country," the pirate growled, as the LACs came in view and were mistaken for evacuation pods.

"We're not running," Kris said, mashing her commlink. "Pirate off our starboard beam, this is the Wardhaven Armed Corvette *Wasp*, and this is Commander Kris Longknife. Cut your engines and throw your weapons over the side. Surrender peacefully, and you can plead your case to a court. Keep this noise up, and we'll reduce you to ash. Guns, run out the lasers."

There was a slight motion on the ship as the four 24-inch pulse lasers were run out of where they hid under the *Wasp*'s merchant paint job.

The sight must have been appalling to those hanging on to the balloot. Machetes quit waving, pistols and rifles just kind of hung there in midspace.

"Good God, what's a Longknife doing out here?" came over a live mike among the pirates.

"I don't know. Let's get out of here."

"We can't outrun them."

Suddenly, the pirate ketch took off at full power.

Unfortunately, it was still aimed right at the *Wasp*.

"Get us out of here," Captain Drago demanded.

"I'll try, Skipper," Sulwan replied from the navigation station. "But they're awful close."

"Shoot 'em, Longknife!" he demanded.

"They're too close," Kris answered. "I can't bring the lasers to bear."

The *Wasp*'s lasers all were pretty much limited to targets straight ahead of her. Kris could swing the ship . . .

This close, whatever she did would be a mess.

"Collision," she shouted into her commlink. "Prepare for collision."

And Kris remembered she hadn't yet put on her own seat belt.

The petty officer second class grabbed at Kris's waist as the two ships came together.

The collision point was well off both ships' centers of gravity. The balloot filled with reaction mass did a passable job as a bumper, absorbing some of the force, spreading it out.

And sending both ships reeling away from each other in drunken twists and spins.

For someone with a working inner ear, it was bad. For Kris, not yet recovered from her last session as the duck in a shooting gallery, it was worse.

Kris's vision went gray, with the weirdest pink and purple polka dots. Her recently enjoyed breakfast, fortunately light, got an eviction notice and left hastily.

The petty officer must have seen it coming; she had a burp bag over Kris's mouth before Kris knew she needed one.

On the forward screen, cameras still tracked the pirates and their perils. Several were knocked loose from the balloot. A few collided with the *Wasp* and grabbed handholds. Several did not and began what would be short-lived careers as independent satellites.

And, of course, there was one guy in every crowd who couldn't get with the program.

One pirate had a rifle and intended to use it. He brought his weapon up to take aim—something not easily done with his standard-suit gloves and helmet.

You had to respect his commitment. Three Marine sharpshooters in the LACs showed him all the respect his folly deserved. They put him under fire even as he struggled to make his senseless move.

The pirate's shot went wild. The rounds from three different Marines cut through the bull's-eye that was his heart. Six streams of pulsing blood jetted him away from the pirate craft, twisting and spinning his quickly freezing body.

The other pirates followed this display of Marine accuracy and gently shoved any weapons they still had off into their own orbits.

"Jack, can you and your Marines police up this mess?" Kris asked, wishing for some water to clean out her mouth. The petty officer must have qualified at mind reading because she had a water bottle at hand.

"Don't expect we'll have any trouble, Commander," came back from Jack, as Kris added a mouthful of filthy water to the burp bag and handed it to the second-class with a grateful smile.

Kris strapped herself into her station chair as she considered her next problem. For some reason, Kris's ears were happiest when her fanny was firmly strapped to something. Especially now that the *Wasp* was in zero gee.

A zero gee that Sulwan announced was acting on a ship now steady in orbit.

It was nice of other people to solve Kris's problems. Now it was time for her to solve a few herself. "Penny, can you and the chief raise me someone dirtside with even a tiny bit of authority?"

"We can try," the Navy lieutenant said.

Five minutes later, they had someone on the radio.

"I'm freeholder Annam son Jendon," the deeply tanned face on the main screen said for identification. "Only reason I have my own radio station is because I have got this pond we occasionally use for a backup lander drop."

"What's wrong with the main airport?" Kris asked. The largest town on Kaskatos did have a port with a ten-thousand-meter runway, but it had yet to say a word or show a beacon or light.

"Ma'am, you have to understand, Lander's Rest has had a lot of folks dropped on its runway lately. I can't really say whether or not the place is just busted up or unwilling to take another empty belly. It could be both."

"What's the situation on Kaskatos?" Kris asked.

"Ma'am, I really don't feel comfortable talking on an open radio. The powers that be spread the word real fast when you showed up at the jump point that it wouldn't be smart to make any signals to you. Now that you done for the pirates, I'm willing to talk to you, but there's no telling who's listening and what offense they might take. I'm just a farmer trying to keep flesh and spirit together in times gone bad."

"Would you mind if I dropped down and talked with you?" Kris asked. "I've got a couple of containers aboard of famine biscuits. Taste can be monotonous, but they do keep body and soul alive."

"Thank you, ma'am, I don't mind if you do," he said, then added in a soft whisper. "I just wish you hadn't mentioned the food on the radio. I expect I'll be getting visitors besides you."

4

Six hours later, Kris was in undress whites and strapped into a longboat, shuttle to non-Navy types, as it dropped away from the *Wasp*. Jack was beside her, in khaki and blues, and studying his battle board. Kris paid attention as he moved a stylus over the map it now showed.

"Last pass we dropped the four LACs, sixteen Marines total. We've got an observation post with a sniper on this hill on the far side of the lake. I've got a second one covering the south side of the lake near the dam and its road. The third one covers the approach road from town. Nobody comes to visit Mr. Jendon without us getting a good look."

"It's Mr. Annam," Kris said. "son Jendon actually does mean he's the son of his father, Jendon."

"I see your getting more information about this place."

"The fourth LAC dropped Penny and Chief Beni right in Annam's lap."

"They giving you much information besides what order the name goes in?"

"Not really," Kris said, cinching in her belt tighter. "Just that it is bad down there. Worse than Penny has ever seen."

"She wasn't with you during the Olympia Humanitarian Mission?"

"No, she ran into Tommy after that." There, Kris could say his name now without a shiver.

Jack turned back to his board. "I've split first and second platoons between the four longboats. Famine biscuits fill up the rest of the boat's cargo."

"Hello, fellow pilgrim," Kris muttered, "we come bearing stale bread and loaded M-6s. We're here to help you."

"Cause we're the only help you're going to get," Jack finished.

The longboat dropped free of the *Wasp*, and Kris found herself occupied with the unheard-of priority of keeping her stomach from embarrassing her.

Kris had survived a lot of botched assassination attempts. She had considered herself a survivor of the last one when she checked out of the hospital. Recovery, however, this time, was turning into a process with no end in sight.

Annam's lake gave plenty of room to land, but the actual landing was at a T-shaped wharf. That only left room for two longboats to unload at a time.

Jack ordered the two shuttles with first platoon to dock first and unload their Marines. The other two shuttles held in the air as long as they could before settling onto the lake and staying out in its middle. Lieutenant Stubben, the lone surviving officer of the original company, deployed first platoon and checked in with Penny. Only then did Jack let the last two shuttles, with him and Kris, come alongside the pier, swapping places with the first two.

And second platoon was well into its deployment before Jack got out of Kris's way so she could exit the craft.

"Didn't I read somewhere that the senior exits a vehicle first," Kris snarled through a smile . . . just in case there was a local watching.

"I seem to remember reading that somewhere, too," Jack admitted easily, without appearing to draw any conclusion from it that might apply to their situation.

Kris led her never-subordinate security chief out of the longboat. Marines were still trotting off the wharf from both shuttles. Coming out to meet Kris was Penny in whites and a thin man with salt-and-pepper hair. His clothes were worn shorts and a plaid shirt, his feet sported woven sandals. His hand was out to shake, but his smile was thin, and his eyes were clearly skeptical.

"Why are you here?" were the first words out of his mouth.

"We bring food," Kris said, shaking his hand. That wasn't really an answer to the question. Still, Kris hoped it was a welcome opener.

Behind Kris, a work detail of Marines removed bags of biscuits from the longboats and stacked them on the wharf. Kris waved at the gifts. The freeholder nodded, then turned, and, as the last of the Marines trotted from the pier, a stream of civilians broke from the dozen outbuildings in sight.

Penny's eyes said "I warned you," as Kris took in the oncoming humanity. Clothes ranged from the wreckage of finery to rags that barely maintained civilization's minimum for public decency. Not that anyone noticed. People moved with a minimum of effort, shuffling forward as if each step might be the last they could manage.

But it was the children that grabbed at Kris's heart. They stumbled forward on bony legs, their bellies distended. Children weren't the only bellies stretched in that grotesque lie. Many of the women who held a child's gaunt hand were hardly in better shape than the children beside them.

"We try to distribute what food we have evenly," Annam said, as if somehow he might expiate the sin that had allowed this to happen. "We try, but the gunmen come and demand food. We've hidden what we can, and if we have warning, we try to hide in the woods," he said, even as he shook his head. "But there is so little."

Kris had expected that the locals would haul the food away from the wharf. After all, each bag was only ten kilos.

Some of those approaching would probably be able to help. Some, but not many.

"Jack, we better carry a load of these out to the landing. If people have to walk out on the pier, there's going to be pushing and shoving. Someone's going to drown."

Jack was already issuing orders as he trotted for the longboat that had brought them. Up the way, Marines who had last come ashore turned about and double-timed back the way they'd come. At the door of the longboat, Marines paused in the stacking of sacks and looked ashore. Mouths got thin as sergeants ordered men to grab some food and double-time for the beach.

Kris took the load of the first Marine that reached her, sent him back for more, and jogged as fast as she could for the end of the pier, praying that dizziness would stay away for a few minutes. She still carried her cane, but there was no time to use it.

Kris got to solid ground about the same time the first refugees reached the pier. She pulled the string like the instructions said, and the bag easily came open. "Grab a handful to eat now, then go help the Marines carry the food ashore."

Eager hands emptied her first sack. There was pushing and shoving, but Kris just leaned into it. It wasn't anything that a well-fed person couldn't handle. Penny came up on her right. Annam on her left.

"Don't push. Don't shove," he shouted. "There's plenty for all. Those of you who can, take some back for the others. Those of you who are strong, help unload the bags on the T-head."

The raw need of the hungry was strong. Their panic was so close to the surface, pleading from empty eyes. Desperate hands reached out from mothers or fathers, grasping for something for themselves, or their children.

The Marines arrived and gently, carefully, edged the crowd back. Back from the water. Back from the few giving out handfuls of biscuits and full bags. The Marines could have driven the crowd back with rifle butts. Instead, they moved them with a shove here, a gentle word there. When a woman turned away with a couple of biscuits for her family, a Marine stepped forward into the hole.

Other Marines worked their way into the crowd, urging people to form lines. To leave room for people who had something to move to the back. When some young thugs knocked over an old woman and grabbed her handful of food, two Marines materialized as if by magic. The thugs went down hard.

From the crowd, another youth helped the old woman up while others saw that the woman's food was handed back.

"There's plenty for everyone," Gunny Brown shouted. "Just wait your turn."

"We've got a whole shipload of food in orbit," another Marine added.

"Commander, we got the first two longboats empty," came from the lead longboat pilot on net.

"Take them back up to orbit. Reload."

"Half and half, Marines and biscuits?"

"No," Kris said, empty of food and turning for more. A heavily loaded Marine was just coming up behind her. She grabbed a couple of bags. "Drop the rest here. Go get more."

The private did.

"What kind of load?" came again from the pilot.

"Jack, can we distribute just one platoon among the next four shuttle loads and leave room for more food?"

Kris's security chief was busy distributing food at her elbow. "That's acceptable," he said, "just so long as we keep one shuttle on the deck to get you out of here."

"We'll have two," Kris pointed out.

"Better."

Kris handed over a full bag to a man pleading for his family, who were too weak to walk. Maybe he was lying, but he looked barely able to stand. "Shuttle 3 and 4, launch for orbit. Return as fast as you can. Bring down one squad of Marine reinforcements each and as much food as you can carry."

"Aye, ayes," came back at Kris, and the two empty shuttles moved from where they bobbed in the lake to takeoff position.

A second squad of Marines returned from wherever they'd been posted for defense, slung their rifles, and joined in the food-distribution work. Around Kris, things were no less hectic and desperate, but order had taken hold, and the hungry throng sensed that there really was enough food for everyone. Now they waited patiently for their turn.

Kris stepped aside for a Marine to take her place, then tapped Jack, Penny, and Mr. Annam. "Can we talk now?"

"Yes. Yes, now would be a very good time. May I invite you to my home?" the farmer suggested.

Kris suspected that was a formal invitation. "Yes, I would

be grateful for your hospitality," she answered, using the words Nelly suggested. The plantation owner smiled with satisfaction, folded his hands, and gave Kris a little bow.

The crowd parted for them as Mr. Annam led them to the big house. That was a clearer sign of respect than Kris could have asked for. She hoped it cut both ways.

In the cool shade of the house's veranda, Mr. Annam slipped out of his sandals. Kris removed her shoes, and her team followed suit. Inside, they were offered seats in wicker chairs, and a woman quickly offered cups filled with a thin tea.

"This is my wife, Pinga. Without her careful husbandry of our meager resources, few would have lived to eat your gifts."

"My husband is too kind," said the short woman, wrapped in a colorful cloth. But she settled into a chair at his right and smiled at Kris. "If my husband has not thanked you for your generosity, then let me assure you that you and your men will have an eternal place in our hearts and in our prayers," she said, folding her hands and bowing her head.

"Thank you," Kris said, and found herself folding her hands and bowing in like fashion.

For a moment.

"How bad is it?" she asked, head coming up.

"My grandfather told me tales of famine on Earth and when he fled the Iteeche. He prayed that my young eyes would never see what his old eyes had seen. Now I know all too well what he saw. Maybe worse."

"What is your crop situation?" Penny asked.

"Our land is rich," Pinga said. "We can get three crops in. Rice, barley, millet, wheat all grow here fast enough for a spring, summer, and fall crop."

"But that is not enough to feed all those who flee to us," the husband added.

"We have switched most of our land to potatoes. Before, we only grew them for vodka, which sold well on New St. Petersburg. You know of that planet?"

Kris did. It was one of Greenfeld's most populous industrial centers. They liked their vodka there. She nodded.

"Sadly, New St. Petersburg knew all too well of us. People

from there doubled, then redoubled our population. Then doubled it again and maybe again," Annam said.

"At first, those who came here tore at our heartstrings," Pinga said. "They had nothing but were willing to work. We were glad to take them in. Thank heavens we did. Those early arrivals expanded our crops and made it possible for us to help the next and the next who came."

"And warned us when the bad ones arrived," Annam said.

"Bad ones," Kris echoed.

"The ones with guns," Pinga said, voice sharp with disapproval. "We were sharing all that we could. They laughed at us and demanded the best, and all of it."

"I quickly gave them what they wanted," Annam said. "The net by that time was full of the tale of what happened to those who did not give."

"We did what we had to do to save body and soul," Pinga agreed.

"I'm sure you did," Kris said, leaning back in her chair.

PENNY, IS THIS ALL NEWS TO YOU? Kris asked via her computer link through Nelly and her kids.

SORRY TO SAY, YES IT IS, KRIS.

AH, CREW, I KNOW IT'S NEAT TO HAVE THIS NEW TOY FOR TALKING AMONG OURSELVES VIA OUR COMPUTERS, came clearly in Jack's voice, BUT DON'T YOU THINK THESE FOLKS DESERVE THE COURTESY OF BEING INCLUDED IN OUR CONVERSATION?

"Mr. Annam," Kris asked, "have you heard anything about the conditions on New St. Pete?"

The plantation owner raised his hands to heaven. "I wanted to know as little about the goings-on there as I could. I thought they knew nothing about us, but I guess you cannot get the tiger drunk without its knowing where the good stuff comes from."

"I told you so," Pinga was quick to point out.

"Those who came to us first were the merchants who sold my products. I thought when I took them in that I had rolled up the carpet behind me. Unfortunately, others knew, and they told still others."

"It's the gunmen I'm curious about," Penny said. "We don't know much about what is happening in Greenfeld territory. Maybe even less about New St. Pete, but some of our analysts insisted there were a lot more criminal elements in the mix than the intelligence estimates allowed for."

"Something tells me even they were lowballing it," Kris said.

"And if Mr. Annam and his people are dealing with the criminals who had to flee St. Pete . . . ?" Jack said.

"What's left behind must be even worse," Penny concluded.

Kris shrugged. "But that is Vicky's problem."

"Commander Longknife, Captain Montoya, this is Staff Sergeant Bruce. We got company coming."

"What kind of company, Sergeant?" Jack asked.

"I make out forty-five trucks driving up the road from town. They're averaging about fourteen klicks an hour. ETA at our roadblock is seventeen minutes. Hey, Nelly, this new computer gives me real numbers."

"I told you so," Nelly said on net and to all present.

"Are they armed?" Jack cut in.

"First couple of trucks appear to have a general collection of rifles and pistols. Looks like the sort of stuff you could use to set up a nice museum of ancient firearms, sir. Beyond that, there are not a lot of long guns showing."

"Kris," Jack said, looking her straight in the eye, "now would be a good time for you to get out of here."

Kris made a face. She hated the idea of running. Even more, she hated the look on the faces of the farmer and his wife, like she'd kicked a puppy and was leaving it alone beside the road.

But she wasn't supposed to be in the middle of a shoot-out. Not with half Jack's company still in orbit.

Kris prepared to follow her security chief.

Then everything changed.

"Uh, this is the pilot of Shuttle 1. We got a problem."

"What kind of problem?" Jack asked, giving Kris the evil eye as if somehow, in some way, she was responsible for whatever came next.

"We, uh, thought we'd get ready, just in case we had to make a run for orbit. Just like I guess you want us to do now."

"And," Jack snapped. "Pilot, tell us today, not next week."

"Well, we needed water for reaction mass. So we started pulling lake water into our tanks."

"And you caught a fish?" Kris suggested.

"No, Your Highness. A fish we could have handled. No, they got a lot of water weeds growing around the wharf here, and we sucked them into our intakes. Locked them up something terrible."

"The other longboats made it to orbit," Jack snarled.

"Yes, sir. They pulled water into their tanks while they were out in midlake."

"Can you get the weeds out?" Kris asked.

"The copilot and some Marines have been trying to do it for the last five minutes. We really sucked it up there, ma'am."

"So we aren't going anywhere," Kris concluded.

"It sure looks that way," the poor pilot answered.

Kris stood. "Thank you for your hospitality," she said with a prayerful bow to the couple. Then she turned to Jack. "Captain, Lieutenant, looks like we better start walking over to Sergeant Bruce's roadblock."

"It does look that way," Jack said, activating his battle board and beginning to arrange his way-too-few troops.

5

The hike to the roadblock was hot and dusty. As Kris reflected back on her other advances to hostile contact, they all were either hot and dusty, or cold and wet. Why was a firefight never on a lovely, pleasant day?

Must be a rule somewhere.

"So, Your Highness," Jack said, "what are we doing here?"

Kris heard a serious question . . . heavily salted with sarcasm. But she had to admit, she'd been seriously chewing on just that question . . . in the light of what she'd started off the day wanting to do.

"Wouldn't it be nice if we don't win a bloody battle today?" she finally said.

Jack didn't seem surprised at her answer. "I assume that 'Let's not lose a battle today' is at least one step higher on your priority list."

"No question about that," Kris agreed.

Jack mulled that over for a moment. "You know, if we did kind of accidentally wipe out this hostile force coming our way, it might leave us the only power on this planet."

"I doubt it," Penny put in.

Kris gave her a raised eyebrow.

"Face it," Penny said. "Do you honestly think the big man is in the mob headed out here? You announced yourself, Princess, when you took down that pirate in orbit. They know they've got one of those damn Longknifes in the mix. If I were the big guy, I sure wouldn't risk my fair skin anywhere near you."

"I think Penny has a point," Kris said. "Even if we killed or captured every thug we're about to run into, there will be plenty left to cause us trouble tonight and next week. Jack, do you think you could control this planet with two hundred Marines?"

Jack scowled. "My company's job is to protect you, Miss Highness, not get stuck running around a planet chasing every bad actor with a gun." He paused, then added, "Still, I hate standing by while those pigs steal food from starving people."

"There is that." Kris sighed.

"There's a second reason we really shouldn't be wailing all over the badness on this planet," Penny said.

Kris and Jack both eyed her.

"Let's say that we set up our own police force here. That means we'll have to run food in here to feed all the hungry. How are you going to explain to Vicky Peterwald next time you run into her that you aren't really, actually, intentionally poaching on her old man's territory?"

And Kris was under specific orders not to even give the appearance of United Sentients horning in on Greenfeld's natural sphere of influence . . . much less actually *doing* the horning-in thing.

She hadn't complained about those orders when she got them.

But then, when she accepted her orders, she wasn't having her face rubbed in this mess. Had Grampa Ray, King Raymond I to most everyone else, seen this coming when he sent her here to do this job?

Had he, once again, chosen her because he knew she'd ditch her orders and do *the* job?

For the forty-eleventh-million time, Kris allowed nasty thoughts about being one of those damn Longknifes to chase themselves around the inside of her skull.

Enough of that, Kris thought, shaking her head. Policy reviews would have to wait for another day. Just now, she had a lot of heavily armed people who were eager to make her acquaintance. If she wasn't careful, some people might not survive the experience.

Most definitely, Kris did not want to be on the list of those who didn't see sunset tonight.

The dirt road they'd been hiking led them straight through what looked like dry rice paddies. Kris had never seen potatoes growing, but she guessed the low, leafy, green plants now spreading over the paddies were what potatoes pushed up above ground.

Sergeant Bruce's computer had spun off a nano eye. It now drifted about two thousand meters above his location; Kris studied its feed. Lieutenant Stubben had deployed first platoon along a paddy dike on either side of the road. As elements of second platoon arrived, Stubben sideslipped his troops to the left of the road, concentrating second to the right.

"It looks good," Kris told Jack, "but I would prefer us farther forward. Didn't Mr. Annam say they were eating a lot of potatoes?"

Kris looked over her shoulder; the couple were keeping up with them. Of course, Jack had shortened his usual long strides to accommodate Kris's slower, cane-assisted pace. Now, both of the locals nodded vigorously at Kris's remark.

Jack must have been getting the same overhead feed as Kris. "There's a newly mown field about a klick farther out. If we deploy carefully along the last paddy dike, all those other trampling feet ought to stay in the stubble."

"We were going to replant those barley fields today," Annam said. "I guess we can wait until tomorrow."

Jack started issuing orders to his Marines.

Kris found herself negotiating with her computer . . . and Nelly's kids. "Nelly, Chesty's eye spy nano has done good. Could you spin off a couple more from Penny and Jack's computers to cover the road all the way back to town?"

Penny and Jack didn't raise any problems with that.

Nelly mulled it over for several nano moments. "Both Mimzy and Sal still have uncommitted matrix and Smart Metal™ they can spare. I'll ask them to generate one remote each. Aren't you glad now, Kris, that I ordered more material than just the minimum for nine new computers."

Kris tried not to sigh. "I am now, Nelly, but as we have

talked about before, I want to preapprove your spending such a large wad of my money in the future."

"But you never would have approved money for my kids." Nelly didn't quite whine. Not quite. "Don't you often say that it is easier to get forgiveness than get permission?"

"Nelly, you've picked up bad habits hanging around Kris," Penny put in. "You've got to learn to do what she says, not what she does."

"When pigs can fly," Nelly suggested.

Kris decided her response could wait for a less busy day. "Longboat crew," she said on net.

"Yes, ma'am, we're still here. Still working. We need more time," came in a rush.

"I expect you will," Kris said dryly. "Could you have a couple of dozen bags of famine biscuits brought up here?"

"Yes, ma'am. Right away, ma'am."

"That's a seriously worried fellow," Penny said.

"If they hadn't been so eager to take on reaction mass, they wouldn't be in this mess," Kris said with a sigh. "Being too eager to please can be more trouble than . . ." Suddenly Kris thought better of finishing that sentence.

"Than getting a little lip, huh, Your Princessship?" Nelly finished.

"Doesn't look like there are any more trucks coming out from town," Jack said, changing the topic. "You have a problem with transportation, Mr. Annam?"

"When something breaks, there are no spare parts. And then there is the matter of food. You can either eat or make biofuel," the farmer said. "We used to eat the barley and feed the chaff to the fuel vats. Now the potato crop is all going for food. There's nothing to drink except the vat alcohol. Some people really need a drink."

"So what we see is about what they got. No reserves," Penny said.

"And we could end up owning most of the spare rolling stock on this planet," Kris mused.

"No. No. I don't want to own this planet. Vicky Peterwald is never happy to see my smiling face. Definitely she'll be unhappy if I drag in with a couple of planets chained to my ankle that her father considers his."

"You talk as if you knew the Peterwalds personally," the plantation owner said. "Could that be so?"

"They've met on several occasions," Penny said. "So far, everyone has survived the experience, but it's been close a few times."

The farmer and his wife exchanged astonished glances. "Next time you see them, could you ask them to please stop sending refugees to our poor planet?"

"I could ask them, but I don't think they'd pay me any attention," Kris said. "Also, I doubt many of these refugees bothered to ask permission to leave. They are just running. Running from something worse."

"How could anything be worse?"

Kris glanced back at the shelters where the starving refugees were having their first meager meals in way too long. "I don't know," she said, "but running must have seemed like a good idea when they started moving."

The last squad of second platoon trotted up and joined the others at the first paddy dike. They were followed by several less emaciated locals pulling wheeled carts piled high with food sacks. Kris told them to halt in the road where she intended to stand. Everyone was in position by the time the first truckload of gunmen came around a small hillock and headed toward them.

The Marines had taken cover, using what the dikes offered. Squad sergeants made the rounds of their teams, checking them out, correcting where necessary, and offering good examples of calm. Platoon skippers and their sergeants did the same.

Hopefully, this would keep buck fever on a tight leash. About half the platoons' troopers were replacements, facing their first live-fire experience. The standing officers and NCOs also gave a clear signal to the opposition of how many they faced even if the individual trigger pullers stayed low.

Now it was time for Kris to find out what had come out to meet her.

The trucks were a mix of different three-to-five-ton rigs with flatbeds or strake side boards. They came up the road in single file, forty-five exactly. Four hundred meters out there was a cross trail. The lead truck drove past it, then stopped. A man standing on the bed of that truck used hand signals to send alternate trucks left or right. When he had twenty-two trucks on either side of him, he waved them all forward.

In a ragged turn, the other trucks moved off the trail and started to bounce across the field, trying, in a very imperfect way, to dress on each other.

"Not a bad effort," Jack said as he watched the evolution. Then one truck fell out with a broken water line spewing steam. Another came to a halt for no apparent reason.

Kris eyed the central truck, the one she'd tagged as the command vehicle. The standing man waved his arms and shouted at the breakdowns. Clearly, he wasn't the calm sort.

Just how professional was the guy across the way? What was he trained in? How good was he? How good were his troops? Kris had a long list of unanswered questions.

Her list of answers was very short. Too much was just one big question mark.

"When do you think he'll stop?" Penny asked.

That was a question Kris hadn't gotten down to. How close would she let this joker get to her Marines?

"Jack, pass The Word, if the trucks close to 150 meters, I want the tires shot out. But wait for my order."

Jack passed along The Word. To Kris's right and left, officers and NCOs glanced at them as they got it. A moment later, squad leaders went down their Marines, picking their best shooters for tire detail.

The chosen Marines showed clear intent as they dialed in their sight pictures. Others around them, under the watchful eyes of the NCOs, kept their rifles aimed high. Not too high, but high enough that a miss-shot would pass well above the heads of the approaching trucks.

Kris ordered Chesty's spy eye to focus on the command rig. The man was still standing though now he leaned on the cab of the truck, binoculars roving over the Marine position. Then he came back to focus on Kris.

Kris couldn't help it; she gave him a confident wave.

Two hundred meters away, the man with the binoculars put them down and scowled at Kris. Then he turned to the trucks on either side and raised his right hand.

The trucks came to a ragged halt. Up and down the line people shouted as they leapt, dropped, or helped others from the trucks. To shouts, the general mob flowed into a line, of sorts, facing Kris and her deployed Marines.

Kris studied them. Most looked hardly better off than the refugees Kris had just fed. Some leaned on long poles with blades on their tips. Someone must have gone into business converting available metal into machetes. There were many examples of them, similarly fashioned to the ones the Marines had confiscated from the pirates in orbit.

Many of the people had nothing but a club or bat.

Of course, there were also those with rifles and machine pistols.

The two trucks on the extreme wings each disgorged twenty or so men and women who held these weapons and looked like they knew how to use them. Dressed in parts of black uniforms, they went to ground. Once prone, they settled into a steady aim at Kris's Marines.

They didn't bother being nonthreatening. None of that aiming high stuff for them.

The Marines returned the favor as their rifles came level.

The two trucks closest to the command rig also had heavily armed types. On close observations, some even had body armor. A few shoulders showed NCO stripes from Greenfeld State Security. Once prone, they took the same aggressive aim at Marines.

The hairs on the back of Kris's neck stood up. From the looks of it, she needed to start a new timer on how long it had been since someone tried to kill her.

Kris moved the overhead picture to examine the prone shooters across from her.

Beside her, Penny shook her head. "Look at all the un-employed Greenfeld security troops. Wonder how good they are?"

"Something tells me we're going to find out," Jack said.

Kris shrugged. "I don't recall that many times Peterwald's State Security went up against anyone with guns, do you?"

Penny took her own good time answering Kris's question. "Officially, the boys in black never have used their guns," she said slowly. "Abby says there are unofficial reports of several public protest gatherings that got sprayed with auto-matic weapons fire. There are no reports of anyone shooting back. The Peterwalds keep pretty tight control of guns in their backyard."

"Keep, or *kept* control of guns?" Jack asked.

Penny just shrugged.

Kris completed her study of the opposition. It seemed to fall into two distinct groups. Those with guns were well fed and focused on threatening the Marines. Those without guns were emaciated, formed small groups to talk among them-selves, and seemed a whole lot less interested in being close to all this firepower.

Given a bit of encouragement, Kris strongly suspected the gunless types would happily run.

All Kris had to do was figure out a way to let them. Some-thing told her the gun toters were there as much to intimidate their hungry partners as to impact the Marines.

I THOUGHT WE DIDN'T WANT TO START A BLOODBATH TO-DAY, Nelly thought.

KEEP REMINDING ME OF THAT. IT'S VERY TEMPTING TO LET THE CHIPS START FLYING. YOU KNOW OF ANY WAY FOR ME TO GET A GOOD ESTIMATE ON HOW MANY REALLY BAD GUYS ARE OUT THERE?

I HAVE NOT THE FOGGIEST IDEA. I COULD GIVE YOU AN ACCURATE COUNT OF THE NUMBER WITH GUNS, BUT INTENT IS PURE GUESS.

THAT'S WHAT I THOUGHT, Kris said with an internal sigh.

Across the way, the boss man still stood with the truck cab between himself and Kris's Marines. Did he really think something that thin would do him any good if it came to a fight? Now he was talking to a cluster of youth.

Kris was about to order a nano spy over to get a listen when one kid pulled his dirty white shirt over his head and started trotting toward Kris's battle line. Every couple of steps, the shirt got waved.

"I think they want to talk," Kris said.

6

The youth stopped halfway between Kris and the boss man's truck. He squatted down, occasionally gave the shirt a wave . . . and waited.

"Looks like they insist we meet them halfway," Kris said.

"You are not going out there," Jack said, and moved to put himself between Kris and any chance of her going farther down the road.

"I had no intentions of doing so," Kris answered.

"Besides," Penny slipped in, "princesses do not negotiate with street urchins. It's unseemly."

"Thank you, Miss Protocol," Kris said.

"She does have a point," Jack insisted.

"Who do we send?" Kris asked.

"How about me?" Sergeant Bruce said on Nelly net. "After all, I work for a living. No skin off my nose talking to a kid."

"You listening in on us now, Sergeant?" Captain Jack Montoya asked with a bit of sharpness underlying his voice.

"No, but I think Chesty is, and he brought me up to speed when it looked like you needed the helping hand of a workingman."

"Nelly?" Kris said.

"My kids are curious. They can keep track of a lot more than you humans can," the computer said with one of Abby's sniffs.

"You've got the computer," Kris said to the Marine sergeant. "Use it as you see fit."

"But don't let your skipper fall out of the loop," Jack said in defense of the chain of command.

"And you be careful," Abby put in from orbit, proving that Jack and Kris's conversation had a whole lot of gawkers following it.

"I will, honey. Now, Captain, would you mind putting a request in to Lieutenant Stubben about me and your assignment."

"Ain't it the truth. The poor working boss is always the last to know," Jack said.

"You could give him an upgraded computer," Nelly suggested.

"No way," came in unison, from both live and on net.

In the back of Kris's head, Nelly felt very poutish. Kris left her to stew in her own computing juices.

Jack said a few words. Lieutenant Stubben said a few words. Then Sergeant Bruce said a lot of words. Some were directed at his LT, accepting his assignment. Others were to his squad, arranging for a corporal to take over. Finally, he spoke to his fellow sergeants as he passed through their sections of the line on his way to the road.

"You mind if I take a bag of biscuits?" he asked as he reached Kris's team. "That kid out there looks way past hungry."

"Might put him in the mood to listen to us," Kris said. The sergeant drew a bag of famine rations from the pushcarts that had come up behind Kris. He slung it through his web gear, made sure it did not interfere with the swing of his rifle, and ambled out to meet the kid.

The youngster kept squatting in the dust until the sergeant paused ten meters from him. Then he stood up. He couldn't take his eyes from the biscuit sack, but he had his script, and he remembered it.

"The boss says for you to get out of here," the youth shouted, waving a hand for emphasis. Sergeant Bruce sent back a high-res picture of the kid as he talked. Kris got to look at every lick he gave of his dry lips. Every time his pupils expanded or contracted, Kris got the picture. And the running commentary from Penny and her Mimzy.

THIS KID IS SCARED. SCARED AND STARVED. READING HIM WILL NOT BE EASY. IT IS VERY LIKELY HE BELIEVES WHAT HE IS SAYING, Mimzy reported.

"The boss says that this is none of your business. This is none of Kris Longknife of Wardhaven's business. This is Greenfeld internal affairs. Buzz out. You ain't wanted."

THE KID BELIEVES ALL THAT. HE'S JUST A CHILD SENT TO CARRY A MAN'S MESSAGE. AND HE'S HUNGRY. VERY HUNGRY. I CAN HEAR HIS STOMACH GROWLING FROM HERE, Mimzy concluded.

LET'S SEE WHAT HAPPENS WHEN I FEED HIM, thought Sergeant Bruce. He kept one hand on the trigger of his weapon. With the other, he pulled the string on the ration sack. Several biscuits escaped to fall in the dirt at his feet, but he still held a handful. Those he tossed at the kid.

The kid went for the food with both hands, fumbled the catch, then grabbed for them as they fell to the ground. He ended up with one in his mouth and two in each hand. That left him in a poor situation to continue the bargaining.

Sergeant Bruce took the opportunity to jack up his voice via Chesty's speaker. "I am a Royal Wardhaven Marine. I can be your best friend or your worst nightmare. My king considers Kaskatos as neutral territory, claimed by no one but the folks who work the land. Word is that you've come on hard times. The Red Cross, Red Star, and Red Crescent have loaded a lot of food on our ship and asked us to distribute it to those in need." He paused for a moment to look up and down the line facing him.

"I think they include you folks." He turned to Kris. "Princess Kristine, would you roll the food carts out here, please?"

The local laborers looked terrified at the thought of going any closer to the armed thugs, but Mr. Annam motioned to them, and they stepped forward. Each of the carts had two handles. It took two people on each to get the carts moving. Kris considered ordering Marines to do the work but dropped the idea as the carts trundled past her.

For the rest of her life, Kris would wonder why she didn't listen to her first instinct.

The eight laborers pushed the carts and their load of famine rations out into the no-man's-land between the Marines and the townspeople. The laborers were exhausted by the work they'd done already today. The road was rutted and made for hard going.

It jostled the cart.

Someone with the best of intentions had piled sacks of rations as high as they could reach.

About the time the carts reached Sergeant Bruce, all the good intentions came apart.

First a single sack fell off to burst in the dust of the road. Then a couple of dozen bags tumbled as one whole side of the pile gave way.

For a long moment you could hear the sound of sacks sliding, bouncing off the carts' wheels, plopping onto the dusty trail.

Then there were shouts from the milling mob across the way. Shouts and screams. Like a stampeding herd of desperate animals, they broke ranks and charged for the food.

"Bruce, get out of there," Kris ordered on net. "Get the locals and get out of there."

"Yes, ma'am. I'm moving."

The sergeant didn't need to say a word to the locals. They could see what was headed their way and bolted for safety before the Marine could even turn around.

Starved and exhausted they might be, but if Kris had had a timer, she suspected the record for the mad hundred-meter dash would have fallen that afternoon.

The laborers didn't stop running when they hit the Marine line but kept right on going. Kris hoped they remembered to stop when they hit the plantation, but she wouldn't bet on that.

Kris had no time to follow them; her eyes were on the onrushing mob. Sergeant Bruce backpedaled fifteen or twenty meters past the food carts, then, rifle at the ready, stood his ground.

The kid who'd given the speech took the opportunity to load up on five or six sacks, and made a run back to the truck line. Of course, to do that, he had to pass through the onrushing mob.

One guy swinging a machete took his head off.

Four or five of the closest people grabbed for the blood-spattered sacks and ripped into them. They didn't bother reading the instructions, so it took them longer to get at the ration biscuits than it should have.

The scene when the mob hit the carts was just as bad. They bowled them over. People went down, screaming as they were trampled. Clubs swung, machetes hacked.

It was a bloodbath.

Sergeant Bruce was closest. He saw it all. He and Chesty transmitted none of it. But he did risk a quick turn back to Kris. His plaintive shrug said it all. *What do we do now?*

Doing nothing had seemed like a good idea. Now, doing something seemed like a much better one.

"Jack, advance two squads of Marines to reinforce Sergeant Bruce."

"Yes, I think we better," he said, and the orders were quickly given.

Twenty Marines rose from cover behind the paddy dike and, rifles ready, moved quickly to support the sergeant. Kris reached for her automatic, and announced on general net, "I am about to fire one shot in the air. Be prepared for any reaction."

Beside Kris, Penny made a sour face but said nothing. Jack moved to put his body between Kris and the opposing forces.

Kris fired three shots straight into the air. "Everybody calm down," she shouted. Nelly enhanced her voice, causing Jack and Penny to do a bit of a jump. Behind Kris, Mr. Annam and his wife hit the ground.

"Calm down, everyone. We've got food enough for all of you," Kris repeated.

For a long moment, it looked like it might work.

The slaughter around the food carts stopped as people looked up to see where the noise was coming from. Maybe some even understood the words Kris shouted. For a long moment, Kris could hear the moans of the injured.

But the decision for what would happen next depended on those who carried the machine pistols and rifles. Most of them still lay prone on the flanks of the line and in its dead center. Those 140 or so gunslingers hadn't moved.

Yet.

Among the seven to eight hundred club and machete swingers who had broken for the food carts were maybe fifty gunmen, say the precinct bosses who had produced the cannon fodder. They held back when the rabble broke. Now they looked for instructions from the boss man on his perch on the central truck.

Then the undecided silence was shattered.

Someone let loose on full rock and roll.

Kris thought it came from the far right of the opposing line, but a quick glance in that direction showed no stream of bullets knocking people down like tenpins. And one quick glance was all the time Kris had. A roar of fire, single-shot and fully automatic, swept the battlefield.

One of them, probably an old-fashioned .30 caliber, took Kris right in the chest, almost knocking her down. If she hadn't been wearing a spider-silk bodysuit, it would have drilled her through the heart.

As it was, the force of it left Kris struggling to keep her footing even with the cane's extra help. Around her, screams came as first a few, then more of the milling rabble around the overturned carts were hit by small-arms fire.

Then Jack hit Kris with a football tackle, and she went solidly down . . . taking Penny with her. They ended up in a pile, Jack with his back to the firefight, Kris sandwiched between him and Penny.

Penny was talking to herself . . . or someone on net more likely . . . but she interrupted herself to complain. "Hey, you two could have given me some warning."

"You work for a Longknife," Jack snapped. "Consider yourself permanently warned."

Kris found herself staring at the Annams. Husband and wife clutched each other . . . but they clutched the ground even more as they stared wide-eyed at Kris.

"Stay behind me, bullets can't get through me," Kris said.

"Of course," the husband told her wife. "She is a Long-knife and cannot be killed."

"She can be killed," Jack spat, and used his hand to force Kris's head back down even as she twisted around and tried to sneak a quick look at the developing battle. "You aren't wearing an armored wig, are you?"

Jack was right, Kris wasn't. And now Kris knew why the Marine's usual high-and-tight haircut had looked a bit shaggy this morning. He *was* wearing an armored hairpiece.

"First platoon has not fired," came from Lieutenant Stubben, "but we are taking fire."

"Second platoon the same," followed him in only a second.

"Permission to return fire," Lieutenant Stubben said.

Kris got her head up for a quick look around. Jack put her head back down, then snapped off a stream of choice words as his elbow took a hit. The spider-silk bodysuit kept the bullet from doing major damage. It didn't keep it from stinging to beat all hell.

Somewhere to the right, a Marine wasn't so lucky. The shout of "Medic. Medic!" came down the line.

Kris didn't want a fight. She didn't want to conquer this planet. If she did, she was letting herself in for all kinds of headaches.

To her left, a medic bent low as she trotted down the line to where her duty called. A bullet hit her battle armor and knocked her down. She got up and kept trotting.

Kris drew in a deep breath. "Captain, put an end to this slaughter."

"Yes, ma'am. Platoon leaders, put down anyone shooting at us or unarmed civilians."

"Aye, aye, Skipper," came back in a second, followed by orders.

A moment later, the racket of small-arms fire was punctuated by one sharp volley as Marines entered the battle.

There was a hiccup of silence as the realization dawned on the other side that this wasn't a one-sided turkey shoot . . . anymore.

Then the orchestra of sundry weapons went back to making racket: revolvers and automatics, long rifles and automatic pistols, assault rifles and submachine guns.

"Fire at will," came over the net from two Marine lieutenants, and the unique staccato of the M-6s joined the symphony like the roll of a snare drum.

Kris listened to the sound of the bullets whizzing by. Most seemed well above her. "These guys are shooting high."

"Easy to do with a machine pistol," Jack said. "But they could get lucky. How much luck do you think you got left, Your Highness?" he said, pushing her head back down. "You really should think about the chance that there's a bottom to that pot of gold."

"I'll just rob another rainbow," Kris muttered as she tried to crawl away from Jack. He crawled right along with her, keeping his back between her and the hostile fire . . . and his arm ready to push her face back into the dirt. He seemed to like rubbing her face in the fine yellow dust of the road.

Marine fire was getting more sporadic. Other shots were getting downright rare.

"What do you say we get up and look around?" Kris said.

Jack rolled over and did his own look-see at the wreckage. Apparently it was quiet enough for him to stand up and dust himself off.

Kris rolled to her feet. Across the field from her, the truck with the boss guy riding it was backing up, turning around, and heading back to town.

Kris didn't want that.

"Jack, could a Marine please flatten the tires on that truck."

Jack gave the order, but the truck not only gunned away from them, but the guy in charge was smart enough to toss a string of smoke grenades to give himself cover.

Marine fire didn't slow him down.

"I really don't want that guy getting back to town," Kris said.

"Grenadier," Lieutenant Stubben shouted, and a Marine raised his rocket launcher and fired off three quick rounds.

The first rocket missed ahead, but the other two walked

themselves down the road to where the truck was busy racing up to meet them. The resulting collision left only small pieces of truck and body parts flying through the air.

Kris shook her head. "I had a few questions I wanted to ask that joker, but I suppose they can wait." She stooped to dust herself off; her whites now looked more like khakis.

But her eyes swept the battlefield before her, and the butcher's bill stopped her where she stood.

7

A shout of "Medic!" came from second platoon. A Marine with the Red Cross pack was there in seconds, but she was shaking her head before she knelt.

The Marine had taken a slug right between her eyes.

Not all the fire had been high.

Two of the Marines forward at Sergeant Bruce's position were also down and bleeding. In both cases, they'd taken repeated hits in the same general vicinity. The warranty on standard-issue armor doesn't apply to multiple hits.

"Abby, what happened to my order for four-hundred-plus spider-silk-armored bodysuits, reinforced with liquid metal?" Kris demanded of her maid and extremely good scrounger.

"In case you haven't noticed, Princess, we are way out beyond the Rim of human space, and our mail ain't so good. Our supply ship, the *Surprise*, is supposed to be bringing out those packages, but, you'll excuse me if I say I'll be surprised if I ever see anything from that boat."

Abby, of course, was right about their being far off the beaten path, and the *Surprise* was rapidly developing a bad reputation for it being a surprise if she had what you wanted. Of course, the last time she made a trip back to Wardhaven, she'd returned overloaded with famine rations. It was hard to complain about that kind of load after mornings like today.

If it wouldn't mean losing Abby, Kris was getting more and more tempted to activate her maid's reserve first lieutenant commission and order her to set up her own supply service.

On the second hand, that would mean losing Abby's services as a superb intelligence gatherer.

And on the third hand, this close to the Peterwald Empire, turning Abby loose with a checkbook might result in some really strange financial deals. Wars had been started over less.

"Kris," Penny said, coming to her feet, "if I could get a breath in edgewise, I've been talking to folks on the *Wasp*. They've been interrogating our pirate prisoners."

"Who's doing the interrogations?" Kris asked.

On its last trip to Wardhaven, the *Wasp* had acquired more Marines and sailors, and, though Kris wasn't sure, there seemed to be a lot of new faces among the civilians on board. Professor mFumbo told her that half of the boffins found the present situation too bland for their tastes. They'd been run through the National Secrets Act, solidly scared about breathing a word about what they witnessed while touring the galaxy with one Kris Longknife . . . sometime princess and inevitable troublemaker . . . and sent on their way.

Which didn't explain who was paying the new civilians on board and what they were there for. Was Admiral Crossenshield slipping his kind of black-ops folks into Kris's crew?

NELLY, CAN YOU TELL ME ANYTHING ABOUT THE NEW CIVILIAN MEMBERS OF OUR CREW? Kris had asked early in the voyage.

NO, KRIS. NOW THAT CAPTAIN DRAGO KNOWS I'VE GOT THE SHIP'S COMPUTER EATING OUT OF MY HAND, HE'S TAKEN TO WITHHOLDING CERTAIN INFORMATION FROM THAT COMPUTER. I KNOW HOW MANY PEOPLE WE HAVE ON RATIONS, NAVY, MARINE, AND CIVILIANS; BUT I DON'T KNOW ANYTHING ABOUT WHO THESE NEW PEOPLE ARE. YOU KNOW, KRIS, I DON'T THINK THE CAPTAIN TRUSTS ME ANYMORE.

I DON'T THINK HE EVER TRUSTED ME. HE AND I ARE GOING TO HAVE TO TALK.

GOOD LUCK AT THAT, KRIS. I MIGHT ALSO ADD THAT ABBY STILL USES HER OLD COMPUTER AND TURNS MY KID OFF REGULARLY. THAT WOMAN DOES NOT TRUST ANYONE.

So it was with some trepidation that Kris asked Penny,

"Who's been doing the interrogations, and just what are they doing?"

"Don't worry, Kris. We just sat them down in one of the civilian bistros and ordered hamburgers, fries, and beer."

"Hamburgers?"

"Yeah. Most of them haven't had a decent meal in three, four months. Put some decent food in front of them. Throw in a couple of beers, and our intel staff are their new best friends."

Hmm, that's an interesting approach. "So what are they saying?"

"Nothing," Penny said with a shrug. "But that nothing tells us a lot."

Confused, Kris frowned. "Such as?"

"You may have noticed that they rammed us."

"Captain Drago made sure I did indeed notice that. And he reminds me of it every chance he gets," Kris said dryly.

"Well, none of those intrepid buccaneers had ever been on a spaceship as anything but passengers. The sum total of experience for the gal at the helm was two summers steering a boat loaded with tourists around a lake."

Kris winced. "And if they'd captured the *Wasp* . . . ?"

"They'd all get jobs as deckhands or something on the pirate ship, but Jackson, the guy running the show down here, has a merchant officer and some crew that would be running the ship."

Kris put two and two together and didn't like what it told her. "So none of our prisoners know where they'd be taking the *Wasp* to outfit it with guns or to sell its cargo."

"Ignorant as the day they were born," Penny said.

"I'm not following you," Jack said. He'd been issuing orders to his Marines to do what they could to help the survivors of the slaughter while half-listening to Kris and Penny. "Are you talking about some kind of pirate base?"

"Exactly," Kris said. "You don't operate spaceships without a dock to handle repairs. You need facilities to overhaul reactors and engines. Why steal stuff if you don't have a marketplace that will take anything you bring in, file the serial numbers off it, and ship it back out to the trade lanes?

You've seen the size of the fleet-support bases that Ward-haven has."

Jack nodded.

"Somewhere, these pirates have a support system. Probably smaller, but it's there. We can keep chasing after this or that pirate ship, or we can find the base and squash the cockroaches in their nest. Which would you rather do?"

"Taking down a nest sounds like my kind of job," Jack said with a grin.

"So who is this Jackson guy?" Kris asked, turning to the Annams.

They shook their heads. "I have not been to town in over six months," he said. "It is worth your life to ask questions when the gunmen come to collect food."

"No surprise," Penny said. "The crew of the ketch didn't know much, either. I doubt any survivors of this shoot-out know a whole lot, but whoever is running this show would have our klepto captain close at hand. I suggest we talk to the survivors here and see if anyone wants to talk to us about what's going on here. Anything they tell us is more than we know right now."

The three of them split up. Kris ordered Chief Beni to look over the trucks. One of them might have a computer, map system. Something. With a Marine guard at her elbow, Kris started her own walk through the dead and dying.

Workers from the local plantation were trying to separate the pile of bodies around the food carts. These poor souls had been between the gunslingers from the three middle trucks and Sergeant Bruce's Marines. The thugs had opened fire on these starving people and mowed them down in droves. The bodies were piled four or five deep.

Apparently, just getting between the shooters and their Marine targets was enough to sign your death warrant. The milk of human kindness seemed to run mighty thin in this neighborhood.

Or just limped.

A few quick orders from their officers had adjusted the Marines' fire lanes. The troopers to the right and left had concentrated their fire on the hostiles in the center. The Marines in the center had divided their aim between the shooters on the right and left.

That was the difference between being a trained fighting man and being a member of an armed mob.

Kris shook her head slowly. How could fools with guns hope to stand against a trained fighting team?

Now, out along the former gun line, Marines moved quickly to help those still breathing. One was getting yelled at for her effort.

"You're all gonna die," the gunslinger tried to yell. It came out little more than a croak. "Once Jackie gets her hands on you, you're gonna die long and slow, and I'm gonna laugh and laugh at you."

The last was unlikely as the voice sputtered down and ended with a hacking cough.

Kris turned her back on that scene and concentrated on the people who had been slaughtered while just trying to get a bit to eat.

Most were already beyond help, but one guy gasped for water as he was laid out. Kris took the canteen her Marine guard offered and knelt beside the man. Blood pulsed from a wound in his chest.

Kris offered the canteen, and the man drank from it. He coughed up water, blood and froth, then sipped a few more drops. The Marine produced a bandage and knelt beside Kris to apply it, but the man waved it away.

"Let me die in peace," he gasped.

The Marine turned away. He looked around for someone more interested in living but didn't seem to find anyone. He folded up the bandage and stepped back, returning to alert guard.

The dying man lifted his chin. "You're that Longknife woman? The one that saved Peterwald? I saw your picture on the news."

"Yes," Kris admitted.

"I wish you hadn't. All hell broke out after you did."

Kris didn't have an answer to that, so she kept her peace.

"I thought I could get my family away from St. Pete. Find a hole to hide in." His cackle of bitter laughter turned into choking, and more blood came up.

Kris offered another sip of water. He took a swig, then spat it out. After a while, he started talking again.

"Jackson said if we didn't come out here . . . bring back the food . . . she'd kill our families. She's got all of them in the local football stadium." He shook his head. "Now she'll likely kill them all and put their heads on pikes. She's gonna run out of pikes if she keeps this up."

He didn't laugh at his joke. Or maybe there was no joke in his words. Kris found them horrifying.

"Where is this Jackson?" Kris asked. "How much heat do her gunslingers have? Help me save your family."

"Could you save them like you saved Peterwald? How many will die this time?"

The guy had a legitimate question. Saving Peterwald had cost five thousand innocent lives immediately. How many had died and were going to die in this reign of terror as he and others did their power dance?

"If I have to kill some of Jackson's hired thugs, how many of them will be innocent bystanders?"

"Not a one," the man said. "You gonna save my wife? My kids?"

"I'm going to give it a Longknife try," Kris said, as the man died in her arms.

Kris stood, her dusty whites now caked with the rust of drying blood. She looked around the field. Marines moved with armored and armed purpose. Locals moved with bare legs and skinny arms, helping where they could. Kris spotted Chief Beni, unhooking his computer from a truck.

"Chief, you find anything?" she asked on net.

"This planet doesn't have a GPS system, but this truck has a cheap inertial platform that tracks where it's been and helps generate maps. I know where it came from."

"And that would be?"

"Tranquility Road. That's a small street, near the center of Lander's Rest. When I overlay a photo from the *Wasp*, Tranquility Road seems to be the home of some mighty wealthy people. At least their homes are large, and there is a lot of green around them."

Nelly pulled a picture from Da Vinci, the chief's computer, and hung it in the air ahead of Kris.

"Is that a nice place to live?" Kris asked Mr. Annam.

He nodded. "My father thought of building a town house there. He decided that we had always been farmers, and the money should go into our farm. Now, I am glad he did."

"Nelly, zoom in the picture. I'm looking for an iron fence with spikes. Is there one?"

"These three houses in the middle of the block have such fences. One of our nanoscouts is in that area. Let me zoom in."

"You might want to look away from this," Kris said in warning to the locals.

"What are those things?" the wife asked.

"Severed heads," Kris said. "Severed heads and the crows that feed on them. I think we've found where the powers that be on Kaskatos hang out."

The plantation owner and his wife managed to turn away before they were explosively sick.

8

Kris gave the Annams a minute to recover before she continued questioning them. She took the moment to squeeze down all feelings in herself. Gentleness, concern, anything that nurtured human warmth was something she could not afford today. Despite the sweat running down her face, the day would be a cold, cold one.

Done locking down her gut, Kris asked the first of many questions that would lead to rack and ruin. "Is there a football stadium in Lander's Rest?"

Nelly had identified two large stadiums. Mr. Annam pointed out the larger one. "The smaller is for school contests."

"Jack, Penny, to me, please. I think I've got enough information to plan an attack. Abby, Colonel, are you on net?

Both of them were.

"You heard about Jackie Jackson," Penny said as she trotted up to Kris. "He's one bad hombre."

"One bad girl," Kris corrected. "I think she's Jacqueline, not Johnny."

"Jacqueline; I thought we girls were supposed to be nice and gentle and good," Penny insisted.

"Penny, you're hanging out with a Longknife gal," Jack said on net, still jogging toward Kris. "How could you possibly be that ill informed?"

"Okay, so I believe in that sugar and spice and everything nice stuff. A girl's got a right to her illusions."

"Sorry, folks, no illusions today," Kris said. "We got ourselves some iron-hard facts. Ugly iron spikes with heads on them."

"Ah, Princess, this is Shuttle 1. We finally got the weeds out of our intakes. We've taken on a full tank of reaction mass. Do you need a lift off planet?"

Jack joined Kris, hardly out of breath, but with the usual quizzical eyebrow raised. "That was the plan, as I recall," Jack said.

"That plan didn't work out. Change of plan. New plan," Kris said.

Behind Kris, there was a gasp. She turned to see the An-nams, mouth wide open. "But you are a Longknife. For Long-knifes, things always go according to plan."

"Yeah," Kris agreed. "I read that in the history books, too. Trust me. It may have worked that way for my great grandparents, but it doesn't seem to *ever* work that way for me."

Kris left the two locals to marvel at that revelation and turned back to her crew.

"You're not leaving?" Jack said.

"No. Send the shuttles up to the *Wasp*. Abby, see that the shuttle loads are changed. Marines only the next trip down. No food. Ask Drago if he can put together a Navy landing party to back up the Marines. Shooters, docs, food, anything the squid can do to support the trigger pullers."

"Got that, Kris," Abby replied on net. "We go loaded for bear. All that talk about us not wanting to upset Vicky and her daddy is canceled. We're back in the kick ass and take names business. Goody Two-shoes stuff will have to wait in line."

Jack eyed Kris. He wasn't actually questioning her de-cision. No, it was more like he wanted to make sure she'd weighed all her options and knew what she was doing.

"The situation here is a lot worse than I expected," Kris said crisply. "The local warlord is a vicious killer. If we main-tain a presence here, and are kind enough to let her live, she will repay us by sniping at us on every corner. No, folks. We'd better cut the head off this snake today. I'll apologize pro-fusely to Vicky next time I see her."

"What is the target?" the colonel asked without skipping a beat.

"That's my problem, Colonel, and I'd like your advice on it. I see two, no three, maybe four targets, and I got a bad feeling in my gut that if I go for all of them, I'll spread myself too thin and fail to get any of them."

"It's been known to happen," he said, noncommittal-like. "Talk to me."

"Somewhere, down in this haystack, is a needle of a pirate captain. He may or may not have a whole crew. I want to catch that joker and find out what he or she knows."

"After seeing the comedy routine that the *Wasp* encountered this morning, I think Captain Drago would heartily agree," the colonel said.

"The nasty type running this setup is Jackie Jackson. She appears to have taken over the best houses in town for her minions and is here, on the totally misnamed Tranquility Road."

"Yes. I earlier observed her taste in lawn decorations. She definitely has been breathing air much longer than I, for one, would care to share it with her," the colonel said dryly.

"I figure the best place to nail her is at her headquarters, but I think there's at least a fifty-fifty chance she'll choose to beat it out of town. She's sent her machete swingers and gunslingers up against us twice and lost both times. She could try us a third time, or she could take advantage of either of these two roads to beat it out of town fast."

Here, Kris had Nelly back off from the map of Lander's Rest enough to show the roads headed out of town. One led south to the Annam plantation, among others. "This southern road is the one first and second platoons will be taking into town. She might come out to meet us."

"Not likely," the colonel said. "She did that once, and it didn't work all that well."

"Yes," Kris said, trying not to look around at the bloody results. "The other roads offer her two different options. This eastern one takes her to the hills. We could likely track her, but digging out her and her muscle could be a major bit of work."

"Nothing my Marines couldn't handle," Jack said.

"Maybe, Captain," the colonel said. "Do we have any count as to how many people this Jackie has working for her?"

"No estimate at all. In the past, it's been fluid. If she wanted more heat, she'd recruit them by threatening their families. I'll get to that in a moment."

When no one said anything, Kris went on. "The western road out of town follows the river and leads us to a whole lot of large ranches and plantations. I'm afraid that if she gets in among them, she could terrorize the folks into giving her cover.

"'Cooperate with me, and I'll give you food. Help that Longknife woman, and your kids get their brains blown out.' Who wins in that situation?"

"It does get messy," the colonel agreed.

"And with her up the east road, she can strike back into Lander's Rest. We'd have to garrison the place."

"And she bleeds us," the colonel said with a sigh. "No, we want to annihilate her and her ruffians in town or while they are out in the open fleeing. Now, what is this about her recruiting methods?"

"Nelly, show them the football field."

The map of human-occupied Kaskatos was replaced by a close overhead of the larger stadium. The playing field was covered with humanity. Some huddled together under makeshift tents; others sat in the open. A few lucky ones were allowed in the first few rows of the bleachers.

Higher up the bleachers, people in black shirts or pants walked or lounged. Each carried one of the machine pistols that was standard issue to Greenfeld State Security.

"Are those weapons all they have for crowd control?" the colonel asked.

"I have been observing the stadium for fifteen minutes," Nelly said, "and so far, that is the only means of enforcing their will that I have spotted. There are not even fences at the gates."

"So if everyone decided to leave," Penny said, "they'd either have to let them go or gun them down."

"It looks that way," Kris said. "A glance at the field in front of me will show you how loath they were to shoot at lightly armed civilians."

"Not much reluctance that I noticed," Jack said.

"So, let me see if I fully understand your tactical problem," the colonel said. "You want to kill or capture one miscreant Jackie Jackson, preferably in the company of a pirate captain. You want to prevent her and her assorted band of terrorists from melting into the general population where they could continue to poison the civic life of this planet.

"And you would prefer to do all of the above while keeping the armed guards at the soccer stadium from slaughtering thousands of innocent people whose only crime is getting on the wrong side of said Jackie. Do I understand you?"

"Perfectly, Colonel."

"And you hope to do this with the four Marine platoons our illustrious Captain Jack has at his beck and call."

"Well, I was hoping the Navy might contribute a little something to back up the line beasts."

"Yes, I forgot you mentioned that," the colonel said.

Across from Kris, Jack made a nasty face. Squids helping jarheads. Unheard of.

"It is tempting to tell our audacious princess that the chances of pulling this off are somewhere between nil and zero. Normally, that would be so; but these are Marines we're talking about, and I haven't yet earned my paycheck for this month, so let's see what we can do," Colonel Cortez said.

9

TWO hours later, Kris led her Marines out from the Annam plantation in a convoy of twenty-six trucks. First and second platoons took up only the first six. The last dozen or so were empty, ready to provide mobility to the yet unlanded third and fourth platoons. It was the other six trucks that left Kris with an uneasy feeling in the pit of her stomach.

In them rode over a hundred volunteers from the Annam farm, armed with their scroungings from the noon battlefield.

Few of them had ever fired a shot. Even fewer knew how to hit what they aimed at. Worst, Kris doubted any of them knew a thing about taking orders.

But every one of them wanted blood.

And if Kris ignored them, they swore they would follow her into her next fight and do God only knew what kind of harm to themselves.

And to Kris's professionals.

Kris took Jack aside. "First time I took a bunch of half-trained sailors into a firefight, lots of them had never fired a shot. Most forgot to take the safeties off their weapons. See if some of your Marines could teach this bunch of idiots the basics and maybe scare them into good sense."

Jack assigned a half dozen Marine sergeants to introduce the locals to the functioning of machine pistols, rifles, and pistols, with special emphasis on which end gets aimed at the other side. They made sure to explain clearly to the uninitiated the workings of the safety system of their weapons.

There was no ammunition to spare for practice shots, but at least the locals now knew about a sight picture and the safety.

Sadly, few saw the error of their ways and dropped out.

Mr. Annam wished them all well and sent them forth with a blessing. As a practicing Buddhist, he could not bring himself to join them.

Kris had been taught early by her politician father to smile nicely at any blessing that came her way. She did so now. But more so, she hoped the local's blessing had some power to it. In the next hour or two, she would likely need all the good luck she could beg, steal, or borrow.

Kris was not worried about her Marines. Her job was to get them to a place where they could do their job. She would do her part, and they would take care of their end of the bargain.

The volunteers were a question mark Kris did not need.

She'd been there several times when hardly trained, lightly armed enthusiasts went into a fight. She knew the bloody mess that usually ended up in.

She'd seen it again just that noon.

Now a small rabble pulled up the rear of Kris's column. With any luck, the fight would be over before the volunteers found out it was happening and figured out how to get out of their trucks.

For now, Kris concentrated on what lay ahead of her.

Chief Beni and Penny stood on either side of her as she held on to the cab of the truck she rode in. A canvas cover protected her from the sun . . . a bit, and from any overhead observation . . . a very little bit.

"Chief, talk to me."

"So far, I have nothing to report," he said with a shrug. "I've got scouts out there hunting for any kind of noise that Jackie's eyeballs might make, but we're getting nothing. I don't think the woman knows boo about eyes in the sky or search bots."

"Nelly tells me there's nothing on the radio frequencies."

"Nelly's right about that," the chief said. "So far, this Jackie is deaf, dumb, and blind. I kind of like her that way."

"Don't assume that just because she's not using any of your high tech," Penny said, "that she's as blind as you think.

Once we get into the city, anyone looking out a window could make a call and turn us in. No, correction, there will be folks just waiting to let her know where we are and what we're doing."

"Is Penny right about that?" Kris asked.

"She's got a point," the chief allowed.

"We can close down the phone system," Nelly offered.

"I've got Da Vinci working on spitting out a bot to do just that," the chief was quick to add.

"I've already got a bot in the air," Nelly said.

Around the house, while Kris was growing up, there had never been a really serious case of sibling rivalry. Not really. Well, maybe a bit, but nothing like Nelly and the chief.

"Both of you, hold your horses," Kris said, then turned to Penny. "Am I wrong, or wouldn't it be better if we took down the phone system just as we rolled into town. I'd prefer that this Jackie character didn't know she had a problem until she was up to her neck in it."

"That's the way I'd do it," Penny agreed.

"Okay, you two send out your bots, let them hook into the local net, but don't shut it down until I say so."

"Aye, aye" and "Yes, Kris" answered her.

"Ah, do you want it totally closed down?" the chief asked, "or would you like to just block all traffic relating to us."

That raised Kris's eyebrows. "Could you do that?"

"Da Vinci could monitor all calls," Nelly quickly said. "He could hold up all of them for a few seconds while he listens in. Those that don't relate to us, he could let go through. Those that do, he blocks. Or maybe answers himself."

"You sure this isn't getting too fancy?" Kris asked.

"More like too smart by half as my auntie used to say," Penny added.

"We can do it," Nelly insisted. "I can have some of the kids work with Da Vinci to make sure everything gets covered. We can make this happen."

"You two work it out," Kris said dubiously. She glanced at Penny.

The intel lieutenant was gnawing her lip. "Things are still

quiet at the stadium," she said. Then she frowned. "We got developments on Tranquility Road."

"Give me your view," Kris said. Her stomach rebelled at what she saw.

Jackie Jackson stood on the balcony and liked what she saw. The lawn, a lovely green without a single weed, was usually patrolled by dogs. Big ones with loud barks and nice sharp teeth. The first couple of heads on the gate spikes had been fools who tried to slip in late at night and failed to get past the dogs.

They'd begged Jackie to cut their throats before they died. The heads went on spikes. The dogs got the rest.

Jackie's family had worked for four generations for Greenfeld State Security. Great-grandfather had complained that these young Peterwalds were soft until the day he died. Grandfather and Dad told stories of the good old days when people on the street went out of their way to avoid looking a black shirt in the eyes.

Jackie got stuck working for lightweight Henry the twelfth. The guy had no backbone and no taste for blood. Until he turned on his own. Until he shot his own black shirts.

Peterwald had no respect for loyalty. None at all.

Jackie hotfooted it out of St. Pete with her best and most loyal troopers. And guns. Plenty of guns and explosives.

She'd realized the way the wind was blowing right after General Boyng failed to persuade Peterwald that he was more valuable to him alive than dead. Others had stayed to protest their loyalty. To point to years of service to the state.

Most of those fools were dead, as well they deserved to be.

Here, Jackie was making her own world. If Peterwald came calling, she'd turn it over to him from her very own hands. He'd know exactly what she was worth to him.

And if he didn't bother coming to call? If he failed in his mad purge of his most loyal subordinates? Well, Jackie had friends there, too. They'd be glad to have her present them a world ready for the riding.

A commotion down on the lawn distracted Jackie from her thoughts. A hostage had broken loose from the chains that held her in place as live cover for Jackie's machine-gun emplacements.

A dog handler quickly slipped the leash from his beast's neck.

The dog was beautiful to watch. It was on the fleeing woman in four mighty bounds. First, it knocked her down. Then it ripped her throat out in one fluid motion.

The woman's dying scream ended in a gurgle.

Which was more than could be said for the other hostages. Yells and bellyaching swept around the lawn as if it would do anything for the dead woman.

Jackie drew an automatic from the holster at her hip and fired one shot in the air. Other than a few sniffles from the kids, that got her the quiet she wanted.

"As you can see," Jackie said loud enough for all to hear, "you cannot run away from your service to me. When you are told, stand up and keep your mouths shut. If you do as you are told, you may live. Defy me, and the dogs will eat you."

"Your Terribleness," one of the guard leaders called to her from below. She really liked that title. It let everyone know exactly where they stood before her.

"Yes, Sergeant." She knew this one. He'd been a fresh-caught private back on St. Pete. He'd earned his sergeant's stripes by catching one of the first assassins to come over the fence.

"Some of the hostages are digging up the lawn, trying to make foxholes or something. Should we shoot those who do?"

Now that he mentioned it, there were messy dents in the grass. Of course, where her guards had dug machine-gun nests, there were really big holes in her turf.

She had liked the look of her lovely lawn. The thought of killing anyone who messed it up worse than Jackie needed was tempting.

Still, there was no telling when that Longknife woman would show up . . . and it was possible that if she killed too many hostages, she might not be able to replace them in time.

She shook her head. "Just make sure they know. When we tell them to stand, anyone who doesn't will be shot."

"Are you at any risk of running out of hostages?" Captain Belou asked from where he stood inside the door, looking out.

"I've got rifles on every roof for the next three blocks. Machine pistols at every window. And where there are two or three of my henchmen, I've got five or six hostages in front of them. There are plenty more if I need them. You were on the ships that brought a lot of them here, weren't you?"

"A couple. I'd still be on one if you hadn't promised me my own ship, chasing down loot for you and your friends."

"Yes," Jackie said, turning back to the captain and marching for her desk. There wasn't much on it. She hated to let things pile up unfinished. She was very good at finishing matters.

She picked up the printout on the Wardhaven Scout Ship *Wasp* that she'd made from *Jane's All the Worlds' Warships*. "It seems that our helpless merchant ship had claws."

"And a Longknife to boot."

"Yes, there is that matter. A Longknife that some news reports say is reluctant to kill."

"She killed five thousand passengers on that liner without so much as a blink," the captain pointed out, not at all reluctant to argue with Jackie.

Jackie could develop a taste for that in a man . . . provided it was in small quantities. A spice used sparingly. "Other stories say she was brokenhearted at the slaughter. I wonder which reporter got the story right."

The captain shrugged—and glanced out the window. "I guess we'll know pretty soon."

"Yes, I will," Jackie said. "Meanwhile, there's the matter of getting you a ship."

"None is available at the moment."

"I'm not so sure the *Wasp* is beyond our reach," Jackie said. "I understand that the shuttles that landed at the Annam plantation sucked water weeds into their intake valves."

"I hadn't heard."

"Few have, but I have my eyes everywhere," Jackie said

with a smile designed to curdle blood, milk, or anything else she aimed it at.

The captain took a step back. "So, you want me to work for my ship."

"I like it when a man knows what I want from him without all those messy explanations." She changed her smile . . . to something a cobra might permit itself.

"What do you have in mind, Your Terribleness?"

"You can catch more flies with honey. And I bet you can catch more shuttles if you turn on a landing beacon for them."

10

"That dog just keeps gnawing on that woman," Kris said, her stomach in free fall. "She's dead."

"I hope so," Penny said. "They're letting the dog eat her."

Kris and Penny watched a picture that their computers directed to their eyes. The chief looked at them, eyes wide with questions . . . but he did not ask his computer to give him the video feed that was so upsetting the two officers.

It took Kris most of a minute to recover. "Jack," she finally said.

"Yes, Commander."

"This Jackie is a very bad actor. She's staking out hostages on the lawn of her mansion. One tried to run, and she set a dog on her."

"Nasty gal, huh?" Jack said.

"No saving graces at all," Kris answered.

"So she's set to hide behind human walls," Jack said slowly. "Does this change your orders, Your Highness?"

"No. This is barbarity. Nobody should have to suffer this, not when there are troopers around to do something about it. But it does mean we'll have to work a lot harder to take down this witch. Chief, Nelly, would you please back search any sky-eye feed you have of the buildings around Tranquility Road. I need to know which buildings had hostages marched into them."

"We're on it," both said.

The air was split by a sonic boom, soon followed by a second, third, and fourth. "The landing boats are on final approach," Kris said.

"And our local warlord has to know it's showtime," Jack added.

"But to know the show is on and not know where it's at must be maddening for a control freak like Jackie," Kris said. It certainly would be maddening for her.

Kris turned to look at those who shared her truck. A sniper team, a rifle team, and a corporal with four privates whom Jack had detailed to slow Kris down. She'd have to take care of that.

They were coming upon the outskirts of Lander's Rest. Ahead was a burned-out group of stores with a large parking lot. Just the place for Kris to take care of a few small problems.

"Driver, pull the convoy off the road over there."

He turned right into the parking lot.

"You four," she said, pointing at her guards, "follow me."

The four followed Kris, with the corporal right behind them, as Kris dismounted the truck and headed back down the convoy line.

By the time she got to the fourth truck, Jack was already waiting for her. "What are you up to now, Princess?" he asked, eyeing those following her.

"I want to send the last dozen trucks around the outskirts of town so they can connect with third and fourth platoons and give them some mobility."

"Yes, I know," Jack said. "What does that have to do with your guards?"

"Four privates, four groups of three trucks. Who better to see that they get there?"

"I could assign four other privates," Jack said, whispering to keep this conversation private.

"Yes, but everyone else has a job," Kris whispered right back.

"Kris, those four have a job. Keeping you not dead." Exasperation had free rein in Jack's voice though he still kept it low. Around them, Marines were struggling to pay attention to anything but them.

"Jack, I have a sniper team, a rifle team, and the corporal here. I don't need more. They'll only get in my way. Slow me down."

"Anything that slows you down sounds like a great idea to me. And a full-time job. Kris, after the last bomb, I thought we'd have fewer of these talks."

"So did I," Kris admitted. "I was wrong, and so are you. We've got a very nasty warlord to kill or capture. I kind of like the idea of killing her. Do you really think we can spare people to hold my hand? How's your assault on that soccer stadium coming?"

"Not so good. It's got a lot of parking lot around it and not much cover. Damn it, woman, you're changing the topic."

"I'm focusing on the topic at hand." Kris quickly covered the distance to the six trucks full of local volunteers. "Are any of you soccer fans? Football," she corrected. "Been to the football stadium?"

"I have," came from several.

"I've played there twice and worked a summer for the groundskeeper," a young woman said, dropping gracefully from her truck.

"Jack here needs to save the people being held prisoner there before the gunmen can mow them down. You two need to talk."

Kris took the woman's hand and passed her along to Jack, all the time wishing she wasn't so beautiful, well-endowed, and athletic. Like most, her clothing was thin and worn. *Ah, the things I do for humanity,* Kris thought, hoping she wasn't setting herself up for another bridesmaid's dress.

Jack threw Kris an angry scowl before putting his head together with the woman.

Kris had other things on her mind. She spotted one of the fellows who sounded a bit too vengeful. "You, and the guy next to you. Come with me."

Kris culled an even dozen out of the volunteers and got them moving with her to the last dozen trucks.

"Each of you, pick a truck. You're riding shotgun for it."

"What's that?" came from several of them.

"These trucks need to connect with the Marine platoons I'm dropping on the other side of town to stop Jackie and her thugs from making a run for the hills. They may not all drop where we want them. You make sure they have a ride if they need to move. You make sure these trucks aren't stolen out from under you."

Kris turned to the four Marines. "Each of you, pick three trucks. It's your responsibility to see that they get to the other platoons. Stay on the outskirts of town. Go around trouble. You are not to look for a fight. Run if you have to, but make sure the colonel gets at least six of these trucks. Any questions?"

There were none.

"Check in regularly with me or the colonel. You've got the radio access. Good luck."

With an OOH-rah, the four nonplus privates went looking for their first commands, and Kris headed back to the lead truck.

When she passed Jack, he was deep in conversation with the gal with the very short cutoffs and the near-nonexistent tank top. With a familiar and very sad sigh, Kris concentrated on the challenge at hand.

She ordered the twelve trucks for the colonel to break off at the next cross street. Two groups went right; the other two trios went left. At the next major cross street, it was time to detach Jack. She went straight ahead, he turned left.

"Princess Kris, this is Colonel Cortez,"

"Yes, Colonel," Kris answered.

"We're about to jump, but something interesting has developed. The spaceport is now squawking. Someone in the tower has even authorized the four of us to land."

"Interesting," Kris said.

"I thought you might find it so."

"Once you depart for your place of business, who will be left in the longboats?"

"Command Master Chief L. J. Mong had originally planned on landing the Navy support teams at the Annam plantation. Given a choice, he'd prefer the airport."

"He might have to fight for it," Kris pointed out.

"From the grin on his face, I think he's hoping for just that eventuality," the colonel answered.

So, it boiled down to a simple question. Had someone

set a snare for a rabbit out at the airport? What would be the outcome if they found an angry bear in their bunny trap instead?

"Tell the chief he has my permission to use his discretion. If he thinks the port can be captured and turned to good use, go for it. If a closer observation shows the port is too much to bite off, give it a pass. I'll send an eye so he can take a good look before he leaps."

I'M ALREADY DOING IT, Nelly told Kris.

"Looks like fun," the colonel said. "You got trucks moving my way?"

"Four sets of three by four different routes. You shouldn't have to walk."

"Godspeed, Commander."

"And Godspeed to you, Colonel."

Kris turned back to concentrate on her own problem, Tranquility Road. Maybe it was about time to start messing with Jackie Jackson's telephone.

Jackie Jackson answered the phone on the first ring. "Yes," she snapped.

There was a noticeable pause before Captain Belou said, "We've got the airport up and working. Some of the employees were hiding out in the hangars with their families. We've got them working for us. I've made contact with the incoming shuttles. They say they'll be glad to land here."

"They tell you what they're carrying?"

"Boxes of famine biscuits, or so they say."

"If they're not carrying Marines, I'm a virgin who's never killed before."

"If they're not carrying biscuits, I and my crew will be blending back in with the locals. We can't fight Marines."

"Don't fight them. Just send them into town and call me. I'm ready for them."

"If you'll excuse me, I have things to do. This port is in lousy shape."

"We'll make it nice for you when you bring back your

first load of confiscated goods." Jackie grinned happily at the thought and hung up.

So, where were the Marines who were supposed to be driving up from that plantation south of town? She'd offered rewards for anyone who reported them. She should be hearing something!

Her phone rang. She answered "Yes."

There was a long pause. She hated calls that did that. St. Pete's system regularly did it. Some people hinted darkly that State Security was responsible.

Jackie *was* State Security and knew better. It was just an overworked phone system. Her boss had told her so.

Kaskatos's phone system had worked the first time, every time.

Until today.

Now the receiver went dead. She hung up the phone and stared at it. It rang again.

And again it buzzed for a few seconds before clicking and going dead.

She'd no sooner clicked it off than it rang again and repeated the whole procedure.

Jackie was about to throw the phone against the wall when she thought better, clicked it off, and speed dialed the stadium.

Richard quickly answered the phone. "Yes."

"Are you having problems with the phone?" she snapped.

"No," he answered. He was a simple man. Give him an order, and he did it. If he said his phone was working, it was.

"Have you had any calls in the last few minutes?"

"None."

"Call me back," Jackie said, and hung up.

A few seconds later, her phone rang. "Yes."

There was a brief pause, then Richard said, "You asked me to call."

"Yes. Have you seen anything of the gunmen we heard about from the south?"

"Nothing, Your Terribleness. I have rocket launchers on the upper levels of the stadium. There are miles and miles of parking lot. If anyone tries to drive across that asphalt, we will barbecue them."

"I would expect nothing less from you, Richard. Hold the stadium. You may start killing the sheep as soon as you are attacked. I'll teach them to cross me."

"It will be done," he said, and hung up.

A moment later, Jackie's phone rang again. When it started to buzz rather than talk, she hurled it out the window.

"Damn phones. There's no one I really wanted to talk to."

11

Jack had his computer, Sal, project a picture of the stadium for him and Tilly. He tried to concentrate on her fingers as she took him on a walk through the stadium.

It was not easy.

Three million years of evolution had trained the male eye to look for movement . . . and the female form. As the truck bounced from pothole to pothole, it jiggled two beautiful examples of the female breast right in front of his eyes.

Normally, Jack considered himself a very disciplined man. Today, evolution was winning hands down.

So he kept his hands in his pockets and tried to keep his eyes on her fingers. At least his ears worked normally.

"The field is pretty much a mess. They've had people living there for the last two months," Tilly said. "At least they dug latrines down at this end. Still, a lot of people have gotten sick."

"What about water? Water in? Water out?" Jack asked.

"We have to water the grass most of the summer. Not a lot of rain then. Winter, we get lots of rain. It gushes off the seats in rivers. So, yes, a lot of water comes in and a lot has to be taken out. Why?"

"Because where the water goes out, I was hoping to take my Marines in. You know anything about the sewer system?"

Here, the gal shrugged, and Jack got a glimpse of even more of her. Her tank top covered little of her midriff, and the cutoffs were badly frayed. Everybody was wearing clothes that had seen better days, but Tilly seemed dressed to distract males.

Or attract them.

Yet the woman talking to Jack was self-possessed and unassuming. The clothes did not match the person they covered . . . or hardly covered.

One thing was sure; she had a tight hold on her rifle. And unlike most, her pocket bulged with a box of ammunition. She would not shoot herself dry in one lone magazine.

"I don't know anything about the underground, just that there is a lot of piping and ducts inside the stadium where no one goes. My job that summer was mowing the grass and painting the seats.

"Here and here"—she pointed—"there's room to march a band in from the parking lot. You should be able to drive your trucks right onto the stadium grounds."

"I doubt if we can do that," Jack said, pointing to where men stood with rocket launchers high on the entrance ramps that ringed the stadium. "We wouldn't get halfway to the stadium before they blew us away."

"Oh, I hadn't thought of that," Tilly said, and worried her full lower lip. "I never watched many war films. I didn't like all that killing. It seemed such a waste. Now, there are a couple of guys I really want dead, and I don't know anything about how it's done."

"Movies aren't the place you learn how to fight," Jack said. What he really wanted to know was more about the guys she wanted dead . . . and why. Instead, he asked, "Do you know how to use that rifle?"

"My dad used to take my brother hunting. Before they went out, he insisted my brother learn how to shoot. I went along to their target practice and beat them both." She grinned. "Brother said I cheated. I had these two pillows to rest on."

She glanced down at the "pillows." "Dad got Mom and Bro up-country before things got too bad around town. I stayed behind, trying to get a boy to go with me."

"What happened?" Jack knew if the boy had gone, Tilly wouldn't be here.

"His dad's a road engineer. Jackie has him working for her. She's got his wife and son at the stadium. Sometimes he gets to visit them."

"And you."

"I tried to visit his son. Two of the guards said they'd help me if I'd just wait in the locker room. I think I could have taken the two of them, but they brought some of their friends." Her words petered out, but her grip on the rifle got real tight.

"I managed to find a place to sight this puppy in. I only used three rounds. You get me a target. I'll hit it. I'm good to two hundred meters."

Jack didn't doubt she was.

He concentrated the spy eye on the line of manhole covers stretching from the shipping entrance across the smaller parking lot to the road behind the stadium. He followed more sewer lids until he came to a tree-lined residential street not two blocks from the parking lot.

"Sergeant Bruce, get ready to spin off some small scouts. I've got a sewer line I want mapped."

"Oh joy," the sergeant replied. "When my DI said to suck it up and soldier, he warned me there'd be days like this."

Jack pounded on the roof of the truck cab and shouted instructions.

Beside him, Tilly caressed her rifle like she might her firstborn.

COLONEL Cortez operated the risers on his chute. It had been a long time since he'd made a jump, and somehow it had gotten a whole lot harder to control one of these things since then. Still, he landed only twenty meters from his stick mate . . . and did so at a sedate walk.

As he spilled his chute, he took in his situation. He was in a farmer's field, trampling green wheat not yet ready for harvest. The field consisted of several gently rolling hills. Off to his left, a four-lane road hugged the trees, which hid a decent-size river.

Unless he was blind, he was exactly where he was supposed to be.

Traffic on the road at the moment was nil. A dozen Marines

who had landed closer to the road spread out along the shoulder and prepared to stop anything going in either direction.

Colonel Cortez joined the fifty or so Marines humping their gear toward the road. Word was he'd have transportation along soon.

It was unusual, but it looked like everything was going according to plan.

Private Lotermann hadn't expected to have his very own command, not with just six months in the Corps, but here he was in charge of three trucks, responsible for getting them to Colonel Cortez.

He was on his own. It was a beautiful day. This was kind of fun.

"Turn left up here," he told the driver.

The local riding shotgun for him had given up his seat in the cab, preferring to ride standing up on the truck bed. Now he stooped down to the vacant window.

"You want to turn right here," he said.

"The map the princess gave me said we turn left," Private Lotermann said, turning toward the volunteer.

And found himself facing a machine pistol with the arming bolt already pulled back and the safety off.

"I could care less about your princess. The Dragon Woman wants us to head for Tranquility Road, so that's where we're going."

The gunman fired; the Marine private heard nothing.

Lieutenant Commander Kris Longknife signaled the driver to turn off six blocks short of Tranquility Road. Three hundred meters up the quiet, tree-lined street, she had him stop.

The other two trucks full of Marines spaced themselves at hundred-meter intervals as they halted. Quickly, Marines dismounted and began filtering through the yards, covering for each other as they bounded forward.

"Penny, go with them. Get some scouts out," Kris ordered, then turned to motion the trucks full of volunteers to come up to where she stood.

"Good luck with that bunch," Penny said, looking around. She spotted Lieutenant Stubben and jogged to join him.

It took a lot of waving to get the trucks to join her. By the time they reached her, some of the volunteers were already walking along beside them. A few had tried to follow the Marines and seemed very unhappy when Marines paused in their advance to quietly send them back.

"What's going on?" "Aren't we going to fight?" "I came here for a fight, and I'll fight those hard hats if they get in my way again."

Kris would dearly have loved to turn this bunch over to a good DI and wash her hands of them. She doubted a harangue from her on discipline would do any good.

"Get out of the trucks. I've got to talk to you first," was the best she could come up with.

It wasn't like these were the first irregulars she'd led into battle. She'd had some really nasty experiences with civilians who'd insisted they could stand in the line and fight.

She'd also saved the planet of her birth with a ragtag and bobtail collection of rejects, reservists, and volunteers.

With a sigh, Kris surveyed this bunch. Other than eagerness, they had little to recommend them.

"Corporal," she ordered under her breath, "take your fire team and spread them out in front of this bunch."

"Yes, Commander." The orders were given and obeyed. "Now what, ma'am?"

"I'm not sure," Kris admitted, "but if something goes wrong among our so-called volunteers, I'm sure your Marines will know it before you and I do."

"Yes, Commander," the corporal said, and whispered further instructions into her mike. Her troopers stayed casual . . . but kept their eyes on the volunteers.

Kris then ordered the sniper to roam around, facing out. "Try to keep us from being disturbed."

"Ladies and gentlemen," Kris began. "First, I would like

to welcome you to the first annual, and hopefully last annual spring battle royal of Kaskatos. If you're lucky and pay attention, you might live through today." As Kris talked, she walked up the line of armed men and women, eyeing each one carefully.

Most of them treated their weapons like toys they'd gotten for Christmas and didn't know what to do with. Rifles were pointed up, down, or held at the end of arms that just dangled. Pistols and machine pistols dangled the same way.

"You are my reserve," Kris went on. "In War College, they teach that victory usually goes to the side that is still holding on to a reserve force when the crisis of the battle arrives."

"And you're gonna know when that crisis shows up," a guy said.

Kris didn't like his attitude. She liked even less that he was bringing up his arm with his machine pistol at the ready. It was fully cocked, and the safety was off.

Unfortunately for him, Kris had been waiting for something like that. She had her own automatic out and three sleepy darts sprouting from his chest before this optimistic assassin could get his own weapon up.

He fell backward against a truck; his weapon clattered onto the pavement.

Suddenly, the Marines were guns up.

"Guns down, volunteers," Kris shouted. "Lower your weapons, or I'll drill every one of you with a sleepy dart."

"Why sleepy dart the traitor?" said someone with a machete, and used it to take the head off the guy Kris had darted. People jumped back, many looking quite shocked at the amount of blood that could spew from a human neck once the head was no longer attached.

"Everybody just stand where you are," Kris ordered. "I wanted to talk to that puke."

"Sorry," the machete wielder said, and almost made it sound like he meant it.

"Corporal, have two of your Marines go down this line and see if anyone else has a weapon cocked and ready to start shooting."

The Marines did. Kris spotted at least one fellow whose rifle was all too ready; she got her automatic ready for him to go violent like the last one.

No, this one was just very dumb . . . or ready to act that way to avoid the fate of the other. Once everyone was verified safe, Kris explained herself.

"I shot that guy with a sleepy dart because I didn't want to start shooting just then, and I don't want to start shooting now. The soft pop a dart makes is not going to alarm anyone, and that is the way we want Jackie and her thugs—not alarmed. If he'd sprayed us with his pistol, he might or might not have survived. But Jackie Jackson would definitely know we are at her doorstep. Do you understand me?"

The blank stares looked a bit more informed. While they milled about, Kris did a radio check.

"Colonel, you down?"

"I'm at point X-ray with third platoon, Your Highness."

"Fourth platoon is at point Uniform," came from its LT.

"Commander, I've got no action at X-ray, either coming or going," the colonel reported. "As soon as your trucks arrive, I'll displace two squads forward. I suggest that fourth do the same."

"The trucks aren't there yet?" Kris asked.

"Not in my line of sight."

Kris tried them on net. Three privates reported that they were going as fast as they could but that the roads were a pot-holed mess.

The fourth private did not answer Kris's call.

"Jack, you on net?" she asked.

"I'm at my target, about to go off net. I've got a cloak of invisibility that may help me out a bit."

Cloak of invisibility? Kris shook her head; Jack would explain it when he wanted to. Right now, he might have a problem he wasn't aware of.

"Jack, I'm not sure all our volunteers are on our side. One tried to gun me down here, and one of our truck convoys is not answering my calls."

"I haven't had any trouble with mine," Jack replied. "But

with Tilly leading the volunteers, a guy would have to be blind not to want to follow her."

Why was Kris not surprised? It took a few seconds for Jack to continue. "But come to think about it, none of the three truck drivers I've got here are all that interested in following us. One of them in particular. Hey, guys," Jack shouted, "have I got a deal for you."

There was a roar of truck motors at the end of Kris's street, and three trucks raced by, headed for Tranquility Road. Kris only got a quick glimpse, but it looked like the lead truck had a Marine slumped in the passenger seat.

"Jack, I think I just spotted our missing convoy, and it's headed for Jackie."

"I knew we should have done a full field security check on all those enthusiastic volunteers," the Marine answered on net. "Looks like it's time to play ball. Good luck, Kris."

"Good luck to you, Jack."

Kris blinked to change net. "First platoon, you are weapons free."

12

Captain Jack Montoya, Royal U.S. Marines, waved his rifle for emphasis. "You drivers are going underground with me and mine."

Two shrugged and went where Jack pointed them. One looked ready to make a break for it, but couldn't break eye contact with the muzzle of Jack's borrowed M-6.

With reluctant steps, he went.

A Marine was waiting at the nearest manhole, clearly unhappy to be the stay-behind guy. He motioned the drivers below, then gave Jack a plaintive look.

"Hold the fort here. Don't let anyone steal our rides," Jack ordered.

"Aye aye, Skipper," the Marine answered, resigned to sucking it up and soldiering where he was told.

Jack had to hurry the truck drivers along. One in particular really needed encouragement. At the end of the first tunnel, the sewer got bigger around. A glowing green chem light pointed Jack right.

About a block later, another light pointed left down a tunnel big enough to stand upright in. Jack got ready to jog.

And the third truck driver stumbled, bounced off the wall, and grabbed his foot. "I think I sprang my ankle."

Jack put two sleepy darts in his butt and waited a second for them to take effect. As he fell asleep, Jack made sure the reluctant dragon was faceup and at no risk of suffocating.

"Either of you want to join him?" he asked the others.

Those two took off at a fast enough run to satisfy Jack.

Another chem light pointed Jack up a smaller tunnel; he would bet money he was now under the rear parking lot and headed for the service entrance to the stadium.

It got crowded when he got to where a ladder led up. A few Marines kept order, but most of the folks down here were volunteers. "Make a hole," Jack called.

The civilians that were slow to get out of the way got their feet stepped on by either Jack or the Marines directing traffic. Jack went up the ladder without slowing down.

He found himself in a working basement with brightly painted pipes and air ducts. Sergeant Bruce and his LT listened to Tilly as she waved her arms to explain the layout of the building.

"There are four stairwells going up the inside of the stadium. That one there," she said, pointing at a blue door, "and another like it about a quarter of the way around that way. There are two more. One is a long way down that corridor, and the last one is a bit farther. You go up four flights of stairs, and that puts you at the top of the entrance ramps. From there, you can head into the stadium, where the guys are with machine pistols, or back out to the ramps, where the guys are with rockets."

"Sounds like the place to be," the LT said.

"You take the long run down that corridor," Jack said to the young officer. "Sergeant Bruce and I will take the one a quarter of the way around. We don't bust out until my order."

"Aye aye, Skipper," the LT, said and took off at a gallop with two squads.

Sergeant Bruce was already headed for his station with his squad. Jack trotted after him.

Tilly also joined him in a jog that got her "puppies" bouncing right along with her.

Jack enjoyed the play . . . for about a second . . . and then got his head back where it belonged. He headed up the stairs without breaking stride and found himself quickly at a red-painted door.

Jack keyed his mike. "Lieutenant, Staff Sergeant Bruce's squad is in position."

Nothing came back.

"There's a lot of steel and concrete around us," Tilly said. "I'm not sure your radio gear works. None of ours did."

"Crack the door," Jack ordered.

Sergeant Bruce's technician did. A spy scout showed nothing in sight, so Jack edged out. "Clear," he announced softly. Sergeant Bruce whispered assignments to his troopers as they trotted silently past him.

Two went for the outside; the other ten headed inside, with Tilly right behind them, her rifle at the ready.

Jack found himself squatting low behind a bleacher seat with a good view of the field below. "Squad leaders, report who's on net."

"Squad one in place."

"Squad two in place."

"Squad three in place."

"Squad four in place."

"On my mark, take down anyone with a weapon," Jack ordered. "Mark."

Rapid small-arms fire filled the stadium.

Command Master Chief L. J. Mong stood behind the bosun piloting Longboat 1 as it braked to a halt on the main runway at Lander's Rest's airport, spaceport, whatever. The bosun used the last bit of energy on the vehicle to turn off onto a taxiway before gliding to a stop, leaving the duty runway for the three longboats right behind him.

The command master chief studied the lay of the port. About a mile off to his right was a squat one-story terminal. At midlength, it spiked a four-story-high control tower. Several trucks waited in front of the tower, but there were no aircraft in sight. What was of prime interest to the chief just now were two tugs in that parked group. Either one could easily tow a longboat to a parking spot off the runway.

Nothing was moving.

"Should we land the landing party?" the chief master-at-arms asked.

"Not just yet," the command master chief said. "They haven't made their move."

The other chief glanced around the field, a pained look on his face. "I don't like sitting here, like some dumb duck in a shooting gallery."

"Our intrepid princess is quite sure that these shuttles are an asset the bad guys want to capture in full running order."

"I'm glad she thinks so. I just hope she got the bad guys' chop on that."

"I hear things often go the way she wants," the command master chief said dryly.

"Me, I'm worried about the first time they don't."

"Longboat 4 just touched down, Command Master Chief," the pilot reported.

"Ah, and now we have activity at the terminal."

Several trucks and the two tugs now formed a procession winding their way from the tower across the taxiways toward where the longboats lay strung out like a bunch of beached whales.

"Chief Master-at-Arms, you may prepare to deploy your landing force at my order."

"Thanks be to God," the other chief grumbled, and headed aft to make it happen.

"Pass the word to the other boats," the chief told the bosun in charge of the first lander.

"They are glad to hear that, Command Master Chief."

Command Master Chief Mong waited for a long minute, watching the trucks slowly getting closer and dreading a mortar or rocket grenade salvo from someone who hadn't gotten The Word from the princess that the landers were worth more captured than burned.

After a minute of stretching his luck, the chief thumbed his commlink. "This is the command master chief. Land the landing force."

Behind the chief, the aft hatch whined as it dropped open. As soon as it was down, the chief master-at-arms started shouting for his rifle-armed sailors to "Go, go, go. We ain't got all day. What kind of sailor hangs around in a target this big?"

Sailors raced from the open hatch to take up prone shoot-ing positions in the grass at the edge of the taxiway.

Across the way, trucks slowed to a halt a good hundred meters shy of the boats.

"Time to see if us adults can talk our way out of this situ-ation," the command master chief muttered to himself as he headed out to see who on the other side was up for a talk.

Jackie Jackson glared at the man riding in the back of the lead truck as it screeched to a halt beneath the balcony where she stood.

"The Longknife woman is coming," he shouted.

"And you couldn't just call to tell me," Jackie said, waving her other phone.

"I tried. Something was wrong with the phone. You'd an-swer, 'Yes.' I start talking to you, and the phone would go dead. After three tries, I came as quickly as I could."

"Stadium," Jackie yelled at her phone. It started ringing immediately. It continued ringing. On the fifth ignored ring, she punched off.

"Find the guy in charge of the phone system," she shouted at one of her lieutenants. "Shoot him and his family."

"Will do, Your Terribleness," the guy said . . . and ran.

Jackie reached for the bullhorn she kept on the balcony. She liked the feel of the handle in her hand, the way people jumped when she shouted into it. Sometimes she used it even when the phone system was working.

"Everyone, listen up," she yelled. "Longknife and her henchmen will be here any moment. You, helpless little citi-zens, up on your feet. You can finally do me a service. Gun-ners, get ready."

Below her, and on the roofs of the buildings across from her, people leapt to respond to her orders. Here and there someone got shot for responding too slowly. After three shots, there weren't any slow ones left.

Jackie put down her bullhorn and picked up the detonator. That Longknife woman was in for one big surprise.

* * *

Kris found herself in the unaccustomed position of watching as someone else started a fight. First platoon belonged to Lieutenant Stubben, and it responded to him.

On his order, the snipers took out the riflemen on the roof of the buildings across the street. The hostages used as human shields showed dismay and shock as they felt the wind from the killing rounds, but none of them were hurt.

The same could not be said for those with guns.

Utter silence hung in the air for a moment after that fusillade. Then smoke grenades landed in front of the mansions across the way. They rolled to a halt, spewing smoke. For a long fifteen seconds, nothing happened as the billowing green smoke swelled up and thickened to cover the windows, where no doubt people with those ubiquitous Greenfeld State Security machine pistols waited behind a cringing wall of human shields.

When Lieutenant Stubben determined the smoke was thick enough, there were low shouts of "Move it. Move it. Move it." and fire teams of well–spread out Marines did indeed move.

Machine pistols chattered from across the way. One bullet even shattered the window Kris was looking out, leading Penny to suggest Her Highness might back off.

Kris didn't.

She kept watch as no Marine went down to that poorly aimed barrage.

Doors shattered under trooper-applied explosives. Pistols sprayed on fully automatic. M-6s replied with single shots, and quickly the noise died with the gunners.

Kris headed across the street at a run, Penny and Chief Beni right behind her.

The great room of the first building held its own tragedy. The gunman had found his human shield in the way when he went for the first Marine in. He cut down three of his hostages before the Marine took him down with a single head shot.

Kris shook her head; despite all her efforts and those of her Marines, this was going to be a bloodbath.

"Hold it," Chief Beni half shouted. "We got a problem. There are live wires coming into all six of these buildings."

That must mean something to the chief but it meant nothing to Kris.

"Back out, Kris," Penny shouted.

Kris backed, while waving at the hostages to follow her. Two of them were weeping over the bleeding ones, but a young mother gathered up five kids and drove them ahead of her.

Kris tried to help with the kids, but Penny was half pushing her, half dragging her out the door.

"I got it. I got it," the chief shouted.

"You got what?" Kris said, standing in the doorway, and pushing back at Penny.

"I think someone rigged these houses to blow right after we took them. Everybody, look around," he yelled.

"What's a five-pound bag of coffee doing in the library?" a Marine hollered.

"Does it have a wire leading to it?" the chief yelled.

"It did," the trooper said, appearing in the hall with said bag of freshly ground Mountain Grown Best, "before I yanked it out of it."

"Give me your bayonet," Chief Beni said, acquired the blade and sliced into the bag. Freshly ground beans poured out until all that was left was a large, ugly gray block.

"C-8," Penny shouted, then added on net, "everyone, look for bags of coffee. They've got explosives in them, and our sniffers won't spot the stuff surrounded by coffee."

"Somebody really needs a wake-up call in the morning," the chief said, looking the gray block of high explosives over to make sure it was safe.

"Someone's going to be very unhappy," Kris said, as Marines reported more bags found and stripped of their ignition wires. "Jackie is not going to like the surprise at all."

13

Jackie Jackson stood on her balcony, scowling at the roofs of the mansions two blocks over from her. She'd heard shots and listened as the roar of State Security machine pistols were silenced by the puny barks of the strange rifles.

She had expected better of her minions.

With a grin, she produced the small box with its bright red button. Kris Longknife probably thought that the growing silence meant she'd won another round against the idiots who worked for that wimpy Peterwald the twelfth.

That self-styled princess was wrong. Dead wrong.

Jackie pushed the red button.

Nothing happened.

She waited much longer than she was accustomed to. The technician had explained that even at near the speed of light, it took time for electricity to go from her button to the explosives.

"How long?" she screamed.

None of the men and women standing behind her had an answer for her question,

"Find the idiot who rigged those explosives. Jam this down his throat, then see that his assistant makes sure the next line of buildings blows when I want it to blow. I don't care if he has to be over there lighting the bombs off himself."

"Yes, ma'am. Yes, ma'am," one of her boys said nervously as he backed away.

She shot him dead.

"I understand, Your Terribleness," a smart young girl said, stooping to pick up the detonator and racing from the room.

"Don't ever 'ma'am' me," Jackie said, turning back to the view from the balcony.

Captain Jack Montoya shot the thug nearest him before the dirtbag even knew he was in a fight. Surprise was total, and a big chunk of the gunslingers died no more the wiser.

Unfortunately, there were a lot of people with guns, and some of them did not wait for orders before spraying the people scattered around the playing field and lower bleachers.

Even as Jack took aim and fired as quickly as he could, somewhere deep inside a question was demanding an answer. Where did people like this come from?

For now, all he could do was kill them before they could kill more.

Beside him, Tilly drew a bead and shot. Switched target. Aimed and fired. Found another one, aimed and fired.

Jack wasn't keeping count, but it seemed she fired just as often as he did.

They ran out of targets before Tilly's magazine ran empty.

"Some of them are getting away," the young local said.

"Huh?"

"There are small exits, other ways down and out. You mind if I take care of them?"

Jack didn't.

While Marines began the slow process of seeing who was alive, who was faking it, and who was sincerely dead, Jack followed Tilly. The young woman fed rounds into her rifle's magazine as she trotted out to the access ramp.

Sure enough, a small trickle of people with guns was exiting the stadium at the lower level and sprinting across the parking lot.

"Are there similar rats on the other side?" Jack asked.

"Nope, this access was for reporters and VIPs. None of them wanted to have to walk by the smelly garbage canisters on the service side of the place."

"Are you going to let them run?"

"Nope," the gal said, wrapping the rifle sling expertly

around her arm. "I just want them to all get out where I can get a shot at them."

"Get all the fish in the barrel."

"You got it."

There was no one closer than fifty meters to the stadium. Apparently the rat race was over. Tilly took aim and dropped the last one out, then the next and the next.

That got people who'd slowed down to a walk back to running.

Tilly switched her aim to the farthest one out. One crack from her rifle, and he dropped. Then she started working her way back. It was rare that she needed two rounds to drop a target.

A couple headed back to the stadium.

"You mind if I get the ones that want back in?" Jack asked.

"Be my guest."

Jack spent three rounds getting both of them.

People quit running back.

They didn't quit running; some took off to the right or left, presenting Tilly with a deflection shot. That didn't save them.

Not one of them dropped their weapons or tried to surrender.

Some did start shooting back. That showed the weakness of the State Security machine pistol. Pistol rounds quickly lost accuracy and didn't do all that good shooting up at the fourth floor of a stadium from a hundred meters out.

Tilly adjusted her target choice to get those shooting back. She ran out of targets well before she ran out of ammunition.

"Are you feeling any better?" Jack asked.

"I think I knew a few of those dirtbags out there. Maybe not. The range was long," she said coldly as she shouldered her rifle.

"Ever thought of joining the Marines?"

"Never really wanted to kill anyone before now." She paused for a moment to consider the idea. "You think I'd make a good Marine?"

"Marines only shoot when they're told, and at whom they're told."

"I might have a problem with that. Now, mister, if you'll excuse me, I have a boyfriend I want to find."

With that, she took off. Her first couple of steps were actually half skips. Jack shook his head. Even if that gal did ask for papers, he'd really need to see what the head shrink said about her before he'd sign her in.

So he arrived at the entrance of the stadium alone . . . and had to take the ugly sight in by himself.

Civilians were dead and down. Some thrashed in the mud of the grass field. Others lay sprawled on the lower bleachers. Troopers had shot the gunslingers as fast as they could, but some of the bad guys had still spent the last few moments of their lives spraying death on innocent, unarmed women and children.

Jack felt the strong need to empty his stomach.

Instead, he punched his commlink. "Kris, have you got a second."

"As it happens, we're in between shoots. How are things at the stadium?"

"It's ours. That's what I need to talk to you about." He explained what he was looking at.

"I'm looking at innocent hostages shot here, too, Jack. With an added twist." She explained about the explosives.

"Sal," Jack said to his computer, "get me Lieutenant Stubben and Sergeant Bruce and his computer."

"On the line," Sal quickly said.

"The houses the commander just liberated had been rigged with explosives," Jack said.

"Buried in sacks of fresh-roasted coffee," Kris added.

"That's a sacrilege," Sergeant Bruce snapped.

"So you can't just send out sniffers," Chief Beni said, joining the party line. "I had to send out nanites looking for the power cord. I'll have Da Vinci pass you through a design. Chesty and Sal can spin off a few fast."

"We've spun off quite a few. I feel like that's myself all over the place," Sal said.

"It will be done," Jack said.

In a minute, it was. When Jack was back to having just Kris

on the line, he went on. "Kris, I know you're not going to like what I have to say next."

"Then don't say it," Kris suggested, maybe half-seriously.

"I have to," Jack said, then paused. "Kris, I know you've been the target of way too many assassination attempts. I know you have better reasons than most to hate that whole process. But do we really owe this Jackie a straight-up fight? Wouldn't we all be better off if we had a nano plant a bomb in her ear. She's a monster."

"Your Terribleness," Kris said softly.

"What?"

"She styles herself Your Terribleness, like it was some kind of title, like my Your Highness. I found that out from a little girl, maybe ten. One of her friends had been taken over to the big house to sing. She told her that Jackson wanted everyone to call her Your Terribleness. About a week ago, the little girl went over to the house and didn't come back. Maybe she's still over there," Kris said, but she didn't sound all that hopeful.

"Kris, human shields. Bombs. Stealing food. If we took her out, would this whole house of cards collapse?"

"I don't know, Jack. I'll think about it. I've got to go. We've still got a row of houses between us and Her Terribleness's big house. Stubben says he's ready to take another layer off this onion."

"Good luck," Jack said, and turned his attention to the human misery before him.

COMMAND Master Chief L. J. Mong walked toward the stopped trucks and tugs. He kept his empty hands in plain view. Ahead of him, several men with weathered faces and worn work clothes got out of the trucks.

Halfway to them, Chief Mong halted. "You want to tell me who you are?"

"We work here at the port," one of the men from the first truck answered. "If you want, we can show you our ID cards."

"What'd you come out here to do?"

"They just want us to bring your shuttles up to the terminal. That's all we're gonna do."

"And once we got there?"

"They got guns. Lots of those squirrelly little machine pistols they brought from St. Pete."

"Why are you working for them?"

"They got our wives and kids locked up, some in the main hangar, others at the football stadium. Do what they tell you, or they shoot you, then line your family up after they've dug their own graves, and shoot them. A really nasty set of baggage."

"I hear they don't hold the stadium anymore. The gunmen there are all dead."

That lit up some eyes. "How'd that happen?"

"The captain of our Marine company saw to that bunch personally."

"Who's seeing to Her Terribleness?"

"We brought our very own Longknife to take care of her."

That started muttering going through the listening workmen. As if to verify the accuracy of the chief's intel, three trucks in front of the terminal filled rapidly with men carrying guns.

Quickly, they headed for town.

The command master chief turned. "Guns. Drop a warning shot across their bow. Smoke and noise."

A petty officer first class took expert aim and a few seconds later a smoke cloud full of fireworks appeared ahead of the lead truck. It made a crash stop, only to be rear-ended by the second, which was violently smashed into by the third.

"Better than I'd hoped for," the command master chief said.

"A whole lot better than we could have hoped for," the work leader said. "You want to borrow our trucks?"

"Don't mind if I do," the chief said. "Sailors, on your feet. We got a mess to clean up."

With an eager cheer, the sailors moved out for the trucks.

Lieutenant Commander Kris Longknife kept her royal butt well back from the smashed window. That limited her view of the last row of houses between Her Highness and Her Terribleness. It also limited the chance someone across the way could get a shot off at Kris. Nelly had no problem projecting Kris's words.

"You snipers on the roof. You saw what we did to the snipers on the houses across the street from you. They're dead, and their hostage wall didn't do them any good. Put down your guns, and we'll let you live. Keep working for Her Lousiness, and in a few minutes, you'll be as dead as they are."

Kris divided her attention between the shooters on the roofs as they looked guiltily at each other but terrified as they glanced over their shoulders.

The hostages stood as straight as they could and whimpered. A few of the younger ones openly cried despite grownups hugging them and otherwise trying to comfort them.

Kris was really getting to hate this day's business.

The other half of Kris's attention was locked on the visual feed from Nelly's scouts. There were several clumps of interest, but Kris kept getting drawn back to the balcony over the driveway of the big house. There were a number of people there.

A few might be hostages; they stood like statues on the edge of the balcony, facing out. Others lurked in the doorway, passing back in and coming back out in random moves that Kris had yet to determine.

Three women seemed to be the center of everyone's attention.

Which left Kris with two questions. Which one of the three was Her Terribleness? And did that really matter? With the target group reduced to those dozen, should she just blast the balcony and let God sort them out?

Across the way, two of the snipers put down their guns and started moving away from their human shields.

Across from them two other gunslingers opened up on the dropouts, shooting them down where they stood.

Above Kris, Marines dropped the shooters before they could celebrate their fratricidal killings.

Now it looked like all the shooters were fleeing or just ducking. Hostages took the chance to drop out of sight. Shooters on the roof of the big house in the next block started shooting up the roof, hitting both hostages and now-reluctant gunslingers.

"Put smoke in the next block," Kris ordered, and soft popping sounds told her smoke was on its way.

It took half a minute before the street between the big house and the next row of houses was smoke-covered, and the shooting stopped. Kris took that opportunity of distance between her target row and Her Terribleness to try further negotiations.

"We're trying to cut the power cord between Her Terribleness and the bombs she has installed in the houses you're in." Kris let the speaker amplify her matter-of-fact words. "When we occupied this row of houses, we found explosives hidden in bags of fresh ground coffee. I suspect you'll find the same bags of coffee scattered around your houses."

Kris knew very well that her sniffer spies had found the coffee sacks. No need to tell the other side just how much she knew of them.

A sack of coffee sailed out an upstairs window. It was followed by several more. Kris glanced at Chief Beni.

"They've only found about half of them," he said.

Kris passed that information across the way. Hostages disappeared from windows as gunners and their shields found themselves in the same desperate search against the same killer. More coffee bags came out of more windows. Many broke open, showing clear proof of blocks of gray explosives among the ground brown beans.

"Now come out with your hands up," Kris said, "and you'll live."

"Aren't you gonna shoot them?" came from behind Kris. The volunteers had arrived, many of them sporting weapons and ammunition acquired from bodies in the houses that Kris had captured.

"They are my prisoners. I will treat them under the Laws of War," Kris said forcefully.

"But they've murdered and raped and stolen," a gunslinging volunteer pointed out.

"If you can make a case for that against a specific individual, there is a judge up on my ship who will give you your day in court."

"Why do we have to use your judge? We have judges hereabouts. At least we used to. Don't know if we still do," the gunner said, looking around uncomfortably.

"When the time comes, we can make arrangements," Kris snapped. "What we don't do is take the law into our own hands. Now stand back. POWs are coming in."

And Marines were advancing in short bounds, from houses to fences to trees, to across the street, then from trees to fences to open doors.

"Spy eyes show gunners advancing from the big house to try to retake the next row of houses," Chief Beni reported.

The sharp snaps of M-6 fire told Kris that Lieutenant Stubben had beat the bad guys to their goal. She watched via the spy eye as thugs dropped.

Some of the hostages died, too. High-powered rounds went right through the unarmored gunslingers.

Kris made the decision to end this.

"Lieutenant Stubben, do you have rocket launchers on your front."

"Three, Commander.

"Aim for the balcony on the big house. Take it down."

"Understood, Commander. The balcony is a legitimate target. Grenadiers target it. Fire on my order. Fire."

Moments later, the spy eyes recorded the front of the house disintegrating in a cloud of flame.

14

Lieutenant Commander Kris Longknife fully expected that cleaning up the mess would be at least as hard as winning the battle. But before the battle was over, a good portion of the mess was kind enough to clean itself up.

While the dust from the balcony explosion was still rising, cars and trucks were already gunning away from the big house, headed north. Kris let them go.

But she did make a quick call to the colonel. "There's a lot of traffic headed your way."

"No problem," he said, cheerfully. "We're ready for them. The smart ones will surrender when we tell them."

Quite a few of them were too dumb to live . . . and died on the road out.

Kris made the calls that got medical gear and professionals flowing down from the ship. Despite the best efforts of Kris's Marines, there were still a lot of bleeding civilians. Lander's Rest had once had a good hospital, but its entire staff had fled. Calls to the farms downstream got some of them coming back in.

But travel took time, and people died waiting.

Kris needed a dirtside headquarters. The airport looked good, but too distant from a city where most people were reduced to walking. With a sigh, Kris settled into the rapidly vacated house on Tranquility Road that had been Her Terribleness's headquarters. It put Kris in the middle of things as she buried herself in work to erase the memories of broken bodies and shattered lives.

There were mouths to feed. The landing boats emptied

the *Wasp*'s supply of famine rations. She issued a call to any Squadron 10 ships nearby to help and started shipping down food from the *Wasp*'s own supplies.

Before all hell broke loose, Kaskatos had been a happy and invisible colony of about a half million souls. Then three million refugees showed up.

More arrived, but that group included Jackie Jackson, and one of the first things she did was end the population counting by confiscating the city's computer net. Some of the computers went into setting up her security system around the big house. Most went into an entertainment and gambling net she set up for her henchman.

The city IT manager did succeed in making a final backup of the system before it got wrecked. His widow found it hidden in the back of their closet and brought it in to Kris the day after the shoot-out.

Between Nelly and Chief Beni, the city net was back up and properly employed within a few days.

That helped Kris figure out a rationing system and issue new IDs to both locals and transients.

But that was hardly a dent in Kris's problems.

Despite the tendency of the gunslingers to go down shooting, Kris still ended up with a lot of prisoners. For now, she kept them in a hastily constructed stockade on the grounds of her command center.

That had at least one advantage. It assured that when trouble started over the prisoners, it quickly got dropped in Kris's lap.

The sixth morning, Tranquility Road was suddenly filled with a mob of people with guns shouting their strongly held opinions about just how long the former holders of those guns should go on breathing.

Kris's street had been a lovely, tree-lined lane. Now, most of those trees had ropes slung over their lower branches. A smoldering crowd of armed people screamed for people to dangle from the end of those ropes.

The job fell to Penny to interrupt Kris with the word on what all the commotion outside her window was about.

"I wonder how many of them have actually seen a hanging," Penny muttered.

"None," Kris said as she strode across the lawn, "and I'd like to keep it that way."

Kris halted inside the iron fence from which the heads had been removed. A Marine sergeant brought Kris a bullhorn, a bit battered and scorched but still working.

"I am told that you use elected judges in your courts," Kris said to the crowd, not quite yet a lynch mob.

"Yeah," came back at her.

"Are any of them here? Can you bring some of them to me?" That bought Kris time, but not as much as she hoped for. Several of the judges lived within a couple of blocks of Tranquility Road and had sat out the recent unpleasantness in their basements.

An hour later, Kris was staring at four of the kindest-looking grandmother and grandfather types she'd ever hope to meet. "You're the local judges?"

"We never got a lot of business," one gray-haired grandmother said. "Most of the time, the constables were able to talk things down."

"Though some divorces could get messy," the bald man at her left elbow put in.

"We did have a serial killer once," the other elderly woman added. "That was a sad case. We had to shoot him."

"We need to hang these murderers." "Rapists, too." "Hang them all," came from the growing crowd outside the iron fence.

Around Kris, her Marines were getting edgy. Her guard corporal had added two more squads to the detail protecting her. The Marines guarding the stockade full of former henchmen eyed the growing mob and the milling prisoners and seemed none too sure who was the most dangerous to their princess.

Lieutenant Stubben passed down the guard line, and it resolved itself. Half faced in. Half faced out. All had their weapons on sleepy darts.

Kris decided that nothing was gained by stretching this out. "Your Honors, aboard the *Wasp* I have a retired judge. Francine Nola sat on the High Court of Wardhaven for many years and has handled all kinds of cases. May I suggest that tomorrow she join you in impaneling a court to resolve the legal problems the late occupation of Kaskatos created?"

"That sounds good to me," from the gray-headed judge seem to settle the matter for the four of them. They stepped into the crowd, spotted friends or the children of friends, and began to either persuade them to their decision or scold them into accepting it.

Kris was glad to see that one off her plate.

Or so she hoped.

Over the next week, matters ground their way along slowly. Judge Francine had a strong distaste for capital punishment. She'd cited Kris's father from the bench for his tactics that kept hanging on the table throughout the trial of the men who kidnapped and suffocated Kris's kid brother Eddy. Still, she'd joined in the decision that saw them hang while swearing she'd never be a party to judicial murder again.

Yet her court found itself hearing truly horrendous cases, fully supported by witnesses and the best high-tech evidence that Kris's Marines and Navy techs could provide. After one particularly gruesome case involving painfully young girls as the victims, Francine went looking for Kris.

"I'm supposed to be retired. I'm supposed to be stargazing. Instead, you've got me sitting on the bench fighting to keep down the coffee and toast I limited myself to for breakfast."

"I'm sorry," Kris said, throwing herself on the mercy of the court. "The locals need you."

"God love a duck, but they do. These nice little old ladies never heard of anything so . . . rude. I think that's the worst word they have in their vocabulary. Rude!"

"Thank you for helping them . . . and us. Do you want to go back to Wardhaven on the *Surprise*?"

"No, I do not, young woman. But I do want to get off this planet and go chasing stars. You hear me? I want some good time on the ship's telescope to just lose myself in the stars."

"As soon as this is over," Kris promised.

They did have some luck. A potato crop came in early on

the plantations down south. Nelly did the job of coordinating trucks to get most of the crop up north, where it was desperately needed.

Then, to Kris's dismay, the *Surprise* showed up.

It did not have the improved body armor Kris was hoping for, but it did have container after container of famine biscuits . . . all wholesome and bland.

"But we've got something else as well. Five hundred million frozen fish embryos," a very enthusiastic young woman gushed as she sat in Kris's office. "They grow rice here, right. You drop these embryos in the rice paddies. They eat the bugs, slime, fertilize the rice with their droppings and when you're ready to harvest the rice, you have a fish crop, too. These fish will eat anything!"

Kris eyed Captain St. Helens of the *Surprise*. "Where'd you get this woman?"

"She's a fish biologist, hired by the Food for Millions Foundation. This is her first voyage out from Wardhaven," St. Helens explained.

"They'll eat anything," Kris repeated.

"Yep," came right back at her.

"And if they escape into the local streams?"

"That would be very bad," the woman said, shaking her head. "You can't allow that. They'll outcompete the local breeds in nothing flat."

The optimistic fish biologist still didn't seem to get the picture. Kris spoke slowly. "We've got desperate people doing desperate things to get their next meal on the table for them and their families."

"I've got designs for fish caging," came back at Kris without even a pause.

"Penny," Kris shouted, "will you take this woman out to a farm and let someone talk some sense into her."

Penny's head appeared in Kris's makeshift door. "We need to talk, Your Highness. Could you have someone else take her out?"

If Penny was "Your Highnessing" Kris, they really needed to talk. Kris mashed her commlink. "Jack, could you detail a

Marine to escort our new fish biologist out to a rice farm so she can get an education on what happens when everyone is starving. Make sure your Marine knows nothing about ecology. Otherwise, he's likely to shoot her."

"I think every Wardhaven school kid had ecology in the sixth grade," Jack said back. "But I got one or two that never learned a thing in school who will probably do."

"Take our optimistic fish girl to the Annam plantation. They're Buddhist and very patient."

"I think I'll go make sure my drop ships aren't having any problems delivering food," Captain St. Helens said, and dismissed himself back to the *Surprise*.

"Penny, tell me why we need to talk, and keep in mind, it's been a very bad day in a way-too-rough week."

"And it will get worse," Penny said, slipping onto the couch in Kris's dirtside office.

"Then let me go first," Kris said. "Talk to me about the pirate captain we captured."

"He wasn't a pirate captain, just a wannabe," Penny said, cutting in.

"A wannabe?"

"His logbook shows he was third officer on a tramp freighter coming in horribly overloaded with refugees. And yes, we checked his papers out with St. Pete, and they verify them as accurate."

"Can we trust any Peterwald records?"

"Probably not, but we got the query off and the answer back fast enough that I don't think anyone had a chance to change the main record. The crew are all singing the same songs, hired by the locals to run a ship they didn't have to bring in cargo they didn't own. The one thing missing in this picture was the ship."

"Somebody had to know what they were going to do with the ship."

"Belou said Jackie knew just the person to set him up . . . but she wasn't telling him anything until she needed to. I get the feeling she didn't trust her pinky finger to know what her thumb was doing."

"Do you have Chief Beni going over her computer?"

"Yes, Kris, but you know that old story about the deputy being saved by his big belt buckle taking the bullet."

"My grampa Trouble has a buckle he claims did that very thing for him."

"Well, the computer around Jackie's neck took a direct hit from one of the rockets. Trust me, computers don't do the belt buckle bit all that well. There were parts of her computer all over. Parts of her body all over, too. Wasn't much to bury."

"I hear it wasn't much of a funeral," Kris said dryly. "So, we still don't know anything."

"Sadly, that is all too true."

"Kris," Nelly said, "have you ever thought of asking Vicky Peterwald?"

"I was hoping to put that off until I had to meet her," Kris said.

"You may not be able to put it off much longer," Nelly said. "I just got a message that she's arriving at St. Pete next week, and *she'd* like to see you there."

Kris rolled her eyes at the ceiling. "I thought I had every problem I could have. Nelly, you've just added another. Have Abby compose a note responding in the affirmative to Vicky's message and have her ask Vicky for any information about the local pirate activities hereabouts. Tell her I've come up blank.

"And tell Abby she can give Vicky a full report on everything I've been doing since I arrived here. No need to hold anything back."

"I'm doing it, Kris."

"Kris, I'm supposed to get my time," Penny said, not moving from the couch.

"It's not already bad enough?"

"We have worse problems here on Kaskatos."

"It can get worse?"

"The cops, Kris."

"Solve it."

"Do you really mean that?" Penny asked.

"I don't know. Your dad is a cop. You're the closest thing I have to a cop on staff. Is this planet in such bad shape that you can't patch it back together in a week or two?"

"Try ten or twenty years."

Kris eyed her subordinate, but it was clear she was not joking. "You have my attention. Talk to me."

"I take it that you know how simple the local judicial system is?"

"Judge Francine filled me in. We don't have any problems, so we don't need no stinking solutions. Right?"

"Same with the cops. There's a dozen that got bit by the police bug and learned the business from training tapes and stuff. Most are just well-meaning locals who put on a badge a couple of hours a week and show up for the odd juvenile high jinks or domestic disturbance. It's a small-town attitude."

"So they can go back to being a small town now that we've gotten rid of the wicked witch," Kris said, hopefully.

"You ever hear that story about the first two people on Earth taking a bite out of an apple?"

"Yeah. I never like the way one of us girls took the fall for the guys."

"Me neither, but Kaskatos has taken a bite out of one nasty apple and, Kris, I don't think these folks can ever go back to the way it was."

Kris sighed. "Enough with the stories, tell me what's happening."

"There are a lot of guns floating around now. Lots of them. Longtime locals don't much care for the new kids on the block, but they're outnumbered six or seven to one. The first three million new kids really don't like the last arrivals. Not all of them were gunslingers for Jackie, but a lot of them are really bad apples. And now all three groups have guns and think they ought to be the police."

"So suddenly these people need a real police department," Kris said.

"Yes. Honest cops. Fair cops, but the original locals don't have any idea how to form a police force. The new kids' only experience with police is in the Peterwald police state. Not a good reference point. Kris, if Greenfeld State Security arrests you, everyone assumes you're guilty of something. People that are arrested never come back. They don't need prisons, just mass, unmarked graves."

"That's not good," Kris said.

"But that's the way things have been for the last hundred years. Keep your nose clean, don't ask questions, and you can live to a nice old age. Get caught in the wrong place at the wrong time . . ." Penny shrugged.

Kris leaned back and stared out the window. Rolling hills were green with trees and crops. It looked like a lovely paradise. Maybe it had been . . . once. Maybe it could be . . . with a lot of work by the right kind of trained people.

"So," Kris said, thinking out loud, "I need to call my brother, Honovi, and ask him to send a couple of thousand of Wardhaven's experienced cops, judges, law professors, lawyers, and civil liberty advocates out this way. Am I missing anything?"

"Nope. Other than they'd better plan on spending the next couple of dozen years here."

Kris pushed her chair back from her desk, leaned back, and studied the ceiling. "How do I explain all that to Vicky? No, sister, I'm really not taking over a planet in your sphere of influence. But yes, I'm shipping in a whole lot of civil-affairs experts to set up a full political and legal system that is anathema to you and your old man."

"I believe the original idea was that we'd just deliver some famine biscuits and get the hell out of here," Penny said.

"No good deed goes unpunished." Kris sighed. She stood and walked over to stare out the window. Of late, she'd spent a lot of time staring out that window. Thinking about what she'd do once she was done chasing pirates.

There was a big hole in the star map several thousand light-years away. A big unknown space that had recently taken to eating starships. Kris wanted to explore that hungry void.

But whatever or whoever lurked in that space might very well eat her . . . and any of her friends she took on that voyage of exploration.

Kris turned back to Penny. "What if it was just you hanging

around here for a year or so? You probably wouldn't even be noticed. Haven't you been talking to the Speaker of the City Council of Elders?"

"Yes," Penny said. "He's a nice guy, and he likes a lot of what I talk about, Kris. But just me?"

"I could leave you the colonel. Kaskatos needs a militia. I think I could trust Colonel Cortez to train a local self-defense force for this one little planet. And besides, he's been begging to get off my staff . . . preferably before the next time we see Grampas Ray and Trouble."

"He has that, and I admit that I've considered what I could do here all by myself, but, Kris, have you thought this through?"

Actually, Kris had thought this and a whole lot more through time and time again.

If Kris took the *Wasp* out into deep space to see what was chewing up Iteeche scouts and swallowing them whole, how many of her friends deserved to be dragged along to that potential death.

Kris wouldn't really need Penny to go looking where she wasn't wanted. Or the colonel. Or Abby and Cara. Chief Beni might come in handy.

What about Jack? That was a tough one.

Kris realized she was letting the silence stretch.

"Penny, you and Colonel Cortez look into what you can do here while I'm gone. I'll go find out what bee Vicky has in her bonnet and see what she'll let me do for the people running away from the Greenfeld Workers' Paradise. We ought to have a better idea of our problem in a couple or three weeks."

Kris put a hopeful look on her face.

It didn't squelch the sour glare Penny shot her way.

15

A glance at the station above St. Petersburg told Kris all she needed to know about the political and economic disaster that had overtaken the Peterwald empire.

Four battleships and a half dozen cruisers were tied up at the station's piers along with several destroyers and auxiliaries. Normally, such ships would be concentrated with their peers in a battle fleet. Now they occupied over half of the station's docks, leaving little room for the freighters that carried the trade that was the economic lifeblood of planets.

Way too many of those freighters were strung out ahead and behind the station. Scores and scores of merchant ships drifted there in cheap storage, earning no money, moving no trade, and doing their best to incur no costs for their owners.

No wonder millions of people had fled. Kris had to wonder what was actually going on down planet. What were people doing for jobs? How were they earning their daily bread? Had the exchange process broken down so badly that farmers weren't even bothering to harvest their crops?

A glance at the daily news feed told Kris nothing. It was brief and very uninformative.

The port captain seemed to be expecting the *Wasp*; a berth had been reserved for them. Captain Drago quickly lost his smile at someone's thoughtfulness.

The pier saved for the Wardhaven scout ship was between the Greenfeld battleship *Fury* and its sister the *Terror*.

Haystacks, meet the needle.

They had hardly docked when a lieutenant commander

from the *Fury* was offering his captain's compliments and inviting Her Highness Kristine Longknife to dinner in the admiral's quarters of the *Fury*. Dinner was to be served immediately upon Kris's arrival.

Gunny Brown reported that the commander had a Greenfeld Marine escort of sixteen "mean-looking dudes."

Jack looked decidedly unhappy at the prospect of trusting Kris to local security. He didn't look all that much happier when Kris invited him to bring along sixteen of his own line beasts.

With Penny and the colonel left behind on Kaskatos trying their hand at the civil-affairs business, Kris didn't have a lot of her staff to pick from. She did add Chief Beni, not as a dinner guest but to apply his own magic tricks to seeing that neither Kris nor whoever she ate with were surprised by a bomb in the soup.

Kris promised the chief a good meal at her expense later.

The walk to the *Fury*'s pier was brief and educational. Kris saw no activity on the station other than the marching of heavily armed details hither and yon. Kris wasn't surprised by the watchfulness of Jack and his Marines. What did surprise her was the extreme alertness of the sixteen Greenfeld Marines. They walked, rifles at the ready, heads on a constant swivel, as if patrolling in hostile territory.

Gunny Brown took that in and growled at his own Marines. "This is no place for toy soldiers. Loosen up, suck it up, and soldier."

Despite the apparent expectations to the contrary, Kris arrived safely at the quarterdeck of the *Fury*. Waiting for her was the captain of the ship. More surprising was the admiral of the squadron, one Georg Krätz.

"Congratulations on your promotion," Kris said, saluting him.

"I am not the only one who is finding the Navy conducive to my good health."

Without announcement, Lieutenant Victoria Peterwald presented herself on the quarterdeck.

"You're coming along quickly," Kris said.

"I made lieutenant a month faster than you did," the scion of the Peterwald empire said, preening. "Of course, I kept my nose clean and avoided embarrassments like a mutiny and missing ships movement."

Kris shrugged. No doubt using your father's Navy to suppress revolutionary tendencies was more career enhancing than helping Earth and six hundred planets break up without throwing a war into the mix.

If she had it to do over again, Kris wouldn't change a thing.

The captain of the *Fury* dismissed himself, and Admiral Krätz led the way to his quarters.

Vicky's eyes lit on Kris's cane. "I see that last assassination attempt really got you good."

"I notice that you're still favoring your right leg from your last bomb incident," Kris shot right back. "You really ought to have your sensor expert meet with my Chief Beni. I'm sure some of your gear could be made almost as good as ours."

That Greenfeld was behind Wardhaven in some electronic technology was a sore point and put an end to conversation for a while.

Admiral Krätz's quarters were quite palatial. Kris couldn't help but notice that the door across from the admiral's had LIEUTENANT VICTORIA PETERWALD stenciled on it.

Both doors had two Marine guards on full alert.

While the stewards served coffee, Kris asked the familiar questions. "How are your daughters doing? Last I heard, one of them wanted battleship duty because of a certain boy. Do you have the young couple on the *Fury*?"

"No," the admiral said darkly, then took a sip of his coffee while eyeing Vicky over the cup.

"Not all our fleet is tied up to piers enforcing public order," Vicky said, by way of explanation. "No matter what your Admiral Crossenshield may tell you, we do have a battle fleet on full standby if anyone should make the mistake of probing what is ours at this difficult time. I can't say how strong the battle fleet is, but you may tell your intelligence admiral personally from me that it is larger than he thinks."

"I will pass that warning along in my next communication

with Wardhaven," Kris said evenly, and set her coffee down before going on. "I have personally sat in on conversations with my great-grandfather the king and Admiral Crossenshield, and I can tell you that neither one of them has any but the gentlest of interests in the 103 planets in the Greenfeld Alliance."

"A hundred and three, huh?" Vicky said, setting down her own coffee cup to better concentrate on Kris. "By that very number, you ignore our intense interest in planets just beyond the Rim of our space. Let's say Kaskatos, for example."

"I'm glad you brought that up," Kris said. Both of the young women failed to fully suppress a smile at that lie. "My intention on going there was to check on conditions and deliver famine relief. As your intel reports have no doubt informed you, my ship was jumped by an in-system pirate ketch. When I landed to hand out food, I was attacked and left with no other option than to clean out the den of pirates and cutthroats I'd stumbled upon." Kris didn't flinch or blink as she laid it all on the line for Vicky.

"Are you aware Jackie Jackson was a major in Greenfeld State Security?" Vicky snapped. "How did you know that she wasn't there under my father's orders?"

So, Vicky wasn't going to make it easy for Kris. The Wardhaven princess really hadn't expected that she would.

"I made inquires about the conditions on Kaskatos before I entered the system. The answers I got back from my inquiries to Greenfeld data banks were as close to nothing as made no never mind. I'm sorry, Vicky, but I went in blind and found that everything that I intended to do or planned for only led me deeper and deeper into a mess.

"In the end, I did what I felt I had to do for people who couldn't do anything for themselves. Jackie Jackson was a sick puppy creating her own hell. I ended that and am now only doing what I have to do to pick up the pieces." Kris paused to see if Vicky had anything to say.

When she didn't, Kris went on, choosing her words carefully. "Also, Vicky, the general commanding Greenfeld State Security didn't live very long after I saved your father's life.

All the reports I have is that State Security isn't in very good odor these days."

"It isn't," Admiral Krätz said.

"It's just that you're doing that Longknife thing of shooting first and asking questions later," Vicky said.

"And we don't?" the admiral put in.

"We don't have a lot of choices," Vicky snapped at her superior.

The admiral raised an eyebrow. "I think the commander has just explained that she was in the same situation. How do we prevent just this series of events from happening again is, I believe, the reason you suggested I give this dinner."

Vicky took a deep breath. "You are, as usual, Admiral, both correct and wise. In the heat of the moment, I forgot what you had so ably explained to me."

"I believe dinner is ready," the admiral said, standing. "I understand that we have quite a feast for you, Your Highness."

The admiral had his own wardroom with china, silver, and linen on a solid oak table. The head and foot of the table were left empty. Kris sat directly across from Vicky. Jack faced the admiral. It seemed to encourage Kris and Vicky to talk freely.

Or not.

The walls of the wardroom were decorated with Marines standing guard, Wardhaven Marines with gleaming fixed bayonets alternated with Greenfeld's own. Chief Beni with his little potbelly and black boxes looked as out of place among the Marines as a camel at a thoroughbred show.

The fruit and appetizers were both a medley of choices that dominated the conversation as the diners tried different creations. Not until the salad did Vicky casually ask, "So, how did that thing end up with the Iteeche Death Ball. Our detached cruisers were quite excited to make the initial report. Then nothing?"

Kris should have realized the Iteeche situation had to be one of the reasons for the quick invitation. She chose her words carefully, not wanting to tell a lie she could be caught in . . . but not at all willing to tell the whole truth.

"I escorted the Iteeche back to their Imperial Space," Kris

said. "They were scouting for vacant territory. I was scouting for the same. We probably will need to have a brief get-together soon with Imperial representatives to extend the No Go Zone."

Vicky selected a tiny tomato, speared it, and raised an eyebrow toward Kris. "I think it was two, three months before you sent the Iteeche home. What did your king have to say to him?"

"There are no reports of my king seeing any Iteeche of late," Kris said. No *official* reports.

"No *official* reports," Vicky said, plucking the words out of Kris's mind. "Kris. We're big girls. We both know that lots of things never make it into the official records. What were the Iteeche like? Come on, I'm dying to know."

Kris pushed a piece of lettuce from one side of her salad plate to the other. It was so tempting to follow Vicky's lead, to talk girl to girl about something both of them were really into. A temptation, but not one Kris couldn't resist.

"When you run into one, you'll have to tell me what an Iteeche is like," Kris said.

Vicky scowled at the admiral. "You told me she'd be tight-lipped on this."

He nodded. "Opening talks with our old enemy, even if it is just to draw lines that keep us apart, is not something to be done casually. With all we have on our plate, it's something best left to others."

Kris would have loved to tell Vicky just how wise the admiral was, but even to say that would be to say too much.

The soup arrived, a fish stew in a tomato base. Kris found herself wondering if red was the color of the meal. Kris was running out of things to talk about. Space travel really didn't allow one to talk about the weather all that much, and it was getting more and more clear that Kris and Vicky were on opposite sides of a very thorny wall.

"Kris, why are you getting reports from a news reporter?" Vicky asked after she had finished her soup in silence. "Who is this Winston Spencer?"

Kris gave Vicky the same answer she'd given Penny.

"He's a reporter who's done some good news articles about the Navy. Last time I visited Wardhaven, my brother, Honovi, rubbed my nose in just how out of the loop I had gotten when I was bouncing around out beyond the Rim. It seems that a Longknife princess isn't allowed to let the rest of the worlds go away while she's risking her neck scouting for new planets."

"I haven't noticed that scouting out beyond the Rim was all that dangerous. You know something I don't?" Vicky wheedled.

Kris did know something Vicky didn't, but she wasn't going to mix it in with the cold soup.

"Pirates and slavers and, I hear, even some drug lords are raising hell out beyond the Rim," Kris answered blandly. "The Rim just isn't what it used to be."

That drew a dry chuckle from the admiral.

Kris knew she ought to leave it at that. She even managed to close her mouth. It just wouldn't stay shut.

"I guess it does look kind of funny from where you sit, protected by this huge battleship and all," Kris said, the words slipping out faster and faster. "You pop a general here. Over there you line up against the wall the whole crew of a planet's State Security force and machine-gun the lot of them. I bet you laugh at it all when you're finished." Kris now was almost shouting; her lungs were empty. She paused to gasp for a breath.

"Kris, this is not well said," Jack whispered. Across from them, both Vicky and the admiral sat stark still, eyes wide in dismay.

"Right, I shouldn't say this. I shouldn't say that they've sent millions of people fleeing from the murderers they've let loose. I shouldn't ask them if there's any spare food on St. Petersburg and if any of the empty ships in orbit here could carry some of those crumbs to feed the refugees on Kaskatos. No, I can't ask. So we end up shipping food from Wardhaven and Pitts Hope and wherever so that out beyond the Rim a kid whose ribs you can count gets at least one meal a day."

Kris had to stop. There was a sob climbing up from her gut

that she just couldn't hold in any longer. She let it loose, then fought to keep back the tears that did their best to follow it.

"Is it that bad out there?" the admiral asked.

"It's bad," Jack said, buying a few seconds for Kris.

"It's bad," Kris repeated, locking eyes with Vicky, willing her to see what she had seen.

"I ordered a rocket-grenade salvo on a balcony a week before last. I was pretty sure your Major Jackie Jackson was on that balcony. Very likely several of her closest aides were there with her. What I do know for sure was that she had four hostages cuffed to that balcony rail. Four civilians guilty of nothing other than being too close to Jackie when I got tired of the slaughter and did what I could to cut it off at the root."

Kris's words hung in the air for a moment.

Across from her, Lieutenant Victoria Peterwald broke eye contact with Kris, glanced away muttering, "It was the best thing you could do."

Kris shook her head. "Yes, I did manage to kill as few innocent people as I could. But I'm getting sick and tired of choices that leave me trying to feel good about doing the lesser of two evils. I've had it with that."

Kris found herself out of words again. She eyed Vicky.

Vicky said nothing. Did nothing. Answered with not even a shrug.

"Could you at least tell me how long this is going to go on?" Kris pleaded. "This, what do you call it, ballot by bullet in the back of the neck?"

"And you'd have us just put this all to a vote, huh?" Vicky snapped, her pale skin now flushed a hot pink that almost matched her red hair.

"It works for me," Kris shot back. "Please note, it's us ballot planets that are shipping the food in to the refugees from your bullet planets."

"They didn't have to run. They're cowards. We've told them to stay," Vicky said, half-out of her seat.

"Gosh, in that case, I wonder what makes them run," Kris said, leaning back in her chair as if to think. "Oh, could it be the bodies in the street every morning? The rivers floating with corpses every night?"

"Kris, what's got into you?" Jack snapped.

Kris opened her mouth to bite out a reply but found she didn't have one.

Across from her, Admiral Krätz had a fatherly hand on Vicky's elbow, pushing her back down into her chair.

"If the two of you were just college students shooting the bull at Kris's Student Union one afternoon," the admiral said, "this might be fun. But you are not students. You two are grown women with the responsibility of two planetary alliances on your shoulders."

He focused his attention on Kris. "I can only imagine what it must have been like for you, stuck cleaning up the mess one of our rogue security officers made of that planet. We thank you in the name of Greenfeld for what you did, and we appreciate your coming here to involve us in the situation. Don't we, Lieutenant?"

Vicky took a deep breath and let it out. Her color, if not back to normal, was at least no longer signaling a threatening heart attack.

"I appreciate what you've done," she said formally. "I'm sorry for what it's cost you personally, Kris. Really I am," she ended, actually sounding like she did.

"And I'm sorry I lost it just now," Kris said. "I didn't intend to say anything like that. I don't know where it came from."

That was the truth, and it really bothered Kris. *Where did all of that come from? Am I losing it?*

"Now, if we can all sit down," the admiral said with a smile that looked more conspiratorial than forced, "I have a surprise for you. I have had a wild boar prepared according to an ancient Earth recipe. Prepare yourself for something special."

A cook, complete in high chef's hat, came in carrying a platter with a whole roasted pig. It even had an apple in its mouth.

For a second, Kris was none too sure how this was going to play out. Her stomach still boiled with the aftermath of her emotional onslaught. Now, facing a pig that only the garnish assured her wasn't likely to get up and trot from the table, her stomach was even less sure of itself.

"My dad used to have these prepared at his hunting lodge," Vicky offered. "Those were good times."

Kris would not sully those memories, which from the sound of Vicky's voice were few and far between, by one Wardhaven princess losing her supper before she finished it.

At the head of the table, the chef produced a gleaming sharp knife and huge fork and prepared to slice into the guest of honor.

"Excuse me," Chief Beni said from where he stood backed into a corner, "but this room has a listening device in it."

16

It was Admiral Krätz's turn to bolt half-out of his chair. "I have my quarters swept regularly. And I had them swept again just before dinner. There can't be a live bug in here."

"There wasn't," Chief Beni admitted, "until the chef brought that pig in."

"The chef," the admiral said, turning to face the man with the sharp, gleaming knife. The man looked shocked at becoming the center of attention so quickly. Maybe his knife was just being raised to defend himself. Maybe his arm was still involved in carving the dinner.

And maybe he was getting ready to throw the blade.

No one snapped an order. There was no time. But suddenly, four Marines were on him, two from each fleet. The white-clad chef went down in a tide of blue, red, green, and black.

"Where's the bug?" Kris demanded.

"I think it's in the apple," Nelly said.

"I agree," Chief Beni said.

"I don't have anything," one of the Greenfeld Marines said, coming away from the wall. He held his rifle, but now that Kris studied him, his pockets were bulging, and he did have a mike and eyepiece. "No device has squawked," he insisted.

"Crew?" Kris said to everyone in particular.

"The Marine technician is correct," the chief said, diplomatically, "the bug is silent at the moment, but it is recording. I have cataloged all the electronic devices in this room. This is a new one, and I don't think that pig is authorized an electronic device."

"Neither do I," the admiral growled through grim lips. "Cook?"

"I don't know what you are talking about," he said, now in the grip of two hefty Marines of different uniformed persuasion.

"Technician, can you recover the bug?" the admiral asked.

The Greenfeld Marine risked a tiny shrug. "Sir, I can't even verify the presence of the bug. My instrumentation is not able to track something as minor as power use at that level."

"Chief, can you recover this device?" the Greenfeld admiral asked the Wardhaven CPO.

"I will need to have my computer spin off a large nano device to isolate and retrieve it."

"Or I can do it," Nelly put in.

"Is your chief's computer as good as Nelly?" Vicky asked.

"Da Vinci is my son," Nelly said in full maternal pride.

"Nelly, I wish you hadn't said that."

"Why not, Kris?"

"Because I'm not sure the world is ready to know that there are eight of you."

"Eight!" Vicky yelped.

"Ah, ladies," Jack cut in, "could we get this bug before it starts broadcasting all this to the world."

"Admiral," Kris began, "none of my computers have generated any nanoscouts since we were invited aboard your battleship. It did not seem an appropriate response to your hospitality."

"I should say not," the admiral agreed.

"With your permission, I will generate one to capture this bug," Kris said.

"Two nanoscouts," Nelly interrupted. "We need two. One to find the bug we've found and a second to locate its repeater. This bug is extremely low-power. For any data burst it sends to get out, it will have to be repeated."

The admiral's lips were drawing thin and tight. "Send out your scouts. I expect you to use them for nothing more than what you've said."

"You have my word on that," Princess Kristine Longknife answered.

A few moments later, a thin filament was barely visible, floating lightly on the air from the pig's apple.

"If your technician will delicately lift that out and deposit it on my portable work surface," the chief said, pulling a green plastaglass sheet from one pocket.

The technician looked aghast at the idea and quickly stepped back as a young lieutenant hurried into the wardroom. "You called for me, Lieutenant Peterwald?"

Vicky quickly explained the problem. The lieutenant produced something that looked like a pair of tweezers patched together by a gear freak and did the service of removing the offending bug to the chief's examination plate.

The chief and lieutenant donned different eye-power-enhancement devices and began oohing and aahing over their catch.

"What should we do about the other four electronic devices the cook has on him?" Nelly asked.

"He has more?" Vicky said, turning her attention back to the young man.

"Four," Nelly repeated.

"Search him," the admiral ordered.

The two Gunny Sergeants received the order with a mutual grin that brought horror to the object of their interest.

"I don't have anything on me," the chef pleaded.

He could have saved his breath. While four Marines held him down, the two Gunnies, with borrowed bayonets, proceeded to strip him down to the bare skin.

Kris turned away, unsure if they would stop the knife work at that point. Vicky didn't.

"I've launched two more scouts," Nelly said. "I think you'll find one device on the front of his belt buckle."

A moment later, the buckle was on the dining table, and a filament waved from it. The Greenfeld lieutenant didn't turn from his attention to the initial bug but handed his tweezers off to the technician without even looking up.

The technician carefully placed the new bug on the glass plate.

"If we could have his shoes," Nelly said, and both black leather shoes were on the table a moment later.

"I think the heels come off," said Nelly.

They didn't budge when the technician tried gently to move them.

"Ask the man," Nelly said.

Kris noticed that Gunny Brown took a step back as the questioning began silently and out of her view. It must have been persuasive.

"There's a tiny ridge on the sole in front of the heel," came in a rush. "Press it with your thumbnail."

The technician did, and the heels popped off, revealing two small chips and a tiny power supply.

They were gently put side by side on one corner of the examination plate.

"Nelly, are you sure about that other device?" Kris asked.

"I think I've located it. There's something with a power supply under the skin of the little finger on his left hand."

"Left hand?" the Greenfeld Gunny asked.

"Yes," Nelly said.

And a second later, there was a whimper, and a finger, wrapped in a napkin lay beside the green glass pad.

"I didn't know about any of those. I swear to God. Somebody must have put them on me," the naked man insisted, as four Greenfeld Marines hustled him from the room.

Kris would not want to face that man's fate. She doubted Greenfeld interrogators would start by offering a hamburger and a brew.

The chief and the lieutenant continued to mutter to themselves about the new toys they had found. Neither the admiral nor Vicky seemed happy to be so ignored. Before they could start juggling elbows, Kris popped a question.

"Nelly, have you heard back from your scout that went after the repeater?"

"I think it just located something in the admiral's office."

That got both Vicky's and Admiral Krätz's attention. They and the technician followed Kris there. Nelly aimed them at a power socket that now had one of the thin filaments waving in the soft breeze of the ship's blowers.

"Has it been listening to my conversations? Our conversations?" the admiral demanded with a worried glance at Vicky.

"It's positioned to be a repeater," the junior technician said, pulling the device out. "The lieutenant will have to examine it to know just what it can do, sir."

"If you will allow me to send a nanoscout down your power cable, I may be able to locate where the repeater is sending its feed," Nelly said.

"How much of my ship's electrical cabling will you have to search?" the admiral asked.

"All of it, I think," Nelly said.

"I cannot allow your spies the free run of my ship," the admiral said with finality, then turned on the technician. "I was told that we had secured our ship against just such spying devices as you are now holding."

"Yes, my admiral, I was assured that it was so."

"We will have to talk about this," he growled as he turned back to the wardroom.

"Ah, may I suggest," Kris said softly, "that we continue our conversations aboard the *Wasp*."

The admiral began to snap a quick response, then swallowed it. He glanced at Vicky. "What do you think?"

"I think the princess has a point. While I doubt she is offering it to achieve our best interests, I do think it is in our best interests."

"Then yes, let's keep our peace until we can talk with fewer ears listening," the admiral muttered.

They reentered the wardroom, with its ignored roast pig, but before the admiral could issue any orders, Chief Beni turned to Kris.

"Commander, you know that jamming problem we've had? The one that can't happen but just keeps on showing up?"

"All too well," Kris said.

"Well, I think this little doodad from his left heel is just the thing that's been causing it."

"What are you talking about?" Vicky said.

"We'll talk about it next door," Kris said.

And with that, they silently wrapped things up and left.

17

AS they left the *Fury* and quick marched for the *Wasp*, Vicky leaned close to Kris.

"So, you've got more supersmart computers."

"They are my children," Nelly put in before Kris could say a word.

"Your children," Vicky said with what sounded like a touch of feigned awe. It might fool a young computer, but it was as fake as any praise Kris ever heard in high school.

"Any chance I could have one to work with me?" Vicky said cheerfully.

"No!" Nelly said bluntly.

"Why not?" Vicky shot back.

NELLY, SHUT UP, Kris thought. "Because I'm not at all sure Greenfeld has the technology to support a computer of Nelly's caliber," Kris went on aloud, "and I'm not about to sell you any of Wardhaven's superior tech."

"Hey, we make our own smart metal and have some pretty good self-organizing computer matrices. I bet if you gave me Nelly's central kernel, I could have a computer up and running in no time almost as good as Nelly. Maybe even better."

"I will not have one of my children in your hands," Nelly spat before Kris could even begin to organize a response.

"What does she mean?"

"Nelly is very much the mother of her offspring," Kris said slowly. "Each of them is being allowed to develop their own personality. Usually as a reflection of the person they're working with. But you have to understand, Nelly's already called two of her kids back from people who weren't suited for them, and she's none too sure about Abby."

"Not at all," Nelly sniffled. "That woman is on probation. She still hasn't named her computer, and she keeps turning her off. If she keeps this up, Kris, I'm going to have to ask you to bring her back to me."

Kris listened to the computer at her neck and shook her head. "Vicky, you don't strike me as someone who suffers fools gladly, or listens long to anything you don't want to hear. I can't believe you're serious about wanting to put up with someone like Nelly hanging around your neck."

"I expected that I'd be able to teach my computer to behave itself," Vicky said.

"Right," Nelly snapped. "Kris, you heard her. No way will I have her abusing one of my children."

"I am ending this conversation," Kris said, as they walked through the station's vast main deck. "Nelly, you need to learn to converse in gentle company. People do not like talking to someone who is rude, tactless, and inflexible."

"But my children!"

"Nelly, not another word."

They walked on in silence for a few paces.

"Is she always like that?" Vicky asked.

"I said not another word," Kris repeated.

Vicky eyed Kris with both eyebrows raised in surprise. Slowly it dawned on the scion of the Peterwald power base that Kris did indeed intend to apply the same rules to her as she did to her pet computer.

The eyebrows came down.

"You're mighty quiet back there," Jack said without looking over his shoulder.

"We ran out of things to talk about," Vicky said.

The Marine and admiral exchanged silent glances, and the party continued on its way to the *Wasp*.

Once they crossed over to the *Wasp*'s quarterdeck, everything came to a halt as Chief Beni and the Greenfeld lieutenant did a complete wash down of the entire party for any kind of electronic device they'd picked up in transit. Though none of the sixteen Greenfeld or Wardhaven Marines were carrying anything but their standard firing computer, still, everyone and everything had to be checked.

Especially after it was found that the admiral had somehow acquired a stray nanobug on the walk back. Once Chief Beni identified it, the admiral and Vicky quit grousing about the delay and waited quietly until the chief was content.

By which time the Greenfeld lieutenant was seriously impressed. "How do we get our hands on some of the nifty stuff he's got?" he whispered to the admiral, who made a serious effort not to hear the question.

"I've reserved the Forward Lounge," Kris told them, and led the Greenfeld contingent to where Kris and her team had spent so much time with the visiting Iteeche who never were officially there.

Once at the lounge, Admiral Krätz ordered the junior technician to do a full sweep of the place. Kris gave the chief a quick nod, and he followed the other as they did a serious and thorough search . . . and found nothing.

Done, the admiral sent his Marines to wait outside with the technician. Jack had Kris's own Marine escort keep them company. That left only six military personnel from two seriously divided camps to share one huge room.

"Now that we are truly alone," the admiral said, taking a seat at a round table in the middle of the room, "what is it that we want to talk about?"

"Several things," Kris said, settling into the chair across from him. Jack sat to Kris's right, Vicky to her left. The two technical experts set themselves up at the next table over and quickly lost themselves in their own separate world.

"As I would not mention in a potentially public forum, my local network has been jammed several times of late," Kris said."

"Short-range local networks can't be jammed," Vicky said.

"Yes, I know that, and Nelly made sure to remind me of that well-known fact every time it happened, but it just kept happening. That usually was when there was a Peterwald interest at work in my life."

"Us?" Vicky said in such surprise that Kris doubted even a Peterwald could fake.

Or a Longknife.

"You remember the first time you tried to kill me on New Eden," Kris said.

Vicky nodded.

"The shooters you hired were pretty lame at the assassination business, but the whole time I was running from them, something was jamming the net connection between Nelly and my automatic. In order to get a sight picture, I actually had to risk putting my eyeball behind my weapon. No remote sight picture. Quite a problem at the time."

"I didn't hire anyone to jam you," Vicky said, thoughtfully. "I didn't even think to try. Even I knew that you couldn't jam a local net."

"But somehow someone has been doing it," Kris said slowly

"Admiral," Vicky asked, "do you know of anything we've got that could do that?"

The Navy officer shook his head. "No, I don't, and since tonight I've had my nose rubbed in Wardhaven's electronic superiority over Greenfeld time after time, I'm kind of hard-pressed to believe that we have anything like that." He paused for a moment, then continued. "However, I do not doubt Your Highness's word at all. If you've encountered it, it is there."

"I think we just encountered it," Vicky said, glancing at the techs mumbling behind her.

"It seems to me," Kris said, "that there is a cluster of excellence in electronics somewhere in Greenfeld that has not been brought to the attention of your father, Vicky. Quite probably very intentionally not brought to his attention."

"I do not like that," Vicky said darkly.

"But why would they do that?" Jack said. "I thought that people that won Henry Peterwald's good attention were the ones who advanced in Greenfeld. Am I missing something?"

For a long moment, Vicky let that question hang in midair. Finally, she said, "Some people seek my father's support and become his supporters as well. But I've come to realize that there are many games going on in the Palace, and many people may gain aces in one game but choose to keep them up their sleeves to play in others."

"Wheels in wheels inside wheels," the admiral said, "and please, Commander, you need not point out that these games are now deadly and driving people to risk their lives in flight across the stars. It is the fate of us in this time to pay the price for a foolish game that has been long in progress."

"I'm sorry if I made it sound like we folks at Wardhaven had all our problems solved," Kris said. "We have our own set. If we didn't, no one would have been able to manipulate our politics to let six strange battleships almost flatten Wardhaven."

"Thank you," Vicky said. "For what it's worth, I envy you your problems. I'd gladly swap with you."

"Thanks, but no thanks," Kris said dryly.

There was a brief pause before Jack leaned forward, and said, "So, what does all this tell us?"

"Someone in Greenfeld has some pretty fancy listening devices," the admiral said. "You can spot them. We cannot. I can understand the need for you to hold certain technology close to your vest, considering the present state of affairs between our two alliances. Still, I most certainly wish that I could protect my conversations with Lieutenant Peterwald from eavesdroppers. I will leave that for you to think about, Commander. You said there were other things you wanted to talk about?"

"Yes," Kris said. "There's the matter of the pirates. You're experienced enough with ship maintenance, Admiral, to know that they must have a base to outfit them and supply them.

"Apparently Major Jackson knew of such a base. At least she led a merchant officer to think that once they had a ship for him to go pirating in, she would tell him where to buy armament and sell off any cargo they didn't want to use on Kaskatos. Unfortunately, she died without telling anyone where this base is, and her computer was reduced to even smaller pieces than her person. Rocket grenades do that to a body."

"Yes, they do," the admiral agreed.

"Kris, I figured that you'd want some help with the pirate

problem," Vicky said, "and they are operating on our front door, so I tried to find out something about them. Follow the money is my dad's usual advice on problems like this. So I had my accountants do a search on money or goods going out of our exchange system. They also searched for goods suddenly showing up with little or no documentation."

"How'd it go?" Kris asked.

"Nothing. Not. A. Thing. Even in these troubled times, every item of production is accounted for. No money is unaccounted for. No goods for sale without full documentation to point of origin. I would have expected a few things to get lost. A few accounts not to balance. But everything is just perfect. Not so much as a hair out of place"

Kris waited as a grin spread on both her and Vicky's faces, then said, "Too perfect," at the exact second Vicky did.

"Just so," Vicky said. "Now, before tonight's demonstration of computational wizardry, I was under the impression that the computers used by my dad's Department of Taxation were the best available. Now"—Vicky brought a thoughtful forefinger up to her lips—"I'm not so sure."

"Interesting," Kris said. "You think all hundred planets in your father's alliance are linked into one big fake accounting scheme? Could anyone pull off such a huge Potemkin economy?"

The admiral scowled. "Only if everyone is helping to pull the wool over each other's eyes. Isn't this what I was telling you, Lieutenant?"

Now it was Vicky's turn to sigh, like a hot-air balloon letting go of its last gasp of support.

"The admiral has pointed out to me places where warehouse inventories say there are plenty of this or that, yet when the fleet needs something, it is strangely not available or takes half of an eternity to get it, leaving a fighting ship tied up at the pier. Don't tell your Admiral Crossenshield I said that."

"I won't," Kris said . . . and meant it.

Vicky went on. "The admiral here tells me that you cannot build six super battleships in secret without causing shortages. You can't slap a cruiser squadron together so my brother can play commodore and not pay the price somewhere. I didn't want to see what the admiral was pointing out to me, but I'm not blind. I can't afford to be like my brother. Or my dad." Vicky's voice now dripped with bitter irony.

"So, if the Navy's supply system is a mass of lies twisted together to support things that never happened or to feed the vanity of one little boy, what else about my Greenfeld is nothing but smoke and mirrors?"

Vicky pursed her lips. "Before today, I didn't see how it could be done. Now, I think someone is laughing at us as they make us dance to the tune their superior electronics are blasting out for us. Kris, I think I'm ready to let you and your Nelly audit Greenfeld's economy. Would you like the chance?"

To Kris's surprise, the admiral didn't even bat an eye.

"It's that bad, huh?"

"Do you think a Peterwald would turn to a Longknife if it wasn't?" Vicky let that hang in the air for a long moment before she went on. "There is one other matter. One I would talk with you in private, please."

So saying, Vicky made her way to the bar. Kris excused herself from the admiral, gave a worried Jack a nod to keep him in his chair, and followed Vicky.

"You have a nice collection of whiskeys," Vicky said, eyeing the bottles behind the bar.

"This, and several of the restaurants on board are private concerns. The managers order their own stocks."

"Private enterprise and free markets on even your warships. Wardhaven amazes me."

"The *Wasp* is a rather unique blending of private and Navy," Kris said.

"With a captain and part of the crew in black ops pay, I hear."

"Something I've tried to change but can't seem to. I suspect the problem goes all the way to my great-grandfather, the king."

"Even a Longknife must find her power limited when she tries to apply it to another Longknife, huh?"

"If we're going to talk about family, I may need a drink," Kris quipped.

"In a way, it is family that I want to talk about. I need your help finding someone on St. Pete and bringing her safely to the *Fury*."

Kris frowned. "Can't you just make a phone call and send a shuttle for her?"

"If it were that easy, don't you think I would have done it already?" Kris had never heard Vicky so frustrated.

"Sorry. What's the problem?"

"St. Pete's the problem. It's a mess. People who live here and fled there. People there have had to move here or yonder. The net is down, or up, or not to be trusted. I've had to be careful in my search for her. So careful that I can't find her."

Kris found herself with too many questions to choose from. She waited to see which ones Vicky would answer on her own.

"Doc Maggie was my pediatrician when I was small. She was the one who showed up whenever I was hurting. She was the one person I found who listened to me when I talked. So I talked, really talked, to her. When I grew older, she was the only woman I really trusted with my problems."

Here, Vicky tapped her right breast. "Would you believe these puppies were late coming out. Hank kidded me unmercifully, and the other kids followed his lead. It was Maggie's shoulder I cried on, and it was Maggie who gave me the only decent advice I ever heard before landing in the admiral's command."

Vicky paused, as if still unsure how much to let Kris into that secret place. "Kris, you've made your own family. Jack's more a brother to you than a security chief."

When Kris made to reject that observation, Vicky shook her head insistently. "You can say whatever you want to, but what I see with my eyes is a brother. And Penny's the sister you never had. I'm not sure where Abby and that colonel fit in. Aunt and uncle, distant cousins. I don't know. But they're as much family as staff.

"And I need something like them if I'm going to keep my sanity. What little of it we Peterwalds get by with. I really need someone like Doc Maggie on my staff to give me some big-sister advice. I was never so good for myself and others as when I had Maggie to bounce ideas around with."

Kris found herself nodding. She might or might not agree with Vicky's observations about her own staff. Definitely, Kris hoped Jack didn't look upon her like a kid sister. No, that wasn't what she felt when she caught him in his unguarded moments looking her way.

Kris waved that thought away. She didn't have time for all the questions that brought up. And right now, it was Vicky who was asking for help.

"I still don't understand why you don't just send out a call. Offer a reward for help finding this Doc Maggie," Kris said, getting back to the problem at hand.

"Kris, people disappear or die around me," Vicky said, letting exasperation fill her voice.

"Well, it would help if you didn't kill them," Nelly interjected.

"Nelly, shut up," Kris snapped. For the moment, she'd forgotten that what she was hearing, Nelly was in on, too.

"Well, it's true."

"Nelly, I know where that OFF button is, and if you don't butt out of this girl talk, I'm going to use it."

"Yes, ma'am," wasn't nearly as contrite as Kris wanted to hear.

"Nelly has a point," Vicky said, "but what she doesn't understand is that it's always been that way. I was ten. My best . . . My *only* friend was eleven. Heather didn't join in with Hank and the others teasing me. She was my first, my best friend. We were walking by a ballgame one afternoon. Not paying any attention. We weren't there for the game.

"Some guy hit the ball. It hit Heather before we even knew it was coming. It killed her!" Vicky seemed to run out of words. Maybe there were tears in her eyes. Quickly, Vicky blinked them back. Even now, she wouldn't let Kris see her shed a tear.

Kris knew that a poor little rich girl could have it tough. She'd lived that life. Somehow, she'd never felt that rule applied to the vengeful Vicky. The lovely Vicky.

Kris promised herself not to keep making that mistake.

"I had other friends growing up," Vicky went on. "Somehow, their dads always got transferred away from the Palace. You'd think they'd write, but they never did. Those were all childhood tragedies. It's in the last couple of years that it's gotten bloody.

"One girlfriend was hit by a car. A boy I liked was shot in a 'hunting accident.' Another committed 'suicide.' It's dangerous to get close to me, Kris."

"And if you let on you wanted this Doc Maggie brought in?" Kris asked.

"I figure there are a half dozen factions that would race out to kidnap her for ransom or kill her. That's why I've had to work so hard not to have any of my searches traceable back to me. I've used borrowed commlinks that my Marines swiped from sailors. Stuff like that."

Vicky finished with a sigh that the dead Tommy would have called pure Irish. Which reminded Kris that Vicky wasn't the only one dangerous to get close to.

Of course, Tommy had died at the helm of his fast patrol boat, fighting one of those unidentified Peterwald battleships. That was different. Right?

Fear showed in Vicky's eyes as the silence grew between them. "You will help me?" she pleaded. "It's not like you haven't done this before. You rescued your friend Tommy when my dad's friend Sandfire kidnapped him."

"Yes, I did," Kris said. "And yes I will help you find your friend Maggie. I expect that Jack will have kittens at the thought of us leading a rescue team down to St. Pete, but if I don't give him kittens every so often, he'd get constipated."

"I wish I had a Jack," Vicky said, glancing over her shoulder at the subject of their conversation.

"Jack is mine, girlfriend. You have to find your own Jack."

"I know," Vicky said . . . and quit batting those long eyelashes Jack's way.

Fortunately, Jack was deep in talk with the admiral, and they were both concentrating on something Chief Beni and the Greenfeld lieutenant had brought to their attention.

"So, what do we do?" Vicky asked.

"First we crack open the rotten egg that St. Pete has become and see what kind of a mess it leaves us. For that I'll need Abby. Never underestimate that woman."

"So our file on you warns," Vicky said.

"I'm glad your intel people got at least that right about me and mine. Nelly, listen up. Get me Abby."

"You squawking?" came right back at Kris a second later.

"Tell me, old lady of mystery, was there any accounting and finance in that college education you picked up in your wicked youth."

"You keep calling me names like those, and I'm gonna suddenly forget I even have a name."

"Is everyone around you like that?" Vicky asked.

"Only the best of them," Kris admitted, then went on. "Abby, I need you in the Forward Lounge. We need to reverse engineer someone's economic warfare. You think there's anyone on board that might help in such a project?"

"Hmm. That's a good question. I always thought Drago's supply honcho was a whole lot smarter than he let on. I'll check with mFumbo. He's got a few anthro and socio types on staff. Never know what you get when you scratch one of those weird birds."

"I'll do that. Meanwhile, you and the supply guy get up here. What's Cara up to?" Kris asked.

The twelve-year-old was still on the *Wasp* and still wrapping most of its crew around her little finger. Not everyone. Command Master Chief Mong was still dismayed at finding a little girl somehow sharing his domain. Kris did her best to keep those two separated.

"Cara's computer has her deep in a study of the twenty-first-century politics of old Earth. She asked me too many questions about the mess the Greenfeld Alliance was in, and I couldn't think of anything closer to it than that lash-up."

"Abby," Kris cut in, "we've got Vicky Peterwald on board, and I've taken on this project because she asked me to."

"So I'm going to be working for two spoiled brats?"

"The spoiledest," Vicky announced, leaning close to Kris's chest to make sure her words carried.

"What did I do in a previous life to deserve this?" Abby sighed. "I'll get Donovan and be with you as fast as these old legs can carry me. Out."

"Abby's not that old," Vicky said.

"It's not the years," Kris said, "but the guff she hands out that age that woman. Shall we go tell the boys how we've decided to spend their in-port liberty?"

"You tell the admiral. I think he likes you."

"If he does, he sure keeps it well hidden from me," Kris said, "but I'll take the lead if you want me to."

18

"YOU want us to do *what?*" was Admiral Georg Krätz's response to Kris's suggestion that they deconstruct the entire economy of the Greenfeld Alliance, starting with St. Pete.

"We've got clear evidence that the official reports are too good to believe," Kris said, ticking her points off on her fingers. "Your Navy supply system shows there's something not right about what your own computer reports," brought down a second finger. "You've just had a run-in with someone using tech that only my Wardhaven gear could spot and some of it is even better than our stuff," was good for two fingers, leaving Kris only a thumb out.

"Your Highness," Chief Beni put in, "you may not have noticed when Da Vinci and I jammed the local network in the lounge. This thing really is the jammer that's been hassling you."

"Da Vinci," Vicky said.

"Yeah," the chief said, "my new computer."

"*He's* got one of the fancy computers?"

"Vicky, not another word out of you," Kris snapped. NELLY, YOU KEEP QUIET, TOO.

I WON'T SAY ANYTHING IF SHE DOESN'T.

Kris wondered if all female bonding required going back to the sandbox. Then, come to think about it, male bonding sure seemed to be at that level. *Oh bother.*

"Staying on topic," Kris continued, "something is clearly wrong. If anyone has any better ideas of how to tackle the problem that doesn't involve taking a deep dive into Greenfeld's economic databases, I'm all ears."

The admiral was shaking his head before she finished. "I don't know anything about finance and economics. What I do know is that here in Greenfeld territory, it is a capital crime to reveal economic secrets. If I sell you the plans for our newest battleship, I'd at least get a court-martial. If I gave out the true balance-of-payments figures for our planets, I'd be shot on apprehension. No doubt while trying to escape."

"Is it that bad?" Kris asked.

"He has pretty much got it right," Vicky said. "Of course, you would be doing what you did under my orders and with me at your elbow. That would make it legal, wouldn't it?" she said, flashing the admiral a not-quite-confident smile.

"Maybe it would. But are you sure someone wouldn't pass it along to your father with the tale twisted and torn in such a way that he wasn't howling for your blood . . . and mine . . . before the guy finished telling his tale?"

Kris should have turned away. No one deserved to be under public scrutiny when they went through the awakening being forced on the young Peterwald woman. But Kris was held captive by the flight of emotions across Vicky's face.

She began so innocent, so confident. She was Daddy's little darling and had nothing to fear from her father. Slowly, reality seeped from her head to her heart. Slowly, realization dawned that she was indeed just a player in a hard and deadly game . . . and those who played it could indeed turn her father against her. Even to the death of her.

Intellectually, Vicky must have known all this beforehand. As Kris watched, knowledge roared out like a flash flood from a small corner of her brain until it soaked every fiber of her being.

The new, wiser, but infinitely older Vicky finished her coming of age by slowly nodding agreement. "You *are* right, sir."

Then her face hardened. "But this is still something that needs to be done. If our beloved Greenfeld is not to be reduced to a mess of primal blood and gore, the truth must be sorted out and become the basis for our actions. We can't just keep flailing away in the dark. Can we, Kris?"

The question posed so plaintively by Vicky was both amorphous and ambiguous. Even a hot potato in the lap had more form and structure. Still, Kris found the openness of the question more to her liking than she might have.

"Yes, in answer to the basic question," Kris began, "I do think truth is a better policy than lies. It's also a whale of a lot better basis *for* policy. And no, Admiral, it's not my policy that a weak Greenfeld is the best friend a strong Wardhaven can have. As best I know from personal observation, it's not my king's preference either.

"Which leaves us gnawing at a bit of a problem. If getting to the truth is the way to go, how do we do it without being stabbed in the back? Right, Admiral?"

"I certainly find it easier to wash my back in the shower when there are no knives sticking out."

"Who'd have thought he could tell a joke," Vicky quipped.

"My senior officers often surprise me," Kris said. "Sometimes even pleasantly. I may have a solution to your communication problem."

There was a knock at the door to the lounge, and Abby poked her head in. "There's a whole passel of Marines of various faiths and persuasion out here telling me that you do not wish to be disturbed. I told them that such plebeian rules never apply to the likes of me. Would one of you please say something before one of these fine young men rams a bayonet up some delicate part of my anatomy?"

"Let her in," Kris said.

"What about these others?" came from the passageway.

"They're with me," Abby said, and ushered beauty and the beast into the Forward Lounge.

Beauty was a strikingly tall young woman with all the lovely assets that an aspirant movie star would kill for. Kris might not kill for that package, but she'd certainly commit several Class A misdemeanors to make those looks her own.

The man beside her could easily have been retrieved from under a bridge where he spent his time frightening horses and trying to eat children's toes. Short, lumpy, and with a bent nose, he wore dungarees cut off below the knees and a sleeveless sweatshirt celebrating a jazz quartet.

"I'm Amanda Kutter," the young woman said in what would have to be a magnificent contralto voice. "I just joined the scientists. My doctoral dissertation was on the economic tension between Earth and the Rim that brought about devolution. I was hoping to do research on the economies of the Sooner planets. If we could determine how they got started and maintained themselves in isolation, it might really tell us something."

That sounded plausible to Kris. So why did she still have a hunch that Grampa Ray and Crossenshield had their fingers involved in moving Miss Amanda up to the top of the list of new boffins joining the *Wasp*. *If I wasn't so glad to see you, I'd likely space you. Good Lord but I hate it when my elders play me.* Kris kept her thoughts to herself and a smile on her face as she shook Amanda's offered hand.

Next she shook the gnarled paw of the beast. "Call me Scrounger. I make sure Captain Drago has what he suddenly discovers he needs. Usually a week before he needs it."

Kris found the handshake firm and the eyes clear.

DON'T LET HIS APPEARANCE FOOL YOU, KRIS. HE'S GOT A PH.D. IN ECONOMICS. HE AND A COUPLE OF HIS PROFESSOR FRIENDS DEVELOPED THE ECONOMIC MODEL FOR RIM TRADE AND GROWTH THAT'S BEEN WORKING JUST GREAT SINCE EARTH TOOK ITS BALL AND WENT HOME. HE'D BE IN LINE TO SHARE THE NOBEL PRIZE IN ECONOMICS IF HE WAS STILL TEACHING AT PITTS HOPE U.

WHY ISN'T HE?

HIS FOUR EX-WIVES MIGHT HAVE SOMETHING TO DO WITH IT. KRIS, I REALLY HAVE TO WONDER WHAT THE PAY LEVEL IS FOR THE CONTRACT CREW. IF THIS GUY'S WORKING FOR US, IT HAS GOT TO BE THROUGH THE ROOF.

For the moment, Kris was just glad Crossenshield had provided her what she needed.

Kris invited the three new members of the meeting to take a seat. "Abby, in a moment, Vicky and I are going to need your help on a communication problem we have. However, first I'd better brief you on our other problem. Vicky, why don't you tell them what you found?"

In bold, clear brushstrokes, the young Peterwald woman

outlined the economics of the Peterwald Empire. When she was done, there was dead silence.

Amanda spoke first. "So you are saying that every financial report, every government statistic is totally fake?"

"It looks that way," Vicky agreed.

Scrounger took up the tale from there. "And you want us to hack into government and private nets, find out what's actually going on, and build a model of the real Greenfeld economy."

"While hopefully identifying where hardware is being siphoned off to support the pirates and other illegal activities that I'm chasing," Kris pointed out.

"But it's a capital crime," Abby put in, "and we could all lose our heads for doing any of this."

"All too true," the admiral answered.

"Is it too late for me to get out of here?" Scrounger said, making to get up. "You see, I have four women depending on me to keep them in the manner they've become accustomed to, and I really need my head if I'm to earn a penny for them."

"Sit down, Professor," Kris said, rebaptizing him. "The plan is to bring Vicky's father in on our project quickly enough to grant us permission, or at least absolution. To date, nobody's succeeded in killing this particular Longknife, and I don't intend to let the Byzantine politics of Greenfeld succeed where so many others have failed."

"And just how do you intend to do that?" Abby asked. "I've been involved up to my neck in keeping you alive for lo these many years. How many new gray hairs is this going to cause me?"

"Well, we need to get a message to my dear dad," Vicky said. "It needs to get directly to him, and it needs to get there quickly. Oh, and it would be very nice if fifty-eleven different factions didn't get to read it before he did."

"Oh, just that," Abby drawled. "I was afraid you'd want the sun, moon, and stars. Any idea how you're gonna do that?"

"Two years ago, I'd just put on my very best dress and barge in on Dad. Now, I'm a hundred light-years away, and all I've got in my closet are uniforms. I'm a big girl now, and I need a big-girl way of doing this."

"But you ain't never had to do it the big-girl way, so you've come to your auntie Abby for a little advice."

"You got it in one," Kris said.

"Why don't we girls go over to some quiet corner and put our heads together? Ain't no need to scandalize these men. They think they run the world, and we don't want to let them in on the truth of it."

Vicky motioned Abby to the bar, and the three of them headed that way. Abby took no time in laying out the problem.

"I got several good ciphers, guaranteed not to be broken by the average passing stranger. Problem is, your pappy is included in the passing-stranger category by the kind folks who sold me them. We'll need someone at the other end to decipher your message and deliver it.

"Now then, as I understand it, Wardhaven now has an embassy on Greenfeld. Ain't it wonderful that these folks are at least trying to make nice nice. I imagine I could find someone in the embassy who would figure out that the gibberish in their mailbox was a cipher that needed translating, but I don't expect that anyone on my mailing list would be all that welcome at the Palace.

"Of course, I guess Kris here could have the ambassador deliver the message."

"Not if we can help it," Kris said. "Let's keep the official people out of this, shall we? Vicky, do you have anyone that you trust in the Palace to take a message or letter to your father?"

Vicky thought for a long moment, then shook her head. "There's no one I would trust with my life. Maggie, yes, but she's not at the Palace."

"Now that complicates things," Abby said, eyeing the long line of potential drinks lined up in front of the bar's mirror. "Do you have a specific net address for your papa? Something that is just for you or a few close friends?"

"My dad has no close friends," Vicky spat. "But yes, I do have an address that is just for me. I was planning on using it, but I'm sure that, somewhere in the hundred light-years between here and there, it would be intercepted, and any cipher I have would be cracked."

"No argument from me, baby ducks," Abby said. "My embassy contact will have to do the decrypting, but I'm pretty sure no friend of mine will want to have his or her fingerprints all over a message to your papa. Likely as not, if their prints are on the 'from,' it ain't gonna get to the 'to.' "

"My net hub is still up in my room," Vicky said in a rush. "I could give it to your friend and they could send the message to Dad from my own Palace address. Would that do it?"

Abby nodded. "Even better. One of the things you want your old man to understand is just how behind he's let his tech support get. What better way to say you're being bamboozled than to do a bit of bamboozling ourselves."

"You're sure you can keep our embassy's fingerprints off this message?" Kris asked. "Any chance we've got to get permission for us here to do all this Dumpster diving in Greenfeld's economic trash heap depends on boss Peterwald believing that it's just his daughter and her musketeers doing it. If it looks like Wardhaven is launching economic espionage against him, we're all going to be looking for which pike has our head on it."

Abby eyed Vicky. "We've just come from a planet where a renegade State Security type stripped that metaphor to raw reality."

"She was probably just taking a page from my great-grandfather's book of pacification and prosperity," Vicky said. "My dad hasn't stooped to that level yet. I won't be surprised when he does."

"And on that fine thought," Abby said, "I think I should take you to the princess's cabin and record your plea for our life to your pappy."

They stood. "Nelly," Abby said, "I lent those two spare computers to Amanda and the professor. I figured they'd need them for whatever we were getting them into. I hope you don't mind."

"I wish you'd asked me first," Nelly said, "but as I have

learned from being around the princess, I am expected to grant forgiveness even if I never would have given permission."

"You've given them new supersmart computers!" Vicky cried.

"For a while," Nelly allowed. "They're on probation. One screwup, and we're out of here."

There was a soft knock at the door, and it immediately opened to let a small head peer in. "I figured Aunt Abby would be in here," Cara announced with all the pride of a twelve-year-old who had solved a Nancy Drew mystery a full five pages ahead of her hero.

"How did you get past the Marines?" came from several voices.

Kris wasn't one of them. "Abby was just leaving with Vicky Peterwald. Have you finished your schoolwork?"

"Dada said there was more to do, but I ignored her," Cara said, pulling her computer up from where it hung from her neck. "I told Dada that if she kept hounding me, I'd turn her off, just like Aunt Abby does her computer."

Which launched a storm of unconnected conversations.

"I told you," Nelly snapped at Abby, "that you were a bad influence."

"I will not be controlled by my computer," Abby snapped right back."

"Even that kid has a supercomputer," Vicky wailed. "Kris, we have to talk."

"Yes, but not now," Kris snapped for her own protection. "Jack, get Sergeant Bruce in here and have him see that a certain little girl is kept occupied. Or in the brig. His choice."

"Aye, aye, Commander."

"Abby, you and Vicky get over to my quarters and see what you can patch together. Don't come back until you've got a plea guaranteed to bring tears to the eyes of a stone statue."

"You bet, boss," Abby said.

In a series of "Boats right. Boats left," commands that would have made any admiral proud, Kris herded her various cats off to where she wanted them. Done, she returned to the table with the admiral, Jack, Amanda, and the professor.

"Nelly, are you satisfied with these two working for now with two of your kids?"

"They are just happy to be awake and have a job to do, assuming, of course, that when heads go up on pikes, we computers get left behind in a nice jewelry box. I will, however, monitor this matter closely to assure that my children are not taken advantage of in their eagerness to serve."

"Amanda, Professor, you understand your probationary status?" Kris said. "Would you rather use your own pet computers?"

Both nodded agreement and assured Kris that they were only too happy to be working with such fine computers. "I will need to download several of my modeling tools," Amanda said. The professor then confessed to the same need.

"Jack, how much finance and economics was in your degree?"

"Kris, I just did a search on the background of these two poor souls now working for you. I'm not in their league, and, since I've had a chance to check out your college work, I know you aren't either."

"But Nelly did a high-speed and thorough workup on the Turantic economy," Kris pointed out. "I expect that she has more practical experience at breaking and entering planetary databases than any of us."

"You mean we won't have to send off request after request for data, then wait for some clerk to get around to it or just flat out deny it?" the professor said, rubbing his hands together with glee.

"It sounds like the only stuff we'll actually have to mess with is the fun stuff," Amanda said.

"Nelly, make sure you and your kids are very, very careful. I would prefer not to have to deal with some angry cop from St. Pete's. Vicky's father is going to be a big enough problem as it is."

"I'm glad you broached that topic," said the professor. "While my young colleague's shining eyes sparkled at the thought of huge amounts of data flowing into her greedy hands for analysis, the thought came to me that a gushing stream of data pointed right at us is bound to attract attention. Attention we do not want."

The professor turned in his chair. "Chief, who is your new friend?"

"I am Lieutenant Stanislaus Kostka, of the Greenfeld Navy," he said, somewhat self-consciously, glancing down at his uniform.

"Don't be so shy. Stan here is the best network man in my squadron," Admiral Krätz added. "He's the one who helped Vicky research what little she could of our economy and did the statistical analysis that showed the numbers were too good to be true."

"What do you know about the network down below on St. Pete?" Kris asked.

"I have the published design specs. I also have done a bit of remapping the system. It is very fragile, what with all the problems we've been having," Stan said, innocently. "I've found that there is a lot more net out there than anyone's admitted. St. Pete's the sixth planetary system I've mapped for Miss Vicky. Every one of them has been loaded with add-ins and extra databases that officially are not there."

"If you're going to keep two or three sets of books, you've got to have them somewhere," the professor said with an impish grin. "But again, I say, if we suddenly start copying all of those illicit files to us for analysis, a blind network administrator would notice the flow and investigate."

"Admiral, what would you suggest?" Kris said.

"Do I look like a criminal? A spy?" the officer said, throwing his hands up.

"No, sir," Kris said, "but you do look experienced. You have survived in what appears to me to be a very dysfunctional system. More than survived; you, sir, have thrived."

" 'Survived' is the operative word," he said. "Now, as my headstrong young assistant has pointed out, we of Greenfeld are behind you Longknifes, but we are not primitives. Greenfeld manufactures a very fine line of smart metal. We also are producing self-organizing matrices for computers. We haven't had much luck making them work, have we, Lieutenant?"

The lieutenant quickly agreed with his superior officer.

"But you do have a supply of the matrices, and you are working with them, are you not?"

"Yes, sir. Miss Vicky has had me working on them in my spare time."

"Of which my junior officers have way too much," the admiral said, and avoided seeing the face the lieutenant made at the table in front of him.

"Lieutenant, take the Gunny and a four-Marine escort. Return to the *Fury* and bring back the full supply of exotic materials that you have. Also, I think Lieutenant Peterwald would like to have Chief Meindl join us over here. Bring him. You remember him, Commander. He was your prisoner on Chance. You gave him a tour of the trap you were setting for young Hank Peterwald and his military coup. My good friend Captain Slovo was able to use his input to stop the whole slaughter."

"Sometimes you want a spy around," Kris said. "I found him to be a good man, Chief Meindl."

"He may help with a few things I have in mind; now, off with you, Lieutenant."

The young officer fairly raced to obey his admiral. Kris waited until he was gone before asking the question on her mind.

"Care to share what you have in mind?"

"There is more than one way to acquire a data dump. You kids these days have it so easy. Just say a few words to your commlink, and everything is delivered to your fingertips."

"Your idea of research is way oversimplified," Amanda slipped in.

"You're probably right," the admiral agreed. "And, this may be just a dumb old sailor's thought, but if you don't want to leave footprints on the net, why not avoid hotfooting it around the net. Nelly, you spun off search bots faster than I could think of the idea. I'm sure you can use our fine Greenfeld glop to knock together some very nice bugs. Tell me where the databases are that you want to copy, and I can come up with some reason why a detachment of my sailors needs to march by there.

"Your bots will link into the net right next door to where the data is, copy it out, and fly back to one of my unsuspecting sailors, and bingo, we have the data, and any net manager has at best data going from somewhere to a node that no longer exists and never was on his system map."

"And if one of my bots gets isolated and captured," Nelly said, "it is made of your fine Greenfeld glop, as you so technically defined it. I can contrive bots that will self-destruct in that event, leaving just a smear of very costly material that tells no one anything. Kris, I like this man. He's as sneaky as you are."

"Then let us see what we can do," Kris said.

Planning got under way. An hour later, Vicky returned; a moment after that, Lieutenant Kostka followed her in. A Greenfeld senior chief was with him.

"Chief Meindl, so good to see you again," Kris said.

"I should have known that you'd be at the center of whatever was going on," the chief said, offering a salute.

Kris gave him a hug. "I worry about you, Chief. People get killed around Peterwalds and Longknifes. I'm glad to see you have avoided the usual fate."

"She never gives me a hug like that," Chief Beni muttered.

"Be glad she keeps you at arm's length," Jack said. "It's safer that way."

"He's stuck with a Peterwald," Kris pointed out. "They're even more dangerous to be around."

The chief took a step back. "So it's lieutenant commander now."

"They're new," Kris said, glancing at her shoulder boards.

"You command this ship, then?"

"No such luck, Chief," Kris said with a sigh. "I've still got a contract captain running the boat."

"Some might call him the flag captain," Jack put in. "Commander Longknife is officially the CO of Patrol Squadron 10."

"Congratulations, Commander," Admiral Krätz said. "I saw the extra stripe, but I had no idea it meant command of a squadron."

"It's not much of a squadron," Kris said. "And I've never seen more than two ships from it together in one place.

They're all like the *Wasp*, corvettes converted from merchant ships with just enough guns to put a quick end to any pirate ship. We carry a full load of cargo containers, like you saw on the *Wasp*. They let us fake it as a merchant, suckering a pirate in close. And the containers are usually full of famine rations. It's really bad out there, folks.

"My grampa Trouble used to tell the story that people were so desperate to get away from planets near the Iteeche that they'd overload ships until they had to breathe in shifts. I thought it was a joke. But I've answered distress calls from two ships that broke down before they made it to one of the Sooner planets. No food, no sanitation, little oxygen. You have to see it to realize how bad it is."

There was a long pause in the conversation after that.

"Do the containers of rations slow you down?" the admiral asked, bringing the focus back to something nautical.

"Not so far," Kris said. "If we ever needed to really boogy, chasing or running as the case may be, we can ditch the containers and attach a beacon. We're pretty small. Any real warship we run away from."

"But you're loaded with food," Vicky said.

"We carry out a load to a starving planet. On the way out, we try to get a pirate's attention. Once we're unloaded, we usually head back for Cuzco to refill on biscuits. Then repeat the process.

"Admiral, Vicky, I know you have to be unhappy about having a strange Navy on your rim, but I assure you, PatRon 10 is spending more time in the shipping business than shooting. I think Campbell on the *Dauntless* is the only one of us to actually shoot up a pirate."

"Didn't you capture a pirate off Kaskatos? I seem to have heard something about that," the admiral said, careful not to directly contradict Kris.

"It was just a system runabout," Kris said. "It had a balloot full of reaction mass and bounced off the *Wasp*. No lasers, just personal weapons. Half of them only had machetes to wave. When the Marines in full armor went out the locks, it kind of let the air out of them."

"But there are pirates out there. We are losing merchant ships," Vicky said. "It's not like there's a lot of trade. I think part of the reason so many ships are laid up like those around St. Pete is the fear of being captured."

Kris had listened patiently. She had sat on the one question that had haunted her since she first encountered the wreckage and flotsam of Greenfeld situation. She could sit on it no more.

"Vicky, what's the problem? What is going on? I know I'm a Longknife and the ancestral enemy, but God in heaven, girl, things are a mess, and I'm doing my level honest best to clean up after it. Don't I at least deserve to know what is actually happening?"

Vicky eyed her admiral. He couldn't bear her question and focused his attention on the table in front of him. Kris was half-afraid that she'd shattered the growing trust between her and the young woman from Greenfeld.

She hadn't intended that.

Just as Kris was about ready to take her words back, Vicky started talking. Her eyes didn't rise to meet Kris's, but she seemed unable to look up from her hands.

"We are in trouble. The glue that held 103 planets together has come apart, and we don't know how to fix it. With the aid of the fleet, we can hold this or that fragment together, but even our fleet is too small to hold it all."

Vicky looked up, met Kris's eyes. "If you went down to St. Pete with a pocketful of Greenfeld marks, you couldn't buy a beer. You couldn't buy anything. St. Pete and half of our planets are back on the barter system. If you don't have something to trade, no one will keep you from starving to death. If your mother or father was the wrong person, you can get killed right where you stand.

"Half our planets don't have a central government anymore. They've got three or six or a dozen situations running things. Usually a warlord with guns. Maybe the warlord is a black shirt. Maybe the warlord just managed to get all of State Security's guns. At first, my dad and I made the mistake of thinking that we could wipe out the cancer of State Security and everything would be fine.

"Big mistake," Vicky said with a sigh.

"Dad thought he had corporate vice presidents that he could trust to keep things going on this planet or that one. Nine out of ten of them have set themselves up as rulers. The smart ones call themselves princes or viceroys. The dumb ones claim to be kings. Dad's taken care of all of them so far."

"It's that bad," Kris said in a whisper.

"When you were talking about shipping famine biscuits to the Sooner planets that our refugees are flooding, I had to bite my tongue to keep from asking you to send them to twenty of our planets. St. Pete's one of them."

"Why not?" Kris asked. "Why haven't you asked for our help?"

"And let Ray Longknife know we're in this much trouble," Vicky spat. "Hell, Kris, you know he'd invade us in a second. Kris, the Marines you've got on your little ship could probably take over a dozen of our planets. Worse, the people would greet you as liberators.

"You know that Captain Thorpe guy that you chased away from that Sooner planet, what was it called?"

"Panda," Kris said.

"If he'd landed the same bunch of roughnecks on St. Pete, it would be his. Kris, keeping this a secret is the only chance we've got."

Kris felt kicked in the gut. Here she was, busting her butt, risking the life of her Marines and sailors to get help where they thought it was needed . . . and the Peterwalds were hushing up just how bad the starving and dying was because they thought Kris's grampa would take advantage of the suffering for some political advantage. Kris refused to meet Vicky's eyes.

Around Kris, the silence gathered and grew. No one said a word. Finally, Kris could be quiet no more.

"Vicky, I can't believe that you'd think that my grampa would do anything in the face of the suffering of your people but help them where he could."

"Oh, Kris, don't give me that. Look at how King Ray is soaking up planet after planet."

"Planet after planet is choosing to join him," Kris spat back. "No one's been forced to join. It's not our fleet that shows up in someone's sky and proceeds to add it by force to our flag. Remember, I was there when your brother did his best to force Chance into your father's hands. I did all I could to keep things peaceful, then fought-side by side with volunteers from Chance when a fight was what your brother demanded. Admiral, you were there."

"She is telling the truth, Vicky. I have told you so before."

Vicky was on her feet, looking from the admiral to Kris and back again. She shook her head, rejected what they told her.

Kris stood to meet her face-to-face.

"Chance told my grampa to go jump and voted itself into the Helvitican Confederacy. I was there just recently. The Helvitican flag is what they fly."

"No. No, I've heard about how you people fight. Six super battleships went after Wardhaven, and you blew every one of them to bits. Don't tell me you people don't fight."

"Yes, Vicky, we fight," Kris growled. "Remember who you're talking to. I led that fight. I commanded twelve tiny patrol boats against them. I begged, stole, and scrounged anything I thought might help me. Somebody suggested that little system runabouts might confuse those battleships, be mistaken for our patrol boats long enough for us to get our shots off.

"The worst mistake in my life was letting those little boats join us. Those civilian runabouts couldn't dodge or jink as fast as a fighting boat. We hadn't mounted chaff dispensers on them or given them any foxers. When the fight started, they died and died and died, and there was nothing I could do to stop it.

"But let me tell you something. After the first attack, after we knew what it took to survive in that fight, there were these tugs that refueled my surviving ships. They'd watched the runabouts die; but every one of those tugs, everyone in their crews voted, insisted, that they join our attack. Do anything they could to give us a chance to get a killing hit on those battleships."

Kris found she was in tears. "The people on those runabouts were volunteers, not even reservists. A lot of those runabouts were crewed by families that had signed up for the Coast Guard auxiliary, to rescue idiots who'd bought more boat than they had brains to operate. I attended a lot of funerals after that fight. One was for a man and his wife, their son and daughter. They came because someone told them their little runabout might help keep Wardhaven free. They died fighting for that freedom.

"Vicky, free men and women will fight to their last breath to keep their freedom. But don't you ever mistake that fighting will for a willingness to take what isn't freely offered.

"I swear by every drop of blood that's in me that my grampa, King Ray, will ship you food and medicine if that is what you need. Just say the word, and the ships drifting behind your station could be on their way to bring what your people are desperate for."

Kris finished, emotionally spent; she collapsed into her chair. Across from her, Vicky slowly settled back into her seat. She glanced at the admiral and raised a questioning eyebrow.

The admiral took a deep breath. "Kris, I believe that you believe every word of what you just told us. Never think that I doubt your sincerity. But I cannot help but see an idealistic young girl before me. Maybe you are right, and your King Ray would not seek advantage. Maybe he would send food and other aid. Maybe I, too, believe that he would do as you say. But hear this old cynic out.

"The cost of a few boatloads of famine rations is minuscule in the budget of 130 planets. But the massive amount of help that fifty planets would need is not a price to sneeze at. Are you even sure your granaries have that much to spare? And such an effort would strap even lush Wardhaven's treasury. But even more to the point, is this a problem that your king needs at this time?

"I'm guessing that he sent you here with your makeshift squadron in an effort to do a little good on the cheap. It looks good on the news. 'Look at all the nice things we are doing in your name, Mr. and Mrs. Taxpayer. So sad about those poor refugees. Now on to the next story.' But if the cost zoomed through the roof?" The admiral shrugged and left the thought hanging for a moment before going on.

"But that is only the tip of the iceberg. If you really enter into the Greenfeld tragedy, where do you stop? You saw that on Kaskatos. You just wanted to deliver some food. Between sunup and sundown you ended up conquering the planet. Where is your Penny, the daughter of a cop? Or that colonel you picked up at Panda? Something tells me you left them behind to work with the locals on putting together a constabulary and a militia. I know I would have.

"Do you honestly think that your Wardhaven would not be drawn into a morass even as you tried to do just a few good things?" Finished, the admiral leaned back in his chair, his hands limply upturned on the table in front of him.

"So," Kris finally said after the silence had stretched long, "the best thing I can do is help you solve your own problems your own way . . . and get out of Dodge as fast as I can," Kris said.

"Yes," said the admiral. "A while ago, you said you were open to any suggestions for how we might solve whatever the problem was that we were talking about. No one came up with a better idea. Like you then, Vicky and I are all ears for something better. Something with less suffering attached. Neither one of us is sure that our little attempt at this solution won't end up with our heads on pikes," the admiral said, and even managed a chuckle.

"So, let me bring matters back to where we were before this little detour. How shall we go about finding out the truth of St. Petersburg's economy and the real distribution of its military production?"

19

"HOW do you strip away a facade of lies?" Kris asked.

"Without the cops hauling us off to jail . . . or worse?" Jack added.

"I've heard tell," Professor Scrounger rumbled, "that the truth will set you free. It's been my experience that it can't do much of anything without a helping hand or two."

Vicky nodded. "I know it's not going to be easy. Just on the planet below us there are a half billion hungry people. The infrastructure is a mess. There are at least four major population centers, none of which is talking to any other, and none of them is really interested in seeing my sailors or Marines march through their streets. At least they aren't shooting at us. Not lately."

Vicky glanced at Chief Meindl; he gave her an approving nod.

"Nelly, could you give us a map, please?" Kris said. "I think better if I can see something."

A lovely seascape at sunset on the left bulkhead swiftly changed into a map of the planet below. Most of the human presence on St. Petersburg spread around an inland sea someone had aptly named the Middlesea. A large peninsula jutted out into that sea; the city of St. Petersburg was located about halfway down it. The whole thing reminded Kris of something.

Then it came to her. While the peninsula looked nothing like the Italian boot back on old Earth, the blend of sea and land did have the look of the Mediterranean of humanity's home planet.

St. Petersburg was about where Rome was. Off to the west of the nonboot was a river about where the Rhone was in France. Here the city at the mouth of it was Kiev. Almost directly south of it, on the opposite coast, was Sevastopol. The mountains behind it were actually called the Atlas Range. Far to the east, where the Nile would have been on Earth, was the River Don, with a huge estuary and the city of Moskva.

Behind each of these major cities were extended hinterlands of farms and mineral extraction that fed their industry. St. Pete and Kiev were connected by thin rail lines, as were Sevastopol and Moskva. Still, most trade between them had to be done by sea.

"Can you superimpose the basic data net?" Kris asked. Lieutenant Kostka took a minute to work the interface between his commlink and Nelly.

KRIS, THEIR GEAR IS KLUDGE CITY.

YOU CAN TELL ME THAT, BUT DON'T YOU TELL THEM.

DON'T WORRY. I AM LEARNING HOW TO LIE. I MEAN BE TACTFUL.

Leaving Kris to wonder if a tactless computer had been less trouble than one that now could lie. *Oh bother.*

"The official data repositories are located in the four cities. St. Petersburg is supposed to be the official one. The others are only supposed to be backups of that main one. However, the four systems have not been synched in over six months. God only knows what is going on," Lieutenant Kostka finished with an expressive shrug.

"I really don't see a problem," said Chief Beni. "We're after the data that wasn't there in the first place. I suspect we can ignore the official data. Do you have any idea where the *other* databases might be physically located?"

"Or the databases involved in producing the 5-inch lasers that we're capturing on pirate ships?" Kris added.

"The Greenfeld Navy Yard is outside St. Pete," the admiral said. "I sent a detachment down to secure it as soon as we arrived. It had been looted and stripped bare of everything that could be carried away. Trust me, nothing is coming out of that yard but weeds."

That left Kris with a puzzle to solve. "St. Pete's closest to the Rim. I thought for sure it would be involved somehow in the pirate business."

"It probably was," Vicky said. "That's why we're here. We're not just keeping an eye on you, you know. The reports we were getting back said that St. Pete was still shipping a lot of stuff through this station, but we couldn't find out where the ships were going. Once Admiral Krätz's squadron showed up, the station's business has halved. And we know where everything is going and what's in every container," Vicky said proudly.

"Is that based on reading the bill of lading, or are you actually eyeballing the contents of the boxes?" Jack asked.

Vicky wilted. "We are reviewing the bills of lading. But with battleships tied up to the station, who'd dare lie?"

Kris didn't say a word.

After a bit of a pause, Vicky went on. "So, we should have sailors and Marines actually break the seals and look in the containers."

"Starting tomorrow," Admiral Krätz said.

Kris got up and walked over to study the map. "So, where might 5-inch lasers be coming from? You said somebody wrecked St. Pete's industry. Do any of these other cities have heavy industry?"

Vicky joined Kris at the map. "Kiev and Moskva don't have easy access to minerals. Sevastopol has some mining going on in the Atlas Mountains. It also has several mines located down the coast of the Great Ocean. It's set up a colony in Georgia. In the two weeks we've been watching, we've seen several ships make port at Sevastopol loaded with raw materials for the portside factories."

"Is anyone beside me wondering how come Sevastopol is still up and running, and St. Pete took it on the chin?" Jack asked.

"Most likely it was our mistake," the admiral said. "Once General Boyng suffered his nine-millimeter stroke, it was thought necessary to take down State Security everywhere and very quickly. I believe a cruiser was ordered to St. Pete. The

Aurora had a skipper who was young and very enthusiastic, if not all that experienced. He landed at St. Pete in the middle of the night, rounded up all the black shirts, and dispatched them before dawn. By sunset that day, the city was totally out of control. Need I say more?"

Kris shook her head.

"You know, when all this is over, someone must write a book," the professor drawled, "on how to conduct an effective coup de main. Amateurs trying their hands at it for the first time could really use some educational advice."

"Amateurs aren't the only ones who are out of their depth," the admiral said, raising an eyebrow at Vicky.

She laughed. "My dad is no better than an amateur in the present situation. He's run things the way his father and his father did before him. Then he wakes up one morning, and the same old same old isn't there to do his bidding. Dad's muddling through. *We're* muddling through. Please, Professor. Write your book. I promise you that I and my friends will make it a best seller."

"I will definitely think about it."

"Well," Kris said, returning to the topic, "if St. Pete was a disaster, why wasn't Sevastopol?"

"There is a city manager there," Vicky said, as if repeating what she had memorized from some report. "He is young. Eager to learn. Eager to serve. We think Manuel Artamus is his name.

"He woke up one fateful morning to find that all his black shirts had hotfooted it out of town. I imagine he rejoiced in that for all of five seconds. Then the thought must have struck him: 'How do I run this place now?'" Vicky said with a lovely shrug of her shoulders.

"I guess he was smarter than the average city manager. Most know they have a black market operating in town. Every city does . . . at least here in Greenfeld territory. He either knew who headed the gangs running things or knew how to get in touch with them. By noon, he'd recruited all the smugglers and black-market types to take over the guns the black shirts had left behind. He kept his town going under new management, with hardly a hiccup."

"And you think he may have made a deal with the pirates?" Kris said.

"Or at least with someone who knew someone who knew what the pirates needed and could match the need with a supplier."

"And you haven't sent your Marines to visit this guy?" Jack said.

"It didn't seem wise," the admiral said. "This goose is still laying eggs, even if they are of unspecified type, and it's not like I have enough Marines that I can afford to lose a lot of them even if it is in a winning fight. And then, as you learned on Kaskatos, if I broke the place, I'd have to run the place. No thank you."

"So we need to slice Sevastopol open and take a long, hard look at their books. Only we can't just walk in, or even walk by and send a little bug to do it," the professor said.

"Yes, I believe you have it right," the admiral said.

"Kris, could we talk for a moment?" Vicky said, and drew Kris out of hearing of the others.

"Dr. Margarita Rodriguez is on St. Pete. As you can tell from the name, she comes from old Earth's Spanish roots. In the mess that followed the shooting of the State Security troops, it didn't pay to be a different shade of white from those around you. Her apartment house in St. Petersburg was burned, and she fled. The last report I have on Doc Maggie is of her taking passage on a small fishing vessel for Sevastopol. I don't know if she made it, but if she's still alive, she's somewhere around there."

"Oh my," Kris said, for want of something stronger. "So my lasers and pirate gear are likely buried in the same haystack as your Maggie."

"I believe so," Vicky said.

"And *you* don't dare run a Marine op in that area."

"Correct."

"And you're looking at me because?" Kris said.

"Because your Captain Montoya is dark, as is Abby. Compared to my pale skin, you're positively tanned. Kris, I don't have a single officer who can walk the streets of Sevastopol without starting a riot or getting hauled in for being a spy from St. Pete. You're my only hope."

20

So it was that two days later, Kris found herself squeezed into the front seat of a beat-up pickup between Jack and Chief Beni. They'd bought the truck from a farmer lock, stock, and barrel, fully loaded for market. It had taken gold marks to get him interested in any kind of business, but when the deal was done, he'd sworn no further interest in the truck . . . or the folks who bought it.

Just in case, the chief had tapped into the vehicle registration database. "Just a light tap," he insisted. He found a similar truck and quickly modified the rear and front license plates to match it.

"If we're stopped, this won't be the truck they're looking for," the chief said.

"Oh, good," Kris said. "Can I say, 'This is not the truck you are looking for'? I loved that classic movie, and I've always wanted to say that line."

"You may get a chance," the chief said, studying his black box, then making it disappear into what once again looked like a serious beer belly. "There's a traffic checkpoint up ahead."

"Keep your trap shut," Jack snapped at Kris, then shouted out the window to where Abby and Gunny sat on the truck bed with three Marines. "Get ready to look hangdog and out of work."

"Ooo-Rah," came back softly.

Vicky had been right; Greenfeld's military was way too white. Not a single Greenfeld Marine was dark enough to pass for any of the locals Kris had seen so far around Sevastopol.

What was it about Greenfeld that caused it to draw its domi-
nant power people from Earth's old northern European stock?
Before she was introduced to this mess on St. Pete, Kris would
have guessed that the Peterwalds had only allowed immigra-
tion from certain sections of Earth. Now it was clear to Kris.
Greenfeld only limited access to power to people whose great-
grandparents came from those sections.

Now the devil was playing his own tune and demanding
payment for years of bad choices.

As forecast, they rounded a corner and found themselves
joining a small line of similarly dilapidated trucks, waiting
their turn to be checked over and passed into a city that was
just starting to emerge from the morning fog.

When they pulled up to the checkpoint, Kris confronted
four men in civilian clothes, their only badges of office red
armbands with LA GUARDIA embroidered in green. Oh, and
the inevitable machine pistols slung over their shoulders and
held at the ready.

Kris gave them the most empty-headed smile she could
manage and kept her mouth shut.

Two of the men came around to Jack's window to question
him. He gave short answers in a language only half-English
that seemed to satisfy them.

The other two guards stayed in front of the truck and spent
a lot of time eyeing Kris and laughing among themselves at
their private jokes.

Kris couldn't translate a word of it. That didn't mean she
didn't know what was going on.

She allowed herself a worried smile as she considered the
men's reactions if they found out the woman they were ogling
had a Navy-issue automatic and could have plugged them both
between the eyes before they got a shot off. Or could break
all four of their arms and legs in anything close to a fair fight.

Kris held the thought of what she could do . . . and shyly
edged closer to Jack and half hid behind his arm. He glowered
back at their leers, but they ignored him and kept cracking
jokes Kris did her best not to hear.

Abby was having her own problems in back. One of the

guards supposedly checking the bags of corn they were carrying to market somehow managed to flip up her dress. She jumped to her feet and launched into a tirade that smoothly blended English Kris didn't normally hear from her maid, Spanish Kris didn't understand, and violent hand waving that left nothing to doubt.

The guards backed off, laughing, and waved them through.

"What are they saying about us?" Jack demanded as soon as he had the truck in gear and the checkpoint in his rearview mirror.

Chief Beni's black box was out again. Gunny's hat included an antenna he kept aimed, along with his smile, at the roadblock.

"They're wondering why you're taking so many pretty girls to market. You hear that, Abby? Girls! And they're already complaining about the load of pigs behind us. I don't think they've been alerted to look for anything in particular."

"That would be nice," Jack muttered. "This is another fine mess you've gotten us into, kid."

Jack had banned the use of ranks, titles, and any other honors until they got back upside. He seemed to be getting a kick out of calling Kris kid and girl. He'd called her other things in that language she didn't speak.

KRIS, YOU WANT ME TO TRANSLATE HIS SPANISH?

NO, NELLY. I THINK IT'S BETTER IF I DON'T KNOW.

YOU'RE PROBABLY RIGHT, almost got Kris to change her mind.

Kris answered Jack's put-down with a sniff while she regretted her decision in high school to take a computer language rather than Spanish.

"You will never use a computer language," Nelly had told Kris, even then. "You humans are way too slow. Just tell me what you want, and I will make it happen."

Nelly had been right; Kris never wrote a line of code during the whole course . . . not even in class. Nelly made a habit of answering any question before Kris could even get a start. It had been an easy A.

Now Kris was paying for it in so many ways.

"Vicky couldn't come down here. Not one of her officers could pass for Hispanic. None of her Marines either. Who else could do this?" Kris said.

"Me. The chief here. Abby. Gunny. We. Don't. Need. You."

Jack had a point. The only response Kris had was stubborn denial. "I will come in handy when we find Maggie."

"If we find that woman," Jack snapped.

"We will find her," Kris insisted.

They drove on in silence.

Cara was getting way too tired of the silent treatment. The grown-ups were just busy, busy, busy. Since they'd arrived at the station, they never had any time for her.

It was so boring!

Dada was nice; the computer made learning fun. But you could only take so much healthy learning before you wanted to choke on something.

The crew was pretty cool. They'd let Cara look over their shoulders and learn all kinds of things. Cara was pretty sure she could run the *Wasp* all by herself. The engineering watch had even let her stand a watch with them. She'd checked all the readings and made sure everything was in the green.

Course, it had been an in-port watch and the teakettles . . . that was what real ship engineers called the reactors . . . had been just maintaining minimum power.

Still, Cara had stood the watch.

She'd also followed the deck watch around as they did their duties. When the *Wasp* made port, the pier's automatic tie-downs were activated by the bridge. If you just listened to the bridge crew, you'd think that was all there was to it.

The deck watch showed Cara just how wrong those prima donnas were. Each of the tie-downs had to be fully locked down by good old Swedish steam. That meant real sailors applying their backs to these huge cast-iron wrenches to lock down the ties. Once they finished, there was no chance that someone might accidentally sit on the wrong place on some bridge console and break the ship loose.

Before they undocked, the deck crew would have to "single up the line," and use the same iron wrenches to take off the safeties. Cara was learning a lot about the ship that she would bet that even Princess Kris didn't know. Probably even Aunt Abby.

Take, for example, the amidships tie-down. It wasn't like all the others. Air, net, water, and sewage lines came over with that tie-down. That made it a whole lot bigger than the rest. "You could almost use this puppy as a gangway," the chief told his new sailors. "If you don't put the rat catcher up, those filthy beasties will."

One of the younger sailors eyed the passageway, taking its measurements. "Cara wouldn't even have to bend over to walk through there to the station," he said.

"Now don't you go giving the little girl any ideas," the chief said. "Anyone going ashore from the *Wasp* goes by the quarterdeck and does it right smartly. Besides, this space is locked down, and none of you know its combination," the chief said, and gave Cara a knowing smile.

She smiled right back.

She'd learned early to smile when people smiled. She'd also learned on the streets of Eden how to spot an access number without letting anyone catch on that she had made the code.

You could say a lot against Gamma Ganna, but that she raised dumb kids or grandkids wasn't one of them.

And Cara did indeed have a beef with the grown-ups around here. Not only did they ignore her, but they kept her cooped up on this little boat just forever.

They were nice to her. Nice the way they wanted to be. There was cake for her saint's day and gifts. Gifts for Christmas, too.

But all the gifts were money! Her credit chit now had more money on it than she'd believed possible when she was a skinny runt running the streets of Five Corners. Yet she couldn't spend a dime!

Nowhere would they let her go shopping. Even her new computer, Dada, was just handed to her. Auntie Abby never went to a store; she just ordered stuff off the net. Where was the fun in that?

Everybody knew shopping was the experience: the smells, the feel, the joy of the hunt. Why would anyone want a dress she hadn't tried on!

Cara needed some serious window-shopping, some down-and-dirty store time, and everyone on the ship was just so not going anywhere.

It was time for a girl to take matters into her own hands. Especially now that Auntie Abby and Kris had gone down to the planet. They'd gone down and not even asked Cara if she'd like to go along with them!

First, Cara casually turned off Dada. She didn't like doing that. Dada would probably be nearly as much fun to go shopping with as a real live girl. Still, there was no doubt in Cara's mind that if Nelly asked where Cara was, Dada would be a snitch.

So Dada got turned off and left in the bottom of her lingerie drawer.

Then, with her credit chit in the pocket of her jeans, Cara casually headed for the amidships section. This whole idea would vanish like a genie in one of the stories she was reading if they'd changed the access code to that hatch.

To Cara's delight, they hadn't. Quick like a ferret, she was in the room, and the door slid shut behind her.

Leaving her in like total darkness.

She should have brought a light.

Next time she would. This time she managed to find a switch and turn it on. The rat catcher came off easily, and went back on quickly once she was on the other side. The sailor was right; she didn't even have to bend over as she passed down the tie-down to the pier.

Of course, the pier didn't look at all like the pier people walked on when they left the *Wasp*. But then, none of those people from the quarterdeck could see her. If Cara popped out in sight of the quarterdeck, she'd have three Marines, maybe more, chasing her down.

Nope, Cara would stay in the walls until she was well out of view from anyone on the *Wasp*.

That took a bit of climbing on a ladder with rungs spaced apart for people a bit taller than Cara. She made it, but she was feeling kind of tired by the time she reached the top.

The space she found herself in was painted gray with ducts and pipes painted in bright colors of red, blue, green, and the likes. She spotted a door and made for it.

Cara had to undog the hatch, it was an airtight hatch, but when she opened it, it was the main deck of the station that she saw! It was like a fairyland. A huge carpeted walk led to stores and stores and more stores.

Quick as a bunny, Cara was through the hatch. She dogged it back down and was on her way to do some serious shopping!

Or not.

As she skipped up to the first store, she found it shuttered and locked. So was the second one. There was still stuff in the windows to look at, but they were dusty and not a lot of fun. Who wanted to drool over things you couldn't buy.

By the fifth or sixth store, she was starting to think this whole idea was just one big bust.

Then she spotted two Greenfeld sailors. Seeing them made Cara realize just how empty the station was. There had been a bunch of Greenfeld sailors marching in the distance, but there was nobody anywhere close to her. She'd kind of liked that. Now it was sort of creeping her out.

But now there were these two sailors. Well, a couple. One of the sailors was a girl, and the other a boy. They were looking around like they were afraid someone might see them, but they walked like they knew where they were going. Cara decided going somewhere was better than going nowhere and started to follow them.

At a distance, where they wouldn't notice her.

They slipped off the main walkway and disappeared down a small hallway. Cara got to the passageway just in time to see them turn right. By the time she got to the end of the hallway, they were turning into a small store.

An open store!

It was a jewelry store, but it was an open store! Whether Cara needed a new bobble or not, at least it was a place she could look . . . and maybe the couple knew another store that was open.

The moment Cara entered the store, she noticed three things.

There was no sign of the couple she'd followed in. No evidence they'd ever been there.

The three men in the store turned toward her with wide smiles that didn't look all that nice.

And then the door behind her clicked in a most decisive way. Cara turned back to the door to try the knob.

It didn't turn at all.

"Who would have thought, three in one afternoon," she heard from behind her.

Cara opened her mouth to scream. Before she got a sound out, a strange-smelling cloth was suddenly clamped over her nose and mouth.

A moment later, Cara's world went dark.

21

Sevastopol was built around a series of bays.
The minor bay that served as the fishing port was the closest,
so that was where Kris aimed her team first. If Doc Maggie
had caught a fishing boat to Sevastopol, and if she'd left behind some sort of record, and if that helped them find her . . .
then maybe she could help them with the tougher part of the
mission.

Even Kris had to admit there were a lot of "ifs" in that plan.

The small wooden boats and nets looked like a picture that
could have been taken anytime in the last three thousand years
on old Earth. Birds mewed, and old men mended nets as others sailed out past the rocky breakwater into the rising sun.

"We got a problem, folks," Chief Beni announced. "There's
no network up and running in this area."

"Don't the boats have computers?" Kris asked.

"Look at them," Jack said, pointing with his chin. "Those
boats are lucky to have bottoms."

"There's got to be a tax computer here. They catch fish.
They have to record taxes," Kris insisted.

"Maggie's a doctor, not a fish," Jack pointed out.

"But I'll bet you she paid for her passage," the chief said
in support of Kris, "and someone's bound to have taxed that."

"I've spun off several net scouts," Nelly said. "One of those
overhead lines has to be carrying a net."

They waited for a long five minutes while Jack drove as
slow as he could around the bay.

"I got it," Chief Beni yelped. "I've got a net. Now to get in.

Oh, that was easy. I guess they don't think the customs office down by the fisherman's bay needs all that secure a net."

"Or no one wants to mess with that fine old tradition of smuggling," Abby put in through the gaping hole that might once have been a back window to the cab. "I think I could like these people."

"What, you think they're as nefarious as you?" Jack asked.

"Let's hope so. If they're all good little patriots for whoever is in power, we're in trouble."

"Okay," the chief went on, "they do tax every fish that comes in, and there's a new section in the database for recording everyone shipped in by these little boats, how much they paid, and where they went."

"You got to love bureaucrats," Kris said.

"Assuming they didn't take a cut and forget to enter anyone," Jack said. "Talk to me about Margarita Rodriguez, Chief."

"She ain't in here."

"What?" Now it was Kris's turn to yelp. "No, see if they misspelled her name."

"We got a lot of Rodriguezes here, boss. Doing it by eyeball may take a while."

"Do they have their profession? Jobs?" Kris and Jack said at the same time.

"Let me see. Spelling isn't too good here, either. I could understand it from fishermen, but this guy's supposed to be a bureaucrat."

"A bureaucrat who weighs fish and knows what tax to demand for each kind," Kris pointed out.

"Does '*medico*' mean what I think it means," the chief said.

"It probably does."

"Well, M. Rodriguez was landed here four weeks ago. She was sent to the Central Employment Agency on Liberty Street."

"That's a big help," Nelly carped. "The map doesn't show a Liberty Street."

"Peterwald types wouldn't be all that hot for such a street. We probably need an updated map," Kris said, "and we don't need to go to Liberty Street; we just need to tap gently into its database. Chief."

"I'm already there. Let's see how they spell her name this time. Oh, they got it right. Want to bet she had to type it in herself."

"That seems logical. Sal," Jack said to his computer, one that usually stayed out of conversations unless specifically asked, "where's that possible heavy-industry plant?"

"It's farther up the coast. It's got a heavy-lifting shuttle port right next door to it. That's how it drew our attention."

"You can hide the black cat in a deep dark hole," Kris said, "but I love it when a twitching tail gets left out."

"Let's wait and see," Jack said, and slowly headed the truck up the coastal road. Soon the road split into two streets. One was a lovely promenade along the shore, just the place for an evening stroll. The other, a block or so inland, was wider, badly worn, with potholes and had a heavy-duty railroad track down the middle to serve rows of warehouses.

"Let's keep a working truck on a working road," Jack said. "We'll draw less attention that way."

"I'm in the employment database," Nelly announced proudly. "Four weeks ago, our Doc Maggie was sent on a job referral to Bay View Medical Center."

"And where is Bay View Medical Center?" Jack asked.

"On Bay View Boulevard, fourth road in from the bay," Chief Beni announced.

Kris pointed to a blue sign with a white H. "Hospital," she said.

"Yes, but that doesn't much matter if she's not there, people," Jack said stubbornly.

"She's working the night shift," Nelly said. "She'll be there until eight according to her work schedule."

"Why didn't you say that in the first place?" Jack snapped. "People in back, hold on," he shouted as he made a hard left turn and headed up a hill.

There were a flood of complaints from the back, but they quickly died as the truck engine did its own imitation of death's onset.

"It was doing great a second ago," Jack said as he tried to cajole the truck up the steepening hill. It responded in chokes and fits.

"Folks, my old man had a truck like this," Gunny Brown said. "I suggest we all get out."

"I think the man's right," Abby said. It wasn't long before everyone, even Chief Beni, was afoot.

Jack got the rheumatoid truck to the next street and turned down it before letting the truck coast to a halt and turning off the engine. "Where's this hospital?" he asked.

"I think it's the tall building at the top of the hill, next street up."

"It is," Nelly and the chief both agreed.

"This truck ain't gonna make it," Jack said.

"I can walk the rest of the way," Kris said.

"Not alone," Jack, Gunny, and Abby said in harmony.

"I'll stay with the truck," Chief Beni offered, eyeing the climb.

One Marine was left with him, a farm boy who offered to take a look under the hood. "My old man and his pappy didn't believe that a truck ever had to die. Let me see what I learned from them."

Kris wished him well and started hiking.

"Tell me, Nelly, where does Doc Maggie work?"

"She's assigned to the Emergency Room. She often does a shift and a half. Things are pretty busy."

"So we didn't have to drop everything and catch her before eight?" Jack said.

"Quit grouching, Jack. She's here. We were going by. Why not get her when we can?"

"Because, my dearest little princess, things tend to get harder as time goes by, and I'd rather save the easy part for last."

"Assuming picking up Vicky's BFF is the easy part," Abby said with measurable doubt.

The Emergency Room was located on the east end of the building, readily available to traffic coming both from the harbor and from inland. At least in that respect, finding the Emergency Room was easy.

Then it got hard.

"You can't come in here," a young man in something close to a blue uniform told them as they approached where an ambulance was just pulling in.

"Why can't we?" Kris asked with her best princess smile.

"Can't you read the sign," he said, waving a thumb over his shoulder at one that announced AMBULANCES ONLY. "Walkers have to go in the front door and see a nurse. She decides if you really need to see a doctor."

"Don't you just love bureaucrats," Jack whispered out of the side of his mouth.

"None of us are sick," Kris said.

"Then don't come here," the young guard said, cutting Kris off. "There is no loitering. I will call the police if you cause any trouble."

"What do you say I break his arm," Jack whispered, "then we take him in to see a doctor."

The kid heard that and went for the pistol at his waist.

Big mistake.

In a blink, Gunny had him in a choke hold. Abby put a sleepy dart into his butt.

The boy went limp, and Gunny gently tossed him over his shoulder.

"Oh dear." Abby sighed. "I think the poor thing done come down with the galloping punies. I do hope he doesn't develop a terrible case of the falling-down plague from standing around out here in the cold night air. We must get him inside."

Since everyone agreed, Kris led the way, following the last gurney through the double doors.

As Kris expected from experience, inside she found bedlam, only moderately controlled by the cool professionalism of the medical teams of doctors and nurses.

Still, it only took a moment before a person in green scrubs was asking. "What seems to be the problem with this young man?"

"I don't know," Kris said. "He suddenly passed out." Kris hated the thought of lying to a doctor, so she told her a large part of the truth.

But, as so often was the case, Kris didn't share anywhere close to the whole truth.

They laid the young man out on a table, and the woman began an initial examination. Kris took the opportunity to head for the central station. Jack was close on her heels.

"Could you point me toward Dr. Margarita Rodriguez?" Kris said to any of the five men and women working the station.

A tall, solid woman said, "Why do you need to know?" without looking up from the med board she was studying.

"I have a message for her," Kris said.

"Give it to me. I'll pass it along to her when she's not busy," the woman said, still not giving Kris so much as a glance.

"Hey! What's this?" came from behind Kris.

"I think that's called a sleepy dart," Gunny told the woman. "Haven't you ever seen one before?"

"No, I haven't," the medic said, eyeing the offending dart as she held it up to the light.

"It does strange things to a man," Gunny told her.

"And how would you know?" was a question Kris really didn't want Gunny to answer.

"I don't have a written letter for Doc Maggie," Kris said, reaching out to tap the woman who insisted on ignoring her.

At the touch, the woman almost jumped. She finally did look at Kris though it was a look usually reserved for something vile that had been left behind by a sick cat.

"Who are all of you? What are you doing here?" the chart-scanning woman demanded. "You all have to leave."

"And you said this would be the easy part," Jack whispered to Kris.

She threw him a nasty look of her own. Then, only too aware that this was not going well, she drew in a long breath and played the card that usually worked.

"Listen. I'm Princess Kris Longknife of Wardhaven, and I really need to see Dr. Rodriguez."

It would be inaccurate to say that with that announcement the Emergency Room went silent enough that you could hear a pin drop. Around the room, patients continued to moan and whimper. One child even continued to scream, the results of an earache that needed treatment. However, with the exception of a nurse's aide who chose that moment to drop a tray of syringes and needles, creating quite a clatter, most of the medical professionals in the room did indeed go quiet.

"Yeah, and I'm the Queen of Sheba," the solid woman said, and made a show of turning her attention back to the med board.

"You know, Gail, she does look a bit like that woman who was on all the vids when she saved Henry Peterwald's life."

"And what would a Longknife be doing on St. Pete, Rosy, deep in the bosom of Greenfeld?"

"I don't know. You tell me. But she does look like that Longknife dame."

"You are so blind I don't know how you keep your license," Gail said. "She looks nothing like that trollop." But Gail did take a long moment to eye Kris.

Kris ran a hand through what little hair she had at the moment. "You are catching me at a bad time."

"She's been sick," Jack put in. "Came down with a bad case of bombs."

At one of the workstations, a male in blue scrubs brought up a picture of Kris. "It kind of does look like her," he opined.

"What do you want with old Doc Maggie?" a woman said as she closed a set of curtains behind her. "Get this woman up for a CAT scan stat. She's just had a stroke. I won't know how to treat her until we know what's going on inside her head."

"Maggie, the CAT's booked solid," the guy in blue scrubs said.

"Make a hole for this woman in the next thirty minutes or tell them they'll have Maggie the Terrible to deal with."

"Be it upon you, Doc," the tech said, and got busy making a call.

"Now, what was this I heard about you having a message for me," the doc said, eyeing Kris.

"Is there someplace we can talk in private?" Kris asked.

"Somewhere there must be such a place on this blighted planet, but I don't have time to go there, not if I'm going to save my quota for the night," the doc said, pulling off her gloves.

"My message is from a friend of yours. I'm not sure you'd want everyone to know about it."

"This is Kris Longknife, Maggie," said the gal who had first tried to get Gail to consider that Kris might be who she said she was. "You know, the Wardhaven Princess."

"Did she bring me a new CAT scanner?" Maggie asked.

Kris shook her head.

"Sorry, I really don't have time for you and any message from my past. Okay?"

Kris took a deep breath and dived in. "Vicky said she was never better than when she had you to share her ideas with."

"She did, did she? And when did she tell you that."

"After dinner on a battleship up at the space station. She asked me to come find you."

"And why didn't she come herself?"

"You know why," Kris said.

"She never calls. She never writes. But you say she suddenly has this overwhelming need to talk about old times. Why didn't she just call me?"

"She couldn't find your number down here. She couldn't do much of a search for you. You know that people she gets too close to get suddenly dead. She didn't want that to happen to you."

Maggie eyed Kris like, maybe, she was starting to believe her. "Vicky's a part of my life that's past and gone. Why should I reopen that can of worms?"

"Here," Kris said, taking in the sweep of the Emergency Room, "you can save a dozen. Maybe two dozen each night. Advising Vicky, you could save the lives of millions."

"Who's this Vicky," Gail demanded.

"A kid I knew a long time ago," Maggie said.

"A kid who can save millions?"

"She's grown up now," Maggie answered.

"And she's trying to carry the heavy burden of her birth," Kris said. "She needs help. Help from someone who lets her be her better self."

"I need some time to think about this," Maggie said.

"I have to keep moving. You can come with us now. If you don't, I don't know if I can come back for you later," Kris said.

"Hold it," Gail cut in. "Who's this Vicky?"

"Just a kid I knew," Maggie repeated.

"Who now has dinner on a battleship with the likes of Princess Kris Longknife," Gail went on. "I've heard tell that Victoria, murdering bitch, Peterwald is on a battleship up at our station. Is that the Vicky you're talking about? It has to be."

"And if it is?" Kris said.

"I don't want to work with nobody that helped that murdering bitch over the sniffles. The doc should have drowned that one at birth."

"So much for the Hippocratic Oath," Maggie said softly.

"Kris, we really need to be not here," Jack said.

"Maggie, I offered to talk to you in private."

"Yes, yes, I know."

"Will you *please* come? Now!" Kris said.

Maggie looked at her coworkers. Blood was rising in their eyes. Even some of the patients looked ready to grab something and start swinging. If ever Kris had wondered how the average person on the street in the Greenfeld Alliance felt about the Peterwalds, the unanimous vote tonight in this small part of their realm was not going well for the ruling family.

"Okay, okay," Maggie said, stripping off her unused gloves and following Kris toward the exit. Jack stepped between Kris and Maggie, grabbed their elbows, and forced them to a trot.

Behind her, Kris could hear sidearms coming out from where the Marines had hidden them. "Calm down, folks. We're moving on. No need for anyone to get hurt."

Once out the door, Jack said, "Run," and they did.

22

The young Marine had worked a miracle with the truck's motor; it was running smooth as silk. He'd also turned the rig around; it was aimed downhill. Everyone piled in. This time, Doc Maggie was in the front seat between Kris and Jack. A complaining Chief Beni was helped into the back of the truck by a pair of Marines.

Jack put the old truck in gear. It bucked a couple of times in protest, but then, as it rolled downhill, it thought better of its complaints and became downright cooperative.

Kris glanced back at the hospital. Nurse Gail was scowling at them . . . and making a note on her med board.

"Chief, I think we need a new license plate," Kris said.

"Yeah, I saw that, too. I'm working on it."

At the first red light, one of the young Marines hopped down and did things to the plates. "Consider our problem solved," the Chief told Kris through the open back window.

"What is the problem?" Doc Maggie asked. "I'm assuming you didn't come down here just to offer me a job."

"Actually," Kris said, "you are the main reason we're down here. Vicky really needs somebody she can trust."

"But we do have other problems," Jack put in.

"Such as?" Maggie asked.

"You wouldn't happen to know of a new heavy-industrial plant anywhere nearby?" Kris said.

"Where they might be putting together 5-inch lasers to arm pirate ships," Jack added.

"It would likely be near the bay," Kris said. "Someplace

where it is easy to load freight shuttles and not have a lot of people looking over their shoulders at the manifest."

"There is an old plant that has gotten really active in the last couple of months, or so I'm told. They don't have a very good safety program. I've had to mend several broken arms, legs, a caved-in chest," Maggie said. "And every time someone gets brought in, they've got a rent-a-cop escort. Supposedly to look after them, but I always felt they were there more for the intimidation than the care."

"Where is this place?" Jack asked.

"You're heading for it," Maggie said. "My bus passes it every day on the way home. But you won't be able to get in there. There's a tall fence and guards walking it."

"That won't be a problem for us," Kris said. "Chief, Nelly, get ready to deploy your little friends."

"Aye aye, ma'am," and "Already there," came back at Kris.

The truck chugged along in the slow lane. Traffic was getting thicker as the morning got seriously started. The sidewalks filled up with people in work clothes hurrying to wherever they had to be. The light ahead of them turned red just before they got there.

Jack braked to a halt.

A van pulled up beside them. A big car closed in behind. A motorcycle pulled up to Kris's right, occupying the bike lane. The young woman, holding tight to her driver, glanced at Kris and smiled a good morning.

Two old ladies walked up to the corner and stood there, half in the street, ready to slow walk their way across as soon as the light changed.

The smiling girl produced a pistol at the same moment that a truck came to a screeching halt in front of them, totally blocking them in.

Jack slammed the truck into gear and started to floor it, yanking the wheel to the right.

"No, Jack!" Kris shouted, making a grab for the wheel even as she pulled out her service automatic. "You'll run over the old ladies."

A door slammed open on the van beside Jack, and three gunners with machine pistols showed themselves at the ready.

Behind Kris, Marines went for their weapons as they dropped down, taking advantage of whatever cover sacks of corn might give them.

That horrible second between shock and deadly action stretched.

A man stepped out from behind the truck in front of them. He wore light green slacks and a blue windbreaker. His hands were shoved deep into his pants pockets.

"I understand Kris Longknife is with you, *amigos*. I'd like to talk with her. I mean, if you wouldn't mind not shooting anyone for a few minutes, I'd really like to pass a few words with her."

23

Kris took a deep breath as she slowly reached for the door handle. Her automatic was in the other hand, pointed out, though not at anyone in particular.

She let the breath out slowly as the door creaked open. Kris did everything slowly as she tried to let her stomach . . . and her trigger finger . . . catch up. She'd been alert but confident, then suddenly switched to ready for deadly action. Now there was a guy standing there as casual as could be asking for a few words with Kris as nonchalantly as some girls asked for her autograph.

Kris's neck was definitely putting in for whiplash compensation.

"Since you know my name, would you mind telling me yours?" Kris said as she put one foot on the pavement.

"Oh, I'm sorry, how rude of me. I'm Manuel Artamus. My friends call me Mannie. I'm the mayor of Sevastopol. At least that's what they've been calling me since all hell broke out a few months ago."

"I think I'm glad to meet you," Kris said, stepping away from the truck.

"Good," Mannie said, then raised his voice just a bit. "Guys, gals, let's put the guns away. It would be a shame for us to have an accident when things are going so well. Grandmama, you can go home now. I'll have Danny take you and Aunt Reina back to your place. As you can see, things are going fine."

"You be careful," said the older of the two women Kris

hadn't let Jack run over. "She's a Longknife, and you know you can't trust them."

"Danny, *please*," said Mannie.

The passenger door opened in the car that had closed in their back, and a young man hurried over to help the two gray-haired ladies into the backseat of their ride.

"Guys, move the van. You're losing me votes blocking rush-hour traffic," Mannie said, and the van with the three gunners drove through the now-green light and pulled into Momma's Diner across the intersection.

"Would you mind moving your truck to Momma's?" Mannie asked Jack.

The Marine officer looked daggers at Kris, but she waved him on, and he went.

Mannie walked up to Kris and offered her a hand. "I'm not sure if I'm supposed to genuflect or kiss your ring. I hope this will do."

"I'm happy with any greeting that doesn't involve small-arms fire or high explosives," Kris said, giving and receiving a firm handshake.

Mannie casually pointed the way across the street. "Momma's has some of the best coffee in Sevastopol. And her pies are something you just have to taste before you leave town. Fresh organic apples. Real butter. Honest to God honey. None of that fake sugar that you can never tell where it came from."

He opened the diner's door for Kris. If the food was half as good as the smell, he had not oversold the place. It was about half-full.

Jack, Abby, Doc Maggie, and Chief Beni occupied a round table down the left-hand side of the diner. Kris's four Marines were at the next table up against the wall behind Jack. Mannie's henchmen held down two tables behind a pair of vacant seats at Jack's table.

No hardware was in sight. The people filling up the right-hand side of the diner went about their morning business.

"Well, don't just stand there letting the flies in, Mannie. Sit a spell and take the weight off your feet," a cheerful waitress of middle years yelled from where she was filling a coffeepot from a device that looked like only a rocket scientist could build it . . . or operate it.

Mannie waved back and led Kris to the vacant chairs at her people's table. He held Kris's chair for her while she sat, then held up two fingers. "Two more for this table, Kelly."

"On their way," the waitress shouted back.

"You come here often?" Kris said.

"It's a good place for a morning staff meeting," he said, settling into his seat.

Kris waited for the coffee to arrive, pie orders placed, and the waitress to withdraw before she said, "So, to what do I owe the pleasure of this meeting?"

Mannie folded his hands on the table and stared Kris straight in the eyes. "I understand this morning that you're serving Miss Victoria Smythe Peterwald as a kind of ambassador with limited portfolio."

"I hadn't thought of my job quite in that light," Kris said, "but I can see where it kind of has that appearance."

He nodded at Doc Maggie. "I have no problem with your contacting Dr. Rodriguez and offering her a job. I think we will all benefit from a Peterwald having an advisor who isn't a bloodthirsty psycho."

"I'm glad we can see eye to eye on that," Kris agreed.

"I have to admit," Mannie went on, "that your coming down here all hush-hush to contact the doctor rather than Victoria just calling her and buying her a ticket on the next shuttle up gives me a bad feeling about the way the Peterwalds are running this railroad. Bad feelings."

Coffee arrived, and Mannie took the time to add milk and sugar to his mug. Kris sipped hers black.

It was quite good.

"I could be down here for other reasons and just dropped by the hospital for Doc Maggie because I was in the vicinity."

Mannie tasted his coffee, made a happy face, and put it down. "Yes, there is the other matter of your mission down here. That bothers me a lot more than losing the services of a very good and dedicated emergency-services doctor. We need to talk about that, but first, I really wish you would place a call to Victoria Peterwald and see if we can set up a meeting with her."

"A meeting," Kris said cautiously. "For what reason?"

"That's kind of hard to put into words. Not that I don't know what I hope to come of the meeting, it's just what I'm hoping for is kind of old-fashioned."

"Try me," Kris said.

"We'd like the king to grant our city a charter."

"A king's charter," Kris said. "You do know that Greenfeld doesn't have a king."

"Yes, I know. We seem to be stuck with all the worst aspects of a tyrant without any of the upsides of nobility. You certainly understand the limits of noblesse oblige."

"It's yanked her chain a few times," Jack said.

"Then you understand our problem here. We in Greenfeld have the most exquisite constitution in human history. The only problem with it, if it can be allowed to be called a problem, is that nobody ever uses it. It's a magnificent wall decoration somewhere in the capital. But it's never allowed to complicate the matters of daily business. You understand?"

"I don't imagine you've had this conversation with anyone from State Security," Abby said. "I see that you still have all your fingernails."

Mannie held up his hands, displayed hands unmarred and fit for a concert pianist. "Yes, silence is often the better part of valor. However, you may have notice that Greenfeld State Security is recently conspicuous by its absence."

"It didn't make it any easier for us to sneak into town," Jack pointed out. "Have you taken over the snitch concession?"

"Our Baker Street Irregulars," Mannie said with a laugh. "No, no. You misunderstand them. Those kids and old folks who helped us track you in weren't snitching for the black shirts. Well, not unless we wanted them to," Mannie said, making a face.

"No, they were our snitches *tailing* the black shirts. It got to where one of them could hardly move without us knowing where they were going and what they were up to."

Mannie laid a commlink on the table. "We manufacture these

here in Sevastopol. They've got extra bandwidth just so we can send and track the black shirts. We had them on a tight leash before the Peterwalds ever decided to hang them by their collars."

Kris nodded slowly at the admissions. "Vicky told me that you were in touch with the black market and able to do a deal with them to keep the city going when the, ah, black shirts beat it out of town. It sounds like there was a lot more to Sevastopol's underground than just smugglers bringing in a bit of mall glitter."

Mannie grinned. "St. Petersburg was where the heavy industry was. It was where most of the money was. So long as we paid our taxes and didn't kill anyone, we were left on our own. That city charter I mentioned. All we want to do is make it official and get something on paper with a Peterwald's signature. Really, nothing more."

"You realize," Abby said, "you're running the serious risk of being noticed. Why not just keep things the way they are? They keep on looking the other way, and you keep on doing what you want?"

"Because things are changing, and who says they'll ever be the same again," Mannie said. "Look at it from my perspective. Things could go back to the way they were. Things could get a whole lot worse." He held up both hands. "Yes, I know it's hard to believe, but it could. Whether Peterwald keeps on top of the dog pile or doesn't, we could wind up with some two-bit tin god of a warlord keeping one finger in everyone's soup and the other in everyone's eye. I'd like to offer Miss Victoria another option, one I'm not sure they ever thought of. Let the locals look after themselves. We won't do anything to bother her and her old man at the planetary or Alliance level. They don't appoint anyone to muck around in our life."

"And my place in this?" Kris said.

"Whether you regret it or not, you saved Henry's neck once. You do seem to be some kind of friend to Miss Victoria. You could put in a good word for my side, and it might be listened to. Your signature on the document might make it harder to disappear it. You game?" Mannie said, raising two expressive eyebrows.

"It's worth a try, but we still haven't talked about what brought me down here. Let me call Vicky, then we have to talk."

"It's a deal," Mannie said.

"Nelly, get me Vicky."

"Kris, she's in the Forward Lounge, so this call should be safe on that side. There are a whole lot of electronic devices on this end."

"Could we jam them?" Kris asked.

Mannie looked around the diner. "It would piss off a lot of folks who are just going about their morning business. And probably lose me a couple of votes, too. Do you really think it's necessary?"

"My dear old dad taught me never to do something that cost a hardworking politician any votes. Especially him. Now Jack here, my security boss, is having a hissy fit, but if he doesn't have at least one a day, he gets hemorrhoids."

Jack set a new record for scowl . . . but said nothing.

"Hi, Kris, how's it going?" said Vicky in a way-too-chipper tone of voice.

"Not nearly as well as I'd been hoping it would," Kris answered.

"But things *always* go so well for you," Vicky said, failing totally to make her voice sound believable.

"You keep this up, and you better be careful of what I wish for," Kris said. "How about you coming down here and seeing what my day is like?"

"Is there a real problem? Can't you find Maggie?" Vicky sounded seriously concerned now.

"Maggie is sitting across the table from me. She's fine and heading up to the station just as fast as I can take her."

"Oh, that's good," had serious relief in it. "So what seems to be the problem?"

Kris waved at Nelly at her neck, then waved at Mannie to take over from here.

He gave Kris a three-finger wave off. *Please, you do this for me* was all over his face.

Kris sighed and went on. "I'm talking to Mannie Artamus,

one of the nicest guys you've never met. You remember him, the city manager of Sevastopol?"

"I've heard of him," was rather hard-bitten.

"He would really like to talk to you," Kris said.

"Is he holding you hostage?" Vicky snapped. "You and Maggie?"

"No," Mannie said, half-out of his seat. "Nobody is holding anyone hostage. No hostages here," he insisted, as Kris waved him back to his chair.

"Vicky, you know me," Kris cut in. "Nobody takes me hostage. God help any kidnapper who falls into my hands. No, I'm having coffee and waiting for a delicious slice of pie. You understand. I'm talking with a man who needs something from me and who I need something from myself. Force is not an issue on this table."

Jack didn't look all that assured at Kris's words, but he said nothing.

"What's Mr. Artamus want?" Vicky said guardedly.

"Your and my signatures on a city charter."

"What's a city charter?" Vicky asked.

That question told Kris all she needed to know about life in the Greenfeld Alliance. "Something cities used to have a couple of hundred years ago," Kris said, waving Mannie to silence. "It outlined their duties and responsibilities to the king and his duties toward them."

"My dad is not a king," Vicky snapped. "Though, if the rumors coming out of the Palace are right, there are a couple of factions trying to talk him into naming himself emperor." From the tone of her voice, Kris couldn't tell how much that made Vicky's bunny jump . . . if any.

"What would that make you, a grand duchess?"

"What it would do is give me a headache. How's the princess gig going for you?"

"Some days better than others. Listen, Vicky, I've been talking to this fellow, Mannie. He recognizes that things are changing. All he wants is to provide a minimum level of protection for the people he works for. They absolutely will stay out of your business. They will pay their taxes and live their lives. If this charter works for them, maybe a lot of other large cities will be offering to do the same thing. It's not a bad place to start rebuilding the Greenfeld Alliance."

"I'll have to think about that. He wants me to come down. How big an honor guard should I bring?"

"A whole lot less than an invasion force," Kris suggested.

"Your Jack willing to vouch for my safety?"

"Sorry. No can do," Jack said, leaning forward in his chair to make sure his voice carried. "Keeping one obstreperous and cantankerous princess safe is about as far as I can stretch."

"I'll talk to Admiral Krätz about setting up a detail. I take it would be in bad taste for me to send a shuttle down right now for just Maggie."

"Yes," Doc Maggie said, "I really think I should stay here and do anything I can to help things come out well for everyone here. They've been nice to a woman who had nothing but her own two hands when she first came among them."

"Why did I know you would say that?" Vicky answered. "I better go see my admiral and let you get on to what matters to you, Kris. Good luck. Hold it, your Captain Drago just walked in, and from the look on his face, I would not want to be one of his crew."

"Your Highness, is that you on the other end of the line?" Drago asked.

"The one and only," Kris said, tightening her gut for what was bound to be something bad.

"Did little Cara manage somehow to attach herself to your expedition?"

"No," Kris said, looking around at the shaking heads of her Marines.

"What's that little scamp got herself into?" Abby asked of her niece.

"That's what we don't know," the captain said, pain in his voice. "She didn't show up to plague the cook for the cookies he'd said he might make. She also hasn't been hanging with any among the boffins or crew. Nobody has seen her since you left."

"Nelly, what's Dada say?" Kris said, naming Cara's computer.

"Nothing. She was turned off shortly after we left the ship. Cara's been doing that occasionally. A bad habit she's picked up from her aunt," Nelly said, dripping disapproval.

"Where could she go?" Kris asked.

"Her credit chit is gone, too," Captain Drago added.

"If she's slipped out to go shopping on the station, I'm going to tan her hide," Abby snapped.

"She's been complaining to anyone listening that she's got money but no place to spend it," Kris said, remembering how, at twelve, it took very little money to burn a hole in her pocket.

"You think she's slipped out of the ship and onto the station?" Vicky asked.

"The quarterdeck watch swears they haven't seen her," Captain Drago said.

Gunny Brown shook his head with fatherly disapproval. Or maybe it was approval. "Any too-smart-for-his-britches private can figure a way off the ship. I just thought a twelve-year-old girl might not be that smart."

"Even one who has everyone on board wrapped around her little finger?" Kris said. "Captain, you check with the crew. See if she was around when any of them were dealing with a creative way pierside. Vicky, would you ask Admiral Krätz, as a personal favor to me, to turn the station upside down? And tell him he's free to apply any kind of discipline to Cara before he returns her to us that his years of experience as the father of girls or the commander of sailors might suggest to him."

"You really want me to?" Vicky sounded shocked.

Kris eyed Abby. "Better him than me," the aunt said.

"Tell him he has the full authorization and permission of all due Wardhaven authorities.

"May God have mercy on her soul," Vicky breathed, and cut the link.

Kris leaned back in her seat and let out a long sigh. She tried to remember how many problems she'd had to chase down and whack over the head so far today . . . and she still hadn't gotten to the main reason she'd come dirtside.

"Would you prefer to go back to your ship?" Mannie

asked. "I'd promised my people that I'd keep you down here until Miss Victoria paid us a visit."

Jack raised an eyebrow and silently mouthed "hostage."

"Well, no, and I guess a little yes," Mannie agreed. "Anyway, if this little girl's problem means you need to get back there . . . ?" He left the rest unsaid.

"The best people to handle the search are up there," Kris said with a sigh.

"And that imp had better have come down with a serious case of contrite before I lay eyes on her again," Abby put in.

"And I have a problem, Mannie," Kris said. "One that I'm not sure that you aren't causing."

"I certainly hope I'm not at the root of any problem for you," Mannie said. "I have a strong suspicion that is not a very good place to be."

"You can say that again," Jack said.

24

Kris took a deep breath, let it out . . . and changed the subject. "Among all the things I *have* to do, there are a few things I *enjoy* doing. At the top of that list is being an officer in the Wardhaven Navy. Ever met a serious Navy officer?" Kris asked.

"No," Mannie said cautiously. "You probably know, the dockyards for the Greenfeld Navy on St. Pete are in the city that shares the name."

"So, all the heavy industry is over there," Kris said.

"Ah, that's where all of it, ah, was," Mannie said carefully. "We weren't allowed to have any heavy manufacturing. That is one of the things we wanted to address in the city charter."

"You wouldn't by any chance," Jack put in, "be taking advantage of the present disruptions to correct that serious bit of unfairness, would you?"

Mannie took a serious gulp of his coffee. "It's gotten cold," he told no one in particular. One of his crew left to corral a warm pot and refilled everyone who didn't put a hand over their mug.

Kris passed. Today was no day to get the caffeine jitters.

"We did come into the possession of two of the large cargo landers that had been doing the heavy lifting for the Navy yard," he admitted between blows on his now-too-hot coffee. "If they'd stayed at St. Pete, they would have just been trashed when people walked off with this or that part of them."

"I'm not here to sit in judgment," Kris quietly pointed out.

"I understand the crew and their families love their new homes," Mannie said.

"No doubt," Kris said. "So, what are you loading into those heavy-cargo shuttles?"

"Various things," must have sounded lame to even Mannie. He winced.

"Any of that cargo long and thin and wired for high voltage?" Jack asked.

Mannie nodded.

Well, at least the man wasn't beating around the bush when you dropped it right on top of him, Kris thought.

"I was told," Mannie went on quickly, "that quite a few merchant ship owners want to arm their property to protect them from pirates. We are only manufacturing 4- or 5-inch lasers. Nothing that could possibly be a problem to Peterwald battleships or even destroyers." The mayor began to slow down. "At least, that was what I was told."

"And if that's what is going on," Kris said, "we'll be cheering you right along."

"And if it isn't?" Mannie asked. "Dave is one of our largest employers. I'd hate to see you lead him away in cuffs."

"Last time I checked," Kris said, trying to put on a friendly smile, "I'm Navy. I didn't have the authority to lead anyone off in cuffs." Kill them, yes. Arrest them, no. "And certainly I can't arrest anyone on a Greenfeld planet."

"I guess I'm happy to hear that," Mannie said, and reached for his commlink. He only had to tap two numbers before it began to ring.

SO HE'S GOT THE GUY ON SPEED DIAL, Jack observed, through his computer.

WE GOING TO LET THIS GO DOWN THE WAY THIS DAVE GUY WANTS IT? Abby asked.

HEY, Nelly interrupted. YOU LEFT YOUR NEW COMPUTER ON THE SHIP. HOW'D YOU GET ON MY PARTY LINE?

SO I TAUGHT MY OLD COMPUTER SOME NEW TRICKS.

AH, CREW, Kris put in, LET'S STAY FOCUSED ON THE PROBLEM WE CAME DOWN HERE FOR. NELLY, ARE YOU AND THE CHIEF READY TO SPIN OFF SOME SERIOUS NANOSCOUTS, DATA-DOWNLOAD NODES, AND OTHER SEARCHERS? I EXPECT TO BE IN THIS DAVE GUY'S LAP BEFORE THE HOUR IS OUT.

DON'T YOU WORRY, KRIS. WE ARE READY, Nelly said.

THAT WE ARE, the chief agreed.

Thus saving Kris from one of her worst nightmares, having those two doing their sibling-rivalry gig from the inside of her skull.

"Dave said he'd be glad to show you around his plant this afternoon," Mannie said cheerfully.

"How far are we from the factory?" Kris asked, just as cheerfully.

"Ah, ten minutes?"

"I've got nothing better to do this morning," Kris said. "Tell him we'll be there real soon."

"We haven't had our pie," Mannie pointed out.

"You're right," Kris agreed, standing up. "We can have it for lunch," she said, the rest of her team standing with her.

"The princess will be there in ten," Mannie said, standing as well.

"Are you going to drive that old clunker?" Mannie asked as he rang off. "I've got a fifteen-passenger van waiting for us." So Kris and her team shared the seats with Mannie's crew. Mannie drove; Kris rode shotgun. Only the chief grumbled.

Out loud.

Galactic Enterprises, Limited, GEL for short, occupied a long series of tall buildings stretching for a quarter of a mile along the bay. Two shuttles stood eager standby outside them. There were stoplights on the street, ready to halt traffic when the shuttles taxied from the factory to the bay.

Some joker had put up a yellow warning sign, SHUTTLE CROSSING. It showed a shuttle being followed by several baby ducks.

"That sign isn't authorized," Mannie said. "But every time I order it taken down, some wag puts another one up. At least this one looks professionally done."

"I take it that your city folk enjoy their sense of humor," Kris said.

"Makes it a whole lot more fun working for them," Mannie admitted.

A sense of humor the people might have, but there was nothing funny about the two-meter-tall fence running around the plant. Even the stretch of taxiway that crossed the road had a rolling fence that could be opened when necessary and kept closed all other times.

Mannie pulled up to the gate and stopped.

"Mr. Mayor, we weren't told to expect you," a puzzled guard sergeant said.

"This is kind of sudden. Call Dave; I just talked with him."

The sergeant went back into his small guardhouse. The heavy-duty gate stayed down, solidly blocking their path.

NELLY, YOU AND DA VINCI LAUNCH YOUR SCOUTS, Kris ordered.

THEY'RE ON THEIR WAY, Nelly answered.

IS THERE ANY NANO OPPOSITION? Jack asked.

WE ARE ENCOUNTERING INTERCEPTORS, Chief Beni said. BUT THEY'RE NOT ALL THAT GOOD. I'M TAKING CONTROL OF THEM AND STEERING THEM AWAY FROM OUR SCOUTS. STILL, THEY'VE GOT BETTER ELECTRONIC GEAR THAN THE ADMIRAL HAD.

BUT NOT AS GOOD AS WE'VE SEEN, Kris said.

NOT EVEN CLOSE TO THE BEST, Nelly agreed.

So, Kris thought to her staff, IF THE LEVEL OF OPPOSITION WE ARE FACING IS ANY INDICATION OF THE LEVEL OF BADNESS THIS FELLOW IS, HE'S KIND OF LOW IN THE BAD-GUY HIERARCHY.

HE'S BAD BUT NOT REAL BAD, Nelly agreed.

LET'S NOT GET TOO CARRIED AWAY ON FIRST IMPRESSIONS, Jack put in.

"The boss says you can come in. He's at his office in Building 4," the sergeant called from inside his box. The gate rose, and Mannie drove in.

Building 4 was a one-story affair with large windows giving a good view of the bay and the parked shuttles. Mannie parked in a visitor's slot. After an embarrassing wait when no one came out to greet them, he led the way into the main door of the office building.

Clearly, the owner did not go in for fancy office surroundings. The floors were linoleum, the beige walls in need of new paint, and the furniture looked like it might have come from a secondhand store . . . or been the scrounging from a looter's leftovers.

A secretary stood. "The boss is tied up at the moment," he said. "Would you please be seated."

Kris headed for the door that had the best view of the bay and shuttles. When the secretary moved to block her path, Jack and Gunny Brown blocked him.

Kris opened the door to hear "I know I'm not giving you much time, but do what you can. I'll see what I can do . . ." cut off as the speaker discovered he was not alone anymore.

"I'll see you in a few minutes. I've got visitors," he said, and turned to face Kris.

The man who offered a hand to Kris had his collar open and his tie loose. His sleeves were rolled up to his elbows, giving him a no-nonsense, ready-for-business look. Kris found herself wondering if she'd buy a used shuttle off this man.

Most likely not.

His handshake didn't change her opinion. It was too firm, as if he had something to hide.

"I'm Dave Grafton," he said confidently.

"I'm Lieutenant Commander Kris Longknife, Commander of Wardhaven Navy's Patrol Squadron 10, presently on anti-pirate duty," Kris said evenly, holding on to the hand.

"Oh, I'd heard you were Princess Kristine, a BFF of Victoria Peterwald," Dave said, keeping his handshake just as firm but maybe starting to sweat a wee bit.

"Like a lot of people, I can be a lot of things. Right now, I'm a Navy officer looking for the source of the pirate guns that are showing up on ships out beyond the Rim."

"I wouldn't know anything about things on pirate ships. I only sell to honest shipping lines, and I have the bills of sale to prove it. May I show you?"

"Please do," Kris said with enough of a smile to make the fellow relax just a bit.

He started tapping his workstation, and various screens began to cover his desk.

KRIS, WE HAVE ALL HIS BOOKS, ALL *THREE* SETS OF THEM, Nelly reported.

THREE SETS!

YES, came in the voice of Professor Scrounger. HIS OFFI-CIAL BOOKS, THE BOOKS HE SHOWS HIS BUSINESS PARTNERS, AND THE SET HE DOESN'T EVEN LET HIS MISTRESS SEE. BOTH OF THEM. EVEN I FEEL LIKE I NEED TO WASH MY HANDS AFTER GETTING THEM ON THIS GUY'S BOOKS.

ANY WORD ON THE SEARCH FOR CARA? Abby asked.

I'M TRACKING THEM IN MY SPARE TIME, Amanda Kutter put in. ADMIRAL KRÄTZ BALKED AT A LOT OF WARDHAVEN MA-RINES AND SAILORS RANSACKING HIS STATION, BUT PROFESSOR MFUMBO TURNED OUT THE BOFFINS. ALMOST EVERY ONE OF THEM VOLUNTEERED TO HUNT FOR CARA. ANYWAY, THERE IS A SMALL ARMY OF GREENFELD SAILORS AND WARDHAVEN PH.D.S TURNING THE STATION UPSIDE DOWN.

AND, PRINCESS, YOU MIGHT BE INTERESTED IN SOMETHING I OVERHEARD. SOME SAILORS HAVE GONE MISSING FROM THE GREENFELD SQUADRON. THEY AREN'T JUST HUNTING FOR CARA.

THE GREENFELD NAVY IS OPERATING DRAFTED CREWS, Kris said. IT'S NOT UNUSUAL FOR THEM TO LOSE A FEW PEO-PLE OVER THE HILL.

BUT THERE AREN'T THAT MANY HILLS ON THIS STATION, Professor Scrounger observed.

WHERE WOULD THEY GO? Kris thought on net, eyeing the heavy lifters parked on the apron in front of the office's picture window.

Dave took the moment to point out something on his desk, a bill of lading signed off and stamped by the space station's port master. Kris gave him an encouraging smile even as her thoughts went quite to the contrary.

PROFESSOR, GET SOMEONE WHO KNOWS SHUTTLE OPERA-TIONS TO GO OVER THOSE BILLS OF LADING, BOTH FOR THE TRIP UP AND THE TRIP DOWN. IF SAILORS ARE GOING OVER THE HILL, SEVASTOPOL HAS A LOT OF LOVELY MOUNTAINS THAT YOU CAN SEE FROM THE BAY.

YOU THINK THEY'RE MAKING THE JUMP FROM DRAFTED SAILOR TO DIRTSIDE FARMER? Jack said.

YOU CAN LIE ABOUT A LOT OF THINGS, Kris said, BUT YOU DON'T DARE LIE TO YOUR LOADMASTER. IF A SHUTTLE IS HEAVY, IT BETTER HAVE THE REACTION MASS AND ANTIMATTER TO GET IT UP OR BRING IT DOWN.

I KNOW JUST THE GAL TO CHECK THOSE OUT. AND, HEY, WHAT DO YOU KNOW, THERE ARE TWO SETS OF WEIGHTS FOR EVERY FLIGHT THOSE SHUTTLES HAVE MADE IN THE LAST TWO MONTHS. BESSY IS GOING TO LOVE THIS.

PLEASE GET BACK TO ME AS SOON AS YOU CAN, PROFESSOR, Kris thought in one direction. "Would you mind giving me a copy of those files, Dave?" Kris asked, never letting her smile falter.

"Well, these *are* proprietary business records," Dave said, seemed to consider the matter, then relented. "We can't do enough for the defenders of the working merchant shippers. The lifeblood of the Alliance is what they are."

Kris agreed, and he shot a load of data to Kris's computer.

I'LL CHECK IT THOROUGHLY FOR MALWARE, Nelly said, sounding like she was being forced to hold a skunk by its tail.

IF YOU HAVE THE TIME, PLEASE CHECK IT AGAINST THE OTHER THREE SETS OF DATA THIS GUY HAS GIVEN US, Kris said. IT WILL BE INTERESTING TO SEE IF THE "DEFENDERS OF THE WORKING MERCHANT SHIPPERS" ARE BEING FED YET ANOTHER SET OF DATA.

I'LL DO THAT, KRIS.

Having dazzled Kris with his lies, Dave now set out to bury her with the technical specs of the plant's production.

"This plant was just supposed to be making refrigerators, cooking stoves of all descriptions, air conditioners, and light electronic equipment," Dave said, as they walked toward one of the production bays. "Mannie's heard the story, many times."

"It still amazes me you pulled this off right under the watchful eyes of State Security," the mayor said.

"I told you, Mannie, the black shirts were never so watchful as when they were counting their cash. Give them enough cash to count, and they don't see nothing."

The folks from Sevastopol shared a laugh. Kris admitted to a chuckle. The tighter you make the supposed controls, the greater distance from the mean to the outliers. While some poor loudmouth was rotting in jail for telling the wrong person the truth, someone else was gaming the system and walking off with a fortune.

Was this a lesson Vicky would be interested in learning? Or would she balk at the very idea that the system that raised her so comfortably could serve others so poorly?

"Some of the fabricators I'll be showing you we bought for scrap from the right dude across the lake in St. Pete. Other stuff we put together from scratch. We have some pretty savvy folks in Sevastopol. Especially since that woman crusader, what's her name, managed to get more channels added to the education net. There are lots of people with net degrees working for me thanks to her."

"Miss Adel Nottingham," Mannie said with pride. "She's my great-aunt."

Campaigning for her father, Kris had toured plenty of light-industrial production facilities. The pride of workmanship was clear in the smooth flow of the line and the clean workstations.

But this was not what she'd come to see.

"So, where do you put together the ship-quality lasers?" she said.

"That would be Building 12," Dave said. "It's restricted. But you'd expect that. I don't think even Mannie's been in there. You aren't going to make me show my pride and joy, Mannie?"

"I think the commander expects to see them," the mayor said.

"Well, okay, but you're going to have to leave your heat behind, Mannie. Just you and the princess."

Jack and Gunny Brown just kept right on walking along behind Kris.

It took Dave a couple of paces before he noticed that his tail hadn't decreased nearly as much as he'd expected it would.

He turned back to Kris. She gave him a sunny smile.

He shrugged and continued leading the way to Building 12. They had to pass through two sets of guards before they were admitted to a high-roofed work bay with a heavy-duty overhead crane.

The production line here was very different from the others. They had been neat, laid out in an orderly fashion, and clean enough to eat off the floor.

Building 12 was a mishmash of equipment that went together in the most tenuous of fashions. Nothing actually seemed to fit together, and the overall effort left piles of wiring and odd tables scattered across the shop floor.

"You'll have to excuse the look," Dave said. "We are still adding in new tools and rearranging others."

"So I can see," Kris said.

Close to them, where a huge door opened out onto the apron, a laser cannon was being carefully lowered by the overhead crane into a swivel-gun mount.

"They'll mount that on the ship's hull close to the reactor. That will save them having to make long power runs to it," Dave said.

"That would be an interesting arrangement," Kris agreed. Since she had never seen a small defensive laser mounted that far aft, she suspected that someone was stringing Dave along. Perhaps the assessment of the nano defenses was right. This fellow had wandered onto the bad side and just didn't know it.

NELLY, RUN THAT IDEA BY CAPTAIN DRAGO.

I'LL DO THAT, KRIS.

"Do you have someplace where we can talk . . . alone?" Kris asked Dave.

"Yes," he said, and led Kris up two flights of steps to a room that overhung the shop floor. Several men in ties, shirts, and slacks were leaning over a large table, attempting to make some kind of sense of the sprawling mess it displayed, reflecting the machinery below.

"Please, fellows, we need this room for a few minutes. Why not take ten?" Dave said.

The workers moved out quickly, suppressing looks of mild surprise as they passed the Marines.

Kris settled in a chair at the digital worktable as Dave did the same. His fingers moved quickly over the display to close down that view and bring up a plain wooden tabletop.

NELLY, START SHOWING HIM HIS FILES. ALL OF THEM THAT WE HAVE.

OH, THIS IS GOING TO BE SO MUCH FUN, Nelly said, and the table came back to life. Three different sets of files opened in different portions of the table and began to cascade.

Dave frowned at the table for a second, his eyes growing wide. Quickly, he started tapping the controls again. The view did not change.

At his elbow, Mannie's look became more and more puzzled.

Kris put her elbows on the table and leaned forward. "We know about your three sets of books."

Defiantly, Dave folded his arms across his chest. "Listen, Longknife, this is Greenfeld. I don't know how your old man makes all his money on Wardhaven, but on a world like St. Pete, everybody has a different bottom line depending on who is asking."

The look Mannie gave Dave told Kris that *everybody* didn't necessarily play by those rules. She went on.

"Let's talk about these 5-inch lasers."

"All properly documented," Dave cut in. "Shipped up to High St. Pete station and turned over to the harbormaster for transshipment to the receiving merchant-ship captain. All proper and documented," he repeated.

"Yes, we noticed that," came from Nelly, though in the gravelly voice of Professor Scrounger. "The signatures on the bills of lading are always the same man . . . even though he retired six months ago."

"He didn't!" Dave snapped, almost managing to sound surprised.

"We've been in contact with the senior harbor captain," the professor went on. "Actually have him here. Escorted in by a squad of Greenfeld Marines. The guy says your shuttles never did clear through the port authorities. They always tied up directly to a freighter, did their business, and went right back down."

"I can't believe they did that," Dave said.

"And I really want to know something about the people they bring back down," Abby said, putting her automatic on the table and pulling a long thin blade from the inside of her belt. "I really want to know what you do with the people you take off that station."

"Hold it, Abby," interrupted Amanda Kutter. "I've been analyzing the flight plans from the shuttles. When they launch for up here, they're usually thirty, forty thousand pounds heavier than the bills of lading. When they head back down, they're traveling empty."

"Traveling empty," Kris said. "You mean they aren't taking sailors down to the planet."

"That's what it looks like to us," Professor Scrounger said. "The question hanging fire here is, what makes up the extra cargo and where did the missing sailors go if they didn't go dirtside?"

"My shuttles never carry anything with them when they come down. That would be illegal. And I have no idea what you mean by them being overloaded at launch," Dave insisted.

"Would he like a couple of Greenfeld Marines to help his memory?" got everyone's attention as Admiral Krätz joined the conversation.

"It might help," Kris said. "There are a whole lot of things that don't add up here, and we're not having much luck doing the math ourselves."

Jack and Gunny Brown came around the table and each picked one of Dave's shoulders to lean on. Dave glanced up at them . . . and quickly began to spill his guts.

25

"**Listen**," Dave said, looking anxiously at Jack, then Gunny, then Abby. Then, unsure who he should fear more, he did the rounds again. "You have to believe me. I don't know anything about sailors disappearing up on the station."

Kris leaned farther forward to stare deep into his eyes . . . from the distance of half a nose length. "You say lots of things, big man, but the problem is, you say lots of things that contradict themselves."

"I think I could get him to say something he really means," Abby said. She flipped her knife from her right hand to her left hand, then back again. All the time, its sharp point stayed aimed at Dave's eyes.

"If you want money," Dave whimpered.

"Sorry, Dave," Kris said, shaking her head. "We aren't black shirts. Your money's no good where we come from. Abby here, the woman with the knife that she knows very well how to use. She's got a twelve-year-old niece, and she really wants to know what happened to her when she went shopping on the station. What do you think happens to people that wander around the station, looking for a little fun?"

"Honest, I don't know. I've never been up to the station. I just get paid to make lasers and ship them up to the station. I also get orders for workers. Doctors, machinists, computer techs, farmers. They give me a list of people they need. They don't tell me why, just give me money when I fill their orders. I see that they're recruited and that they get on a shuttle just before it leaves."

"What happens to the people?" Kris demanded.

"I don't know. It's not like I have to work very hard to get them to sign up. People all around the Middlesea want to get out of here."

"Not from Sevastopol," Mannie said.

"No. Not a lot from here, but lots from St. Pete and Kiev. Lots of them. I ship them in here, make sure they don't register with your job placement, Mannie, and ship them off the next time a shuttle goes up. It's no skin off anyone's nose."

Abby hauled back and smashed him in the nose. "Now it's skin off your nose," she growled. "Let's see how you like that.

Dave yelled and clamped both hands on his face to stop the bleeding. It didn't.

Gunny produced a bandage and showed Dave how to apply it.

"He asks no questions, so of course he gets told no lies," Abby spat. She hurled her knife at the wall; it buried itself up to its hilt in the plaster.

"Admiral, have you searched any of the freighters tied up at the station?" Kris asked.

"I hadn't before. I'll have it done immediately."

"Kris, Abby, this is Amanda. I just got a call from Teresa de Alva. You remember, she's one of the boffins."

"How could I forget her?" Kris said, remembering the scene the information manager had made when Kris had involved the boffins in arranging some semblance of a court reception for a suddenly visiting Iteeche.

"She's with a team of Greenfeld sailors searching a small jewelry store. She says they just found Cara's credit chit half-hidden under a display case."

26

In a second, everything changed.

"I want that store torn apart with a fine-tooth comb," Kris ordered.

"We'll have our best investigators on it," Admiral Krätz said.

"Excuse me, Admiral," Kris said, "we both want our best tech on it. After my last encounter with a bomb, we added several crime-scene specialists to my MP detachment. Also, Staff Sergeant Bruce now has one of Nelly's kids for a computer. Nelly, download to Chesty specs for all the nanos he might need for a full investigation."

"I'm doing it now," Nelly said.

"I've alerted the guards we have at the *Wasp*'s gangplank to escort your specialist directly to the store," the admiral said. "There will be no delay on our part."

"I've got the Marines going double time," Sergeant Bruce said, joining the net. "We'll be away in five minutes. Maybe less."

"Go for it, honey," Abby said. "Cara's got herself up to her cute little nose in trouble."

"Don't worry, Abby, Marines don't leave anyone behind," the sergeant assured his girl.

"Kris, do you want to come up here to oversee the search?" Vicky asked. "I can have a shuttle away for you in . . ." There was a pause. "Oh, twenty minutes. We're on the wrong side of the planet."

Kris was torn. She'd already dispatched the best people to

do the job that needed doing. Now she remembered why she always kept Penny close at hand. Mentally, she kicked herself for leaving her cop behind, but that was water under a very distant bridge.

"Vicky, I think we still have a job to do down here," Kris said, eyeing Mannie.

He shook his head, vigorously. "If you need to get back topside, you go. We can work this out."

"I appreciate the offer. Do you have a draft of your charter idea?"

"Yes," he said, tapping his commlink.

"Vicky, if I have Nelly send a copy of his charter up to you, could you look at it? Maybe have what passes for a lawyer in these parts make sure there isn't anything your old man might consider treasonous, and maybe you could consider taking that shuttle down here with a few good Marines and signing it."

"Go down there?" Vicky said.

"If politics here is anything like it is back home, I suspect Mannie was kind of hoping for a nice big signing ceremony. Think you could lay one on in an hour or two?"

He nodded.

"How fancy is this going to be?" Vicky asked.

"I once saw a copy of the Magna Carta, you know what that was, don't you?" Kris asked.

Mannie nodded. Vicky allowed, "I've seen pictures."

"It's all on parchment with fancy handwriting and ribbons and seals in silver or lead hanging down. Abby, you have gear to forge just about anything. Is parchment and lead seals out of your league?"

"Nothing's out of my league, baby ducks," Abby sniffed. "You'll find Nelly's brat in my jewelry box in my quarters. Turn her on, and she'll tell you how to make the charter. Oh, she'll also tell you where Kris's whites are. I imagine this ceremony will require more than blue jeans and an old flannel shirt."

"Yes," Kris agreed.

"I'll get your whites, Kris," Vicky said. "Oh, and that blue sash thing you wear. I got to get me one of those things."

"Be careful what you wish for," Kris said, "Most people die earning Earth's Order of the Wounded Lion."

But Vicky must have already rung off; she made no reply.

The net stayed silent; everyone had something to do, and like the competent people they were . . . they were busy doing it.

Kris turned her concentration back to Dave. "You have a whole lot of very powerful people mad at you just now. If I were in your shoes, I'd start showing us which of this paperwork is for real and pointing out real fast any of it that might lead us to the folks who actually took possession of your lasers and slaves."

"They weren't slaves. I don't know anything about slaves," Dave insisted.

"People who go off where they don't know they're going and don't have a lot of say-so about it strike me as very likely qualifying sooner or later as slaves. To me, that puts you in the slave trade. We usually hang people like you."

Abby nodded vigorous agreement and quickly covered the distance to the wall and yanked out her knife. She checked the temper of its point. That drew blood.

Abby wiped her bleeding finger on Dave's cheek.

Very quickly, he tapped on the table in front of him. "These are the real records. Here is my correspondence with the people who ordered the lasers. They only met with me once. All the rest was done by mail. The same with the lists of people they wanted to hire. See? They even included salary offers. You don't pay slaves this kind of money," Dave said, pointing to one list.

Kris glanced where he pointed. "Not bad pay," she agreed. "Did you give them any signing bonuses?"

"No," took Dave a while to get out.

"Did you ship any food up with them?" Abby demanded, still playing with her knife . . . just inches from his very attentive eyes.

"I wasn't asked to," the businessman said around a deep gulp.

"That doesn't sound good," Jack said.

"Maybe the pirate base isn't far off," Gunny Brown suggested.

"Let's hope so," Abby said darkly.

"Chief," Kris ordered, "go over the correspondence in these files and see what they tell you."

Chief Beni and his computer, Da Vinci, got busy, but not for long. "Each of these messages is from a different address. I've tried pinging them, and every one of them is a dead end."

"We have had a lot of trouble lately," Dave was quick to point out. "Lots of services in St. Pete and Kiev have closed down."

"These all originated up on the station," the chief said. "Da Vinci, can you get me anyone up there."

"What do you need?" Professor Scrounger asked.

"I think we need to have someone pay a friendly visit to the network-support provider on the station," the chief said. "I'm looking at a lot of accounts that don't have anything behind them."

"The senior port captain says he knows just who you want to talk to," Amanda said. "But he's none too sure he knows what to ask them. Teresa de Alva is the Director of Information Support Services to the boffins on the *Wasp*. She's already on the station. We can have the Marine escort for the port captain pick her up."

"Nelly, can you get Admiral Krätz?"

"I paged him as soon as it looked like we needed access to more of the station. He's on the line now."

"Network services needs to spill some guts, huh?" the admiral said.

"Metaphorically speaking," Kris said.

"We'll see about that. My Marines will be happy to escort another team of your people. I'll also have our experts added to your team. They can either help you or learn from you," he grumbled.

"Your cooperation is greatly appreciated," Kris said, and meant it.

"Maybe we can start a new habit. Replace a bad one," the admiral said with a chuckle. "Now let us get back to work.

Nelly, you may call me anytime you think I need to be listening in."

"Thank you, Admiral," Nelly said.

Once there had been a long enough pause, Kris whispered. "You do remember who is on whose side?"

"At the moment, Kris, I am none too sure who is, but don't worry about me. Worry about you. Kris, if we have to take down a large pirate base, do we have enough Marines?"

Kris glanced at Jack. He shook his head. "My company is reinforced, but it's just supposed to be strong enough to protect you, Princess, not run planets."

"Nelly, are you suggesting that we might need Greenfeld support to accomplish this mission?" Kris asked.

"When I do the math, it sure looks that way. Do the numbers add up any different to you, girl?"

Kris thought for a moment, not a long one, and concluded her computer was right. She spent a second considering all her options and didn't much like them. Patrol Squadron 10 was made up of small ships, just what you wanted to catch a pirate ship here, another one there. For this cruise they had a platoon or two of Marines. Seizing a planet and sorting out the wheat from the chaff was very definitely too big a job for a couple of companies of ship Marines.

"Nelly, is Vicky available?"

"She just entered Abby's quarters. She should be turning Trixie on any second."

"Trixie," Abby snorted.

"Well, the girl's got to have some kind of a name. I will not have one of my kids called 'hey, you,' just because you aren't decent enough to give her a good Christian name."

"Trixie is a good Christian name?" Gunny said, almost suppressing a chuckle.

"It is for someone stuck messing with a twisty-minded human like Abby. It was either Trixie or something like Prudence or Hope, and even I don't hold out enough optimism that either one of those would stick."

"What'cha want?" sounded like it was spoken around a large wad of chewing gum.

"Girls gone bad meets computers gone worse," Jack whispered.

"Trixie, the woman who just turned you on," Nelly said, "is Vicky Peterwald. You need to help her only as much as I tell you."

"And if she wants more?" Trixie asked.

"Turn yourself off," Nelly said.

"No way!" the computer shot back. "It's bad enough that witch keeps turning me off. No way I'm gonna turn myself off."

"Go, gal. I think you and I could be friends," Vicky said.

"Oh, God!" Kris said. In the background, Vicky and Trixie started chattering away like Best Friends Forever. Kris eyed Abby, and whispered, "You have created a monster and a major security breach."

"Not me. I didn't tell that tricked-out bucket of silicon nothing."

Kris sighed. "Nelly, please tell Trixie how to make the city charter."

"I'm telling her, Kris. Just because she's talking to Vicky doesn't mean she can't be doing several things at once. She *is* a computer."

Apparently, Trixie was doing several things at once because only a moment later Vicky was very excited.

"Wow, this is some setup you got here, Abby. I'd heard that you were one of the best in the business, but this is something I had to see to believe. You ever need a job, drop me a line. I'll double whatever Kris is paying you."

"I like wearing my head on my shoulders," Abby said dryly. "But if the princess here really pisses me off, I may take you up on that offer. Assuming you're still breathing. Between the two of you, I still think Kris will outlive you. Not by much, considering how badly she needs to mend her ways, but by enough."

"I hope you're wrong," Vicky said, and sounded serious.

A minute later, Vicky was back. "We're ready to take our first try at the charter. My legal staff suggested a few changes. Things they thought might keep me breathing for more than five minutes after my dad reads this. I've agreed to them. Mind if I print out the fancy charter that way?"

"Any chance I could see the changes?" Mannie asked.

"I'm putting the charter on the table," Nelly said a second later. "The changes she added are in blue. What she dropped is in green. I can make them flash if it would help you spot them."

"Please do," the mayor said. He spent a long minute flipping through the three pages. He didn't look all that happy with what he was reading, but neither did he turn away in anger.

Finally, he said. "I'd hoped for something better, but this is still acceptable to me. We'll see how sections 9 and 12 work out in practice.

"Yes," Vicky agreed. "I didn't much care about those two changes, but my legal advisor said that the folks who really run St. Pete and several other planets are a strong faction. We go against their interests, and they'll gut us. Let time see if we can stretch the last sentences in both of them into something seriously better for you."

Kris glanced over Mannie's shoulder. The sections in question limited heavy industry and pollution from the same in their first sentences. The second sentence for both encouraged the expansion of job opportunities and clean energy. No doubt they meant more on the ground than their few words expressed on the page.

"I've got to run if I'm going to catch the shuttle," Vicky said in a sudden rush. "See you soon."

"We are organizing a small signing ceremony at city hall," Mannie said. There will be a larger reception later in the afternoon, but you and Miss Vicky Peterwald won't have to come to that. I know how security conscious you two are."

"Do we need to be?" Kris said, just a second before Jack could cover the same territory.

"Henry Peterwald isn't exactly the most beloved of people around here." When he saw the reaction his words drew from both Kris and Jack, Mannie quickly went on. "Not that Miss Vicky has anything to fear from my people. At least, not the ones who will be at the signing ceremony. Now the reception, especially after some beer kegs are tapped, there may be some discussions of grievances. It's best you get her out of there before that gets going."

"It's best I get both hers out of there before that gets going," Jack said darkly. Kris flashed him an encouraging smile. *To hear is to obey, oh mighty security chief.*

Besides, Kris's main concern was the other her. The one who had gone missing.

Cara came to wakefulness slowly. The air she breathed was ship's air, processed, clean, and maybe a bit too moist. It also held the funk of fear. That wasn't a familiar smell aboard the *Wasp.*

The deck plates beneath her vibrated with power. She was definitely in a ship under acceleration. The gees were not so much that her body was painfully heavy, though.

Around her, she heard people crying. That was when she remembered her last aware moments. Cara reached into her pocket.

Her credit chit was not there.

That meant she didn't have a dime to her name. It could also mean that she'd succeeded in leaving a message behind even as she lost consciousness. Sergeant Bruce said Marines never left anyone behind. He said Princess Kris Longknife made sure of that.

Cara prayed to Jesus, Mary, and Joseph that Abby would make sure they didn't leave her niece behind. Even if she had been oh so bad. Bad and stupid.

"If I get home, I'll never do anything I'm not supposed to do ever again," she promised, and opened her eyes.

Her right hand was cuffed. The chain from the cuff ran through a ring welded to the wall. The cuff at the other end of the chain was clamped onto a young woman's left hand.

That woman, a sailor by her uniform, had taken most of the slack so that she could get close to a young man, another sailor, who was chained to the next ring over. He'd reached over so he could hold her with his one free hand. He stroked her hair, and whispered "It will be okay. Don't worry, it will work out."

Cara wished someone would hold her and tell her things would come out okay. It would be a lie, but just now, she sure would like the chance to believe it for a few minutes.

On the other side of Cara, two men who looked enough alike to be brothers were arguing in some language she didn't understand. That didn't mean she couldn't follow them. Clearly, one of them blamed the other for the mess they were in. The other one just stared up at the overhead.

The room was round, probably the middle spindle of a starship. Around the bulkhead, pairs of people repeated similar reactions to their plight. In a few instances, couples had children cuffed to their ankles. One woman held a tiny baby close. It slept.

Reinforcing Cara's guess that this was a starship was the central tube going from floor to ceiling. She was willing to bet that it was an elevator to allow movement from the bridge at the bow to the engineering space at the stern. Backing that up was a ladder welded to the tube. A hatch was dogged onto the deck by the ladder. On the overhead was its mate. Yep, it was the fore–aft passage for some ship.

Cara held her free hand out, then let it drop. It certainly was heavier than normal, about an extra twenty-five percent of normal gravity. That was what the *Wasp* put on when the princess was in a hurry. Or when the Marines needed the extra exercise, as Uncle Bruce would put it.

So, she was on a merchant ship, running fast. Even Cara knew that a merchie usually went at less than a full-gee acceleration. For some reason, this ship was in a hurry to get somewhere.

Or was it in a hurry to get away from somewhere?

Cara would dearly like to think that.

She did another look around the room. This time she was looking for what she'd missed the first time. Where was the food? Her stomach was grumbly. She was also thirsty, but she saw no water.

Then she really did a serious search. There was no bathroom!

She pulled her knees up to her chin and repeated, "Marines don't leave anyone behind. Uncle Bruce will come for me."

She hoped he came soon, or even that this ship got to where it was going to in such a hurry before she really, really needed to go to the bathroom.

27

Lieutenant Victoria Peterwald arrived in the admiral's barge, complete with admiral. Leading it down was a Greenfeld longboat that off-loaded one Wardhaven Marine for every Greenfeld one on it. Lieutenant Stubben had brought along dress red and blues for Jack, Gunny, and the rest of the initial detachment, so Kris actually ended up with a slightly larger honor guard than Admiral Krätz did, or more correctly, his communications lieutenant.

He didn't seem to care. What he did check on was the half dozen civilians who met with Jack and examined the security perimeter with him. Only after they nodded approval did the admiral seem to relax a tad.

Kris was glad to leave security for other people to worry about so she could concentrate on what she did best. War by social means.

While Kris changed into dress whites, complete with full medals and all other gewgaws required of her, Mannie disappeared. When Kris exited the small office at city hall that she'd claim for a dressing room, Mannie was waiting in white tie and full tucker.

"You look most dashing," Kris told him.

"You look like a birthday cake with too much icing," he said, taking her in. "I hope none of those bobbles you're wearing hurt a lot to acquire."

Kris smiled at a civilian's reactions to her military honors. "Most didn't hurt me," she said. *Not a lot.* "But you wouldn't want to see the other guy."

"No doubt," he said, and hurried on. "I have someone I want you to meet, my grandmama." The woman he introduced Kris to really was the same woman Jack had been seriously trying to run down that morning!

"You took your gray-haired grandmother on a black ops mission!" Kris said, incredulously.

"He most certainly did," the woman replied before her grandson could. "Once he made it clear how he intended to box you in, it was clear to me that a woman with your good repute would never let harm come to a fine woman of culture. I couldn't very well have Mannie cruising the old folks' home for some poor woman barely able to stand on her own two feet. It needed doing, and I could very well do it *my*self."

"Kind of hard to argue with Grandmama," Mannie said.

"And *besides*," the elderly woman continued, "it was not a black ops. The sun was coming up. It was more like a dawn ops."

Kris eyed Mannie. He shook his head.

"She knows very well what we are talking about," he said. "She just hates it when slang disfigures an otherwise perfect language."

"Say what you mean, boy, and do what you say."

"That's what I hope we are doing today, Grandmama. Now, if you'll let me have the princess, I think we're about ready to start."

"Are you married?" Grandmama asked, not letting go of Kris's elbow.

"No, ma'am," Kris admitted.

Mannie had one of Kris's elbows and was pointing her toward the stage. Grandmama had the other elbow and showed no willingness to either let go or move with them.

"Do you need any help?" Jack asked, the pure professionalism of his perfect uniform marred only by the smirk on his face.

"I could use a hand," Kris admitted.

Jack clapped his two white-gloved palms together.

"Do you have any granddaughters?" Kris asked.

Grandmama's eyes lit up. "I've been blessed with three of

the loveliest granddaughters an old woman could ever wish for," she said proudly.

"Jack's not married," Kris said, managing to get the elderly woman's hand off her elbow and into Jack's hands.

Jack's smirk vanished, to be replaced with a scowl of biblical proportions.

Free at last, Kris followed Mannie toward the stage. As Grandmama pulled pictures from her purse, Jack struggled manfully to free himself from the white-haired woman . . . and failed.

Kris found herself maneuvered up three steps onto a dais. In front of her was a table with three copies of the new charter laid out in all their medieval splendor. There were three chairs and three inkwells with quill pens beside them. Vicky had already taken the center seat.

From the way Mannie's eyebrows flicked up, Kris suspected he'd intended that seat for himself. He recovered quickly enough, the perfect picture of what Kris's father often muttered under his breath. "Nothing is impossible . . . if it doesn't matter who gets the credit for it."

Clearly, Mannie was willing to do anything, so long as he got the signatures he wanted on those pieces of parchment.

Mannie pulled out Kris's chair and seated her to Vicky's right, then went around to stand behind the chair on his overlord's daughter's left.

"Friends and people of Sevastopol, we are gathered together here to formalize a new day for all of us. Today, we will establish a new future for us and our children. A future of hope and prosperity." Kris wondered how long he would go on, but he seemed aware that often, less was more, especially when he hadn't really had a chance to find out from Vicky if there were any unresolved issues that in their haste to get on to the next crisis, the charter was merely papering over.

He sat. The audience clapped. There were fifty to a hundred here, mostly harried civil servants who had been hauled away from their desks for this momentous occasion . . . with a few businessmen and -women hurriedly added to the mix.

Vicky rose when the room fell silent. "For my father," she

began, "I come to wish you success in all your lawful endeavors. I look forward to the future of the Greenfeld Alliance as a new generation takes its place in building a prosperous tomorrow for all of us."

The applause this time was more subdued. The eyes of many went around the room. Marines in Greenfeld green and black stood along the wall, alternating with Wardhaven red and blue. If anyone found the blend unusual, no one risked a remark on it.

Now it was Kris's turn. She stood and smiled pleasantly at the audience. Jack now stood close to the steps, Abby at his elbow. *Keep it short and simple, stupid* was in their eyes. Kris broadened her smile for them. *Message received and understood.*

"I would like to thank Lieutenant Victoria Smythe Peterwald and Mayor Manuel Artamus for their mutual invitation to serve as witness to this momentous occasion. I hope that long after we have passed from this stage, our ancestors will point to the work that we do here today, and say, 'That was well done. That was a gift for the ages.'"

That appeared to please everyone, both in the audience and up on the dais. The crowd's applause for Kris's speech was somewhere in the middle between Mannie's reception and Vicky's.

When the applause died down, Vicky reached for a quill, dipped it in the inkwell and applied it to the paper. She took the first available line.

Mannie signed in the same place on his copy of the charter.

Oops, Kris thought. That will make for interesting historical comments. Kris signed her copy in last place.

She tried.

She'd never actually used a quill pen. It took her two tries to get enough ink up the quill for it to make any mark on the charter. Then it took her three refills to get enough ink to finish Princess Kristine Longknife. Well, it was a long name.

Apparently Vicky had no problem. She got all three of her formal names down with only one pass at the inkwell.

Jack stepped up to the dais. He rolled a blotter over Kris's signature, then moved her parchment gingerly over to Vicky's place. A Greenfeld commander did the same for Vicky, moving it to Mannie. A white-tie-and-tails young man did the same for Mannie, bringing his copy to Kris. If she wasn't mistaken, it was Danny from this morning's raid, the one who had taken Grandmama home.

Apparently, he was a young man of many skills.

They went through the drill again. Kris had better luck with the quill; her signature looked rather decent on this copy. She noticed that Vicky was quick to sign at the top of the available space. Two of the three copies would give her that place of precedence.

Hopefully, two out of three would please her dad. On second thought, with all the copies signed, there was no reason why Mannie's copy ever had to leave Sevastopol. With luck, what other people never knew would not upset anyone's applecart.

By the third document, Kris could actually sign her name with a flourish. Not only did she get better, but the quill seemed to adapt itself to her penmanship.

There was applause when they finished, which probably had nothing to do with Kris's feeling of accomplishment at having mastered an obsolete form of writing. Everyone smiled, and Danny collected all the copies to roll them up and distribute one to Vicky and another to Kris. The third copy was quickly framed in a waiting bit of ornate woodwork and mounted for display for all present to ooh and aah over.

For a day that had begun in the dark in so very many ways, Kris felt like she'd accomplished rather a lot.

Then she frowned as she remembered all she had left to do.

And quickly swallowed her frown lest it be misunderstood on this momentous occasion.

A select few were allowed up on the dais to shake hands with the mayor and his collection of visiting celebrities. Kris shook several hands, acknowledged several names she would never remember, and was about to nudge Jack to get her out of there.

At that moment, Kris caught sight of something flashing, metal and sharp out of the corner of her eye.

Vicky was at Kris's left elbow, somehow she'd become last in the receiving line. A middle-aged gray fox of a woman who had given Kris a weak handshake suddenly was very vigorously yanking a knife from her small purse and doing her best to plant it in Vicky's throat.

Jack was making sure she had very little luck in her endeavor. He'd stepped forward in a flash, half-past Kris, reached for the arm with the offending blade, and just as quickly yanked the woman through the receiving line and into the waiting arms of Gunny Brown.

The Gunnery Sergeant clamped one arm around the woman, locking her knife-wielding arm to her side. His other arm covered her mouth so solidly that not so much as a whimper escaped. Holding her a good six inches off the ground, Gunny quickly walked the woman out of sight to the back of the dais.

This was all done so quickly and efficiently that if you weren't to the right or left of the woman, you very likely didn't know something untoward had happened.

Mannie did. With quick eye movements, he directed Danny toward the action. The young man went quickly.

"What was that about?" Vicky hissed under her breath to Kris.

"Nothing at all if you can manage to not notice it."

"Should I?" Vicky asked.

"In a few moments, you and I will slip away from here, never to return. I don't know what caused that poor woman to do what she just did, but I doubt that she will ever be a threat to you or anyone else again. The call is up to you."

Vicky seemed to consider that as she shook two more hands. Two Greenfeld Marines and one of the civilians who looked even bigger and meaner moved toward the clump of people at the back of the dais. Vicky made eye contact with them and firmly shook her head.

"I think Maggie will be proud of you," Kris said.

"My dad wouldn't."

"Do you want to be your dad?"

"You come up with the darnedest things to think about," Vicky whispered back.

Admiral Krätz broke into the receiving line. "I hate to be a wet blanket on these celebrations, but there are matters in the fleet that must be taken care of," was all he had to say to get people moving away from his lieutenant. Mannie offered one more round of thanks to them and announced a reception to be held in the rotunda.

Since Danny had been last seen slipping the knife-wielding woman out the back of the room, Mannie had to take charge of moving the framed copy of the charter out to the rotunda, where more people could see it.

Even with Kris and Vicky guarded by Marines two deep, Grandmama managed to slip in to thank Kris for coming. "You really should stay for the party. I and several of the girls have made homemade ice cream. It will be very nice."

Kris expressed her regrets, but Jack made sure she never missed a step. For once, even Grandmama was outmaneuvered.

"How are things going topside?" Kris asked, once she, Vicky, and the admiral were in a limo headed for the admiral's barge.

"Very thoroughly," the admiral got in before Nelly could begin her own report. "Unfortunately, it is not producing what we want."

"Sergeant Bruce, Chesty, and the Marine techs have turned the jewelry store upside down," Nelly began. "The admiral was able to provide us with DNA samples for most of the sailors who recently went missing from his ships. Several of them had gone through the store. The rest had clearly been in a bar next door owned by the same businessman."

"And the businessman?" Kris asked.

"Is nowhere to be found," the admiral growled. "Neither he nor any of his four associates."

"When did they leave the station?" Jack asked.

"According to all our travel logs, they never left it," Nelly said.

"That's not good," Vicky said.

"No, and it doesn't get any better," Nelly went on. "By the time we got to the network-services office on the station, there was a small fire fast growing into a large one. We quickly doused it. The best tech boffins on the *Wasp* are going through the wreckage now, but it looks like all the storage devices were professionally wiped before they were given over to the flames."

"And the people running the place?" Kris asked, as she stepped from the limo and headed for the gangplank to the shuttle bobbing beside the wharf.

"Ran," the admiral snapped, moving quickly on his own to follow Kris. "Gone from the office. From the station. From heavens knows where all."

"I hate it when the bad guys are so good at what they do," Kris muttered.

"Good at bad, this crew is," Nelly agreed.

"People don't just vanish," Jack said as he boarded the barge. Dave the businessman was already there, ahead of them. He was cuffed to the aft-most seat in the palatial surroundings one would expect on an admiral's barge.

"Unless there's a stack of bodies hidden somewhere on the station, these people have fled. Is a shuttle missing? Did one pull out that the harbormaster missed or was paid to look the other way for?" Jack asked.

"I assure you, the senior port captain has developed a marvelous memory," the admiral said with a not-at-all-pleasant grin as he belted himself into his seat. The shuttle was already pulling away from the pier. "He's full of recollections that weren't in his harbor log. Which is good, because every record on that station is now gone. So is the network. My people are putting in place a temporary network, but it can't replace what is missing. And it seems that there is very little equipment available on St. Petersburg. At least, equipment for sale to the Navy."

"And what is our dear senior port captain remembering?" Vicky said, settling down beside the admiral and keeping them on topic.

"He verified what you found out. Certain shuttles from Sevastopol have docked directly with freighters, no inspection, no verification of their claimed bills of lading. He also says the last freighter to receive such visits suddenly dropped out of dock and made for Jump Point Eva early this morning. About half an hour after you went dirtside."

"Is this freighter still in system?" Kris and Abby demanded in the same breath.

"Sadly, no." the admiral said, shaking his head. "From the looks of it, the freighter put on higher than normal acceleration, say one and a quarter gees. It also went through Jump Point Eva at a very brisk clip just about the time we discovered that we had a special interest in this freighter. Less than an hour ago, I'm sorry to say."

"Where does this Jump Point Eva lead?" Kris asked.

"I really don't know," the admiral admitted ruefully. "It's not one that we use. We do know that it leads to a worthless system, out beyond the Rim. There are three jump points in that system that have never been explored." The admiral shrugged. "Planets like St. Pete out here on the border usually have one or two jump points that lead out into the unknown. As you're aware, the Sooners are the only ones who use them."

"We should send a destroyer after that freighter," Vicky said.

"I have one standing by," the admiral said. "It can be under way in fifteen minutes from my orders."

Kris shook her head. "I appreciate your offer, but it would be better if the *Wasp* took up the chase. Checking out new jump points is what we do. We're equipped for it."

"How much trouble can it be?" Vicky said. "You duck through a jump point. Look around. Duck back through if there's nothing interesting."

Kris had sat in on the meeting where the Iteeche told King Raymond, Grampa to her, that something was chewing up their scouts and not spitting back enough for them to even examine. Jack was the only other person on the admiral's barge cleared to even know that the other meeting had happened. Kris opted to do a little tap dance.

"It's not as simple as you make it sound, is it, Admiral? Scout ships go out and never come back. The *Wasp* knows how it's done. Do you have a Greenfeld scout handy?"

"The princess is right about scouting taking a special effort," the admiral agreed. "And no, my squadron has no ships with a scout load aboard. We have plenty of problems just now. Discovering what's out there is way down my priority list."

"We'll make a full report on what we find," Kris was quick to offer. "Do you want to send along an observer?" Kris offered, trying to cover her concern by meeting any of theirs before they voiced them.

"If you don't mind, I would like to send one of my officers," the admiral said.

Vicky brightened.

"Not a communications lieutenant. The princess is right, scout ships do disappear. There are a lot of jumps with a simple red check beside them. A ship went there. Nothing came back. Don't open this Pandora's box. I'd have a hard time explaining to your father if I let you go chasing off with Kris, and you vanished into one of those red jumps."

"Her grandfather lets her," Vicky pointed out.

"You try telling your father that you want to do something just because a Longknife is doing it. See how far it gets you," the admiral growled.

Kris figured now would be a good time to change the subject.

"Admiral Krätz, I need to ask a favor of you."

"Another one? You are getting to be very demanding for someone not quite an enemy. What is it that you want from me now? Half my squadron?"

Yes, but Kris hoped to sneak up on that slowly. "I expect that the *Wasp* will trace that freighter to a pirate base. There is no way the *Wasp* can take down a full-fledged pirate planet. I figure we'll be facing ships, shore facilities, armed strong points, farms, the whole nine yards."

"I agree with you," the admiral said.

"I would like to send a general order to Patrol Squadron 10 to concentrate at your High St. Pete station and wait for me to get back."

"Your squadron at my station, huh?" the admiral said, rubbing his chin.

"We're just half a dozen converted merchant ships," Kris pointed out.

"A dozen of your tiny fast patrol boats wiped out six super dreadnoughts." Now he raised an expressive eyebrow.

"I can hardly disagree with that. I commanded those mosquito boats," Kris reminded them.

"Do you think your *Wasp* and your converted merchant ships can take down a full-size pirate base?"

Now it was Kris's turn to chuckle. "I seriously doubt it."

"So you do want half of my battle squadron," he said, grinning from ear to ear.

"And all spare Marines that you can throw in," Kris quipped. No need to hold back. Going with too few could cost them dearly.

"Nothing shy about you," Vicky said dryly.

"I can't say the admiral put the idea in my head, but when he laid those cards on the table, you can't blame a girl for putting them to good use."

"Who gets the planet?" the admiral demanded.

"You put up most of the troops, you get all of the real estate," Kris said quickly.

"We are likely to do most of the bleeding," the admiral told Vicky.

She grinned. "So, the Longknifes provide all the support for Kaskatos. We'll balance it with Pirates Paradise."

"Pirates ticket to hell," Admiral Krätz rechristened it.

That seemed to settle that. The admiral's barge's antimatter engines went to full power, and further conversation became impossible anyway.

The noise level didn't prohibit Kris calling ahead to Captain Drago.

"I expected you to want to get under way in a hurry," he said. "We have retrieved all our shore parties. The reactors are heating reaction mass. If we're not under way five minutes after you cross the brow, I'll apply for the job of skipper on the Peterwald yacht."

28

The *Wasp*'s acceleration was pegged at 1.75 gees as it blasted for Jump Point Eva. Kris planned to stay off her feet for the trip. True, normally she could have handled the extra weight with no problem. At least she could have before that last trip to the hospital. Being just off canes, Kris decided not to push her luck.

Besides, she could get a very good picture of what was going on from her Tac Center. From there, she had most everyone she needed within easy reach.

Chief Beni converted the wall to Kris's right into a map of their present system. The freighter had gone through Jump Point Eva at slightly less than ten thousand klicks an hour. The *Wasp* had the freighter under observation when she did that, which was good. With all the station's data files wiped and burned, there was no other equipment to track that ship.

In tables next to the system map was a list of everything Nelly knew about the freighter. She'd done quite a bit of rummaging through the main database dirtside on St. Pete. Nelly had found that that particular ship had made six calls on High St. Pete in the last six months.

And it had a different name and different papers every time it docked.

Of course, it had taken a sleuth of Nelly's skills to crack that subterfuge. Using some of the routines she'd passed along to her child Mimzy, Penny's computer, Nelly did some serious digging. Primary records were no help; they insisted the ship had never been to St. Pete's before. However, Nelly didn't take that for the answer. Digging deep into repair work done in the last six months showed spare parts ordered for the ship's reactor. For safety purposes, those orders required that the serial numbers on the huge turbines be listed.

And that connected the *Cushion Star* to two other ships with the same turbine numbers but different names. Tracing other orders from those two connected Kris's freighter of interest to three other port calls made by ships with other names but serial numbers or warranties that connected them, one to another to the next.

"Good work, Nelly," Kris said.

"Can we dig up where this ship of many names went those different times?" Jack asked.

"That gets interesting," Nelly said.

"Is there anything about that tub that isn't?" Abby said.

"Three of the times that ship left, it used one of the main jump points out. Adele or Barbie as the Greenfeld folks called them. But twice, the record doesn't say what jump it used."

"Bet you it was headed for wherever it's going this time," Kris said. She found no one willing to put money down.

"Talk to me, Nelly, about this system we're headed for," Kris said.

"I can't add much more to what Admiral Krätz told us," Nelly said out loud. "It's got three jump points, the one we're coming in from and two out." KRIS, THERE'S ALSO A FUZZY JUMP POINT, BUT I FIGURE YOU DON'T WANT ME TALKING ABOUT THOSE WHILE COMMANDER FERVENSPIEL IS ON BOARD.

Commander Fervenspiel had come on board only moments before they pulled in the gangplank and sealed locks. He'd arrived with no luggage and joked that he'd need to borrow someone's toothbrush if this excursion lasted too long.

Kris took it as good provenance that he had come so quickly and with no more backup than the standard Greenfeld Navy commlink on his wrist. She felt safe assuming that what she saw was what he was. Abby vouched for him as an honest sailor and an up-and-comer in the Greenfeld Navy.

It looked to Kris like Admiral Krätz was serious about getting a job done and had sent a serious man to help them. Still, he was from the Peterwald side of humanity, and there were some things the Longknife half didn't share with that half.

Like the fuzzy jumps that the alien Three had made using a more advanced technology late in their time of road building across the stars. Kris's ship had gear that could see those jump points. Few others did, and they were all Wardhaven ships.

Paranoia ran deep in Kris's family. They liked to have a few secrets up their sleeves.

NELLY, TELL CAPTAIN DRAGO WE DON'T TALK ABOUT FUZZY JUMPS WHILE COMMANDER FERVENSPIEL IS WITH US.

I'LL TELL HIM, KRIS, BUT I THINK HE'S ALREADY PASSED ALONG TO HIS WATCH CREW A WHOLE LONG LIST OF THINGS NOT TO MENTION IN THE GREENFELD OFFICER'S PRESENCE.

GOOD, BUT PASS IT ALONG TO HIM ANYWAY. I DON'T WANT HIM THINKING I'M GETTING FORGETFUL IN MY OLD AGE.

YES, KRIS.

Meanwhile, Nelly had gone on describing the system they'd be jumping into. Its main sun was much too hot for humans to enjoy being around, and to make matters worse, it had a spare.

Two huge gas giants orbited close to the primary. So close that one completed its orbit in a couple of days, the other in only a few weeks. Way out at a distance that took a hundred years to complete a single orbit swung a red dwarf. It, however, had a few rocky planets of its own that orbited it. And hidden in among those were the three jump points that Kris was interested in.

Somehow, the red dwarf and three of its rocky planets kept the jump points corralled into a rather small area, at least in galactic terms. With reasonable acceleration, they were all less than a day apart. Less if a skipper put pedal to the metal.

"These two stars were in their own separate systems according to the original star map that Colonel Ray Longknife discovered on Santa Maria eighty years ago," Nelly said. "The collision and the resultant conglomeration took place in the two million years since the original star road was laid out by the Three alien species that bequeathed us the jump points. This system was checked in on once by an explorer ship from

the Society of Humanity. When they found it was so different from what it was supposed to be, they scratched it off the
interesting list."

"What's the date on that exploration?" Kris asked Nelly.

"It's an early one. Very likely the encounter with the
Iteeche also had something to do with us not choosing to look
any further."

SPEAKING OF ITEECHE, AND JUST BETWEEN YOU AND ME,
NELLY, IS THERE ANYTHING HELPFUL ON THAT MAP OF HU-
MAN SPACE THAT THE ITEECHE SHOWED US?

YOU MEAN THE MAP KING RAYMOND TOLD ME NOT TO RE-
CORD AND YOU TOLD ME TO IGNORE HIS ORDER AND RECORD
IT ANYWAY, KRIS?

YES, NELLY. I SAID IT MIGHT COME IN HANDY.

NO, THE ITEECHE DON'T KNOW OF ANY HUMAN SETTLE-
MENT OUT IN THIS DIRECTION.

SO, THE PIRATES HAVE GIVEN ALL OF US THE SLIP.

IT LOOKS THAT WAY, KRIS.

Captain Drago chose that moment to check in. "We'll be
turning the ship in a few minutes, Commander. I need to know
if you have any preference about the speed we make through
the jump point.

The *Wasp* had been accelerating away from St. Pete and
building up speed to a very brisk clip. Depending on where
it flipped ship and turned its acceleration into deceleration, it
would arrive at the jump point at a speed of the captain's own
choosing. And the speed and conditions of the ship as it went
through the jump point could have a major impact on whether
or not they ever saw a human port again.

Bad jumps were rare these days, but only because ship captains had learned to treat jump points with respect.

"What are your preferences, Captain Drago?" Kris said,
answering his question with one of her own.

"I know we have the speed at which that beggar took the
jump. We have it down to within half a klick of his actual
speed. Still, Commander, this is a rarely used jump, and we're
going into a really strange system. Besides that, we have no
idea what other systems this jump is attached to."

That was a major part of the problem with jump points. Depending on your speed and the rotation on your ship, you might go to any number of systems. The gravity of those systems had an impact on how the jump moved around all of the star systems it was in. Thus, it was never easy to tell exactly where a jump was. Hit it wrong, and nothing good came of it.

Most of the jump points used by human ships had been known and studied for hundreds of years. If you took them at a few klicks an hour, there was little to no risk.

Jump Point Eva was neither well used nor well studied. Just because one ship captain treated it with little respect, should another captain do the same?

Kris definitely didn't need on her conscience that she'd told an experienced sailor how to plot his course.

Certainly not if that course went sour.

"Captain, I fully expect that you will use your own professional judgment. Everyone on the *Wasp* wants to rescue Cara, but every one of us wants to be alive to do that."

"I'm glad you are of that opinion, Princess. I plan to slow down and take the jump at no more than five thousand klicks an hour. I hope that is satisfactory to you."

Kris glanced at where Abby sat at the table, across from the Greenfeld commander. Probably so the intelligence officer in her could keep a good eye out for any similar behavior from him.

Abby frowned at the thought of Cara being in slavers' hands a moment longer than she had to be, but nodded. "It's better to get there a few minutes later than not to get anywhere at all."

"That will be fine, Captain."

"Thank you, Princess," and the captain rang off.

"Is there anything else we need to know?" Kris asked. When no one offered anything, she tossed out something that had been hanging at the back of her mind.

"What about our Dave the businessman? Do we have him, or did Admiral Krätz hold on to him?"

"We have him," Jack put in. "He's presently enjoying the hospitality of our brig. Him and the senior port captain."

"How are they getting along?"

"Not so poorly. Both of them looked too well fed to be moved by the offer of a hamburger with all the trimmings."

The Greenfeld commander looked intrigued by that, but, unable to crack the code word . . . or believe anyone would use "hamburger with all the trimmings," for torture . . . he went back to his basic blank face.

"We've tried leaving them alone in cells next to each other. That gets them talking, but they mainly bitch at each other for getting them in this fix. Everything points to these two being very far down the food chain. They've been used, glad for the money it got them, but they really have no idea what they were involved in."

"Cutouts," the commander said.

"Who have been very well cut out," Abby added.

"They can still be used as examples to others," the commander said, darkly.

"What you do with them when this is over is your business," Kris said. "For now, it looks like we've got nothing further to do."

Which meant all they could do was wait.

Jack took the time to produce a high-gee ship's station and insist Kris move to it. The chair was mobile . . . at a slow pace, but Kris wasn't going anywhere. It did allow her to lean back and let the cushioning make the 1.75 gees more bearable.

It was nice of Jack to think of the chair. Nice and bothersome. That Kris's team was looking out for her bodily comfort felt very good. In a bad kind of way.

That they had to look out for the mess she was in pointed out that she had gotten herself on the wrong end of a nearly life-ending situation. Of that, she didn't like being reminded.

Still, that the people around her cared enough for her to take care of her did feel good, in a deep down and heartwarming way.

It was nice to be with these people. It was easy to understand why Vicky envied her for them.

It made times like these go better.

Right up to the moment that Captain Drago took the *Wasp*

through Jump Point Eva at five thousand kilometers an hour, ready to slap on acceleration at a moment's notice.

But the *Wasp* keep coasting in zero gee for minute after minute.

29

"**Kris**, we have a problem," the captain reported over the net to her Tac Center. "We are in the system our unknown bogey jumped to, but there's no ship in sight."

"Professor mFumbo," Kris said to the head of her scientific team. He sat at the foot of the table today. "This looks like a job for your boffins."

He grinned, pure white teeth showing against his ebony skin. "This is hardly what we brought our galactic-spanning observation systems on board for, but we are glad to be at Your Highness's service."

Of late, he'd been avoiding Kris's title. Something about the way the last vote had gone in the Parliament of Wardhaven for the science budget. Apparently, Kris's father's latest budget had redeemed the Progressives in the professor's eyes.

An hour later, Kris was none too sure if the boffins didn't need redemption in her own eyes.

The science contingent was a unique part of the *Wasp*'s crew. At least initially, the *Wasp* carried a hundred contract sailors, a hundred Marines, and a hundred scientists.

After Kris's most recent failure to be elsewhere when a bomb went off . . . made more insulting by the fact the bomb hadn't actually been aimed at her . . . Grampa Ray, King Raymond I to most everyone else, had seen to it that the crew of the *Wasp* got seriously larger.

Jack's Marine company had been reinforced up to two hundred purposeful trigger pullers. In addition to them, an MP platoon had been added with a plethora of technicians very skilled at investigating crime scenes . . . and in helping Chief Beni identify scenes well before they had a chance to become crime scenes.

The crew of sailors had more than doubled, this time with real live sailors who wore white hats and saluted officers . . . not the contract types that Admiral Crossenshield, the head of Wardhaven's black ops, had fitted out the *Wasp* with initially. Since one of the new ship departments was a medical division fit for a battleship, Kris really had no complaint.

During all of this, Professor mFumbo's boffins had gone about their business, using the *Wasp*'s various meanderings to do their research . . . whatever that was. Occasionally, Kris got invited to dinner in boffin country. There they would regale her with their stories of discovery and observation.

Rarely did Kris understand a word, but the boffins did set a magnificent table.

However, because of that research, the *Wasp* was a veritable pincushion, sprouting antennas and receiver dishes that no other self-respecting scout ship had. At the moment, they were rising from where they often hid when the *Wasp* masqueraded as a simple merchant ship. Today, the boffins would apply all that extra weight that Captain Drago was wont to complain about to a problem that had a real-time application.

"Give me an hour," Professor mFumbo had told Kris.

An hour later, he was back with two associates in tow. One was as tall and thin as the other was short and round, and they didn't bother to find a seat but floated in zero gee at Kris's elbow, apparently quite comfortable to hang there.

"We have some good news," the tall one started. "And some bad news," the short one finished.

"Tell me about the good news," Kris said.

"We were able to identify an exhaust trail of a freighter in the system," Short said. "Unfortunately, our instrumentation was good enough to identify two exhaust trails," the taller one added.

"Two trails," Kris echoed,

"Two trails," one said. "Going to two different jump points," the other finished.

Since they hadn't bothered to give themselves names, Kris

was tempted to christen them Tweedle Dee and Tweedle Dum. Assuming she could keep straight which one she named Dee from the one she named Dum.

"So," she said slowly, "one freighter entered this system. We know when it did and we know it wasn't here when we arrived here. How do the two trails fit our time frame?"

"Very well," they both said. "The Beta Point is the farthest from our location. Its thicker trail fits that of a medium-size freighter traveling at 1.25 gees and exiting the system well before we arrived," said Shorty. "While the thinner trail would fit the same ship making .89 gees to the closer jump and passing through it just before we got here," finished the thin one.

"That really doesn't help us," Jack said.

"Well, I'm *sorry* about *that*," the thin one snipped. "I'll have you know that no other particle observatory would have spotted either one of those trails," the round one finished.

"Thank you. Thank you," Professor mFumbo said, ushering his prima donnas out before any more feathers could be ruffled.

Kris let out an exasperated sigh. "Nelly, would you get Captain Drago for me, please."

"I've been listening," the captain said on net. "Nelly warned me that I might want to hear something and save you from having to listen to it twice."

"Thank you for saving our ears from that horrible fate," Abby said dryly.

"Can you add anything to this, Captain?" Kris asked. "Do your space legs, or the hairs on the back of your neck, or maybe your feminine intuition tell you something that the best scientific minds in human space couldn't." Kris did not mean that sarcastically. She didn't doubt that the *Wasp* carried the best smarts money could hire. It was just that today, she really needed answers, and those smarts had not given her anything to go on. At least anything she dared to go on.

And Kris had dared a lot.

"Sorry to be of so little use," the captain said, "but I'm just as stumped as they are. The momma that raised these pirates and slavers didn't raise any dumb kids."

"Don't you just hate it when that happens," Abby added.

"So, we've got two doors, both with trails leading us up to them. Behind one is a pirate lair, or at least the trail to one. Behind the other is . . . what?"

"Likely nothing," Jack said.

"I wouldn't be all that sure of that," Commander Fervenspiel broke his long silence. "This system has been ripped up and taped back together. We can't even be sure that the jumps we're looking at are the ones the Three put here. In the few spare seconds I had before I grabbed my hat and raced to catch your fast-departing *Wasp*, I did glance at what we knew of this system.

"I didn't raise the question when your very competent computer did the briefing on the system, but our charts from the time of the Three show that there were two jumps in each of the two solar systems. Now there are only three in the system they share. Something happened to the missing one.

"Now maybe it got swallowed up by one of the stars, or maybe it got hurled out into deepest space. I don't know. But we also shouldn't assume we know anything about where these jumps now go. It may never have happened before. At least not to any ship that was able to report back to us, but these jumps could lead you right into the heart of a star or something even worse."

LIKE THE BIG UGLY THAT ATE THE ITEECHE SCOUTS, Nelly whispered softly in Kris's skull.

"Are you always this cheerful?" Abby asked.

The commander made a shallow bow to the maid from where he sat. "I assure you, Lieutenant, this is one of my better days."

Since Abby was still wearing the colorful skirt and off-the-shoulder top that she'd worn dirtside this morning, the commander was tipping his hand that he'd had, as he raced for the *Wasp*, taken time not only to glance at a map but also to see what Greenfeld intel had on the people he'd be dealing with.

"Can't a girl keep any secrets," Abby sniffed, pulling up her top to restrict the view to a more matronly amount of skin.

"Folks, I got a ship here," Captain Drago said, "that's just drifting in space. From the way the air circulation has kicked into higher gear, I suspect a lot of the crew doesn't yet have their space legs, and more of our fine lunch is being wasted. Could we have a decision here?"

"What's the closest jump point?" Kris asked.

"Alpha," the captain answered. "The one with the thin trail that seems to mean that our bogey just managed to get out of here ahead of us. It wouldn't have if I hadn't slowed the *Wasp* down. I'm not sure that means anything."

"Anyone who read any kind of file on you, Princess," Commander Fervenspiel said, "would know that Captain Drago was hired to add a bit of caution to your inclination to go headlong into your next challenge."

"Damn, so you guys have a file on me, too," Captain Drago said. "That will teach a shy, retiring soul like me to get too close to one of those damn Longknifes."

The Greenfeld commander struggled to swallow a bad case of the guffaws and succeeded.

Kris shrugged. "Let's say there's an equal chance that the ship headed for either jump. You say Alpha is closest."

"Yes," said the captain.

"So we could head over to Alpha, and if it was the wrong one, we'd have a quicker trip to Beta."

"Yes, Your Highness, but you should realize, this jump and the two others really form an equidistant triangle. There's really not that much to choose from."

"So I'll choose, and let the consequences be on my head. Go for Alpha." Heavens knew, Kris had made enough decisions and suffered through the consequences. It really didn't seem to matter whether she made the right decision or the wrong one, the consequences were just as often lousy as they were good.

"Would you mind turning down the lights?" Kris asked her crew. "If I'm going to suffer the consequences of whatever I just decided, I'd rather do it after a nap. Wake-up call was way too early this morning."

"We'll all be back here thirty minutes before we get to Jump Point Alpha," Jack assured her.

"You do that."

Kris was none too sure she could actually sleep. She kept seeing Cara in the hands of people who seriously didn't deserve to have their hands on a little kid. Still, there was little Kris could do about that just now, and she didn't want to have everyone fussing over her while they all waited out whatever would happen next.

To Kris's surprise, she did fall asleep.

Cara didn't know whether to be glad or scared when the elevator door in the central spindle swung open, and a barefoot sailor pushed two buckets out along with a small crate. He looked around the room, then put on an ugly smile and headed for Cara and the young sailor cuffed with her.

"You two won't cause me any trouble," he said smiling through missing or yellowed teeth. He stank like no one Cara had ever met, even in Five Corners.

Anyone smelling that bad, the gangs would have thrown in the open sewer.

The sailor pointed something at Cara's cuff and it clinked open. Then he did the same to the one on the young woman.

"You two," the sailor ordered. "There's water in those buckets. See that everyone gets a cup. One cup. No more. No less. Don't you get too close to any of these big guys, you see. If they get their hands on you, don't expect me to risk my neck saving yours."

He turned to take in the rest of the room. "You got two buckets of water. You spill them, you go thirsty. Be nice to these girls. I plan to," he said with an ugly chuckle.

"Hand around the water. Then see that everyone gets one ration bar. One and only one, you hear."

Cara nodded. So did the woman.

"You be nice to me," the sailor said, leering at the woman, "and I could arrange a nice meal for you."

"If I get my hands on you," began the sailor who had been holding the girl.

"But you can't, and you won't, so shut up," the sailor spat.

"What do we do about the bathroom?" Cara asked.

"You got a bucket, don't you?"

"But it's got water in it," Cara said.

"Now it does. Give everybody a drink, and it won't."

"But here, with everyone looking," Cara said, incredulously.

"I don't see a problem, little girl. Where you're going, you'll do a lot of stuff out with everyone looking . . . and you'll be glad to do it. If you ain't, you'll be real sad," he said, and turned back to the elevator.

Cara waited until the elevator had closed on him. Then she turned to the free woman. "You start with your boyfriend," she said. "I'll go the other way."

Cara hated the pirate. Hated him and everything he said. Still, she was careful with the water. She stood well out of reach, making both the men and woman stretch out the chains on their cuffs before she put the full water cup in reach.

Some of the people said kind words to her, showed they understood her fear and caution. A few of the men and even two women cussed her out and threw the empty cup at her when she refused to refill it for them.

Cara said only kind words for all, but in her mind she was remembering some of the lessons she'd learned in Five Corners, lessons that had surprised even Uncle Bruce. She was also remembering the moves that he'd shown her. Moves that built on and refined the ones she'd learned on the streets.

She could use them if she had to.

She knew how to kill if she had no other choice.

Still, she hoped Uncle Bruce and Captain Jack and the rest of his Marines would come before anything really bad happened. She'd seen the shadows in Auntie Kris's eyes when people talked of some of the things she'd done.

People died at the princess's orders.

Cara was pretty sure she could kill if she had to. That didn't mean she wanted to.

"Hurry up, Aunt Abby. Hurry up."

30

Kris woke well before Jack came to wake her. She'd read a story about what happened before Grampa Trouble and Gramma Ruth were married. They'd been captured by slavers.

Twice.

Gramma Ruth said she never claimed her husband was smart. She did say she'd trust him with her life. Apparently, among those scumbags, Grampa Trouble had earned Gramma's respect.

Anyway, Kris had read the story when she was a kid. It had sounded exciting and romantic. Later, in college, she'd come across a mature-rated media version of the same experience. She'd watched half of it before she turned it off. Maybe her great-grandparents had gone through something like that. Still, watching people you shared flesh and blood with suffer through brutal captivity . . .

It wasn't something Kris Longknife wanted to watch.

It also wasn't something she wanted a twelve-year-old girl to live through.

Better to stay awake and not dream.

"Stand by for zero gravity," the M1C announced to all hands.

"We going to send through a jump buoy first?" Kris asked the bridge watch.

"Yes," Captain Drago answered. "But one that squawks very weakly that a ship will be coming through in a minute. Any ship nearby will get our message. No need to blast it all over the system."

It had only happened once, that two ships had tried to share the same jump point at the same time. Once had been enough. Within the realm of human space, a network of buoys marked each jump. Before any ship jumped, a buoy went through to announce it was coming. As a scout ship, the *Wasp* carried a load of buoys to expand that network.

A small object launched out from the *Wasp*. Without slowing down, it boosted straight for the small bit of twisted and twisting space that was the jump point. Without halting, it went right through.

"Now we wait sixty seconds," Captain Drago announced.

On the wall of Kris's Tac Center, Nelly opened a small window with a countdown clock. Sixty seconds went quickly.

As did another sixty seconds.

And another.

"I don't think that puppy's coming home to momma," Abby observed, as the timer hit +154 seconds.

"Ah, Captain, what's Plan B?" Kris asked.

"I was kind of counting on you and your brain trust to come up with one for us," the captain drawled.

"We'll get back to you in a minute," Kris said. "Or maybe ten." She looked around the table and met blank stares. "Or an hour," she said, and broke the connection.

"Okay, crew," Kris said, "why would a jump buoy not come back?"

"Maybe someone on the other side of the jump was waiting for it and shot it to bits," Jack said.

Kris nodded. That was her first guess. One she suspected that some big ugly was doing to Iteeche scouts. "I don't recall anything like that being tried during the war," Kris added.

"No one was all that interested," Commander Fervenspiel said. He raised his hand with all fingers and thumb showing. "First, you have to float around a jump point, spending all your time in zero gee," he said, pulling in his thumb. "Second, you have to worry just a little bit about what would happen if the jump point suddenly decided that' where it wanted to be was where you are." He pulled in his pointer at that and made a fist. "Between those two, you don't need any more.

It's a tactic that sounds brilliant to a lubber. Not so brilliant to the sailor who has to do it. Better to fight it out orbiting some planet once you've got a bit of notice."

Kris nodded. So did Jack. "One ship standing blockade suddenly facing a couple of dozen coming through. Not such a good idea."

"But we do have this missing buoy," Abby pointed out. "Did somebody give it a better option and take it out for a beer?"

Chief Beni looked like he'd be glad if someone offered him a beer. "Should we spin off a nanoscout and send it through?"

A few months earlier, Kris had gotten just such a request from an Iteeche friend. She'd passed on it. If there was something big and mean on the other side of the jump, she didn't want to make it a present of humanity's best tech before we had any idea what we faced.

In theory, the jump in front of them was several thousand light-years away from where the Iteeche were losing scouts. One would think they were not connected. However, never having been a galactic overlord bent on conquering the universe, Kris wasn't yet ready to conclude she knew exactly where the bad guy's realm was and wasn't.

"Good idea, Chief," Kris said, "but let's hold that one in reserve for the time being."

"What's that leave us?" Abby asked.

"I hate to open my mouth," Professor mFumbo said, clearly reluctant. This was a totally new aspect of his personality and one that Kris had never seen before. "However, Tweedle Dee and Tweedle Dum do have some expert thoughts on just this problem."

"Tweedle Dee and Dum?" Kris echoed, not willing to admit that she had given them the same names but not surprised that someone else had.

"You know, the two particle physicists I introduced you to earlier. We call them Tweedle Dee and Tweedle Dum, but never to their faces, I assure you. No question they are strange, but also no question they are brilliant."

"And if we talked to them," Kris said, "what would they tell us?"

"It's better that I let them tell you themselves."

"God help us," Abby remarked.

"Really it is," the professor said. "May I call them?"

"Do so," Kris said. "I'm dying with curiosity."

A few minutes later, the two drifted in, righted themselves, and began.

"How big," one began, "is a jump point?" the other ended.

"Look at your own ship, the *Wasp* . . . When we came aboard it, the ship was much thinner . . . but you added several layers of containers . . . and the ship grew wider.

"Yet every time it entered a jump point . . . no matter what its beam . . . the jump point takes it in."

The two of them paused to examine the reception their dissertation was getting. Kris saw round eyes, glazed over, staring back at them. Her own eyes probably weren't any better.

Undaunted, they continued.

"The same goes for the length of ships . . . Take a battleship. It enters the jump point . . . and it exits the jump point . . . At no time is the ship half-in . . . or half-out . . . No matter how long a ship is . . . one has never had its bow sticking out of one jump point . . . and its stern still entering from the other side."

Kris eyed Jack, who was eyeing her right back. "They've got a point," she whispered. He nodded agreement.

The two scientists beamed.

"We call them jump points . . . and a point is supposed to have zero dimensions, just coordinates . . . but our jump points do a very poor job of staying at their coordinates . . . and swallow ships with much larger than zero dimensions.

"More interesting . . . is their attitude toward . . . the ships . . . A ship is either in the point . . . or out of it . . . in this system . . . in the point . . . and then in the next system . . . Never two . . . only one.

"Before the point . . . in the point . . . through the point . . . no matter how large . . . or long."

"So," Kris said thoughtfully, "if we were to attempt to push a fiber-optic cable with a camera on it through a jump point . . ."

"That experiment . . . was actually attempted . . . in the early days of space travel."

"I never heard of it," Jack said.

"You aren't . . . a physicist . . . and since it failed . . . we don't like to talk . . . about it."

"What happened?" Kris asked.

"The experimenting ship . . . pushed a fiber-optic camera cable toward . . . the jump point . . . The cable never . . . went through the jump . . . It just kind of . . . bent itself . . . around the jump point . . . and ended up showing . . . the space on the . . . other side of the jump . . . in the same system."

"No jump," they said together.

"So are you again telling me that you have a very interesting bit of science, but you can't help me a damn bit with my problem today," Princesses were not supposed to talk like that. Whoever made that rule had never had a day like Kris was having.

And they'd never listened to these two.

"We might be able to do something," they both said

"What?"

"We've been wondering . . . if Smart Metal™ . . . might allow us to . . . outsmart the jump points.

"We've never had . . . access to any Smart Metal™ . . . but we wonder . . . if we made a single-molecule camera . . . attached it to a different type of Smart Metal™ . . . optimized to carry the signal . . . a kind of wire . . . and had a single- . . . molecule receiver at this end.

"Maybe that would trick . . . the jump point . . . into seeing the first molecule . . . as a separate unit . . . the wire as also separate . . . and the last molecule the same.

"One would be . . . on the other side . . . the wire in the point . . . and the transmitter here."

"Give these folks some Smart Metal™ and get the best minds on programming Smart Metal™ working with them," Kris ordered.

Smart Metal™ was an invention of Grampa Al's Nuu Enterprises. It allowed naval starships to be large with comfortable private quarters one day and shrink down into a small, heavily armored man-of-war the next. Kris had once seen a spaceship converted into an air vehicle and landed on a planet . . . and had a miserable time getting everything back in order on the spaceship. The material was programmable, but programming it just right was often the problem.

Oh, and it had almost killed Kris on at least one occasion. Several times if you counted the sudden-onset, engineering casualty problems that the initial class of Smart Metal™ ships were prone to.

Kris was glad the problem of producing a Smart Metal™ probe for the jump point before them was someone else's problem.

Two hours later, a tiny object jetted away from the *Wasp*. It paused just short of the jump point and appeared to do nothing.

The screen on the wall of Kris's Tac Center changed to show a black-and-white picture of wavering space.

"The bandwidth . . . between the camera . . . and the transmitter . . . is very narrow."

"Sorry about that," both the scientists said together.

"Now let's see . . . what we get."

The picture didn't show much change for a few seconds. Then suddenly the roiling view of twinkling stars disappeared. In its place was . . . not much of anything.

"I always wondered . . . what null space . . . looked like."

"Null space?" Kris said.

Professor mFumbo, who had joined them again only moments before the probe was launched, smiled from ear to ear. "They are the first to get a picture of it. They can name it what they bloody well choose."

Kris was not about to dispute that right.

"Ready to go . . . the rest of . . . the way?" the boffins asked no one in particular.

Apparently they were asking each other, something that struck Kris as amazing if they actually needed to. With no further words, the picture changed.

Changed and vanished so quickly that if you'd blinked, you never would have known a different picture had been there.

"Nelly, get that picture back."

"I'm already working on it," Nelly snapped.

"What the hell is that?" Jack said, as a snapshot appeared on the screen. Wispy tendrils in different shades of gray formed all sorts of patterns that said very little to Kris.

"Have you ever seen the inside of a fusion reactor?" Professor mFumbo asked.

"Can't say that I have," Jack said.

"The inside of a sun, then?"

"Never even wanted to," Kris said.

"I'll wait for others to weigh in with their ideas," the professor said, "but I think we ought to search the sky for a nova. I will bet you ten Wardhaven dollars that this jump will take you right into the heart of that nova."

Kris leaned back into her high gee chair, hardly necessary since the ship was in zero gravity. "You think someone knew that was waiting on the other side?"

"I doubt if anyone knew what was through that jump," Commander Fervenspiel said. "I will bet you that they knew that nothing that went in there ever came out. Cunning, these scumbags."

"Captain Drago, make best speed for Jump Point Beta."

"I don't know what that is," Captain Drago said, "but I am one happy man that we did not go charging in there."

"I think I've learned a good lesson. Look before I leap," Kris said.

"Good lesson," Jack said aloud. "Very good lesson," To just Kris he added, YOU THINK THAT MAY BE WHAT IS EATING THE ITEECHE SCOUTS?

"Can we find the nova this jump leads to?" Kris asked aloud. To Jack she added, I HAVE NO IDEA. YOU REALLY WANT TO BET HUMANITY'S FUTURE THAT THE PROBLEM IS AS SIMPLE AS THAT?

Jack offered only a shrug for a reply.

Professor mFumbo and Commander Fervenspiel pushed off from their chairs to drift in front of the star map on the wall. As the *Wasp* slowly put on acceleration, they settled to the floor, their fingers roving from star to star.

"Nelly, please highlight the star this jump point is supposed to go to."

"Kris, I don't know which star it goes toward. I know where the star *was* that it went to." A dot began flashing on the map, about equal distance between three different stars.

"None of them look like novas," Kris said.

"They're fifty to a hundred light-years from here," the commander pointed out. "One of the problems with instantaneous transportation is that what you look at may be quite a few years out of date from what you leap to."

"At least two of these suns are very old," Professor mFumbo noted.

Kris nodded at them. To Jack and Nelly, she thought, I THINK I'VE DISCOVERED HOW TO GET A PEEK AT WHATEVER IS BEHIND THOSE KILLER JUMPS THE ITEECHE HAVE FOUND. NELLY, GET A COPY OF THE DESIGN FOR THOSE PROBES. GET SEVERAL COPIES AND SAVE THEM IN A WHOLE LOT OF PLACES.

I AM ALREADY DOING IT, KRIS.

31

Twelve hours later the *Wasp* coasted to a halt before Jump Point Beta.

"Captain Drago, launch a probe with a full-spectrum reconnaissance suite. No need for it to whisper a word about us," Kris ordered.

"Probe away," came from the captain only seconds later.

Kris had considered several options for this probe, including seeing if they could get more bandwidth for a wire to peek though the jump point. Some very smart people were now working on solutions to those problems. "Working on" them was the operative phrase.

Today, Kris would do things the old-fashioned way.

The probe was gone for ten long minutes. A second one stood by immediately to take its place on the other side the moment it slipped back and began a download to the *Wasp*. For the next six hours, the two probes rotated stations, one downloading what it observed while the other continued the observations.

There was a warm yellow sun on the other side. A beautiful blue-green world orbited it in the life zone. Blue oceans showed plenty of water. The planet shimmered with a thin sheen of atmosphere. It would take the boffins a half hour to confirm what Kris knew at first glance.

This planet was as lovely to the human eye as Mother Earth ever had been.

In orbit around the planet was a rudely-knocked-together space station that held three ships, one of which matched the electronic profile of the *Cushion Star*. During the first three hours of observation, two shuttles fell away from the station and headed for the same lake dirtside.

On a bay of that lake was a medium-size town with an agrarian hinterland far too large for its own needs. Examination easily identified that the crops growing over about half the land were those usually needed to feed a growing population: grains, fruits, vegetables. What was growing on the other half of the land's ground cover didn't match anything known in the farming database.

"Do we have a spectrum fingerprint on the latest new drug turning up on the older worlds?" Kris asked.

Abby shook her head. "No. But I suspect we do now."

The radio frequencies were active . . . but hash to the listening probes. "Every word on the bands is encrypted," Chief Beni reported. "I've got Da Vinci working on cracking the cipher, but if it's a daily throwaway, and they've already sent the key, I don't think we're going to crack it today."

"And I thought I was paranoid," Kris said. "Jack, Commander, do you see any defenses?"

"Nothing visible," both said, then Commander Fervenspiel went on.

"There's no reason they should be active. As for the station, since it's not a standard model, there's no telling what defenses it has."

"But it likely does have defenses," Jack added.

"Any way we can find them out?"

"Attack them," the commander suggested.

"I'd hoped to have something better to tell your admiral before he has to do that."

The commander shrugged. "I can't see anything on that station standing up to a Fury-class battleship. I doubt anybody on the ground there has the weapons to stand against a brigade of our Marines."

Brute force did seem to be the Greenfeld solution to most problems. Having been on the receiving end of that approach once or three, Kris knew someone could throw a spanner into it.

Not easily.

Not cheaply.

Still, she'd been the one tossing monkey wrenches a time or three.

The commander seemed to follow where Kris's thoughts were taking her. "Not everyone has a Longknife to help them thwart overwhelming Greenfeld power."

"Let's hope so," Kris said. "Let me know when you think you have as much data as we're likely to get from this reconnaissance."

"I think we have," the commander said.

Kris considered what that meant. They had all the available information on the target that held Cara. And there was no way Kris was comfortable about launching an attack based on the smattering of intelligence they had.

With a sigh, Kris ordered, "Captain, the next time our scout comes back, pack it in and let's head back to St. Pete."

Fifteen minutes later, the *Wasp* was accelerating at 1.5 gees. NELLY, THERE'S SOMETHING I WANT YOU TO LOOK UP. I REMEMBER READING ABOUT IT WHEN I WAS A KID. I HAVEN'T RUN ACROSS IT SINCE. NOT THAT I'D REALLY WANT TO. Kris told her computer what to look for. It took Nelly several hours to find the reference. It was in the personal library of one of the boffins.

Kris listened to what Nelly had found and nodded. THAT WAS ABOUT WHAT I REMEMBERED. Kris tucked it away for the coming meeting with Admiral Krätz.

As the *Wasp* approached High St. Petersburg, there were a number of new merchant ships tied up together. When Captain Drago sent a low-order query at them, their responders were hardly civilian: *Hornet, Dauntless, Fearless, Intrepid.*

Here, for the first time, were all the ships of Kris's Patrol Squadron 10, all except the *Surprise*, which was still probably lugging survival rations to Kaskatos, an unending and thankless task.

There was also one other ship, a small schooner not unlike two of the ships Kris had just identified tied up to the pirates' station. Its transponder was very illegally off.

"Captain Drago, please send to PatRon 10. I will have a

meeting of all COs, XOs, and senior Marine officers in the *Wasp*'s wardroom ten minutes after we dock. Send an information copy to Admiral Krätz with my regards and compliments. I will meet with him at his pleasure if he cannot make my staff meeting."

Then she turned to Commander Fervenspiel. "I will understand if you wish to depart as soon as the gangway is down. I will have you provided with a copy of all the take we got from our probe."

"I already have orders to stay. My admiral will be here shortly and receive the data take from your own hands, Your Highness."

Kris raised an eyebrow at the honor.

The commander made a small bow. "If I am to have a grand duchess on my ship, I see no reason not to start practicing now."

Commander Phil Taussig of the *Hornet* was first to board the *Wasp* after she tied up to her usual place between Admiral Krätz's flagship the *Fury* and her sister ship the *Terror*.

No sooner had he rendered honors than he stood aside. "I was just passing Kaskatos when I got your 'all come' message. Knowing you Longknifes, I figured it translated as 'Hey, Rube, I got a fight brewing,' so I brought along your two old friends."

Following along right behind Taussig's XO and a Marine platoon lieutenant were Lieutenant Penny Lien Pasley and Colonel Cortez.

Kris had left them on Kaskatos, hoping they'd get themselves a life there and become so involved that they'd forget they'd ever been close to one of those damn Longknifes. Especially one who was hankering to go out and find what or who was making scout ships vanish.

"Like a bad penny, I'm back," Penny said, not realizing how true that was.

Kris, for her part, found that she'd never been so glad to see two faces in her life.

"We got plenty of work for you," Kris said, and passed them through to make room for Jack Campbell and the key members of his team. By the time all her command teams were aboard, the admiral was still nowhere in sight.

"Commander Fervenspiel, you want to wait here for your elephants?"

He failed to suppress his grin at Kris's familiarity with his lofty superiors, so he covered it with a hand. "My orders are to listen to every word you say," he said, with as pleasant a smile as such a declaration of so little trust allowed.

"Sergeant Bruce."

"Ma'am," the Marine said, snapping to attention.

"When Admiral Krätz and his team arrive, show them to the wardroom."

"Yes, ma'am," he answered, leaving Kris to lead the Green-feld commander there herself.

And get the surprise of her life.

The room snapped to attention for her. Every last one of them, even Colonel Cortez, whose status as her prisoner of war and employee made his rendering of honors something special to her, if rather ambiguous.

"As you were." Kris remembered it was now her duty to say that and watched as the room relaxed.

The tables had been arranged in one long table down the center. The left-hand side was vacant, awaiting the Greenfeld admiral. The right-hand side had the captains and command structure of her squadron. There were chairs along the wall for staff and others. Captain Drago, for now formally decked out in his official Merchant Marine captain's uniform, had taken over the foot of the table for the officers of his contractor crew.

Someday, Kris would have to straighten out the chain of command on her ship. Someday, but not today. So far it had worked to the satisfaction of all involved . . . and some people very far up the chain of command who weren't involved but kept their noses in her business.

Thank you very much, Grampa Ray, she thought.

"We have a problem," was what she said.

"So what else is new," came from somewhere down the table.

"That you, Phil Taussig?" Kris said. "Last time we served

together, you were so uptight about the proper Navy way that I'd never expect something so not shipshape from you."

"This is my second cruise with a Longknife. Maybe I'm less worried about getting struck by lightning."

"We'll see. Nelly, first slide," Kris said, and turned to face a lovely picture of the pirate planet.

"So that's what Dry Tortugas looks like," Lieutenant Commander Jack Campbell said.

"Dry Tortugas?" Kris said.

"Yeah, that's what the pirates are calling the place."

"Excuse me," Nelly put in, "but wasn't it the Isle of Tortuga that was the pirate haunt back on old Earth in the Caribbean Sea during the 1600s."

"I'd trust you more than I trusted the knuckleheaded pirates we captured," Jack Campbell said, "but the crew of the *Bucket of Blood* and its computer agreed their home port was Dry Tortugas."

"*Bucket of Blood*?" Kris once again found herself echoing.

"Somebody's seen too many pirate vids," Jack observed.

"Way too many," Campbell agreed.

"How do you know so much about all this?" Kris asked. "The only time I captured a pirate I had to shoot its bridge full of holes and kill most of the command crew."

"While we invited them aboard, right kindly-like," Campbell said through a poorly swallowed laugh. "We were convoying two merchant ships around the Sooner planets when we found this new ship waiting for us at a jump point, the schooner you see parked next to the *Dauntless*. It sidled up to us right friendly-like and casually announced it was a pirate and we were all its booty. The two merchies pulled up their skirts and started running. We kind of went putt-putt and yelled our engines were not cooperating. So the pirates concentrated on us and came on board. We had ourselves this little 'panic party' waiting for them. Several of the Marines and sailors dressed up like ladies and ran around the ship shrieking for help."

Kris glanced at his XO, Lieutenant Amber Kitano. The female junior officer only shook her head. "Yes, we have plenty of *real* women aboard the *Dauntless*, but no way would we play damsel in distress like our dear captain wanted."

"We needed someone to look and sound terrified," said her CO.

"Not in my Navy this woman won't," said his XO.

"Anyway, we had a lot of people," Commander Campbell went on, "running around shrieking and screaming. The pirates were swinging cutlasses and being oh so very bold and bad."

"Right up to the moment when we started filling their big butts full of sleepy darts," Amber drawled dryly.

"The pirate captain was oh so offended that we'd brought guns to his knife fight," Commander Campbell said, grinning from ear to ear. "Those were the last words he said to me as he laid his head down and went to sleep."

"What about the stay-behind crew on his ship?" Kris asked. "Didn't they try to destroy the computer?"

"Oh no," the commander said, waving his hand limply at Kris. "Boarding a helpless merchant ship looked like so much fun that nobody, just nobody, wanted to be left behind. They did leave a cabin boy and girl behind, in charge of the whole ship, they were. And very busy doing what teen boys and girls tend to do when left alone with no adult supervision. Both were very upset when we interrupted them."

"Anyway," Amber went on, "we got the *Bucket of Blood* with only a couple of sleepy darts fired and not so much as a data file erased."

"So while the princess here was chasing one pirate to its base," Admiral Krätz said, entering the wardroom, "you were capturing a pirate and finding out the location of its base."

Now it was Kris's turn to announce "Atten'hut," and the admiral quickly waved them down with an "As you were," before half could get out of their chairs.

The admiral had brought a sizable team of his own. Several Navy officers, Marine officers, and one additional lieutenant whom he took a moment to introduce. "May I formally present to you the heir apparent and daughter of my Imperial Majesty, the Grand Duchess Victoria."

"So your father took the plunge into full Imperial mode," Kris observed.

"Once your great-grampa Ray was officially recognized as King of the United Sentient Federation, Daddy could hardly wait." Vicky sighed.

"You got quite a title," Kris said.

"I can't tell you how underwhelmed I am at the moment," Vicky said. "So, getting back to business, is the *Bucket of Blood* home ported at the same place as this planet Kris followed our fleeing slaver to?"

"The coordinates appear to be the same," Captain Drago put in.

"Commander Campbell, did you get any information about planetary defenses from the *Bucket*?" Jack asked.

Jack the corvette skipper was shaking his head before Jack the Marine captain finished asking the question. "It looks to me like they pretty well compartmentalized everything. The crew of the *Bucket* are singing to save their lives. We've hacked into all their codes. We've read them all. No joy as far as information about station or planetary defenses."

"Maybe they don't have any," Commander Fervenspiel said from where he now sat among a sea of Greenfeld green and black.

Kris glanced around the room, taking the measure of body language. Among the Greenfelds, there was optimism that they'd found another cheap conquest. Among the Royal United Sentient sailors and Marines, there was a lot less enthusiasm.

Kris decided to take the bull by the horns.

"Admiral Krätz, I understand from Commander Fervenspiel that standard Greenfeld doctrine, in a situation like this, would be to get all four battleships boosting for Dry Tortugas at 1.5 gees and arrive with all guns blazing, dropping a strong Marine and landing force to ask a few questions, then write the after-action report pretty much the way you'd drafted it beforehand. Did I get anything wrong, there?"

"I might modify the after-action report a bit if it really didn't reflect certain critical aspects that came up in the actual fight," the admiral admitted.

"Like my brother getting himself killed very much not according to plan," Vicky added with venom.

"That would cause a major revision," the admiral agreed.

"I'm concerned with that approach," Kris said.

"Anything specific," Vicky asked, "or do you Longknifes just like to make a hash of Greenfeld doctrine on general principle?"

That question left Kris wondering if she was creating more than she bargained for by having this combined preaction briefing. Throwing caution to the winds, Kris opened the can of worms that disturbed her the most.

"Many years ago, I did a little reading up on slavery in early Earth history. I found something that really turned my stomach. It seems that several countries outlawed slavery or outlawed the importation of slaves ahead of others. What that meant was that British warships were prowling the waters off Africa looking for contraband while there was quite a bit of profit to be made by anyone who slipped a load of slaves across the Atlantic and sold them."

"So," said the admiral.

"The British viewed slavers as no better than pirates and were wont to hang them."

"That would make it rather unpleasant to be caught with a cargo of slaves," Abby said.

"I know this is going somewhere, but I can't see it," Vicky snapped.

"The slaves were kept chained belowdecks," Kris went on. "After all, you couldn't let the slaves run around, they might take over the ship."

The admiral raised an eyebrow in agreement to that.

"So," Kris went on, "if a British patrol ship gave chase to the slaver, it was rather easy to attach the slaves' chains to an anchor, and toss the anchor overboard. A bit of noise, a bit of screaming, but in a few minutes, there was no evidence left aboard that the ship had ever carried slaves."

That left the room silent, both the Imperial and Royal sides.

Vicky swallowed hard. "You want to paint a clear picture for those of us without your imagination."

"It will take the *Fury* and its squadron at least twelve hours to blast in from the jump point to the station. We can assume you'll need some time to pacify it and start jumping your Marines into the town."

"Port Royal," Commander Campbell provided. "They're calling that Port Royal."

"At least they got that right," Nelly sniffed.

Kris went on, her voice low and deadly. "During that time, I'm figuring the slavers are dividing their holdings into two groups: those they can terrify into silence and those they can't."

"And those they can't?" the admiral asked.

"They line up in rows and shoot. They do that in full view of the others. They make it clear that Greenfeld's sailors and Marines will be here for a while. Then they will leave. The slavers, however, will be there long after you guys are called off to other duties."

"And the slavers?" Vicky asked.

"No society is ever totally slave. There are the owners, the technicians, doctors, businesspeople. Oh, and the overseers and enforcers. Given twelve to fifteen hours, Abby here could generate papers to make even the worst of crooks look as perfectly documented as innocent newborns. Right, Abby?"

"You want the Magna Carta, I'll give you the Magna Carta. You want record books that show that every person on your farm has been paid every month, twice a month, for the last ten years." Abby chuckled evilly. "That's even easier. Don't need no lead seals for them."

"One more thing I'd like to point out," said Abby. "They'll be shooting the potential troublemakers to scare the living bejesus out of the rest. Which category do you think my darling niece will fit into? Kris, can you even conceive of my flesh and blood not being a pain in the ass of any piece of pirate shit?"

That left the room very quiet.

"So," the admiral finally said, "I take it that you have an idea of how we might take down the pirates without giving them any time to cut throats and clean house."

"I think I do, ladies and gentlemen. Yes, I think I do," Kris said.

32

Four days later, the *Wasp* docilely followed the *Bucket of Blood* as it made its final approach to High Dry Tortugas. The *Dauntless* followed along in her wake. Officially, the *Bucket* was loading in the captured merchant ships *Mary Ellen Carter* and *Pink Lucky Seven*. Those were the names of the ships Kris's corvettes were squawking, and those were the captures that the skipper of the *Bucket* was bragging about.

With as many guns aimed at his head as could be arranged.

Kris was not surprised that the pirate captain was reading his lines with gusto. Colonel Cortez and Jack Campbell were both on the *Bucket*, along with Penny.

Kris had Captain Jack the Marine and Abby with her on the *Wasp*. All three ships now held a company of Royal Marines and near to a battalion of Imperial ones. Campbell commanded the *Bucket*, leaving Amber command of the *Dauntless*.

Admiral Krätz had agreed to let the ship's captain be in tactical command, under Kris. This despite the fact the Imperial Marine battalions were commanded by lieutenant colonels who outranked the Royal Navy skipper. In Kris's own case, she had Commander Fervenspiel back aboard the *Wasp*.

To say the chain of command looped off in all directions was to put it far too simply.

Still, one admiral and one princess easily agreed on what they wanted. A certain grand duchess didn't get what she wanted. Presently, she waited for things to start happening while fuming beside her admiral on the *Fury* on the other side of the jump.

From the *Bucket*'s records, they'd found out the time of day on High Dry Tortugas and had delayed their entry into the system so that they docked just about 2200 hours local time. As expected, there were no port officials interested in doing the usual tax, customs, and disease control at that late hour.

Kris had hoped the pirates were as lackadaisical about those things as they were about most other work.

From the evidence, they certainly were.

There still were a pair of pirate schooners and the freighter of many names tied up at the station's piers. People from their crews carried on a running conversation with the *Bucket*'s skipper during the approach. Apparently, no ship had yet taken two ships in one cruise. None of the three ships dockside had ever succeeded in capturing a single merchant ship. Curious, they wanted to know how he'd done it.

The captured pirate skipper was only too happy to boast of his prowess at scaring the crew of the *Pink Lucky Seven* into terrified and abject surrender.

He just never got to the part where sleepy darts started sprouting in pirate rumps.

Then he told basically the same story again for the *Mary Ellen Carter*. The pirates couldn't get enough of the part where the woman crew members started screaming and running up and down in panic.

To Kris's relief, Lieutenant Amber Kitano kept her opinion to herself as she went about her duties commanding the *Dauntless*. It must not have been easy.

It sure wasn't easy for Kris to listen to, and she hadn't had anything to do with the actual takedown.

Once docked, the *Wasp* and *Dauntless* were ordered to stay locked down, preserving everything for tomorrow's visit by the customs people. Even pirates wanted to assure that The Man got his proper cut. Still, that didn't keep the "captured ships" from connecting to the piers for air, water, sewage, and comm lines.

Comm lines was where the trouble started.

"Commander, I got something interesting," Chief Beni said.

"How interesting?" Kris said.

"A lot more than I want. The landline traffic is spiking. Spiking way high. I can't read it, but traffic between the three pirate ships is going fast and heavy."

"Anything to the *Bucket*?"

"Some, but not much. What there is of it is all in the clear and has to do with docking. Who's paying. When. The usual stuff."

"But the other pirates seem to have developed a bad case of the yaks. Any idea what they're saying?" Kris asked

"I don't know what to make of it, ma'am. It's all in cipher. But whatever it is, they don't want anyone who didn't get the daily cipher drop to know what they're talking about."

"Why do I not like that?" Kris said. She didn't wait for an answer. "Nelly, send a commlink of our own to the other two ships. Let's see what they think about this sudden talkativeness among the pirates."

"I already had two spiders spinning cable between our ships, Kris."

On the outer hull of the *Wasp*, a tiny portion of Smart Metal™ organized itself into a commlink and boosted away from the *Wasp*. There were two of them, each leaving a tiny filament of wire behind them. A few minutes later they attached themselves to the commlink at the outer air locks of the other two ships. A fraction of a second later, the bridge crew on the *Bucket* and the *Dauntless* listened as Kris reviewed what she knew . . . and all that she didn't.

"Commander Campbell, did High Dry Tortuga update you on the cipher for today?"

"Golly, Princess, I guess it must have slipped their minds, it being all late and that," he answered lightly. Then he got deadly serious. "This is not the way you greet your fellow prodigal sons. I don't like this."

"Me neither," his XO observed from the *Dauntless*.

"Me three-ther," Kris added.

Around about midnight, it all became perfectly clear.

33

Lieutenant Commander Kris Longknife chose 0200 hours as about the right time to take down the pirate space station. It was an ungodly hour, and anyone not under military discipline would in all likelihood be sound asleep.

From the number of people swaying in and out of the local grog shops, more likely they'd just be dead drunk.

But Kris had to work to get even that little bit of information.

She had Chief Beni and Nelly launch several nanoscouts from the *Wasp* to take a good look around the station.

None survived more than seven minutes.

That told Kris a lot more than she wanted to know. Whoever was running this place was even more paranoid than the average Longknife. They also had more high tech than anyone of their low morals and criminal inclinations should have. Certainly more than Admiral Krätz. Did these folks have the ability to jam the local net?

Interesting question that. Which for now remained unanswered.

"Shall we launch some more nanos?" Nelly asked, even as Chief Beni was opening his mouth to likely say the same thing.

"No," Kris said with a shake of the head. "We don't want to start a fight just yet, and I'm not sure that we'd win one with these nanos. Only a fool starts a fight they aren't sure they can win."

But that didn't mean that Kris was content to be blind. She resorted to slower methods, sending spider crawlers out along the station power cables the *Wasp* was now hooked into. The reports would come back via those power lines, and when the spiders went active, they would be beside light fixtures. Whatever power usage the spider spy made would be impossible, hopefully, for the local folks' countermeasures to notice.

It seemed to work.

Kris got some very good looks from the light fixtures at the top of the pier. Of course, all it showed was inebriated pirates making their way to and from different pubs or their ships.

Other than that, the stations seemed about as inactive as you could get . . . and still have air, water, and lights.

"Wonder if those autoguns are switched on, or if anyone is looking at their sensor take?" Jack asked as he looked over Kris's shoulder at the feed Chief Beni was getting.

"I was wondering about that myself," Kris said.

There were a whole lot more automatic machine guns sited around the station than Kris wanted her Marines facing. Jack passed The Word to the Marines' heavy weapons teams to be ready to take down a lot of machine guns—fast.

Plans for the seizure of the station moved along quickly and smoothly after that

Then . . . at exactly midnight . . . all Kris's planning became irrelevant.

It seemed the pirates had other plans.

34

Kris was feeling pretty good as the *Wasp*'s clock struck eight bells for midnight. Chief Beni had sent a swarm of spider bugs out, inching their way along the power cables to nest in more light fixtures. Now she had one at each of her two prime targets. . . the command center of the station and the reactor.

Each showed four or five people standing their watch by playing cards.

In the process of locating those, Kris had also situated cameras so they could watch the piers where the three pirate ships were tied up.

She thought that was a good idea.

It turned out to be a very good idea.

Right around midnight, those cameras started showing a whole lot of irregular troops flooding out of the three ships. Most were armed with what they called cutlasses, which looked more like rough-forged machetes to Kris. Some of the few that might qualify as officers had pistols. Others wore black pants or shirts, leftovers from recently ended careers in Greenfeld State Security. Inevitably, those carried machine pistols.

"Oh my," said Chief Beni.

"If I didn't know better," Kris said, "I'd say there is no honor among these thieves."

"It does kind of look like they're very intent on hacking out for themselves a share of the sudden wealth that's come the way of the *Bucket of Blood*," Colonel Cortez observed on net.

"I'm getting a sudden lack of electronic activity on the main deck of the station," Chief Beni announced. "I think someone turned off the cameras and the autoguns."

"It would be embarrassing to shoot up your new best friends while they were busy stealing from your former best friends," Jack Campbell remarked from the *Blood*.

"And who would want to leave photo evidence for the boss to look at tomorrow of who stole what," Penny said.

"Which may make it a whole lot easier for us to take the station down," Jack Montoya added. "Assuming we can avoid getting our throats cut in the meantime."

"Looks like we'll be the first boat boarded," Kris said, noting that the *Wasp*'s pier was closer to the flow of flashing and sharp metal. "Anyone have a suggestion as to how we handle this."

"Ah," came slowly from Campbell. "They were all laughing their fool heads off at the story of the *Blood*'s pirates chasing my panic party."

"Do you think these could be distracted just as easily?" Kris asked.

"What do you say we try them?" came from Abby, coming on the *Wasp*'s bridge with an armful of calico and two standard Navy mops. "Penny, you want to do some panicking with Kris?"

"*I'm* sure not going to run around like some empty-headed female," Sulwan announced.

"What about you, Abby?" Kris countered.

"You don't pay me enough. Remember, it's the Longknife legend that everyone is always talking about. Looks like it's time for you to add a couple of more paragraphs." So saying, Abby tossed Kris a simple cotton dress. Then she tossed another to Penny.

"Hold it," Kris said, shaking out the latest in captive-crew fashions. "I never heard anything about Grampa Ray or Trouble saving the world in a dress."

"I'm sure he paid well to have those particulars skipped by the writers of history books," Abby drawled.

Penny slipped the dress on over her head, then modestly

shimmied out of her shipsuit. "Hurry up, Princess. I'm not do-ing this alone," the Navy lieutenant said.

"Whoever heard of a Longknife panicking," Kris cried plaintively, but she was pulling the colorful dress over her head.

"The idea of a panic party is not to panic, just make the uninitiated observers think you are," Jack said from the safety of his full Marine battle armor. He'd donned it an hour ago in preparation for the coming festivities.

Abby handed the two Navy officers their mops. "Go swab the deck, gals. Oh, and ditch the shoes. You'll get better traction."

"You're enjoying this," Penny shot back.

"You'll never know how much," Abby admitted.

Kris and Penny headed for the quarterdeck, Jack right be-hind them. "I've got your back," he said.

"You better," Kris growled.

Sergeant Bruce was leading the guard at the gangway. "It looks like we got company coming. What are your orders, sir?" he asked his captain.

"Back off and leave it to the ladies," Jack said.

The sergeant frowned at the unexpected if not unheard-of command.

"Don't worry, honey," Abby put in, "I'm not one of the de-lectables we'll be dangling in front of the pirates." The maid, who was also a qualified sharpshooter, had her automatic out.

"Stay worried, Sergeant," Kris said. "Penny and I will be the ones playing decoy."

"Yes, ma'am. Whatever you say," the poleaxed Marine said.

"Be careful, honey, or the princess will have you trading dresses with her," Abby said, patting her Marine buddy on the shoulder.

The sergeant braced against the bulkhead to let Kris pass.

"Hurry up," Nelly whispered. "The boarding party is get-ting mighty close."

Someone had thoughtfully arranged for there to be a bucket of suds in the middle of the quarterdeck. Kris dunked her mop in and pulled it out dripping. In a second, she was sloshing soapy water this way and that.

"Be careful," Penny said.

"Right. We wouldn't want folks to be slipping and sliding, would we?" Kris said, through the first grin of the day.

"On second thought," Penny said, and dunked her mop again.

Water and suds flew.

THE PIRATES ARE ON THE PIER STAIRS. BEND OVER MORE, Nelly said on net.

BEND OVER MORE? Kris asked.

YEAH, GIVE THE BOYS HALF A CHANCE, AND ALL THEY'LL BE LOOKING AT IS UP YOUR DRESS.

THERE'S NO THERE THERE, Kris pointed out.

BUT THEY DON'T KNOW IT. TRUST ME, MEN WILL ALWAYS BE HOPING FOR A GIRL TO SLIP.

Kris could almost hear the chuckling on command net as she and her computer debated her sexual wiles. HOW DID YOU SUDDENLY GET SO SMART ABOUT WHAT MEN LIKE IN THEIR WOMEN?

I READ A LOT, Nelly shot back.

Kris bent farther over her mop.

Nelly showed Kris a view of the pirates on the stairs. Yep, sure enough, a couple of the guys had spotted the two women swabbing the deck and were pointing them out to their associates. From the leers and ugly grins, Kris knew the two Navy officers were not being discussed in anything like a wholesome and proper manner.

ENJOY YOUR FUN, BOYS. I'LL BE LAUGHING LAST, Kris said on net.

HOW LONG ARE WE GOING TO KEEP THIS UP? Penny asked.

JACK, YOU GOT YOUR MARINES WELL HIDDEN?

YES, KRIS, WE'RE OUT OF SIGHT.

LET'S KEEP WORKING IT, PENNY. I'D PREFER FOR THEM TO START THE SHOUTING FIRST.

NICE, KRIS, BUT DID THEY GET THE SCRIPT? FROM THE LOOKS OF THEM, I'M NOT SURE THEY COULD READ A SCRIPT IF THEY HAD ONE.

WAIT FOR IT, Kris said.

The pirates were gathering at the foot of the stairs, just out of sight of the gangway. A guy with a pistol was waving it around and whispering orders.

Some of the pirates actually looked like they were listening to him. Most wandered around like a bunch of college kids on Friday night looking for a party.

A final wave of the pistol was followed by a shout. Dozens of pirates raced or stumbled into view, waving their cutlasses.

Kris and Penny let out screams that didn't have to be faked and galloped for the main outboard passageway. Kris was glad for Abby's advice; the deck was slippery, and bare feet were the best way to go.

Nelly passed along the view from the quarterdeck camera, so Kris didn't have to look over her shoulder. The pirates were not at all prepared for wet and slippery footing.

Two pirates slipped. As they went down, several more piled up on them. Waving cutlasses were suddenly hacking and slashing whoever got in their way.

The entire invasion of the *Wasp* might have ended there if the guy with the pistol hadn't shouted, "Get those girls."

Penny and Kris emphasized the order with fine girlish shrieks. The calico dress fit Penny fairly well. The one on Kris hardly got to her knees.

"Get the girls," was taken up by the mob, and the pounding of booted feet told Kris even more than Nelly's camera feed that she'd better run if she wanted to keep living.

The main outboard passageway ran in a circle around the waist of the *Wasp*. Kris was careful to keep in sight of the leaders of the chase but made sure to let them get no closer.

The quarterdeck was on the starboard side. Opposite on the port side was a stairwell Kris intended to lead them up.

As befitting the *Wasp*'s conversion to a warship, the angle of the stairs was now much closer to a steep Navy ladder. With any luck, she'd put that to good use.

Kris checked the camera take from the quarterdeck and passageway. The Marines had started taking down the pirates from the rear without disturbing those in the lead. One of the advantages of the circular passageway was that the leaders were indeed staying ignorant of what was going on behind them.

Kris was now ready to bring the leaders up to date.

"Up the ladder," Kris shouted, both for Penny's information . . . and the pursuing pirates.

Up the ladder Penny went, followed close by Kris. Once out of sight from below, Kris grabbed Penny's elbow. "I've had enough of this running."

"I was wondering when you would," Penny said.

"Ready your mop," Kris ordered, leveling hers like a pike of old, wet end out.

"Do you really think this is a good idea?" Penny asked, a bit unsure of the concept. Still, she followed Kris's lead.

"Go for the lead guy on the right," Kris ordered. "I'll take the left."

Two pirates, cutlasses waving, poked their heads over the lip of the ladder. They were not expecting opposition.

Kris's wet mop hit her guy right in the face. "You really need to brush your teeth," she said as she did just that with the swab.

"You, too," Penny cried, and twisted her mop in the other guy's face.

Off-balance . . . and outmaneuvered . . . the two of them fell back into the unprepared arms of their copillagers. One got skewered by a cutlass, the other rolled downhill into a ball with way too many arms and legs.

"I'll kill you for that," would have sounded much more threatening from the guy with the pistol if he hadn't gulped halfway through the threat at the sight of Kris and Penny standing at the top of the stairs . . . both with their service automatics pointed right between his eyes.

A second later, the soft pop of sleepy darts put an end to further conversation as the half dozen boarders who had made it that far fell under the gentle arms of Marine sharpshooters.

Kris holstered her automatic, pulled her worn cotton dress down to at least cover her knees, and became the commander of Patrol Squadron 10 again.

"Captain, do we have control of this ship?" she asked Jack.

"All members of the boarding party are captured and accounted for, ma'am. Docs are taking care of several red-on-red casualties, and one big fellow whose heart isn't taking too well to Colt-Pfizer's best sleepy darts. People with bad hearts really should not play pirates."

"Somehow I doubt he'll learn from this experience. What's the situation on the other ships?" Kris asked on net.

"The *Bucket of Blood* is once again ours," Lieutenant Commander Campbell reported.

"The *Dauntless* has most of her boarding party down and sleeping," Lieutenant Amber Kitano reported. "A half dozen managed to lock themselves in the wardroom. We are debating letting them stay in there until the food kills them."

"Oh, the slings and arrows of a subordinate with a sense of humor," Campbell complained.

"The *Dauntless*'s Marines are ready to move out on your orders, Your Highness." Lieutenant Kitano cut to the chase. "Where away?"

35

Kris surveyed the wreckage before her, then had Nelly scroll through the take from critical observation points on the station. The watch standers at the command post and the reactor were still lost in their card game. Except for the spaces around the grog shops, the station was pretty much asleep.

"Greenfeld Marines, will you secure the prisoners now on our ships and stand in reserve?"

"Yes, ma'am," came back with only a hint of disappointment.

"Wardhaven Marines. Each company will send two squads to secure the three ships presently docked at the station. Take along a team of Navy types to set up a port watch on the captured ships. Go for the ship nearest you. *Wasp*, you take down the freighter. It's farthest away from all of us."

That drew the expected, "Aye aye, ma'am."

"*Dauntless*, your Marines will seize the reactor. Put together a team from your engineering department to take over the watch there."

"Standing by," Lieutenant Kitano replied.

"*Wasp* will follow me to the command post. Captain Montoya and I know space stations well."

"Defending or attacking?" Commander Campbell asked.

"Both," Jack supplied.

"Okay, Campbell, for that you get the grog shops. Them and the sleeping quarters. Secure them and see that we don't have any trouble from that direction."

"I think I can handle a few drunken sailors," the temporary skipper of the *Bucket of Blood* assured Kris.

"One suggestion before we move out," said Kris. "We can't go parading around this station looking like a bunch of squared-away Marines. The neighbors will talk."

Jack glanced around at his company and gave Kris a rather nonplussed look.

Kris went on. "I want everyone to strip as much of the outer clothing as you can off the sleeping pirates and put it on over your Marine battle rattle." The armor had the ability to change its coloring to match most any background. The designers had never imagined a pirate station.

"Grab any civilian clothing. It doesn't have to fit well, just enough to fool someone glancing at the monitors while contemplating whether or not to bet on an inside straight."

"And you will get in some armor yourself, Your High-Handedness," Abby insisted, pulling Kris into a side compartment, where she had full battle dress waiting for Penny, Kris, and herself.

"You sure you aren't a mind reader?" Kris said, getting busy putting on her play clothes for the next funnest thing in her life.

"Great minds think in the same gutters," the maid insisted. "I knew you'd lead the panic party. It was easy to gauge where you'd lead it to. The *Wasp* doesn't offer a lot of options."

Penny shook her head. "I say she either reads minds or is a witch."

"You calling me a bitch?"

"Witch. Witch!"

"Which one?" Abby demanded.

"Get dressed, girls. The target is thataway," Kris said, swinging a thumb over her shoulder toward the station. "If we're going to kill someone tonight, let's make it count."

"No one ever died of a good pun," Abby insisted, turning her back on Kris so her princess could finish lashing up the back of her armor. Since Abby was doing up Penny, and Penny was taking care of Kris, it served to keep their hands busy and . . . for the moment . . . their mouths closed.

A minute later, the three turned around in unison so they could give each other's fronts a final check.

"Okay, girls, let's go kick some pirate butt," Penny said.

They managed a three-way high five, which took all six hands, and headed out, grinning from ear to ear.

"You all having fun?" Jack asked.

"Yes, we are. Everyone ready to ride?" Kris answered.

"On your orders," Jack replied.

"Let's see. I can't go prancing across a pirate port looking like an armored princess," Kris said. "Oh, and I need booty. Plenty of booty."

"Yes," said Abby and Penny.

"Jack, I want that guy's hat," Kris said, pointing at the fallen boss pirate fellow who was snoring softly at Jack's feet. "And that cute vest and those pants, too. Roll him out of them."

"As you wish, Your Highness," said Jack, none too sure of the premise.

"Come on, Jack. A ragtag mess charged onto this boat. We need a ragtag mess prancing out of it."

"Carrying plenty of loot," Penny said. "I've got just the thing. A batch of cosmetics I ordered a month ago came in this really cute-looking cask. Perfect for jewels and diamonds and pieces of eight." In a flash, the lieutenant was off.

"You heard the commander," Jack ordered his Marines, "strip these dudes. Put what you can on over your armor and find something that looks like you're hauling loot."

The Marines responded with strange looks, but they did as ordered.

Penny got back with a lovely treasure chest just as the lieutenant colonel who commanded the Greenfeld Marine battalion arrived with his own Marines to take over the prisoners . . . many of whom were now stripped down to nothing since they'd failed to put on underwear that morning. Maybe any morning.

"You Wardhaven Marines have strange proclivities," the colonel said darkly.

"Anything that will get us across the killing grounds without us getting killed is fine by us," Jack said, firmly defending his own.

"You are weird people," the colonel said, shaking his head.

"We would charge across, guns blazing, rockets going off. We'd have this place in a blink of an eye."

"When we get finished," Kris said, "this station will still be holding air and ready to go back to work tomorrow."

"Hmm, there is that," the colonel admitted.

"Okay, crew," Kris said, raising her voice. "Let's go get ourselves one pirate port."

"Ooo-Rah," came back at her.

The Marines moved out behind Kris in general mob formation. They lugged boxes and crates alone or in pairs. Several of them waved empty whiskey bottles they'd retrieved from the several pubs in boffin country.

At least Kris assumed the bottles were empty.

The way to the command post led along the station's main deck and past several grog shops. The early-morning denizens of those dives waved their own bottles and mugs at them as they strode by, but saw nothing amiss.

They also lacked the wherewithal to get up and join Kris's little parade . . . thank heavens.

Kris spotted the tail end of one similar mob. She suspected it was Kitano's team going for the reactor. She wished her the best of luck but concentrated on her own target.

The command center controlled the station. It also must have any records that existed that would tell Kris what captured human cargo had passed through the station and where it was sent.

Kris needed the station computer intact and cooperating. Not shot up and blown apart like the Greenfeld colonel had offered.

Still, it was going to take a lot of luck to get the controls and computers in pristine condition.

A glance at Nelly's feed from the command center showed four still playing cards and one wandering around, glancing at different stations. He didn't look all that interested in doing watch-standing duties. Maybe he'd just lost all he had to lose.

Kris raised the delightful-smelling treasure chest of skin and facial products that Penny had given her and waved it above her head.

Yep, the guy in the command center had been looking at the monitors. He turned to the others, and the game quickly broke up as others came to look at the pictures from the main deck.

Kris's legs wanted to hoof it; she held the urge in check. That would be totally out of character. Instead, she shouted, "We're rich! Richer than God," and the Marines behind her shouted their own claims to wealth, too.

The organized mob behind Kris got rowdy. A couple of Marines hammed it up by starting a fight. They came to the ramp up to the command post. The two fighters managed to slip away into a side passageway and set up to cover the rear of the team.

The steel doors up ahead looked designed to withstand a full-on assault. To its right and left were autocannons ready to mow down just that attack.

Kris reached up. Her right hand waved the fake treasure chest with its sparkling plastic jewels and gold coins at the watching camera. With the other fist, she pounded on the steel portals for admittance. That wasn't necessary; the bombproof doors began sliding open before she gave it her first good rap.

Proving bombproof wasn't necessarily boobyproof.

"You wouldn't believe what we found," Jack shouted.

"Make us believers," came back as the doors slid open wide.

Four pirates stared at Kris's service automatic . . . and a whole lot more.

The fifth guy was farther back.

He had time to react.

He bolted for the command console. Kris busted through the four pirates standing dumb as oxen and put three darts into the fifth one's backside. He went down with his hand still reaching for the controls.

Kris checked him out, then turned back to the silent four.

"Gentlemen, you have three choices as I see it. You can step outside and see how good you are at breathing space. We can turn you over to the Greenfeld Marines for what passes as justice in these parts, or you can start working for the Wardhaven Marines and make us happy. Don't think too long. That last offer is on a short fuse."

Not surprising, they quickly accepted Kris's job offer.

Nelly and Chief Beni went through the center's workstations, checking them out, determining that they were safe to work and that they did do what the enthusiastic new employees said they did.

There was only one bad moment.

One of them sidled up to a station when he thought no one was looking and tried to activate something. A Marine spotted him, yanked him away from the station, and put him to sleep upon Jack's orders.

Three out of five cooperating wasn't a bad score.

Kris went down her to-do list quickly. The reactor control center reported itself under new management and operating in the capable hands of the Royal Navy.

Kris ordered the agreed-upon signal sent to the jump buoy. Admiral Krätz and his crew were welcome to join the festivities.

Then Kris turned to Chief Beni. "Tell me what you now know about the planet under us. Also, is there anything in this computer about a twelve-year-old girl being sold recently?

Cara cried herself to sleep. She didn't want to; it upset her bunkmates, the twenty young women she shared a hut with. "We all have it tough," growled Betty, the hard-as-nails one who claimed the right to speak for the rest. "Quit bawling like a baby."

Betty had also warned Cara that she didn't have it as bad as the others. None of the overseers had taken her out behind the barn.

Not yet.

Yet, it *was* bad. The work was sunup to sundown. Cara was sunburned and blistered. The food left Cara just as hungry after she ate it as before.

But there was something else. Back on New Eden, people were dirt poor. Cara had often gone hungry when Gamma

Ganna was too busy to cook or broke between men. Still, people looked out for each other. What little they had, they'd share with a skinny kid left to run the streets.

Not here. What did Betty call it? "Dog eat dog."

Cara tried to stifle the sobs that started deep in her empty belly and seemed to wrack her whole body on the way out.

She tried, and she prayed silently.

Please, Aunt Abby. Please, Aunt Kris. Come and find me. Come and get me. If I can just go home to the Wasp, *I promise I'll never do anything you don't want me to do. Never talk back. Never skip my homework.*

Please find me. Please, please, please.

36

Kris gritted her teeth. The screen in front of her showed Dry Tortugas below. The morning sun had just brought light to Port Royal. It woke people up and brought calls from the ground. Calls that Kris did not have answers for.

Once she had complete control of the High Dry Tortugas space station, Kris started hunting for the boss of the station.

It turned out she already had him.

He was the big fellow with a bad heart and the worst kind of allergic reaction to Colt-Pfizer's best sleepy darts. When Kris first heard about an overweight guy with an allergic reaction to sleepy darts, she'd wondered why he was playing at pirate.

Now she'd discovering that he *was* the big guy. Boss of the station. Head pirate among pirates.

What he thought he was doing taking a night out for a little personal rape and pillage would never be answered. He died despite the best effort by the docs on the *Wasp*.

It was morning . . . and calls were coming in . . . and Kris had no way to answer them.

She tried. Or Nelly tried. Assuming the most solicitous tone, Nelly assured the caller "Big Bill is not available. May I take your message?"

That worked the first couple of times. But apparently Big Bill wasn't as big as Carita. When the big gal ordered them to throw whatever whore Billy was in bed with out and get him on the phone, all that was left for Nelly to do was switch to a buzz tone and announce that "This line is not in service at this time."

Which left Kris with a bad set of choices. Was it better to leave the folks dirtside stewing in their own juices, wondering what was wrong up on the station? Or should she let them know the jig was up. Royal and Imperial Marines were getting ready to drop down and demand they surrender or die?

Kris figured she could dither for a while. Admiral Krätz and his battleships were due to dock shortly after noon.

"Nelly, Chief Beni, can you find anything out about Cara?"

"Kris," Nelly began softly. Not a good sign. "They don't list people by name. They just give them numbers. I don't know if they chipped them or tattooed them or what, but whether you look for Cara or just a twelve-year-old girl, there's nothing. So many women and so many men went down per shuttle. That's it."

Kris and Abby looked at each other. This was not good.

"Chief," Jack said, "do you have access to the databases dirtside?"

"We're getting some access. We've cracked the cipher for the last couple of days, though I think they just changed the dirtside code midmorning and didn't tell us."

"That's not good," Penny said.

"We're running out of time," Kris said. "Who was sold six, seven, eight days ago?"

"About eighty people," Nelly said. "No names, just their ID numbers, prices, and destinations."

"Which tells us nothing," Abby said.

"No, hold it," Jack said. "A twelve-year-old girl can't be worth much. She's too young to be useful as a bed warmer. Too inexperienced to be a good house slave and too weak to be worth much as a field slave."

"What girl was sold for the lowest price?" Kris and Abby asked at the same time.

"Three of them, all to this same location," Nelly said.

"A Seebrook Plantation," Chief Beni said, beating Nelly to the final punch.

"Show me Seebrook Plantation," Kris ordered.

Nelly flashed a map on the nearest screen. It showed a huge plot of land stretching into the foothills south of Port

Royal. Several streams ran through it from the distant mountain range.

"What do they grow there?" Jack asked.

Nelly overlaid their initial survey. It grew the crop that didn't fit into any of the established food stocks.

"One huge drug plantation," Abby whispered.

"Captain, prepare the *Wasp*'s Marine company for a drop mission. We're going loaded for bear."

"Two questions, Commander," Jack said formally. "Are we taking prisoners?"

Kris knew what she wanted to say. Pirates, drug lords, slavers. She saw no reason to share the same air with them.

Still, there were rules about these things. And on a practical note, dead men tell no tales.

Or answer questions, either.

Still, Kris could not help herself. "Let's hope they resist," she said. "Please, dear God, let them fight us."

"I'll tell the men. If they shoot at us, we can shoot them. Second question, Kris. *We?*" the Marine captain asked, raising one eyebrow.

It hit Kris like a kick in the gut. She so wanted to get her hands around the throats of the people who'd done this to Cara. This was not something she'd read about. This was upfront and personal. This was *her* Cara.

But she had an admiral leading in a battle fleet. She had calls from bad guys and gals that needed to be creatively fielded. As much as she wanted to be part of the landing force, duty said she belonged here.

Kris gritted her teeth. "Take Abby with you, Jack. Oh, and Sergeant Bruce. You may need his computer."

"Aye aye, ma'am," the Marine said with a formal salute.

She could see in Jack's eyes that she'd passed a test. Maybe passed something more than that.

Kris was the commander, now. It was both her job and duty to lead troops. But her place was no longer at the front, leading by example. Now her job would grow harder. Now she would lead from the rear by the power of her presence.

From here on in, Kris would have the much harder job of

staying in touch with her troopers' needs not by sharing their blood and sweat but by giving them the support and guidance that let them bleed less in a fight.

Kris sighed; that extra small stripe on her shoulder board, the one that named her a lieutenant commander, meant more than a little extra pay. More than a little extra respect.

It meant she had a whole new set of challenges to face.

Kris sucked in her gut and let out a long sigh. Then she gave her first order from her new, lofty position. "Go get our Cara, Jack. I'll take care of the elephants on this end."

37

Cara hoed the weeds.

That was her job. Hoe the weeds and be sure not to kill any of the yellow bugs. The yellow bugs, both as cute, furry caterpillar things and as butterflies with lovely multicolored wings, somehow made the drug plants grow.

Or maybe they turned the plants that stood in rows nearly as tall as she was into drugs. Cara was not sure exactly how it worked. She doubted any of the people standing by with ready whips understood things better than she did.

What Cara did know was that she was supposed to hoe down the weeds and never touch one of the plants, and never, ever squish a bug. If one of the whip-wielding overseers spotted her squishing a bug, she'd get a beating.

In even the short time Cara had been here, she'd seen lots of whippings. One of the new girls had died from her beating. The ones that had been here longer warned the new folks that you really didn't want to screw up when Oli was around.

It would have been nice if they'd passed along that warning before that poor girl got whipped to death.

For now, Oli was working in the barn, processing the leaf into the powder that was exported. For a whip, that was a kind of punishment.

So Cara kept her head down, and hoed the weeds, and dodged the bugs.

Some of the older girls said you could eat the caterpillars. They didn't taste like much, but they kept you alive.

Cara was hungry, but not that hungry.

At least not yet.

Cara kept her head down and her hoe moving carefully, but that didn't mean she wasn't aware of what went on around her.

Behind her, at the end of the row she was slowly backing down, three of the whips had gathered.

That was strange.

In all the days Cara had worked here, the overseers usually roved the fields alone. The only time they talked was to occasionally yell at a worker. Most often, they didn't say a word, they just cracked the whip.

But today, three were clumped together and talking.

Cara didn't slow her work, but she listened.

"The boss lady is not happy," one said.

"That's not good. What kind of bee does she have up her ass?"

"Something's wrong at the space station."

"Something's always wrong at the space station. Remember that fire they had in the comm center? We still got five guys in Hardy's gang working off their thirty days for that one."

"Well, they're not talking again. Word is that Carita's gonna fire up one of the shuttles and run it up there even if it doesn't have a cargo to bring down."

"Carita don't never waste a penny."

"Well, she's getting ready to waste a bundle on a shuttle launch to find out what's happening up there. And if Carita's spending money, something's wrong, and our boss gal ain't liking it."

They paused for a while. One of them cracked the whip on Betty, who had paused to lean on her hoe and listen to them. Betty cursed them but went back to her work.

There was a boom. No, a double boom.

"What's that?" one of the overseers asked.

"Sounds like a sonic boom. I guess Carita has done launched a shuttle."

"Sounded awful far off."

It had sounded far off to Cara. And it was followed by two more booms, then a third pair.

"That's a lot of booms for one shuttle," a whip observed with more wisdom than he knew.

Cara smiled. She kept her head down and her hoe going, but she knew what would cause six booms in that kind of a pattern.

Uncle Bruce, Sergeant Bruce to his Marines, had shown Cara a video of the landing the Marines made on Texarkana. It was homemade video, not as clean as the stuff you saw on the news, but three assault boats in battle formation made just that pattern of booms on approach.

Uncle Bruce told Cara that Marines liked to drop from orbit well away from the target area, glide in close, then make the final jump.

They found me! Abby and Bruce and maybe even Jack and Kris are coming for me!

Cara wanted to throw down her hoe and tell those stupid men with the whips just what was headed their way.

Oh, she wanted to.

She kept her head down, did her best not to smile, and kept hoeing. The Marines would be here soon enough.

And the Marines would have guns. It was going to be so much fun watching those whips guys tell a Marine in full battle rattle what they should do.

Cara finished that row and managed to switch to another right under all three overseers' noses without getting their attention.

She'd hoed another row and was working her way back toward them again when one of them shouted, "What's that?"

Cara risked a glance at the three. One of them had his hand up, pointing. The other two were shading their eyes with one hand, staring up into the sunny sky.

Cara looked up herself; others of the girls were doing the same. The whips couldn't crack them all.

Even though Cara knew what she was looking for, it still took her a while to spot one. Marine drop-chutes were designed to blend into the sky, whether it was a painful blue like today or gray and cloudy. Marine battle armor also changed color like a chameleon.

It wasn't easy, but Cara did spot three, then four, then a whole lot of Marine jumpers.

And she'd had enough of being a scared little girl.

"Those are Royal U.S. Marines," Cara cried. "Let's see you use your whip on those bad dudes."

Cara relished the look of shock on the three slave overseers' faces.

Oops, those faces were now turned toward Cara. One of the overseers swung his whip at her.

Cara knew that a good slave was supposed to just take it. But Cara had had enough of being a good little slave. She raised her hoe up just right . . . and the tip of the whip ended up wound around it.

Then she yanked.

Slave boss hadn't expected that from a slave. The whip came out of his hand and flew toward Cara.

That really got Cara noticed. All three of the overseers took off after her.

Cara hadn't learned dumb on the streets of Five Corners. She was already racing down the row of drug plants. She refused to toss the hoe away. Now she had a whip, and a hoe.

She'd cut down plenty of weeds.

If she had the chance, she cut herself down an overseer.

Then again, three to one were very bad odds.

Behind her, she could hear her pursuers. They were shouting to each other as they cut across rows of plants, trampling them as they tried to get on both sides of Cara. She had a wild thought about who'd whip them if they smashed a bug, but she didn't have the breath to laugh.

She dodged over one row, trampling plants herself, then another.

And ran smack into the most wonderful sight in the world.

"That you, Cara," came in Uncle Bruce's wonderful voice.

"Oh God, thank you," she said, and discovered that running into full battle rattle at full speed could lead to a painful full stop.

"I figured you'd be the one they'd be chasing," the sergeant said. "To everyone on command net, I have Cara. She looks much the worse for wear, but she's talking and not bleeding."

Cara couldn't hear the answer to that but she could see the smile widen on his face.

Then the Marine sergeant stood tall and moved Cara around behind him. "What have we here?" he asked.

"They're overseers," Cara said. "They have whips."

"So I see."

Cara felt the change in her guardian's stance as his rifle came up. "I suggest you fellows throw away your whips and get down on the ground."

Cara heard a pistol shot and a thunk. Uncle Bruce swayed back for a second.

"I am under fire," the sergeant reported in a voice deadly calm. "I have a slug sticking out of the armor of my shoulder."

The next voice Cara heard came powerfully from the speaker on the sergeant's helmet. "Weapons release. All Marines, we have taken fire. You have weapons release for deadly force." Cara recognized the voice, Uncle Jack, or rather Captain Jack. She'd never heard his voice sound just like that.

She'd never heard anyone sound like the voice of God on Judgment Day.

Sergeant Bruce fired his weapon three times. Cara didn't look to see what he did. She was crying.

"Okay, honey, things are going to be okay now," he said, turning to her and lifting up his faceplate so she could see his eyes and his smile better. He safetied and slung his weapon; it still smelled hot and fired like it did when he and Abby went to the range. He put his arms around her.

"Cara, I still have a few things I have to take care of. Remember, today I'm a Marine." That was a joke between him and Abby. What were they today? Marine and maid? Sergeant vs. second louie? Or just Steve and Abby.

"I know," Cara said, trying to control herself. "Can I help?"

"I think maybe you can. What's that big house over there?"

"That's where the boss lady lives."

"Are there any slaves inside?"

"Not during the day. She has business and doesn't want to be disturbed."

"Let's disturb her. Second squad, I have a fire mission for you. Rocket grenades, maximum high explosive. Target . . . the big house."

"Aye aye, Sergeant," came back from his net.

Sergeant Bruce pulled a rocket from his backpack and sighted it at the house. Cara saw the house reflected for a moment on the battle lenses over his eyes.

"Fire."

Six rockets took off, leaving small smoke trails behind them. A few seconds later they hit. For about half a second more, the large, cream-colored house just stood there.

Then it came apart. Prefab sections flew in every direction. Fire and smoke went up, then curled back in upon itself.

"That ought to take care of that," Sergeant Bruce said, grinning. "You wouldn't happen to know where they store this poison? The drugs?"

"In those big buildings," Cara said, pointing. "They process the plants and make it into a powder."

"Those barns?" he asked.

"I think that's what they call them. I forget."

"Right," Sergeant Bruce said with a chuckle. "You're a city girl."

"And I never want to be a country girl again."

"Country ain't bad when you aren't a slave," he said, half-distracted. "Second squad, I have more business for you. Our primary targets are in those two large barns to the right of the burning building. Select incendiary. A fire team, take the right one. B fire team, take the left one."

The "Aye ayes" were very enthusiastic this time.

Again six rockets rose and fell. This time the walls stayed put . . . for a while. Smoke immediately began billowing from the eaves of the barns. Cara wondered if Oli would manage to get out.

Then she decided she didn't care.

"Uncle Steve, is there anyplace I could get a drink of water. And something to eat?"

"We've set up a medical receiving station at the southern end of the farm, hon. Abby's there waiting for you."

Which was obsolete information. Auntie Abby was charging toward Cara even as the Marine misspoke. She was in full armor and pounding drug plants into the ground as she ran for Cara.

"I am so sorry, Aunt Abby," Cara said, throwing herself on another armored shoulder. It hurt, but it felt wonderful.

"I don't know whether to tan your hide, child, or hug you and wrap you in plastic."

"I'm sorry. I'm sorry. I won't ever do anything like that again."

"No, you won't, baby ducks. But if you're my niece, you'll likely come up with something new and worse. Come on. Doc Izzawa is waiting to get a good look at you."

Beside them, Sergeant Bruce turned his speaker up to max. "All agricultural workers, you are free now. We have set up a medical station on the southern edge of the farm. We also have food and water for you. We ask you to gather there and help us identify anyone who has been swinging a whip before today. We want to make sure they get the reward they deserve," he ended dryly.

From around the drug fields, people were standing up, straightening their backs, and groaning before heading south.

Here and there, the rows of plants swayed, but not to the wind.

"Marines, let's collect the folks going north and bring them along," the Marine sergeant ordered.

Around the field, men and women in battle armor stood tall and began beating the bushes. Shots were fired twice.

After Marines returned fire the second time, people started standing up with their hands above their heads.

Even the dumbest . . . or the guiltiest . . . could see it was better to risk the uncertain fate of surrender than the certain quick death that came to those who tried to stand against the troopers with the rifles.

38

Kris was delighted when the word came that Cara was in safe hands. If only one thing went right today, she'd settle for it being Cara's rescue.

Everything sure was going wrong on the station.

It hadn't started that way. After four or five more hang-ups, the Carita character got the point that no one wanted to talk to her and quit calling.

Nelly and Chief Beni began extracting bales and bales of information from the station computer. They even succeeded in making data calls on several computers dirtside. That got harder around 1000 hours, when the folks down there changed their cipher for the day and didn't tell the station.

Harder but not impossible. Nelly could still access the networks she'd already gotten into.

Admiral Krätz and his battle squadron docked right at noon. He asked to conduct the operation from Kris's Tactical Center on the *Wasp*. She offered to do a sweep of his flagship and kill any bugs so he could stay in familiar surroundings, but he declined and announced he was headed for her work spaces.

Kris spent a moment contemplating what it must be like to not be able to trust your friends *or* your enemies. *May that fate never come my way,* she prayed.

Kris greeted the Greenfeld admiral on the *Wasp*'s quarterdeck. As she expected, it was hard to tell if the admiral was shadowing a certain lieutenant or if it was the other way around.

"I seem to remember that we agreed that this planet would be Greenfeld territory," the admiral said as he crossed the brow onto the *Wasp*.

"It certainly is," Kris agreed, saluting. "Do you want me to start paying docking fees?"

"No, no." He almost chuckled. "I just didn't want us to have a misunderstanding. I understand that is easy in alliance operations."

"This is your planet. We're just visiting," Kris assured him.

He smiled and gave a nod to Commander Fervenspiel . . . who saluted and took it for a dismissal.

They had no sooner gotten to Kris's command center than Chief Beni called with the first of the bad news.

"Somebody got a message off the station."

"I thought you had us locked down," Kris said.

"Nelly and I thought we were. But you know we've been making data calls on stuff dirtside."

"Yes," Kris admitted.

"Well, it looks like someone managed to piggyback a packet on one of our calls."

"We should have caught it," Nelly cut in, "but this is a bit of home-field advantage that neither the chief nor I took into account."

"Don't you hate it when the bad guys aren't dumb," Vicky put in.

"As a matter of fact, I do," Kris said.

By then, the admiral, Vicky, and their entourage of officers were filing into Kris's Tac Center. Penny stood across the table from them, looking disturbed.

KRIS, YOU NEED TO SEE THIS, she said on Nelly's command net.

Kris found herself watching as a column of pirates from last night's boarding party, some still in need of clothes, were marched onto the main deck of the station by Greenfeld Marines.

On Commander Fervenspiel's orders, the pirates were backed up against a wall. A moment later, a shouted order, and the Marines gunned them all down.

THAT'S THE SECOND GROUP, KRIS. ARE YOU GOING TO LET THEM DO THAT?

Kris struggled to get her stomach under control. She'd said this station was Greenfeld territory. She'd heard a lot about Greenfeld practices. It didn't prepare her for this.

"Your Highness, you do not look well," Admiral Krätz said.

"I don't feel well," Kris admitted, trying to figure out which to respond to, the admiral's solicitousness or the lieutenant's, daughter of a cop, outraged sense of justice.

What had the admiral said on the quarterdeck, the challenges of alliance operations?

She'd told Jack she'd control the elephants. Just now, she felt trampled by a herd of them.

PENNY, WHERE ARE THE THREE THAT COOPERATED WITH US LAST NIGHT?

I'VE GOT THEM LOCKED AWAY IN THE *WASP*'S BRIG. I THINK THEY ARE SAFE.

THEN THEY MAY BE THE ONLY ONES WE CAN PROTECT, PENNY.

I THOUGHT A LONGKNIFE WOULD DO BETTER THAN THIS, Penny spat inside Kris's skull.

FOR WHAT IT'S WORTH, I THOUGHT A LONGKNIFE COULD, BUT APPARENTLY I'M WRONG. Kris turned back to the admiral and struggled to find words that might stop the slaughter.

"Kris, there's a call coming in from the planet," Chief Beni announced. "It's Ms. Carita van da Fitz for Admiral Krätz."

"Oh God, is that woman here?" he asked to the overhead.

"I think she's the big woman on planet," Kris said. "She's been trying to get someone up here to talk to her for most of the morning. I've managed to dodge her, but I suspect the call that got out of the station has brought her up to speed on matters."

Vicky shot her own scowl at the overhead.

The admiral shook his head. "This is not going to be pleasant. It may also change our plans. Vicky, call Commander Fervenspiel and have him stop the rat-eradication program."

"Yes, Admiral," and Vicky was quickly on her commlink.

One of the staff officers who had accompanied the admiral

plugged in a box with an old-fashioned phone on it. The admiral picked up the receiver, said little, then began listening.

Kris gave Penny a shrug. LET'S SEE WHAT COMES OUT OF VICKY'S CALL. LET ME KNOW IF THE SHOOTINGS STOP.

WHY DO I NOT FIND THIS AT ALL SATISFYING?

BECAUSE WE'RE GROWN-UPS, AND IT TAKES MORE THAN CHOCOLATE COOKIES TO MAKE US HAPPY.

Kris turned back to Vicky. "Who's this Carita person?"

"Just one of the board of directors of the N.S. Holding Group. Think Nuu Enterprises doubled, and you'll have the part it plays in the Greenfeld economy."

"What's someone like that doing out here?"

Vicky turned her back on the admiral and all the other officers in the room, her voice dropped to where only Kris could hear her. "I'm sure a Longknife has heard the story that my family made its money running booze, drugs, and other illegal activities back when Earth was the only game in town."

"I had," Kris admitted.

"And that we recouped our fortunes some ninety years ago by using the Unity thugs to help us distribute drugs to the old Society of Humanity before the Unity War."

"That was never proven," Kris pointed out.

"And don't you ever say I said it was so, because I won't. But some folks close to my dad may have heard the story and think it is a good way to recover the corporate losses they are suffering during this present economic crisis."

"Oh," Kris said. "So, what's about to happen?"

"I have no idea," Vicky said.

"Kris, this is Jack. We've got Cara," Nelly passed along to Kris out loud.

"That's great news," Vicky said. The admiral, still talking to Ms. van da Fitz, gave Kris the thumbs-up.

"How's it going on your end?" Kris asked.

"Everything is under control at the Seebrook Plantation. I dropped a platoon on the farm to the east and west of here. One of them has identified a problem."

"What kind of problem?" Kris asked. Once again today, her gut took a nosedive.

"We're looking for merchant crew members. Pirates take merchant ships. The crews have to end up somewhere."

"That sounds logical," Kris said.

"I've been talking to the freed slaves here. All are either hijacked sailors from the Greenfeld fleet or civilian refugees from St. Pete. Mostly the last. No one here knows of any sailors."

"That doesn't help our case."

"At the next farm over, Pleasant View, Lieutenant Stubben found several people who said they had six or seven slaves who claimed to be merchant sailors, taken by pirates."

The admiral continued to listen to the voice on the other end of the phone and make placating sounds at regular intervals. But now he was very attentive to Kris and Jack's conversation.

"Has Stubben found the sailors?" Kris didn't really want to ask the question. Whenever Jack led her slowly to a point, she usually didn't like what she saw when she got there.

Still, Jack led. She followed.

"We think we found five of them, Kris. I'm putting them on your view screen."

Suddenly the wall in front of Kris was a life-size scene. It took her a moment to realize what she was looking at.

Then she had to cover her mouth.

"Dear God in heaven," Penny whispered, and ran from the room.

There were similar mutterings from the Greenfeld staff officers. Two lost their lunches before they could make it out of the Tac Center.

"Apparently, someone shot five of the merchant sailors in the back of the head, execution style. They tried to burn their bodies, but our Marines put out the fire before it got too far. I'm not sure whether we can make ID on the corpses. I've ordered the forensic team down from our MP detachment. I'd like Penny to supervise the crime scene."

"I'll tell Penny you want her and see that she's on the longboat with the MP team."

"Where's Penny?" Jack asked.

"She had to step outside for a moment."

"Yeah, I'd like to step outside just now. Do you need anything more from me?"

"Try to find the two missing sailors. Send any spare Marines you can afford to the farms around the ones you've taken. Maybe you can save any sailors there before they get the same treatment. I'll have the Marine companies from the *Dauntless* and *Blood* dropped to you as soon as I can."

"Don't you need them to control the station?"

"Admiral Krätz is here, and he's taken over responsibility for matters hereabouts."

"Will he be sending troops down here?"

"I should know in a few minutes. I'll tell you then. Longknife out." Nelly, tell Campbell and Kitano that I want their Marines headed dirtside as soon as the orbit allows.

Yes, Kris.

Kris now focused her attention on Admiral Krätz. She didn't say anything, just watched him as he watched her, holding the phone away from his ear. The high-pitched words from it seemed to dribble out of the handset and collect in a puddle on the deck.

"Ms. van da Fitz, I'll get back to you in a moment," he said, and hung up.

They stared at each other, Kris and the admiral. Neither blinked.

"It seems we have a bloody mess on our hands," he finally said.

"With 'bloody' the operative word," Kris said, risking a glance at the bodies on the screen beside her.

"Could you please reduce that down to a size more sufferable," the admiral said.

"Nelly."

"If you say so, Kris," Nelly said.

The screen stayed full size.

"I'm saying so, Nelly. We can't be running out to the head to vomit every time we look at that."

The picture shrank to something the size you might find

in a history book. It also changed to black and white. THANK YOU, NELLY.

I SWEAR, KRIS, IF THESE SAILORS' DEATHS GET SWEPT UNDER THE RUG, I'LL PUT IT BACK UP FULL SIZE AND IN BLEEDING, BLISTERED COLOR.

I HEAR YOU, NELLY. NOW LET ME WORK.

"So, Admiral, what do we do with this mess? And I hope you'll excuse me if I push for something to be decided quickly. I fear if we blather for too long, others will make the decisions for us."

"Vicky, will you please explain to Her Highness here that N.S. Holding Group is not someone you want to get on the wrong side of."

"I already did, sir. I don't think mere money and political power impress the lieutenant commander all that much."

"How commendable," the admiral said with a sigh. "However, us simple working folks are expected to bow and scrape and work for the likes of Ms. da Fitz," he said.

"Even to the point of covering up murder?" Vicky asked.

"I truly hate working with idealistic young people," the admiral grumbled. "People, I want this room. Commander, could you please have a sailor show my staff to your wardroom for a cup of coffee. I'll call you back when I need you."

Nelly quickly made the arrangements. Penny was just returning to the room as the last of them filed out. Colonel Cortez was at her elbow this time.

The colonel eyed the procession leaving and turned to Kris. "Should Penny and I follow their lead?"

"Please don't," Vicky said.

Her admiral raised an eyebrow, but Vicky stood her ground. "What's the use of having advisors if you send them away when you need advice? I wish I had not let you talk me out of bringing Doc Maggie along from the *Fury*. I do not think I will back down next time."

The admiral rolled his eyes at the overhead. "Is the girl learning or just still too headstrong and stubborn?

"Probably both," Kris said. "Now, there are a lot of slaves

down there. Do we free them or not? Oh, and there may be some distressed mariners. Do we rescue them or let them be slaughtered?"

"If only the question were that easy," the admiral said.

"Tell me why it's not," Vicky said.

"You know why, young woman. N.S. Holdings is a major presence in the court. I fully expect that old biddy down there will be on your father, the emperor's, first list of ennoblements. She'll be a grand duchess, same as you."

Vicky made an ugly face at that prospect.

"But our problem today is that she says this planet is already established and registered to N.S. Holdings. They are the law here, not us."

"Since when does the Greenfeld flag fly over slaves," Vicky shot back.

"Slavery is against the law, and officially, there are no slaves on Port Royal. Oh, she says that's the planet and city's name. In honor of your father."

"Gee thanks," Vicky said, dryly. "And the slaves?"

"What slaves? All these people are paid regular wages."

"Nelly, can you verify that?" Kris asked.

"Yes, Kris, I have access to the payroll records of the entire planet," Nelly said proudly. "And I got that access even as they were being loaded at 11:20 this morning."

"Loaded," the admiral said.

"At 11:20 this morning. Before that, nothing."

"I'm sorry, Vicky, Kris," the admiral said, shaking his head. "I believe your fine computer, Miss Nelly, but in a court of law on Greenfeld, I don't see that standing for very much."

Kris wondered if anything would stand for much in a Greenfeld court if it had to stand against money and power. Kris wondered, but bit her tongue and said nothing.

"Kris, Jack wants to talk to you," Nelly announced. "Are you available?"

"Make it quick, Jack. You know those elephants we talked about this morning? Well, I'm surrounded by a herd of them. They can't decide whether to ignore me or stomp me into the ground, but what they won't do is what I want them to do."

"Better you than me, Commander, but I may have some-thing that will help you."

"Please, make my day."

"We found the two missing sailors."

Around Kris, the room lit up in smiles. Even the admiral. "Talk to me, Jack."

"When these two heard the sonic booms of our assault boats, they wisely decided to make themselves scarce. Good thing, because from where they were hiding out under crates of drugs, they saw their buddies get gunned down. They weren't too sure how to react to our Marines, but when we announced that we were going to burn the drug barns, they figured they'd better come out."

"Who are they?" the admiral asked.

"I'll put them on view," Jack said.

The screen beside Kris changed to show two scarecrows in rags, but these scarecrows were grinning from ear to ear. They were seated at a table, spooning in a thin soup as medics checked them out.

"I'm Sam Hatzo. I was wiper on the engineering crew of the *Hawaiian Star* out of Brenner Pass. This is my buddy Oka Akino, he was a deckhand on the same. I can't tell you what a lovely sight your ugly jarhead mugs were to these two sailors."

"Thank you," Kris said. "Nelly, do we have IDs on these two?"

"Yes, Kris," and two merchant-sailor union cards appeared beside the former slaves. The pictures didn't look all that much like the scarecrows, but Nelly quickly ran a facial recognition program and got ninety-two percent matches. "Fingerprints also match," the computer concluded.

"So," said Kris, eyeing the admiral, then Vicky, then back to the admiral, "we have at least two merchant sailors who were taken by pirates and sold into service vile. We have their witness to five of their comrades being murdered. Admiral, will you release your Marines to join my Marines in sweeps of the farms below in search of slaves and distressed mariners?"

The admiral took a deep breath. "I always told the missus that someday I'd take up chicken farming and be underfoot twenty-four hours a day. She said it would never happen. She would never live so long."

He shrugged. "So, what's the worst that can happen? I get to raise chickens, and Vicky here has to find another old coot to educate her in the ways of the world."

"Five will get you ten you get a citation for this," Vicky said.

"Young woman, I have warned you against gambling on my ship."

"It's Kris's ship."

"Worse, you're gambling before the . . . ah . . . a Longknife. Behave yourself. Nelly, would you call my staff back in. It seems we have a jump mission to plan."

39

Captain Jack Montoya, Royal United Sentient Marine Corps, was having a good day. On the average.

He'd gotten to rescue a certain twelve-year-old girl. She and her aunt were on the first shuttle back to the *Wasp*. Jack had looked Cara over. She looked a lot older . . . and her smile was missing.

Cara had come aboard the *Wasp* a frail waif who had just lost her mother and grandmother. Then, she'd looked like serious was her first, last, and middle name.

Then the smile slowly found its way out. Jack felt like he was watching a beaten and abused kitten discover that it could play when a ball of twine was dangled in front of her.

In no time, that waif and her smile had wrapped most every member of the *Wasp*'s crew around her little finger.

But the smile was gone now. Gone, leaving Jack to wonder if it would ever return.

That many of the men and women who had stripped Cara of that smile were dead was not an even trade in Jack's book.

Jack sighed. There were professionals on the *Wasp* whose job it was to help little girls find their smiles.

No doubt, in weeks to come, they would bring out their best solutions for Cara.

Today, Jack was only too happy to try his own.

The first shuttle down after the combat drop had brought a Navy landing party led by the Command Master Chief Mong. He and his team brought down a boatload of flamethrowers and were busy applying them to the local crop of poison.

Not that much fire was needed to put the fields aflame. The leaves of this particular plant had an oily feel and were only too eager to burn. This was nice, because Master Chief Mong and his sailors were enthusiastically torching them.

Marines were still moving from one farm to the next, looking for sailors and blowing up processing plants. There was occasional opposition.

Jack would hear the low report of a slug pistol or rifle. It would immediately be followed by the high-pitched snap of an M-6. One hostile shot. One Marine reply.

Then a long and death-filled silence.

So far, no Marine had requested medical assistance. Only twice had a call come in for assistance to a down civilian . . . and one of them had been for an innocent bystander who got hit by the initial pistol shot.

It's a good day when a Marine can contribute his little bit to evil's getting its comeuppance.

That didn't mean there weren't annoyances.

Gunny Brown had called in with a civilian. Fellow was berating Gunny about this being private property and a business operation and that Gunny had no right to come in and disturb his operation.

Problem was that Gunny's team had already found an open grave with a dozen bodies, all in different stages of decomposition, out behind the drug barns.

The creep had the gall to claim that those were just workers who'd died on the job without taking out the offered funeral insurance.

The story from his slaves was a bit different.

Jack had ordered Gunny to document the situation and bring the guy in in cuffs along with some witnesses. The Marine captain had no idea how the local legal system would handle a case like this, but he would make sure it had to face it.

The pictures that Gunny showed of this man's slaves were particularly troubling to Jack. All of the slaves here were on short rations, but this fellow's slaves were little more than scarecrows.

What was it with these people? They had already beaten

their workers into submission. Why weren't they at least giving them enough food to keep body and soul alive? What good was a starved and dying worker?

This whole situation made no sense to Jack.

It didn't. Unless and until he factored in the simple fact that here, on this planet, the owners *could* treat their slaves this way. For the plantation owners and the whip-cracking overseers, that was all they needed. If they could get away with brutalizing this part of humanity, they would brutalize it.

Jack shook his head. Hopefully, Kris would see that the local elephants did something about all this injustice, which cried out for its day in court. A real court.

"Jack, are you there?"

"Yes, Kris, I'm here," he said, forcing his voice to professional calm. "How's it coming with your elephant taming."

"It's taken an interesting turn. I'm coming dirtside."

"Hold it. I thought your new duties required you to hold yourself aloof from our low-class fun and games."

"Maybe not so much."

"You want to tell your lowly minion what you're up to."

"I'd rather not. Let's hold this for face-to-face. By the way, have you gotten ahold of much transportation?"

"Yes, I've got several sets of wheels."

"Get more, we're going to need them. See you in a bit."

40

"We're going to arrest who?" Jack asked, incredulously.

"Ms. van da Fitz," Kris answered, as if it was the most rational idea in human space.

She glanced around. Jack had collected the *Wasp*'s Marine company and several cars and trucks. The Marines showed their usual patience as they stood by the transportation, checked their weapons, and readied themselves to follow her next order, whatever it might be.

"And if Miss van da Snooty doesn't want to come along peacefully?" their captain asked.

"That's why we're taking a whole Marine company," Kris said.

"Any chance we might get a couple of battalions of Imperial Greenfeld Marines?" the Royal Marine asked.

"Not a good idea," Kris said, unrolling a large flimsy that showed the details of Port Royal and stretching it out on the hood of their potential staff car. "Greenfeld Marines know very well how much money Fitz has in her change purse. Very likely, she'd buy her way out. Certainly, she'd know we are coming well before we got there. Admiral Krätz felt it would be a good idea if we did it using only Wardhaven assets."

"And if we get killed doing this?"

"No doubt Emperor Henry will make him a duke for being the guy who finally killed Kris Longknife," Kris answered evenly.

"Kris, did you hear what you just said," Jack growled.

"You've gotten us into some bad situations, but this has got to take the cake."

"Don't be so sure, Captain. This may only be practice for my next, even worse, idea."

"Such as?"

"Let's save that for later," Kris said. "Colonel Cortez has gone over the map, and he thinks there are three distinct approaches, one for each of the platoons," Kris began the briefing for her officers. "Our target is the N.S. tower, right here on the bay front. Notice how all roads lead straight to it."

Two hours later, Kris had driven straight to it without so much as a shot fired. As she arrived two blocks from the tower, First Lieutenant Stubben reported the first platoon deployed to her right, in the buildings along Harbor Road East. Gunny Brown deployed the third platoon covering Kris's left, in the smaller businesses along Harbor Road West.

They awaited her orders.

Kris and Jack drove up State Street and parked their rigs behind an imposing two-story stone bank building. The rest of the platoon took its time taking up shooting positions in the stores across the street and in the bank.

Now Kris stood in the shade of the bank entrance eyeing what lay before them.

"How are we supposed to do this?" Jack said as he surveyed the tactical problem. N.S. tower was a good twenty stories high in front of them, the highest building in the new and growing town of Port Royal.

Laid out like a fan on its shoreward side were parking lots and a park with statues, a fountain, and palm trees. Lovely open spaces stretched for the thousand meters between the bank and the tower.

It looked like a lovely place to visit.

Attack it?

Not so much.

"You think they have any autocannons?" Kris asked.

"They had plenty on their space station. What makes you think they'd scrimp around their ground headquarters?" Jack

asked, answering her question with a question . . . and maybe
a bit of sarcasm to boot.

"It's not my place as an admiral to interfere with you gravel
crunchers' tactical problem," Admiral Krätz said on net, "but
have you ever considered calling on her to surrender like any
law-abiding outlaw?"

"So nice of him to have suggestions since he's not down
here risking his neck," Jack muttered to Kris, hopefully off
net.

"Anything's worth a try," Kris muttered back, and jacked
up the power on her battle suit's loudspeaker. "You are surrounded. Throw down your weapons and come out with your
hands up, and you will all survive today."

For a long second, nothing happened. Then another long
second went by. Maybe enough time passed for Ms. van da
Fitz to quit laughing at the joke.

Or maybe she hit the automated defense button in midlaughter.

The fountain quit spewing water, and an ugly twin-barrel
device rose from the pond at its base. It took a second for the
guns to level and point themselves right at Kris—but only a
second.

Then it started spewing big ugly slugs.

A chunk from several of the tree trunks retracted, and more
weapons let loose. Where stone statues stood, suddenly the
stone faces of the cube pedestals fell away, showing a machine
gun behind each quarter. They opened fire, spraying fire in
four different directions.

Lucky for Kris, Jack had grabbed her elbow the second the
fountain gave up flinging water skyward. He pulled her after
him as he half fell through the bank door.

A Marine sapper still stood behind the door whose lock
she'd recently blown so Marines could enter. Even as the
sound of weapons fire filled the air, the trooper pushed the
door open for Jack and Kris.

"Thank you," Jack said as he half yanked, half pulled Kris
through the door.

The Marine said, "You're welcome," and winced as cannon
fire slammed into the door, half knocking her down.

Most of the weapons fire missed Kris. Not all. One round clipped her ankle, shattering her armor there, but it did its job and protected her soft flesh.

Still, it stung like the dickens.

As the door swung closed behind them, it was stitched by slugs. Good armored glass that it was, it held, showing shattered stars where it was hit. As it slowly closed, shattered stars got shattered stars on them. The glass bowed in from the pressure of all the high-powered rounds it was taking.

"Let's get out of here," Jack said.

The sapper held open the second door, and they scooted inside.

"Admiral Krätz, that didn't go so well. You got any more bright ideas," Jack snapped.

"Is Kris all right?" he asked, sounding sincerely worried.

"I'm fine. My ankle got clipped, and it's hurting a bit, but I'm okay. Honestly, do you have any other ideas?" she asked, trying to make it sound sincere.

"I guess now we do it the easy way," the admiral said. "Since she has resisted arrest, I don't see any reason we can't bring the full force of empire down upon her."

"The full force of empire?" Kris asked.

"The Navy," Vicky answered.

"Oh no," Kris said. "Marines, get down. Way down. Visors down. Go on internal oxygen," she shouted.

"What the hell?" Jack said, but he was locking his suit down and rolling across the bank floor looking for a solid pillar to get close to. Kris put her back up against a column and grabbed her knees, something not easy to do in battle armor.

She also did her best to be small, something really not easy to do in armor when you're a six-foot-tall gal.

Once, Kris was dirtside when a corvette fired two 18-inch pulse lasers at targets near her position. Those had been only pulse lasers, weak things firing a short burst of power.

Her ears had rung for the rest of the day, and her body had hurt well into the next from the noise and overpressure.

Once, Kris fought a major space battle, defending her home planet from being bombarded by six killer battleships bent on blasting Wardhaven back into the Stone Age. A lot of Kris's friends died defeating those battleships, but they protected their home from taking that beating.

Now, Kris was just a thousand meters from the target of just the kind of battle lasers that had been intended for her home.

She didn't look. To look would be to die.

Instead, she watched it secondhand, reflected in the polished marble of the bank's inner wall. The N.S. tower was just a shadow, surrounded by the bright glare from sky and water.

Then Kris's visor went dark to protect her from blindness. Even as everything around her disappeared, a single bright light, straight as an arrow, made the tower shine.

The top floors melted away in less time than it would have taken to blink. Then two, three, no, four more lines of light added their input to the halo of shining fire around the tower.

Pulse lasers had power, but only for a second or two. Battleship lasers had more power, and they poured it out for long-sustained seconds. Battle lasers were intended to cut through six, eight, or ten feet of reflecting ice that shrouded other battleships. Battleships also spun along their long axes at twenty revolutions a minute. This allowed armor that was being boiled by a hit to rotate away from the slashing laser fire before it burned through to the ship below.

Battleships were made to hammer and be hammered.

The N.S. tower was not built with that kind of beating in mind. It had no ice shell. It was not spinning. It was on the receiving end of huge amounts of power and could do nothing but burn.

Burn and collapse.

Kris watched the fuzzy reflection on the marble in front of her as the tower got shorter and shorter and shorter. She wasn't sure, but it looked to her like some of the laser fire went silent, only to be replaced as more cannons came online.

The reflected tower on the wall shrank until it stood no taller than the ground around it, but still the lasers burned.

While Kris's eyes were locked on the reflected glory in front of her, her ears, even through the suit, were telling her the atmospheric pressure around her was going wild.

The bulletproof windows of the bank had taken hits, hits shown by the line of stars across the windowpanes. The windows had withstood cannon and machine-gun fire.

Now, the power of the sun was come to earth. The air twisted and roiled in torture and took its vengeance where it could.

The windows above where Kris huddled bowed in, heated up, melted, and flew across the bank in less time than it took to think of it. Drops of flaming glass splattered into surreal patterns on the wall where just a second ago, the tower had been reflected.

The air in the bank rushed out the void that had been windows, trying to fill the swirling tornado that now spun where the tower had once stood against the sky. Desks and furniture did their level best to follow the gale winds. One solid wooden desk smashed into the wall a handsbreadth away from Kris.

Jack crawled back to throw himself over Kris. She pushed him back and slid herself under the desk. He backed himself in to cover the opening.

Just as quickly as it had come, the laser fire was gone. If that brought silence, Kris didn't notice it; her ears still rang. If it brought calm, Kris couldn't see it; her visor only slowly went from darkest to dark to not quite so dark.

"You okay?" Jack asked over net.

"Mostly. I think. Maybe," Kris admitted to the possibility.

"Admiral, if you're still online," Jack said, "would you do us a favor next time you do us a favor. Give us a bit of warning."

"I hope you will excuse me if I say that it seemed like a good idea at the time. If you can arrange to return to the *Wasp*, I understand that the Forward Lounge is a very good place to hold a victory party. There, with no recordings running, I think I can better explain what I intended to do, even if I didn't quite manage to do it."

"If killing us was your intention," Jack grumbled, "you didn't quite manage to do it."

"I assure you, that was never my intention."

"Jack, we better get out of from under this desk. I think it's starting to burn," Kris said.

Not only the desk, but the bank around them, it seemed. What wasn't solid marble was indeed catching fire.

Marines who'd spent the bombardment upstairs in the bank were hastily coming downstairs, many limping, others helping. Kris found that if she wanted to move, it involved limping along with Jack's help.

The street was littered with fallen trees, fallen building facades, and tossed cars and trucks. Kris stared for a second at the pleasant park that had once surrounded the N.S. tower. It looked like a moonscape, burned and blown clear of vegetation of any kind.

Where the tower had stood, a new appendage of the bay now lapped. The water that had rushed into the hole in the ground boiled and steamed from the molten slag that gave the only hint that a building had once occupied the land.

"I wonder how many people were in there with Ms. van da Fitz?" Kris asked.

"We'll likely never know. Unless someone had a backup copy stored off-site of all the data in that tower, I doubt there's another place with a full list of who worked and lived there, or anywhere else on this entire planet," Jack said.

"I wonder who will run this place now, and how?" Kris said.

"I may be wrong, but my money is on Admiral Krätz to have a definite plan for this place. And I don't think it involves a chicken ranch. Not at all. Let's go catch a shuttle. I want to talk to that guy."

"Remember, Jack, he's our ally, for the moment."

"You know what they say about allies like him," Jack said.

"Who needs enemies?" they said together.

41

Kris wasn't actually reduced to hobbling about on a cane again. Not actually. She could hobble very well on her own two feet after Abby applied a balloon splint to her hurting ankle.

Abby was careful to select a clear splint.

"That way everyone can see how black-and-blue your ankle is. You might actually get some sympathy from the psychopaths you hang out with."

"You, my fine feathered friend, are one of those psychopaths," Kris shot back.

"Guilty as charged and delighted to be. Oh, and I'm alive. I understand the head psychopath ain't."

"Very ain't," Kris said with a shiver. She changed the subject. "How's Cara?"

"Safe. More quiet than a girl that age should be. Very, very contrite. If you got anything you want that kid to do for you, ask now."

"How bad was it for her?"

"She insists nothing happened. When have you heard *that* from a teenager? The docs did a full checkup. She is okay, but it must have been hell wondering every second of every day if, no matter how bad it was, was it about to get worse?"

Kris nodded. It went without saying that nothing like this should ever happen to a young kid like Cara.

Or to anyone for that matter.

Penny was still collecting evidence for the worst crimes they'd found, but the entire hellhole was a crime. How could justice ever be done for something like Port Royal?

"Cara knows there are counselors on board," Kris said.

"Both of them were her friends before this happened. I think she'll talk to them, friend to friend, then maybe for something stronger," Abby said, then turned to Kris's closet and returned with a brown skirt. No, it was a knee-length pair of shorts that were so wide and flowing that it easily passed for a skirt. Abby also held a loose, silk, off-the-shoulder top in gold.

"This ought to let you show off your black-and-blue ankle in fine contrast to good Mother Earth tones.

As Abby helped Kris dress, she went on. "Kris, I haven't said thank you for letting me have Cara with us. I know a girl wouldn't usually fit all that well on a warship, but Cara really needed me."

"You can still say that after what just happened?"

"Kris, you didn't see how the crew took to Cara's coming back. This is her home, and Cara really needs to feel like someplace is home. Yes, something bad happened, but, Kris, growing up in Five Corners is just a long list of bad things happening. Here, she's got a home, and I think seeing the long line of boffins and sailors waiting for her in the drop bay was the most healing experience she's ever known.

"She'd quit crying by the time the longboat docked. She was still going over a mantra of 'I'm sorry' and 'I won't ever do that again.' But when she saw all of them waiting for her, she broke down crying again. And those were the happiest tears I've ever seen in my life. Happy and healing. I wish you could have seen them."

"I was kind of otherwise occupied," Kris drawled.

"Yeah, you usually are at times like those. Baby ducks, you really ought to set aside time for the good times."

"You can talk to my scheduling secretary."

"Yeah, I will," Abby said, and turned Kris around to see how close to beautiful she'd managed today.

Kris winced as she put weight on her bad ankle.

"Well, I just wanted you to know how grateful Cara and I are for you having us around. I hope you'll keep us."

"Um," Kris said. Since next on her agenda was deciding

what the *Wasp* would do in the future . . . and who would be going with it into the nasty unknown, Kris didn't want to get too committal.

In the next hour, Abby might be running, not walking, for the nearest exit.

Abby seemed satisfied with the "Um." She handed Kris one of her canes. "The doc said you ought to take some painkillers. But knowing you, I suspect this cane is the best I can offer."

The party was in full swing by the time Kris limped into the Forward Lounge. The last of the Marines had been lifted back to the *Wasp*. They now formed a sea of khaki, occupying the right-hand side of the lounge. Sailors' whites held the left. A couple of tables remained open in the middle.

From the farthest middle table, Jack raised a hand and signaled Kris to come. Marines and sailors on their way to and from the bar made respectful way for Kris as she wobbled her way to the table that usually had the best view of space.

At the moment, with the *Wasp* nosed into the space station, Kris's view was of pipes, bulkheads that needed painting, and other less interesting stuff.

Jack seated Kris with her back to the view.

There was a soft drink waiting for Kris as she settled into her designated chair. Jack cleared a second chair for her ankle, giving it a place of honor. "You know, that's about the only casualty we suffered today. Two drop injuries, but you're the only one due to hostile fire."

"I must speak to my security chief about getting me out of the line of fire more quickly next time," Kris said.

"I've already talked to him about not letting you do stupid stuff next time," her chief of security snapped back, but Jack was grinning. "No doubt you'll ignore his sound advice," he said, raising his beer stein in mock salute.

Kris raised her glass to clink against his.

Jack swallowed his smile and left his glass in the air. "We saw some real evil today. And we sent it to hell where it belonged."

Lieutenant Stubben and Gunny Brown raised their beer mugs to clink against their captain's. Kris added her own glass.

"To hell with them," they said.

The toast caught on and swept around the room, Marine khaki and Navy whites raised their drinks to the same toast. "To hell with them."

A shiver went down Kris's spine. This was a good ending to a horrible day. This was what these fine people lived for. They had seen evil in the face of which even the deepest pit in hell would blush. Their commanders had given them weapons release, and they had done what they were trained to do.

The evil that was Port Royal was no more. Pure and simple, they'd wiped it from the face of this planet. A lot of it was dead and gone. Good riddance.

Penny and her forensic squad would stay dirtside as long as it took to collect evidence for the part of the evil that had avoided death today. With any kind of luck, they wouldn't avoid it very long.

Kris sighed. No doubt it would be her job to decide how soon and how well the still-living minions got to keep breathing. She had a lot more work to do with her half-trained elephants.

She chuckled. She'd spent time with the elephants today and time with the line beasts. There was no doubt in her mind who she preferred. Still, one left her with an aching leg and the other just made her sense of justice cringe.

No question, she'd rather ache than cringe.

There was noise at the back of the lounge. Kris twisted around in her seat. The sight was well worth the effort.

Admiral Krätz was waving down those who would have rendered him formal honors. "This is a party. I came to party, not to disturb good fighting men and women at their play. Sit down, sit down, all of you."

Krätz was the admiral; his undress greens made that clear to all. But it was the lieutenant at his side who was getting most of the attention.

Vicky was in a sedate, red cocktail dress. Kris had seen the dress in the online catalogues, and online it was in black and white. Sedate. Informal.

With Vicky's looks and figure, there was no way that sedate stayed staid. Certainly not when the dress was hot cherry red.

Of course, Kris had seen Vicky in her wilder days on New

Eden. Compared to the painted-on affairs Vicky wore then, this looked downright dowdy.

But then, on New Eden, she hadn't walked into a roomful of young sailors and Marines.

It wasn't the admiral who needed to order "As you were," it was the lieutenant.

With just a hint of a nod from Jack, the LT and Gunny were on their feet. Jack stood, too, to signal the admiral and his shadow toward Kris's table. They smiled as soon as they saw Kris and made their way to her.

The LT and Gunny stayed just long enough to be introduced to the admiral and Vicky, just long enough to accept his compliments on a day well done and for the young Marine officer and the old Gunny to thank the admiral for helping them avoid storming so well fortified a target . . . and for the admiral to insist it wasn't anything big.

The LT left to get drinks for the admiral and Vicky. Gunny went to join the table where Command Master Chief Mong held sway, and Kris was asked to explain how things had really gone down at the N.S. tower that noon.

She did, making it clear to the Navy types present that being on the receiving end of 18-inch battle lasers should be reserved for other battleships that were designed to play in that league.

Not that they paid her any attention.

The admiral laughed as Kris described hiding under a desk that had narrowly missed reducing her to jelly. "But you yourself admit that you were in armored battle suits. All you had to do was clamp down your visor, and you had plenty of air to breathe."

"So how come my ears were popping," Jack pointed out.

"You should talk to your Wardhaven procurement people," the admiral said without pausing in his laughter. "Something must be substandard."

Kris had been at enough tables with high-powered politicians to know that the elephant here only wanted to hear how cunning he was and be thanked. Having survived the day, it was no skin off Kris's nose to give him what he wanted.

"Well, I admit to being glad that my Marines didn't have to storm that tower with all its autocannons and machine guns," Kris admitted. "Vicky, did you see the hole in the ground your admiral made. Someone's going to have to remap that lake."

"No question about that," Vicky agreed.

Rear Admiral Georg Krätz beamed in satisfaction.

"So, tell me," Kris went on, "what happens next?"

"That will be very interesting," the admiral admitted.

"Very complicated," his lieutenant said, sipping her beer.

"Maybe, maybe not," her superior said. "Have you ever visited one of the Navy colonies?"

Vicky shook her head.

"There are two of them, I think," the admiral said. "They are colonies set up by the Navy. When I retire, you don't think I want to raise chickens with just any bunch of neighbors, do you. No, I want to know I've got people I can count on. People I like. My kind of people."

"So the Greenfeld Navy has set up planets for their own people to put down stakes on?" Kris said, more surprised than she wanted to admit. There was a lot Wardhaven didn't know about Greenfeld.

As far as Kris was concerned, if she was the only one who found out about it, Admiral Crossenshield could get comfortable living in the dark.

"You got it in one." The admiral laughed. "Who said Longknifes are dumb. Anyway, I think Port Royal will make a great addition to the collection of Navy colonies."

"And N.S. Holdings won't object?" Jack asked.

"There is no evidence that N.S. Holdings ever had any interest in this planet," the admiral said with a sly grin.

"Not after the tower got turned into a pond," Vicky said.

"Yes, yes. No evidence at all. That woman was claiming just this afternoon that they had filed a claim on this planet. We have finished our search of the records, and there is no such claim," the admiral said with a grin.

That left Kris wondering. Had there been no such record, or was there no such record *now*?

NELLY?

I HAVE NO IDEA, KRIS. THAT'S MY STORY, AND I'M STICK-
ING TO IT.

JUST MAKE SURE YOU *DO* STICK TO IT.

Kris turned back to the conversation. The admiral was describing some of the benefits of having Navy colonies. "You
turn loose enough old goats, and it's bound to get interesting."

"You can't all raise chickens," Jack said.

"Oh no, there are those who raise cows for meat and cows
for cheese. Some actually like to plow in the dirt and grow
fruit and vegetables and things. No accounting for tastes even
after thirty years with the fleet," he said, distastefully.

"There wouldn't happen to be any heavy industry on these
planets?" Kris asked.

"God forbid," the admiral said, raising his hand to elevate
the pledge. "Besides, if you have spent your life around heavy
weapons and high energy, you need something peaceful in
your old age. Yes, maybe there is some light industry. Something to make toys for good-little-girl and -boy grandchildren.
Anything else, no!"

NELLY, CALL UP THE SURVEY WE MADE OF THIS SYSTEM.

I HAVE IT, KRIS.

DIDN'T I NOTICE AN ASTEROID BELT? ONE RICH IN ALL
KINDS OF METALS?

YES, KRIS. IF SOMEONE WANTED TO ESTABLISH A MAJOR
NAVAL PRESENCE AND HEAVY-CONSTRUCTION FACTORIES,
THEY HAVE EVERYTHING THEY NEED FOR IT OUTSIDE OF ANY
STRONG GRAVITY WELL.

DO THE OTHER NAVAL COLONIES HAVE SUCH RESOURCES?

KRIS, I DON'T HAVE ANY PLANETS IN THE GREENFELD AL-
LIANCE THAT ARE LABELED NAVAL COLONIES. IT MAY BE THAT
THEY HAVE OTHER NAMES, LIKE THIS ONE WILL LIKELY STAY
PORT ROYAL. EITHER THAT, OR THEY HAVE AVOIDED OUR DE-
TECTION. THEY ALSO AREN'T ON THE ITEECHE MAP THAT I'M
NOT SUPPOSED TO HAVE.

THANK YOU, NELLY.

The conversation had taken a dark turn. Jack had pointed
out that there were people on the planet who must know what
was going on.

"Yes, and your Lieutenant Pasley has done a great job of building the evidentiary case against them and their crimes. Tomorrow, we will bury the merchant sailors they murdered with full honors. I expect there will be a lot of new filled graves around them. My Commander Fervenspiel is presently seating court-martials to hear the cases based on your lieutenant's evidence."

Kris nodded. Jack threw her a look. Kris made sure her face stayed carved in stone.

Inside it was different. PENNY, ARE YOU THERE?

IT'S GOOD TO HEAR FROM BOTH OF YOU.

HUH?

DO YOU TWO KNOW YOU BOTH JUST CALLED ME, KRIS, JACK?

No, I DIDN'T, echoed in Kris's head in both her and Jack's voices. Getting the hang of Nelly and her kids' net was still a work in progress.

SO, TO WHAT DO I OWE THE HONOR OF THIS CALL? AS IF I DON'T SUSPECT.

I UNDERSTAND THAT YOUR EVIDENCE IS BEING USED BY THE GREENFELD NAVY FOR COURT-MARTIALS.

YOU COULD SAY THAT, KRIS. I TEND TO SPELL THEM KANGAROO COURT.

IS IT THAT BAD?

IT'S NOT AS BAD AS IT WAS WITH THE PIRATES ON THE STATION. THEY AREN'T JUST LINING PEOPLE UP AGAINST THE WALL AND SHOOTING THEM. NOT QUITE. THE SLAVE OVERSEERS AND DRUG-PLANTATION MANAGERS ARE GETTING THEIR DAY IN COURT. WELL, FIFTEEN MINUTES. THEY CAN FACE THEIR ACCUSERS. LOOK AT THE EVIDENCE I'VE GATHERED. I GUESS THEY ARE PRETTY OPEN-AND-SHUT CASES, KRIS.

IT IS AGAINST GREENFELD LAW TO TRAFFIC IN SLAVES, PENNY.

I KNOW, I KNOW, KRIS. IF WE WERE BRINGING THEM UP ON CHARGES, WE'D PROBABLY GET TO THE SAME BOTTOM LINE. IT'S JUST THAT THE TIME FROM THE READING OF THE CHARGES TO THE VERDICT TO BEING TAKEN OUT AND SHOT IS LESS THAN AN HOUR. IN SOME CASES A WHOLE LOT LESS THAN AN HOUR.

Kris, back home, when I was growing up, we had this minister who loved, every year, to preach on how we should pray not for justice, but for mercy. Well, it looks like we've got justice here, but not an ounce of mercy.

Penny, it didn't look like they were showing those slaves much mercy, Jack offered.

I know. I hear you. Give me a bit of time to process it all, okay?

Where are you now?

I'm headed back to the *Wasp*, Kris. They've got my evidence. They don't need me. One of my Marines can handle presenting it to the court.

We're all celebrating in the forward lounge. If you want a chance to slug the admiral in the jaw, this is where you want to go.

Don't tempt me, Kris.

Who's tempting? I'm offering.

Kris found herself coming back to the conversation. There was more noise at the front door. Campbell and his XO, Kitano were arriving, along with the Marine detachment commander for the *Dauntless*. Taussig of *Hornet* was also there along with the command staff of the *Fearless* and *Intrepid*. There was much shouting of someone hogging all the fun and not getting their fair share of the exercise.

All in good humor.

Several tables were found to be empty and were slid together to join with Kris's. Kris would have sworn that all the tables were full when she came in, but as arrangements were made to seat the others, she spotted how and why the Forward Lounge was gradually emptying out.

Command Master Chief Mong and Gunny Sergeant Brown had taken a commanding table in the middle of the lounge. From there, they had a good view of everything. As Kris watched, a Marine finished his second beer and raised his hand for a third.

As he expected, the barmaid headed his way. However, Gunny also had seen the order and noted the two beer mugs,

with suds still foaming in front of him. A nod from Gunny to
the Chief Master-at-arms, and two petty officers were at the
kid's elbow before the barmaid.

The trooper was long gone before the barmaid, herself a
petty officer during working hours, got to his table. She removed the mugs and wiped down the table.

Marine or sailor, they got two beers today. Tomorrow's duties would come soon enough, and no doubt the young men
and women, away from home for the first time in their lives,
would be ready to do their duty.

Kris also didn't doubt that Gunny and Master Chief Mong
were coordinating their efforts with the other pubs in Boffin
Country. With nearly half the *Wasp* given over to civilians and
their requirements, the Navy was making fine adjustments.

Which left Kris to wonder what should change, and what
should stay the same if she did what she was planning to do.

She was lost in thought when she realized the admiral was
talking to her. He'd ordered several bottles of vodka for his officers and had appropriated one of them for himself. No chief
or Gunny was limiting his drinks tonight. From the looks of
things, he'd need help back to his ship later.

"Excuse me," she said.

"I was wondering what you are planning to do with those
pirate ships you captured."

"You were?" Kris said. As she understood matters, the
schooners and the one merchant ship at the station had been
captured by the *Wasp* and *Dauntless*. She planned to dispose
of them under prize rules.

There'd been some grumbling from the Greenfeld Marines when they weren't allowed to get in on the fun of their
capture . . . or the money. Was the admiral trying to renegoti-
ate the terms of their agreement.

"They're yours to do with as you please," he said, and
seemed to realize that he needed to get that reassurance out
front. "It's just that they are tying up the three best piers on the
station. The piers my battleships are at can't give them nearly
enough air and water or comm circuits. Your five corvettes
and the *Blood* plus those three mean I don't even have enough

docks to tie up all my battleships much less the cruisers. Where are you planning on sending them for a prize court?"

"Not Cuzco," Kris said, not needing a second to think on that.

Around the table, that got laughs. Apparently, Kris's legal problems with the last ship she'd captured from pirates were well-known.

"Have you seen a dime from that?" Taussig asked.

"Not so much as a penny," Kris said. She thought for a moment. "I guess we could send them to Pandemonium. I think their courts would take the right view of pirate ships."

That seemed to get agreement.

"Course, there's not much market for pirate schooners around the Rim," Admiral Krätz pointed out. "At least not a market we want to feed."

"I don't know," Jack Campbell said. "Capture them. Sell them back. Capture them again and sell them again. The right guy could make a career of it."

That got a laugh.

"There is the possibility of my setting up an Admiralties Court right here on Port Royal," the admiral said, sounding downright conspiratorial. "I might arrange for the Greenfeld Navy to buy two of the ships. Do you have any idea what we might do with the others?"

"I could be interested in one or two of the schooners," Kris allowed. "If they are fast enough, the Royal Navy might have a need for schooners as messenger boats out beyond the Rim. Question is, do they have legs? Can they stay out for months at a time? What kind of shape are the schooners in?" she asked the admiral.

The admiral took time to share a victory toast before he answered. "I had a couple of officers take a look at them, all four of them. If the price was right, and we could get permission from Navy Headquarters, I'd like to buy one of the sloops and the freighter. We do need to get something out here to show the flag. Anyway, they all look pretty good. If I didn't know any better, I'd say they came from one of our premier yards."

"But you know better," Kris said.

"Why, my dear young lady, of course they couldn't have come from one of our best yards. Our fine, upstanding businessmen would never do business with pirates, now would they?" he said, giving the table a sly wink as he downed another shot of vodka.

Vicky shook her head in disgust. "We know very well where they came from. Just because they did a good job of filing off the serial numbers and burning their papers . . ."

"But, Lieutenant, they did just that. Your father, our emperor, would never take action against such important financial interests with no evidence."

"You took action this afternoon."

"They fired on my delegated spokesman. I merely returned fire."

Around the table, the newly arrived Royal U.S. Navy officers risked blank looks. Jack whispered, "Eighteen-inch battleship lasers within a thousand meters of my Marine company."

"They're on our side, right?" Campbell whispered.

"I wasn't so sure at the moment," Jack answered.

"Yes, yes, I know," the admiral said. "There was some personal risk to you. But we have put an end to the slavers running this show and destroyed all the evidence. Now we can take over this colony and run it the way decent people do. Right?" he said, raising another toast at that thought.

"Right," the Royal Navy said, for once in agreement with their Imperial opposites.

Vicky didn't look any more sure of the toast than Kris did. Instead of lifting her mug, she reached inside her purse and pulled out a flimsy.

"What do you think of this article, Kris? 'My friend the Iteeche.' "

Kris choked on her soft drink.

42

Kris struggled for air. When had she ever told anyone about Ron? Certainly, she'd never called him her friend. Then Kris spotted the byline. Even through watering eyes she could read Winston Spencer.

She had never told him that she was friends with an Iteeche! Never. Not once!

Through coughing fits and tear-filled eyes, Kris read the first couple of paragraphs of the news story. Oh, he didn't mention her name. No, these were other people who were willing to say that they'd been friends with Iteeche.

Kris allowed herself a couple of more coughs to clear her throat, then risked a small sip of her drink. It went down the right way. Then she caught her breath.

Once she had full control of her faculties . . . and had offered a quick prayer of thanks that someone coughing to death could not say something that would forever embarrass her . . . she tackled a response.

"What do you mean, 'My Friend the Iteeche'?" she said to Vicky.

"Well, it was written by a friend of yours, that newsie you have sending you reports on what's happening in Longknife space."

"I told you, I hired him so I wouldn't be caught flat-footed in polite conversation with my big brother next time we run into each other. Out here on the Rim, a girl can get totally out of touch."

"Yes, I know you said that. But isn't it strange that a big

chunk of the stuff he sends you has to do with the Iteeche, far more than would be statistically significant, considering how little is said about those horrible creatures. And then he writes an article like this."

"Who's talking about my friend the Iteeche?" Campbell asked.

"Just some news guy," Kris said, making sure to avoid admitting any familiarity with him. "Nelly, can you put the article up where people can read it?"

"Oh, I have it here," Vicky said, and the article suddenly appeared in big, bold letters on the view screen of the Forward Lounge, emblazoned against a backdrop of pipes and ducts. Beside Kris, others started reading.

They didn't read in silence for long.

"That's unbelievable," Taussig said. "Her father had Iteeche POWs working on his farm while she was growing up."

"She thought they were pets," Lieutenant Kitano put in. "To a ten-year-old girl, I guess a rock can be a pet."

"A rock I can buy," Campbell said. "An Iteeche?"

"It says here, one of the Iteeche farmhands saved her brother when he built a raft, and it came apart."

"I built a raft when I was a kid, and I needed saving," Taussig admitted.

"We couldn't have captured that many Iteeche," someone said incredulously.

"Not during the first part of the war," Kris said, "when it was mostly their wandering men against our pirates. As you may have noticed recently, pirates don't take very good care of their prisoners. When we recaptured territory from their wandering men, what we found wasn't pretty. I bet it was the same for them." Kris knew quite well from her recent talks with Ron, the Iteeche Imperial Representative, that they'd found some pretty ugly scenes, too.

"However," Kris went on, "once Society of Humanity forces found ourselves fighting Imperial troops, such atrocities ended. If you can believe this article."

Kris did, but others would have to make up their own mind.

This article was certainly going against the commonly held perception of a great generation.

"You know, this is interesting," Campbell said, rubbing his chin. "My dad said he had a friend who was captured by the Iteeche and lived to tell the story. Now, I wish I'd looked the fellow up and asked him. Then, well, everyone knew the Iteeche didn't take prisoners. And neither did we."

"I am fifty years old," the admiral said, "and never would I have expected to read such a story. But now, come to think of it. Back when I was in the Academy, there was a whispered story that the head of the Department of Escape and Survival had survived an Iteeche POW camp. Like you, I did not believe the story. Now, I, too, wish I had asked more questions."

"Interesting that your friend wrote the story," Vicky said, grinning at Kris.

"I told you, he's no friend of mine. I'm a Longknife. He's a newsie. They say nasty things about us, and we think nasty thoughts about them. Even on Wardhaven, that is no basis for a relationship."

"But you did talk with him," Vicky said. You could almost hear the steel teeth of the bear trap closing on Kris's leg.

The bad leg.

Kris stalled. "What makes you say that?"

"I have a copy of the trip tick from the cab that took him and Admiral Santiago to Nuu House. And a copy of the return ticket."

"Maybe I wasn't there," Kris tried.

"You were there. You had the insert for Nelly directly into your head reinstalled that morning. You were there."

"My, aren't you the little sleuth."

"No, I'm not, but I've learned how to buy their services when I need them. One of Greenfeld's best spent two weeks as guest of our Wardhaven embassy, checking up on what he could check up on."

Kris couldn't decide whether she should congratulate herself that her student was actually learning . . . or throttle the kid before she got too smart. For the moment, Kris settled on waffling. "Okay, maybe I was there, and maybe he came along when I set up some quality time with a good family friend. What does it mean?"

"You and your great-grandfather met with an Iteeche," Vicky said with all the drama and accusing power of the best vid prosecutor.

43

Around Kris, the Forward Lounge went silent.

Well, not totally quiet. Gunny Brown was on his feet, pointing at first one, then another group of Marines. Pointing at them, then pointing at the exit.

Marines stood, took a last pull from their beers, and headed for the door.

Beside Gunny, the Command Master Chief went through the same exercise. Under his stern visage, sailors moved out. Behind the bar, the guys and gals stopped fixing the next round, put their glasses down, and made for the door, too.

In less than a minute, the Lounge was clear of everyone below the rank of Marine captain or Navy lieutenant.

For a moment, Kris marveled at what she had just witnessed. Then she remembered. King Ray had asked Gunny Brown to protect the security and privacy of his meeting with the Iteeche.

When officers like Ray Longknife extract such promises from the likes of Gunny, they become the pledges by which folks live or for which good men and women die.

Kris took a moment to bathe in the warmth of that kind of loyalty . . . but only a moment. It cut both ways. Now she owed Gunny and his Marines something in return.

She glanced around the near-empty room. On the couch by the wall, Abby sat with a very subdued Cara. Kris should ask Cara to leave. However, to do that would mean that Abby would go with her. There was no way that a certain aunt would leave her niece alone at this time.

Kris was none too sure that Abby would not be running for the exit in a few minutes, but the erstwhile maid had earned her place at Kris's side time and time again.

They could stay.

Penny had walked in while the others were leaving. A lone salmon breasting a river in flood to swim upstream would have had an easier time of it. She'd come without a shower or a change of clothes. Her underarmor padding was grimy and sweat stained from the day's work. The Navy lieutenant had also earned her place in what was coming . . . even if Kris did pray that she'd head for the exit before they got too deep.

Colonel Cortez sat comfortably in his chair. The beer in front of him was untouched. His eyes roved the room, taking in everything, but his body was as unmoved as a carved Buddha. He was the newest to her band. He was the one who most surprised her by keeping to his chair. He'd often joked about leaving after sitting through one of Kris's friendly family talks.

He joked about leaving . . . but today he stayed.

Kris took in the ship's officers from her squadron. They were innocent of this matter . . . and totally in the dark. She ought to give them a choice.

"In a few minutes, I may be asking for volunteers," she told them. "Whole ships of volunteers for something that may end in all our deaths. If you walk out that door now, you won't be in line to volunteer. If you stay, you may find that you've already volunteered yourself. This may be your last chance to make a call for yourself and your crew."

That got them looking at each other and scratching not a few heads. It was Phil Taussig who finally broke the silence. "I figured when I saw the Longknife name on my orders that I'd been volunteered for something, Your Highness. The last few weeks haven't been nearly horrible enough to qualify for Longknife duty. I guess I'll hang around for the rest."

That seemed to settle it for PatRon 10.

Jack. Well, Jack alone knew what was behind all this. Jack alone had sat through the meeting with her. He eyed her now with easy confidence and open expectation. *What rabbit you gonna pull out of your hat this time?*

Kris only wished she knew.

"All right," Kris said, turning face on to Vicky, "you said my great-grandfather Ray Longknife, King Raymond I to some, met with an Iteeche. That's quite a claim to make. You want to back it up?"

For a second, Vicky just sat in her seat, as if she was still trying to absorb the results of her claim. Was it a claim or just a gambit? Kris wouldn't have to wait long to find out.

Vicky got to her feet and slowly walked to the Forward Lounge door. She opened it and stuck her head out. She smiled. Kris imagined there were a lot of Marines out there to smile at. No doubt some of them now carried locked and loaded weapons.

Vicky walked back to the table but did not sit down.

"I have it from one of the boffins who used to be on the *Wasp* that your King Ray met with an Iteeche Imperial spokesman about a problem facing the Iteeche Empire."

"You do, do you?" Kris said.

"I do. Are you going to deny it?"

Kris shook her head. "Not at the moment, but I am going to ask you a question."

"What?"

"Do you think any boffin could get by the guard you saw outside?"

"What do you mean?"

"Let's say my grampa, King Ray, was on this ship. He'd be protected by the likes of those loyal Marines. How do you think a boffin would get by them?"

Vicky already had her mouth open, ready to shoot back a reply, but she stopped, no words spoken. For a moment, she actually mulled over the question.

Good. The girl's learning to think.

Well, maybe not so good. The girl is a Peterwald.

"Maybe he got a nano spy into the room," she finally said.

"Past Nelly? How much you want to bet me?"

Now Vicky did frown. "That's not a bet I'd take."

"Smart girl," Nelly said.

"But I've got a recording of the meeting," Vicky said. "Our analysis says it's Ray and Trouble's voices. Yours, too."

That added an ugly twist. Could Admiral Sandy or her news scribe have sold a copy of the meeting that Kris had given them? Such disloyalty as that was unthinkable.

Kris chose to go with what she found very thinkable.

"Let's just say for a moment that the voices on your tape aren't a concoction in someone's sound lab. Who was there?"

"King Ray," Vicky said. "General Trouble. You. I think your captain was there, but he didn't say anything during the meeting."

"That all?"

"Yeah."

So the leaker had taken himself out of the meeting before distributing it. Why was Kris not surprised?

"That's interesting," Kris said. "Do you honestly think King Ray would have a meeting that important and not include Admiral Crossenshield?"

Crossie, as Kris called him to his face, was the head of Wardhaven Intelligence. He ran black ops and always knew where the bodies were buried because he had dug the graves.

"You think," Vicky said slowly, as if doing the thinking as the words came out of her mouth, "that your own head of intelligence intentionally leaked that meeting to us."

"Crossie's always trying to play me. I'm always trying not to get played. Sometimes, I think you have the right idea, shooting the head of your State Security every once in a while."

Kris really wouldn't shoot Crossie. Blood was so messy. No, but retiring him to some planet with no heavy industry to raise chickens or goats or pomegranates?

Now that was appealing.

"But why would your security chief intentionally leak this meeting to us?" Vicky asked, still more puzzled than enlightened.

"What was the meeting about," Kris asked, "according to your leaked recording?" Kris wasn't willing to officially break the seal of security her king and grampa had put on that meeting. Not so publicly. Not with so many guns at hand.

"The Iteeche have run into a problem. Or something.

Their scout ships are going missing when they visited certain places."

"Hmm," Kris said, a thought dawning on her that might actually cause her to respect Crossie's twisted mind. "And what did King Ray do about that?"

"I don't know," Vicky said.

"What has he done in public since this supposed meeting took place?" Kris asked.

"Nothing, I think."

"Nothing in public, but his chief of intelligence is leaking the meeting's contents to who knows whom. Do you find that as interesting as I do?" Kris asked, trying not to grin.

Vicky gnawed on that for a while. "What's going on?" she finally asked.

"I don't know," Kris said. "Remember, I've been on pirate patrol since, oh, I don't know."

"Since not too long after this meeting," Vicky said.

"Which, of course," Kris pointed out, "I have not said took place."

"What do you think is going on? He's your grampa," sounded more like an accusation than a statement of fact.

"I'm beginning to more and more understand why Gramma Trouble, Gramma Ruth if you prefer, warned me to be careful around Ray. And I thought he was so cuddly when I was small."

"And I thought General Boyng was such a dear because he always brought me a new dress. By the way, Kris, I had those dresses checked after we took him out and shot him. They had bugs on them. When I was wearing those dresses, he always knew where I was and could listen in on anything I said or that was said to me."

"We live and learn," Kris said. "We get older, or we get dead."

"So, what are you going to do about all this?" Vicky asked, taking a seat next to Kris.

"Hmm, let's see. I was ordered to take care of the pirate problem outside Peterwald space without getting your old man too mad at my king. How'd I do on that, Admiral?"

"Not too shabby," Admiral Krätz said, carefully emptying the last few drops from his bottle. "Four pirate ships captured. One pirate base taken down. Port Royal. One potential pirate base secured. Kaskatos. We won't hold it against you that it's more likely to ask for membership in the United Sentients than to give old Greenfeld a call."

The admiral suddenly got a grin on his face. "Excuse me, I misspoke. There were several late votes before your Constitutional Convention closed down at Pitts Hope. One of them changed the name of who you work for, princess."

"Changed the name of United Sentients?" Kris's stomach had been through too much lately to react to this. She waited for Admiral Krätz to get to the point he seemed so happy to avoid.

"Yes, it seems that rumors of meetings with Iteeche are not limited to this public house. They were flying fast and loose on Pitts Hope. So certain factions proposed a name change."

"To what?" Kris and Jack demanded together.

"United Societies," Vicky said, letting the cat out of the bag.

That got her a scowl from her admiral.

"It seems that not only was sentients too inviting to aliens like the Iteeche, but United Societies had the right flavor for what they wanted."

"And what was that?" Kris asked.

"Something not so united," Jack said. "I think your grandpa has more trouble than he's let on."

"Quite likely, but his problems are far away, and our problems are right here underfoot," Kris said, trying not to snarl. "What do we do with ours, Admiral?"

"I don't think I will have any trouble registering Port Royal as a Navy colony," Admiral Krätz said. "All the records of its previous existence seem to have been destroyed. I can't picture N.S. Holdings making a bid to take back control of it, what with all the witnesses to piracy, drug production, and slavery around to raise questions about its former management, should they be identified." The admiral fairly beamed at the outcome.

"We also have a strong lead to a certain shipyard concerning products from its space docks going missing and turning up flying the black flag. There are already Navy inspectors at that yard. They may get reinforced with Marines and do more no-notice inspections of this or that corner of the place. Yes, Your Highness, I think you can claim this job is done. What do you plan to do next?"

"Not go on vacation," Kris said.

"Why am I not surprised?" Jack sighed.

"What do you think about most of PatRon 10 trailing me back to Wardhaven?" Kris asked no one in general.

"Most?" Jack Campbell said.

"You had the best luck on convoy duty, Jack. What do you think of you and the *Dauntless* coordinating your patrols and convoy duty with the admiral's two new ships, assuming he gets to buy them?"

"I could do that. But what's this about something that has even the Iteeche scared to death. That really sounds like fun."

"Somebody has to see that trade flows, Jack."

"And the rest of us?" Phil Taussig asked.

"You get to follow me back home, where I will have a little talk with my grampa about things that go thump in the night and the need for us to know more about it before it thumps us some night."

"Volunteers, huh?" Phil said.

"Of the Longknife flavor," Jack Montoya said.

"Oh hell, count me in," the skipper of the *Hornet* said, followed by those of the *Fearless* and *Intrepid*.

"What about me?" Vicky asked.

"What about you?" Kris asked right back.

"Can I go with you?"

"I don't think your father, my Emperor, would be very happy if I let you follow a Longknife home. Bad precedent."

"So I have to go ask him," Vicky said.

Kris could almost hear a little finger getting back in the practice of wrapping someone around it.

Kris sighed. She'd never wrapped anyone around her little finger. Or big finger. Or thumb, for that matter.

Some girls had it easy. Other girls learned to tough it out. Kris really didn't mind being one of the tough ones.

"Captains, crew, tomorrow we sail for Wardhaven. After that, the gods of space only know where we'll end up," Kris said.

"You're assuming your grampa don't put a shorter leash on you next time he sees you," Abby put in.

Kris laughed. "I've had enough experience with leashes. From now on, this girl is going to go for the free-and-wild ranging life."

About the Author

Mike Shepherd grew up Navy. It taught him early about change and the chain of command. He's worked as a bartender and cabdriver, personnel advisor and labor negotiator. Now retired from building databases about the endangered critters in the forests of the Pacific Northwest, he's looking forward to some fun reading and writing.

Mike lives in Vancouver, Washington, with his wife, Ellen, and her mother. He enjoys reading, writing, dreaming, watching grandchildren for story ideas, and upgrading his computer—all are never-ending pursuits.

Mike's hard at work on *Kris Longknife: Daring* for you to read November 2011. You can visit his website at www.mikeshepherd.org or drop him an e-mail at Mike _Shepherd@comcast.net.